JEEVES AND WOOSTER: THE EVOLUTION OF GENIUS

The Full Text of Right Ho, Jeeves and
My Man Jeeves, with Essays on the
History and Development of Jeeves and
Wooster, The Technique of
Wodehouse, and Biographical Notes

Right Ho, Jeeves and My Man Jeeves

JEEVES AND WOOSTER: THE EVOLUTION OF GENIUS

ISBN-13: 978-1495292002
ISBN: 1495292002

Right Ho, Jeeves and My Man Jeeves

Contents

Wodehouse, Jeeves and Wooster in Historical Context

It is astonishing to think that Pelham Grenville Wodehouse initially breathed life into his creations of Jeeves and Wooster in 1915. Four further stories appeared in 1916. I for one find it surprising that this creation, this "idyllic world that can never stale" in the words of Evelyn Waugh, first appeared in the same year as the First World War battles of the Somme, Verdun and Jutland. While the nations of Europe were immolating themselves in the most catastrophic war the world had ever known, Wodehouse was creating his stories for us to delight in.

Of course, Wodehouse had already been dividing his time between Great Britain and the United States since he went to Greenwich Village in 1909, and we cannot blame him for choosing to spend the war years in New York.

In terms of his earnings from writing, Wodehouse only "hit the big time" in 1914 and 1915. Although at 34, he was not too old to fight, we have to remember that America, where he had worked for the last five years, was not even at war.

Wodehouse, it seems clear, was a deeply apolitical person, and blissfully oblivious of the Great War, and it shows in his writings.

There are plenty of precedents for this kind of thing of course, Jane Austen being the most obvious. The romantic intrigues of Britain's best loved novelist take place at the same time as the titanic struggle of the Napoleonic Wars of the early 19th century; yet there is no allusion to the conflict, death and destruction in Austen's writings, merely the odd officer or sea captain coming or going in the background. In the same way, Bertie Wooster is delightfully free of any worries about conflict or conscription, or for that matter any real worries at all.

We could even conjecture that the timeless idyll which Bertie Wooster inhabits is a reaction on the part of Wodehouse to the cataclysm engulfing the world around him. The United States, of course, also entered the war in 1917 while many of the early, one might say prototype, Jeeves and Wooster stories were being written.

Was this Wodehouse's response to the cataclysm? It's the kind of question or conjecture which journalists and critics often put to writers, but with PG Wodehouse there was never any chance they would receive a straight answer; and any case it's highly unlikely Wodehouse would take anything so seriously.

When PG Wodehouse does allude to political developments in the world around him (and it is not often) it is always to gently mock or make fun of them, or bring out the humour in them. In the Jeeves and Wooster books, "The Code of the Woosters" has a memorable character named Spode who appears to be 1930s fascist type. Spode is the kind of man who "goes about in footer bags [soccer shorts]" like the Brown Shirts in Germany or the less successful Black Shirts of Oswald Mosley in Britain. Against a threatening background of impending war, and with Fascism on the rise, this political fellow Spode was merely the stuff of ridicule to Wodehouse.

(Later on in life, this extremely apolitical attitude on the part of Wodehouse was to go disastrously wrong for him. At the start of the Second World War, Wodehouse was living in Le Touquet on the Channel Coast of France for tax reasons. He could easily have escaped back to Britain when the Germans invaded, but apparently took no notice of the news and completely underestimated the seriousness of the situation. As a famous cultural figure, he was captured by the Nazis, released after a year, and taken to Paris for the rest of the war.)

It is against the background of Wodehouse's life in New York, then, that we must see the first Jeeves and Wooster stories, and in fact the embryonic story where Bertie is Bertie Mannering-Phipps - this original story being "Extricating Young Gussie", published in the US newspaper "The Saturday Evening Post" in September 1915. This first story, included as a bonus in this edition, was later published as a single short story in the collection "The Man with Two Left Feet" in 1917.

It seems clear that that the character of Bertie Wooster was conceived by PG Wodehouse while he was living in New York during the First World War. The first Jeeves stories to be written, that is the four included in "My Man Jeeves", all take place in New York City, whereas the other four stories included in that collection are set back in Wodehouse's native land of Britain. These four other stories do not contain a butler, although it has been said that the narrator, Reggie Pepper, is very much the Bertie Wooster forerunner. Again, it seems to me that the British Reggie Pepper stories pre-date the first four Bertie Wooster stories in this collection – though we will never know for sure.

These four stories from "My Man Jeeves" were adapted and slightly rewritten to be included in the collection "Carry On Jeeves", published in 1925. This was in itself after the first full Jeeves and Wooster book, "The Inimitable Jeeves" which published in 1923.

Now you may consider this chronology to be somewhat confused. Why would PG Wodehouse rewrite and republish stories after a period of eight or nine years? From a writer's point of view, however, it is not so strange. Writers and especially prolific writers such as PG Wodehouse have many projects and stories on the go. In this period between 1917 and 1930, Wodehouse was simply sweating great stories, and also penning lyrics for musical comedies. The job of reorganizing and setting into coherent collections must have fallen by the wayside – especially considering that Plum's mainstay would still have been serialized stories in the Saturday Evening Post in the USA and The Strand magazine in London. Small wonder than any organization of the stories had to wait until the 1920s.

It seems clear to me that Wodehouse loved the character of Bertie Wooster in particular as a narrator, a "narrative voice" as writers put it, and also must have conceived at least some of the other stories from the 1925 "Carry On Jeeves" as early as 1915 or 1916. In some ways, "Carry On Jeeves" is a work which ties up some loose ends for Bertie Wooster and his writer. Wodehouse only decides in the 1925 work to "introduce" us to Jeeves in the first place in the story "Jeeves Takes Charge". This has led many to assume that this was the first Jeeves and Wooster story, yet this is far from being the case. It came nine years after the first Bertie and Jeeves story.

"Jeeves Takes Charge" is the first story in "Carry On Jeeves" and includes a truly masterful introduction to the best known domestic servant of the last 100 years. I shall write more in-depth later in these notes about the writing technique of PG Wodehouse, but suffice it to say that the character creation in the first two or three pages of that story would be beyond the technical ability of virtually any other writer I can think of, with the possible exception of Evelyn Waugh.

As Wodehouse decides to "restart" the Jeeves and Wooster narrative in 1925 with "Carry On Jeeves", it is only surprising to me that he did not decide to edit and rewrite the story "Extricating Young Gussie" which was the first Jeeves and Wooster story, appearing on its own, back in September 1915 in the Saturday Evening Post in the USA.

The other surprise is that although Wodehouse clearly loved his creation of Bertie Wooster and his faithful valet, and came back and back to them, he wrote relatively few stories in the first 15 years after "Extricating Young Gussie". The reason for this is surely that he was an extremely busy man at the height of his powers, writing books and stories and lyrics galore, and indeed much in demand in writing for the theatre in New York.

This is what Wodehouse himself has to say on the matter in 1930.

"It is now some fourteen summers since, an eager lad in my early thirties, I started to write Jeeves stories: and many people think this nuisance should now cease. Carpers say that enough is enough. Cavillers say the same. They look down the list of the years and see these chronicles multiplying like rabbits, and the prospect appals them. But against this must be set the fact that writing Jeeves stories gives me a great deal of pleasure and keeps me out of the public houses."

The man was surely exaggerating, for a couple of dozen short stories in a period of fifteen years is hardly "multiplying like rabbits". Compared to his output of Jeeves and Wooster stories in the following ten years, it is a positive dearth of material for the public, who by this stage could not get enough of Bertie and his valet.

Placing Jeeves and Wooster back in their historical milieu, we see Bertie and his friend Bingo Little in the early 1920s, surrounded by suggestions of social unrest, and the (for Wodehouse) rich comic potential of Russian Communism. The alternative title for "The Inimitable Jeeves" was "Comrade Bingo" because of Bingo's involvement with a Bolshevik sympathiser mischievously named Charlotte Corday (after a particularly blood-soaked French Revolutionary). This, remember, was in the Europe immediately after the First World War, where even Great Britain was a place of profound disillusionment, and very many working people were seduced, intellectually at least, by the idea of the Communist Revolution in Russia.

As usual, Wodehouse pours gentle scorn on the socialists in his stories, and it's all part of the fun, treated slightly less seriously than a wagering scheme involving the length of the sermons spoken by Church of England ministers.

It was in the 1930s that PG Wodehouse really hit his mid-season form with Jeeves and Bertie Wooster. Between 1930 and "The Code of the Woosters" published just before the Second World War in 1938, Wodehouse published the collection "Very Good, Jeeves" in 1930, and "Thank You, Jeeves" in 1934, which was his first Jeeves and Wooster novel. Perhaps the apogee of the Bertie Wooster stories is "Right Ho, Jeeves" set at the Brinkley Court country house, and published in 1934. This work has been included in this volume as arguably the best of the Jeeves and Wooster books. After 1938, Jeeves was not seen again until "Joy in the Morning" in 1946, which was understandable given Wodehouse's wartime captivity. Thereafter many Wodehouse aficionados believe that the quality of the stories never regained the dizzying heights of "Right Ho, Jeeves" and the other work of the 1920s and 1930s.

The last Jeeves and Wooster book of PG Wodehouse was "Aunts Aren't Gentlemen" published in 1973, when Pelham Grenville Wodehouse was well into his 90s. As such we cannot expect it to be as fabulously and intricately written as the books from forty years earlier. Nonetheless, you'd have to be an experienced Wodehouse reader before you really noticed the difference. It lacks a little sparkle in the turn of phrase, and Wodehouse uses a few more words than he might have done in his youth. Nonetheless it is writing of the very highest quality, and quite staggering given the age of the writer.

It is often argued that the first two "complete" Jeeves and Wooster books outshine the others – that is "The Inimitable Jeeves" and "Carry On Jeeves". They are indeed delightful books, and they introduce us to some of the most memorable characters, including Roderick Glossop, Claude and Eustace, Honoria Glossop, Bingo Little and of course Aunts Agatha and Dahlia. Nonetheless, when Wodehouse began to branch out and weave together a whole novel from his characters, we see that his talents extend beyond the witty, clever turn of phrase.

The critic Bernard Levin once said that to criticize Wodehouse "would be like taking a spade to a soufflé". How true. In "Right Ho, Jeeves" we see this filigree of perfection before our eyes. We have the hilariously clever language and concise description of ten years before, and the wonderful dialogue; but now in "Right Ho, Jeeves" we can add in a greater cast of hilarious but essentially sympathetic characters. Bertie himself is slightly softened compared with the man in "The Inimitable Jeeves", and the action is based solidly around the two protagonists to a greater extent. Furthermore, in the longer novel form, Wodehouse shows his ability to construct a fabulous comic set-up from a distance, such as Gussie presenting the prizes at Market Snodsbury.

Wodehouse is primarily a comic genius who has given pleasure to countless millions. Yet he is also a genius in his use of language, who was envied (and often criticized) by more "serious" writers. Many, many are the writers who have loved the work of "Plum" and attempted to write something like it. I know of none who has come close. It's too difficult.

As I shall explain a little later, the interlaced layers of characterization, voice and description are so dense, that his style is impossible to copy. This, surely, is sign of true genius. Read, and enjoy.

The Genius of Jeeves and Wooster: The Peerless Writing Technique of P G Wodehouse

"You don't analyse such sunlit perfection, you just bask in its warmth and splendour."
English writer and broadcaster, Stephen Fry, who played Jeeves in the BBC Jeeves and Wooster televison productions.

"English literature's performing flea…" *Irish writer Sean O'Casey referring to Wodehouse in a letter to The Daily Telegraph of London*

I've already said that to criticize Wodehouse's work is to take a "spade to a soufflé". However, I do not propose to criticize or even deconstruct what Wodehouse has done – still less to suggest that his writing could actually be done better. I do think it is a joy however, to take a look at a short passage from Wodehouse and notice how many clever writing techniques are happening *simultaneously.*

Let us take this example, from early in the story "Jeeves Takes Charge" from the collection "Carry On Jeeves". The idea is to introduce us to Jeeves, even though his stories have already been around for some years.

I shall always remember the first morning he came. It so happened that the night before I had been present at a cheery little supper, I was feeling pretty rocky… I crawled off the sofa and opened the door. A kind of darkish sort of respectful Johnnie stood without.

'I was sent by the agency, sir,' he said. 'I was given to understand that you required a valet.'

I'd have preferred an undertaker; but I told him to stagger in, and he floated noiselessly through the doorway like a healing zephyr. That impressed me from the start. Meadowes had had flat feet and used to clump. This fellow didn't seem to have any feet at all. He just streamed in. He had a grave, sympathetic face as if he, too, knew what it was to sup with the lads.

"Excuse me, sir," he said gently.

Then he seemed to flicker, and wasn't there any longer. I heard him moving about in the kitchen, and presently he came back with a glass on a tray.

'If you would drink this, sir,' he said, with a kind of bedside manner, rather like the royal doctor shooting the bracer into the sick prince. 'It is a little preparation of my own invention. It is the Worcester Sauce that gives it its colour. The raw egg makes it nutritious. The red pepper gives it its bite. Gentlemen have told me they have found it extremely invigorating after a late evening.'

I would have clutched at anything that looked like a lifeline that morning. I swallowed the stuff. For a moment I felt as if somebody had touched off a bomb inside the old bean, and was strolling down my throat with a lighted torch, and then everything seemed suddenly to get all right...

'You're engaged!' I said, as soon as I could say anything.

A couple of years ago I was preparing to teach a Creative Writing class on effective characterization, and I flipped open my well-thumbed volume of Wodehouse to find this passage at the beginning. For the same study exercise, I had used passages from a dozen other world-renowned writers including Muriel Spark, Pierre Boule, Dan Brown, Stephen King, Charles Dickens, Thomas Harris and others. Each passage had one or often two strong ways to create the character in the reader's mind, using voice, dialogue, physical description, metaphor, simile, language, actions, interesting slang, contrast with other characters, impactful "signature phrases" and so on.

I realised on studying this three-hundred-word piece of text, picked pretty much at random, that Wodehouse had used not two or three but *all* of the above literary techniques to introduce his two characters in that short passage. And yet... Does the passage seem dense or laborious to read? Quite the opposite. Furthermore, when we talk about impactful and arresting phrases and creative, memorable use of language, we could pick a number of instances from that short passage.

Here are just a few examples:

Impactful "signature phrases": *like a healing zephyr, just streamed in, shooting the bracer into the sick prince, touched off a bomb inside the old been strolling down my throat with a lighted torch.*

Physical description: *grave, sympathetic; kind of darkish sort of respectful Johnnie; with a kind of bedside manner.*

Simile: *as if somebody had touched off a bomb; didn't seem to have any feet at all; like the royal doctor; seemed to flicker; as if he, too, knew what it was to sup with the lads...*

Irony: *a cheery little supper; extremely invigorating after a late evening; I'd have preferred an undertaker.*

Contrast: *Meadowes had had flat feet.*

Signature dialogue: *All* dialogue here is signature dialogue to the two characters. There is no let-up in the quality of this language through the entire canon of Jeeves books; it starts simply with 'I was given to understand,' and finishes with 'extremely invigorating after a late evening.' It is quintessential, unmistakable - yet not a word is wasted. Take the latest attempts to reproduce Jeeves' dialogue by Sebastian Faulks for instance. It's so long-winded in comparison. The real thing is so concise; it's as light as a feather.

Slang: *kind of darkish sort of respectful Johnnie; shooting the bracer; a bomb inside the old bean; stagger in.* These are all Bertie-signature words and slang of Bertie Wooster's milieu. They contrast entirely with Jeeves.

Ironic, self-pitying tone, especially in the choice of verbs: *clutched; crawled;* comparing himself to a *sick prince.*

Voice. Above all the character of Bertie Wooster is created by the voice in which he narrates the whole. It never relaxes, never comes close to being ordinary, or giving an ordinary description. One of the most delightful aspects of this passage is the faintly self-regarding way he describes himself, when he is suffering from and entirely self-inflicted hangover. It's gentle though, suggestive of a dilettante who sees the humour in it all, and indeed in himself. He has had a "cheery little supper", and now he feels like the "sick prince". Jeeves meanwhile is the royal doctor, grave and sympathetic, who "knew what it was to set up with the lads."

Who else would describe a hangover with this lightness of touch and with all the nuance of characterization that Wodehouse crams in? And he does it all while making us smile, even laugh as we go.

(One of the print editions of "Carry On Jeeves" includes a very short editor's introduction which describes Bertie in this seminal scene as having a "raging hangover". This kind of commonplace, obvious use of language makes the point, doesn't it? Bertie Wooster would never have used a phrase like that, and we sense he would never have thought it either. He really does believe himself "the sick prince").

This finely-wrought filigree of a passage could be used as an example to aspiring writers across the English-speaking world – but it won't be. In a sense, it would make most writers want to give up! It's too good. It is so far beyond the compass of even famous, professional writers, that it becomes a pointless exercise to "write in the style of".

And all this comes after Bertie has begun his narrative only a hundred so words before with: "Now touching this business of old Jeeves – my man, you know – how do we stand?" This is a fabulously disingenuous beginning, as if Bertie can't write a narrative to save his life. And yet we are then plunged almost immediately into prose of such honeyed richness and joyful rhythm that we don't notice any of the elements that have created it. What's more it's not just a one-off couple of pages, but the whole of the rest of the book! Wodehouse keeps up this stratospheric level of writing, page after page after page.

The other thing to note about this work is that, although the writing is incredibly dense with characterization and beautiful language, no one would imagine Wodehouse had done it on purpose, planning out his tropes and similes and slang. It just came out of his typewriter keys, let's face it.

As we read the stories in "My Man Jeeves", it becomes obvious that the work becomes more concise and denser – and therefore paradoxically feels lighter – between the very early stories of Reggie Pepper and the later, sun-kissed prose of "Right Ho, Jeeves". This would not have been a result of conscious work. More likely Wodehouse just became more and more immersed in the character and voice of Bertie Wooster, and made it work for him better.

Moreover, speaking the narrative through one of the main protagonists in the plot has many advantages. Wodehouse thereby creates the character without effort. Compare this with the Mr Mulliner stories, where the narrator is back in bar, removed from the episode. Characterisation becomes a much bigger task.

It is interesting that as the Jeeves and Wooster books move on, it becomes less and less a matter of "extricating" a chum from some scrape or other, and Bertie himself is at the centre of the action. Compare "Extricating Young Gussie" and the four stories of "My Man Jeeves" with the strength of Bertie's voice in "Right Ho, Jeeves".

Something else that the imitators of the Jeeves books don't quite grasp is that while Bertie is allowed to go on at some length, and use natural language that no line editor would normally permit (for example: *a kind of darkish sort of respectful Johnnie*), Jeeves, by contrast does not waste his words. Jeeves does not waste his words, even when he sounds pompous or learned. Jeeves' dialogue is a long, long way from simply shoveling in some "Jeeves-like" words, as the imitators seem to think. It would be easy if you were trying to recreate some Jeeves dialogue to make him simply verbose by over-use of certain words.

Consider this exchange in "Right Ho, Jeeves":

"Newts, Jeeves. Mr. Fink-Nottle has a strong newt complex. You

must have heard of newts. Those little sort of lizard things that charge about in ponds."

"Oh, yes, sir. The aquatic members of the family Salamandridae which constitute the genus Molge."

This is quintessentially Jeeves of course, but not because of any particularly Jeeves-like words; and the continual contrast between Bertie and his man is there again in the way they describe newts.

***

Finally there is the issue of "euphony" which, put simply, means sounding nice and rolling off the tongue. It comes from rhythm and phrasing and having an "ear" for what sounds good when spoken, and it is intimately connected to poetry, lyrics, or at least verse.

This is what the Simon Callow (an English actor with a suitably cut-glass accent and sonorous voice) said about Wodehouse's writing in the Jeeves and Wooster books:

'I've recorded all the Jeeves books, and I can tell you this: it's like singing Mozart. The perfection of the phrasing is a physical pleasure. I doubt if any writer in the English language has more perfect music.'

It's hard to disagree with this, whether you're a layperson reader, or an actor, or regard yourself as some kind of literary expert. Certainly plenty of poets would be up there with him, along with Evelyn Waugh, Scott Fitzgerald and Oscar Wilde; but the point is this. PG Wodehouse did it all, and he was an extremely prolific writer. His technical brilliance almost defies belief, and yet the words flow like they were written by an angel gliding on a snowflake – millions and millions of them.

Whichever way you look at it, the writing of Wodehouse represents a staggering human achievement, and with "Right Ho, Jeeves", you are reading the man in midseason form, speaking through voice of what must have been his favourite character.

Enjoy.

The Evolution of Genius – Development of Technique and Character in the Early Jeeves Stories

As I mentioned earlier, four of the stories in "My Man Jeeves" are repeated in the publication eight years later of "Carry On Jeeves". Because of this, not only can we take our impressions of what might have changed in Wodehouse's approach in those years, we can look at what he wanted to change (if anything) in his own work.

One thing that is fairly noticeable if you read both versions, is that the story has been edited to become shorter. It is only a little shorter, and it's not as if it's been line-edited to get rid of superfluous words. As you can imagine, there weren't any superfluous words. So why has it become shorter? And more importantly, how does it *feel* shorter and with a better flow – because it does.

The answer is that mostly Wodehouse is more judicious in his characterization of Jeeves himself. Bertie is allowed to go on at length, as narrator, in fact at much the same length as he did before – except for one thing. Crucially, Bertie limits the amount of words he devotes to describing and characterizing Jeeves himself. With Jeeves, concision is the name of the game.

Take the example of "Leave it to Jeeves", the first story in "My Man Jeeves". Bertie begins early on in the story with a little exchange as follows:

...it isn't only that Jeeves's judgment about clothes is infallible, though, of course, that's really the main thing. The man knows everything. There was the matter of that tip on the "Lincolnshire." I forget now how I got it, but it had the aspect of being the real, red-hot tabasco.

"Jeeves," I said, for I'm fond of the man, and like to do him a good turn when I can, "if you want to make a bit of money have something on Wonderchild for the 'Lincolnshire.'"

He shook his head.

"I'd rather not, sir."

"But it's the straight goods. I'm going to put my shirt on him."

"I do not recommend it, sir. The animal is not intended to win. Second place is what the stable is after."

Perfect piffle, I thought, of course. How the deuce could Jeeves know anything about it? Still, you know what happened. Wonderchild led till he was breathing on the wire, and then Banana Fritter came along and nosed him out. I went straight home and rang for Jeeves.

Incidentally, I love the line *"...for I'm fond of the man, and like to do him a good turn when I can..."* How wonderfully trivial and self-regarding! How perfectly Bertie Wooster.

Anyhow, as you will have guessed this exchange has been excised from the later version of the story, incidentally now called "The Artistic Career of Corky". Why? Well, firstly because it was a little redundant to the story at hand – although it's short enough that that shouldn't have stopped it altogether. More likely PG Wodehouse thought that the characterization itself was a little heavy-handed. It's not necessary. Jeeves is defined by his dialogue and his actions, and also to a large extent by his dynamic with Bertie. There is a dynamic in this exchange between them, but it's too obvious. Bertie does not need to say that Jeeves' taste in clothes in infallible. Wodehouse demonstrates that in the stories, but it is left unsaid.

The point becomes more obvious in the following passage from the same story. The words underlined were removed from the later version.

<u>Jeeves is a tallish man, with one of those dark, shrewd faces. His eye gleams with the light of pure intelligence.</u>

"Jeeves, we want your advice."

"Very good, sir."

I boiled down Corky's painful case into a few well-chosen words.

"So you see what it amount to, Jeeves. We want you to suggest some way by which Mr. Worple can make Miss Singer's acquaintance without getting on to the fact that Mr. Corcoran already knows her. Understand?"

"Perfectly, sir."

"Well, try to think of something."

"I have thought of something already, sir."

You see, actual descriptions of Jeeves are few and far between, and for a reason. They're not necessary. The interplay with Bertie, and the dialogue and the action are what matter for the character of Jeeves, and for that matter for the joy of the character. The voice of Bertie is the thing that makes these books tick. In this little exchange we have the contrast of Bertie's confusing description of events, with Jeeves intelligence and brevity.

Only later in the Jeeves and Wooster stories do we see the narrative stream establish itself at greater length. For one thing, during the First World War and the early 1920s, Wodehouse was earning his living mainly from magazines and newspapers, so self-contained short stories were the order of the day. These days, short stories are almost impossible to sell, although millions and millions are written. Probably more short stories are written in a year than any other literary form bar none, and they are not an easy form to master. One hundred years ago, short stories and serialised stories were a mainstay of working writers in English.

In the 1920s, Wodehouse begins to weave together the stories into a narrative stream of episodes, particularly in "The Inimitable Jeeves", which continues its cast of characters other than Jeeves and Wooster throughout pretty much the whole work, coming and going, including Bingo Little, Charlotte Corday, Roderick Glossop, Claude and Eustace and Honoria Glossop. We sense in this collection that Wodehouse is building up Bingo Little as an enduring character – "as woolly-headed a blighter as ever bit a sandwich", as Bertie describes him.

In terms of what writers call "mix of characters", Wodehouse must have realised that building so much around a character like Bingo Little had its limits. There is already "woolly-headed blighter" in chief in these stories, and his name is Wooster. There is not too much room for any more. Of course further Jeeves and Wooster stories are full of the Bertie's foolish and flawed chums in one kind of scrape or another – Gussie Fink-Nottle being an obvious example – but they are satisfying different from Bertie. If anything, Bingo Little was too similar to Bertie.

This process of making the stories "Bertie-centric" continues to a kind of sublime perfection with "Right Ho, Jeeves", which smoothly creates a whole novel based on roughly equally-sized episodes. This is no mean feat as anyone who has tried to write an episodic novel will attest – but I guess it shouldn't surprise us that Wodehouse pulls it off so perfectly in "Right Ho Jeeves", "Thankyou Jeeves" and to a lesser extent, "Very Good Jeeves".

As the years and episodes go by, Wodehouse settles into a pattern of allowing Jeeves to be characterised indirectly. Bertie tells us early on that Jeeves looks as if he knows "what it is to sup with the lads." And indeed he does. It comes through in small, indirect glimpses that Jeeves is not at all the older, austere, aloof looking fellow he is often portrayed to be on television. His language is reserved, but he is human at the same time as guarding his English reserve and his hauteur of speech.

In "The Aunt and The Sluggard", Jeeves volunteers to spend his nights visiting the nightspots of New York in order to help out Rocky Todd. Says Bertie:

For the first time in our long connection I observed Jeeves almost smile. The corner of his mouth curved quite a quarter of an inch, and for a moment his eye ceased to look like a meditative fish's.

"I should be delighted to oblige, sir. As a matter of fact, I have already visited some of New York's places of interest on my evening out, and it would be most enjoyable to make a practice of the pursuit."

Jeeves is indeed one of the lads. He is a player. He is, for instance, an astute gambler, and though he is a loyal servant, he often gets the better of Bertie and profits by it personally. Jeeves is anything but the boring, middle-aged stiff of the TV shows and illustrations. He is a man who throws himself into the pleasures of the proletariat when he has the chance – he doesn't talk about it himself, but it often slips out. The running joke is that Bertie thinks he understands Jeeves – but really, in common with others of his class at the time, Bertie has no idea about Jeeves or the others of the servant caste.

Oddly, it is often written that Jeeves' character develops in the early stories, whilst that of Bertie emerges fully formed and does not change. I don't buy this. It is also said of Reggie Pepper, who makes up the narrator of the other four stories in "My Man Jeeves", is "the same character" as Bertie. Again, I don't see this. Bertie has many qualities, including being dilettante, foppish, self-regarding and easily swayed. He is, however, at most times, an extremely kind and sympathetic individual, and in some ways he develops this more and more as the go years by, into the 1930s.

In "The Inimitable Jeeves" of 1923, when a visitor turns up unannounced, Bertie is intrigued, but turns to Jeeves and asks,

> *"Jeeves, would care to give a sporting two-to-one that the man is not a blighter or an excrescence?"*
> *"I should not like to venture such liberal odds, sir."*

The same language by Bertie – a little too harsh and judgmental – would be unthinkable by the time of "Right Ho, Jeeves". He has become a more empathetic character – though I'm not sure if we like him any more or less. It probably just dovetails better with the character of Jeeves, who is wise and sharp.

Bertie's appeal in the midseason stories we all admire so much, is his generosity of spirit, his gallant gentlemanliness. He hasn't an ill-tempered, mean-spirited bone in his body, and apart from some mischief while under the influence, Bertie is always a perfect English gentleman. Wodehouse's language, and Bertie's peculiar slang, neatly reinforce all of our hero's claim that "the Woosters are always magnanimous."

The brief excursion of Bertie's character into something slightly below the standards of the perfect gentleman, in "The Inimitable Jeeves", may not be all that noticeable, but Bertie very soon moves back to being the kind-hearted, sappy knight errant we all know and love. In many ways, "The Inimitable Jeeves" is seen as one of the best collections on the basis of its hilarious stories – "The Great Sermon Handicap" and "Comrade Bingo" are surely right up there with anything Plum ever wrote. But the character of Bertie is not quite the one we know and love.

"Right Ho, Jeeves" has everything in my view: wonderful story lines including Madeline Bassett and Gussy Fink-Nottle, and that heavenly generosity of spirit that is so important to the "idyllic world (that) will never stale," as Evelyn Waugh so memorably put it.

Biographical Notes on P G Wodehouse

PG Wodehouse is thought of as a quintessentially upper-class English author, but he spent much of his life outside the UK, and indeed, most of the formative moments of his career as a comic writer occurred in the USA. As we have seen earlier, Wodehouse conceived the characters of Jeeves and Wooster while living in New York, and in fact his first well-paid "break" came in that city.

Later in life he opted to live first in France and then after the Second World War in the USA. He took US citizenship in 1955 and never returned to his native land. Americans have surely just as much right as the British to claim him as their own, if not more. However, the fact is that the stories seem to anchor Wodehouse in his Englishness.

Wodehouse, called "Plum" (abbreviating his first name, "Pelham") by most family and friends, was born in Guildford, England to Eleanor and Henry Wodehouse. His father Henry was a judge in colonial Hong Kong, and merely visiting Great Britain with his wife at the time of the writer's birth.

When he was just three years old, Wodehouse was brought back from Hong Kong to Britain and placed in the care of a nanny. He attended various boarding schools and, between the ages of three and 15 years, saw his parents for barely six months in total. At age 10, it became time for him to move to a preparatory school, a kind of middle school in the English private school system. Wodehouse's first "prep school" was Malvern House which specialised in preparing boys for entry to the Royal Naval College at Dartmouth, England. Wodehouse spent two unhappy years at Malvern House before finally persuading his father to send him to Dulwich College in South London. Dulwich College now has a library named after him.

At Dulwich College, Plum was successful both as a scholar and a sportsman: he was a member of the Classics Sixth Form (traditionally, the preserve of the brightest pupils aged 16-18) and a school prefect; he edited the college magazine. PG Wodehouse would have gone on to Oxford University like his older brother, but unfortunately his retired father's pension was paid in Indian Rupees, which fell in value at this time, leaving the family without the means to finance Pelham's education. Plum's father secured him a position in HSBC Bank instead, where he was bored and "never learned a thing about banking". Some of his experiences in the bank were recounted in the early stories of "Psmith in the City".

As writers tend to do, Wodehouse wrote constantly in his spare time while working in the bank, and in 1902 became a journalist with "The Globe" taking over the comic column from a friend. He contributed items to "Punch", the English "Vanity Fair", "The Daily Express" and "The World". He also wrote his first published novels and four playlets at this time, and by 1907 had branched out to musical lyrics in the musical comedy "The Gay Gordons".

The big change for Wodehouse was to come after he decamped to the USA. During 1909, Wodehouse visited Greenwich Village in New York City and "sold two short stories to *Cosmopolitan* and *Collier's* for a total of $500 – much more than I had ever earned before." He resigned his job and stayed in New York, where he became a regular contributor to the American "Vanity Fair". However "the wolf was always at the door" and it was not until "The Saturday Evening Post" serialised "Something New" in 1915 that Wodehouse really made it as a full time writer. The "Saturday Evening Post" and "The Strand" in England began to serialise his work, including "Extricating Young Gussie", the first Jeeves story, in 1915, and PG Wodehouse never looked back as a writer.

In 1914, Wodehouse married Ethel Wayman and gained a stepdaughter named Leonora. He fathered no children of his own.

In the quarter century after his big break in 1915, Wodehouse kept up a staggering output of work, including many short stories, novels, involvement in 30 musical comedies and even two stints as a Hollywood scriptwriter.

In 1934, he took up residence in France, to avoid double taxation on his earnings by the tax authorities in both Britain and the USA.

He set up home with his wife in Le Touquet, an upper-class holiday resort just over the English Channel from London.

Wodehouse was uninterested in politics and world affairs, in fact to the point of gross naivity, and by an unkind twist of fate this was to prove his undoing. When World War II broke out in 1939, Wodehouse remained at his seaside home in Le Touquet, France, when he could have easily made the short journey to Britain when the Germans invaded, or even escaped South to neutral Spain. Wodehouse apparently failed to recognise the seriousness of the conflict. He later said that his wife couldn't bear to leave their dog. This naivity and openness of spirit was to have far-reaching consequences for him.

The Germans in occupied France interned Wodehouse as an "enemy alien". He was held first in Belgium, then at Tost, a town formerly in Germany, now in Poland.

While at Tost, he entertained his fellow prisoners with witty monologues. Under the Geneva Convention, Wodehouse was released just before his 60th birthday. He lived for a time at the Hotel Adlon in Berlin, before moving to Paris, which was still under German occupation. It was at this time he drafted the text of five humorous broadcasts to the USA (then not at war with Germany). It was these broadcasts that landed him with accusations of collaboration many years later.

In essence his detractors claimed that Wodehouse had broadcast for the Nazis (even though he had made fun of them), that he had received money from them, and that he had done a deal for early release from internment. In other words, his broadcasts, although entirely innocent in content, had been part of a deal with the Germans.

In reality, Wodehouse's release was down simply to his age, under the Geneva Convention, and the money paid to him was from his own earnings in neutral countries, merely channeled through a German bank. He had no other source of income. The broadcasts themselves were not noticed at the time, being aimed at the neutral US; nonetheless they were dragged out and laid against him after the war, in Great Britain at least.

A thorough investigation by British Secret Services exonerated Wodehouse, but the report was never published until after his death.

The investigation concluded that Wodehouse had been very naïve and indeed foolish to write the broadcasts, but that he had gained nothing by them, and was in no sense treasonous or even disloyal.

Whatever – inevitably, some of the mud thrown at Wodehouse stuck, and in the postwar years he had some loud detractors in the UK.

Wodehouse never returned to Britain, living out his days, and continuing to write, in the United States, where he took citizenship in 1955.

The accusations against Wodehouse for his wartime conduct rankled with him throughout the rest of his life, and he was himself particularly bitter that the British Secret Services would not make public their report on the affair. If it weren't for this unmerited stain on his character, Plum would surely have been honoured in Britain long before his knighthood, which was bestowed only a month before his death in 1975. Nonetheless, Wodehouse did accept the honour, although he did not live to collect it in person.

In many ways, America has more claim than Great Britain on PG Wodehouse as one of its own. He had more success there, lived there for many years and died an American citizen. Despite that, Plum's style is indisputably, in fact quintessentially, English as indeed was his worldview.

The literary heritage of PG Wodehouse is timeless. It will be celebrated for centuries to come wherever English is spoken and appreciated. It is now one hundred years since Wodehouse began to be widely read, and he has as many followers as ever. Very, very few writers can claim this growing popularity and stature one hundred years on.

Perhaps the biggest accolade we can give to the man is that PG Wodehouse is read and reread simply for the joy and pleasure he gives to his followers. His work is not prescribed by schools or universities, or learned professors. Perhaps we should be grateful for that.

RIGHT HO, JEEVES

P. G. WODEHOUSE

**Scholars' Library Press Edition
With Historical, Biographical Notes and and Essay on the
Writer's Craft by Thomas Aston MA (Cantab)**

To

RAYMOND NEEDHAM, K.C. WITH AFFECTION AND ADMIRATION

-1-

"Jeeves," I said, "may I speak frankly?"

"Certainly, sir."

"What I have to say may wound you."

"Not at all, sir."

"Well, then——"

No—wait. Hold the line a minute. I've gone off the rails.

I don't know if you have had the same experience, but the snag I always come up against when I'm telling a story is this dashed difficult problem of where to begin it. It's a thing you don't want to go wrong over, because one false step and you're sunk. I mean, if you fool about too long at the start, trying to establish atmosphere, as they call it, and all that sort of rot, you fail to grip and the customers walk out on you.

Get off the mark, on the other hand, like a scalded cat, and your public is at a loss. It simply raises its eyebrows, and can't make out what you're talking about.

And in opening my report of the complex case of Gussie Fink-Nottle, Madeline Bassett, my Cousin Angela, my Aunt Dahlia, my Uncle Thomas, young Tuppy Glossop and the cook, Anatole, with the above spot of dialogue, I see that I have made the second of these two floaters.

I shall have to hark back a bit. And taking it for all in all and weighing this against that, I suppose the affair may be said to have had its inception, if inception is the word I want, with that visit of mine to Cannes. If I hadn't gone to Cannes, I shouldn't have met the Bassett or bought that white mess jacket, and Angela wouldn't have met her shark, and Aunt Dahlia wouldn't have played baccarat.

Yes, most decidedly, Cannes was the *point d'appui.*

Right ho, then. Let me marshal my facts.

I went to Cannes—leaving Jeeves behind, he having intimated that he did not wish to miss Ascot—round about the beginning of June. With me travelled my Aunt Dahlia and her daughter Angela. Tuppy Glossop, Angela's betrothed, was to have been of the party, but at the last moment couldn't get away. Uncle Tom, Aunt Dahlia's husband, remained at home, because he can't stick the South of France at any price.

So there you have the layout—Aunt Dahlia, Cousin Angela and self off to Cannes round about the beginning of June.

All pretty clear so far, what?

We stayed at Cannes about two months, and except for the fact that Aunt Dahlia lost her shirt at baccarat and Angela nearly got inhaled by a shark while aquaplaning, a pleasant time was had by all.

On July the twenty-fifth, looking bronzed and fit, I accompanied aunt and child back to London. At seven p.m. on July the twenty-sixth we alighted at Victoria. And at seven-twenty or thereabouts we parted with mutual expressions of esteem—they to shove off in Aunt Dahlia's car to Brinkley Court, her place in Worcestershire, where they were expecting to entertain Tuppy in a day or two; I to go to the flat, drop my luggage, clean up a bit, and put on the soup and fish preparatory to pushing round to the Drones for a bite of dinner.

And it was while I was at the flat, towelling the torso after a much-needed rinse, that Jeeves, as we chatted of this and that— picking up the threads, as it were—suddenly brought the name of Gussie Fink-Nottle into the conversation.

As I recall it, the dialogue ran something as follows:

SELF: Well, Jeeves, here we are, what?

JEEVES: Yes, sir.

SELF: I mean to say, home again.

JEEVES: Precisely, sir.

SELF: Seems ages since I went away.

JEEVES: Yes, sir.

SELF: Have a good time at Ascot?

JEEVES: Most agreeable, sir.

SELF: Win anything?

JEEVES: Quite a satisfactory sum, thank you, sir.

SELF: Good. Well, Jeeves, what news on the Rialto? Anybody

been phoning or calling or anything during my abs.?

JEEVES: Mr. Fink-Nottle, sir, has been a frequent caller.

I stared. Indeed, it would not be too much to say that I gaped.

"Mr. Fink-Nottle?"

"Yes, sir."

"You don't mean Mr. Fink-Nottle?"

"Yes, sir."

"But Mr. Fink-Nottle's not in London?"

"Yes, sir."

"Well, I'm blowed."

And I'll tell you why I was blowed. I found it scarcely possible to give credence to his statement. This Fink-Nottle, you see, was one of those freaks you come across from time to time during life's journey who can't stand London. He lived year in and year out, covered with moss, in a remote village down in Lincolnshire, never coming up even for the Eton and Harrow match. And when I asked him once if he didn't find the time hang a bit heavy on his hands, he said, no, because he had a pond in his garden and studied the habits of newts.

I couldn't imagine what could have brought the chap up to the great city. I would have been prepared to bet that as long as the supply of newts didn't give out, nothing could have shifted him from that village of his.

"Are you sure?"

"Yes, sir."

"You got the name correctly? Fink-Nottle?"

"Yes, sir."

"Well, it's the most extraordinary thing. It must be five years since he was in London. He makes no secret of the fact that the place gives him the pip. Until now, he has always stayed glued to the country, completely surrounded by newts."

"Sir?"

"Newts, Jeeves. Mr. Fink-Nottle has a strong newt complex. You must have heard of newts. Those little sort of lizard things that charge about in ponds."

"Oh, yes, sir. The aquatic members of the family Salamandridae which constitute the genus Molge."

"That's right. Well, Gussie has always been a slave to them. He used to keep them at school."

"I believe young gentlemen frequently do, sir."

"He kept them in his study in a kind of glass-tank arrangement, and pretty niffy the whole thing was, I recall. I suppose one ought to have been able to see what the end would be even then, but you know what boys are. Careless, heedless, busy about our own affairs, we scarcely gave this kink in Gussie's character a thought. We may have exchanged an occasional remark about it taking all sorts to make a world, but nothing more. You can guess the sequel. The trouble spread,"

"Indeed, sir?"

"Absolutely, Jeeves. The craving grew upon him. The newts got him. Arrived at man's estate, he retired to the depths of the country and gave his life up to these dumb chums. I suppose he used to tell himself that he could take them or leave them alone, and then found—too late—that he couldn't."

"It is often the way, sir."

"Too true, Jeeves. At any rate, for the last five years he has been living at this place of his down in Lincolnshire, as confirmed a species-shunning hermit as ever put fresh water in the tank every second day and refused to see a soul. That's why I was so amazed when you told me he had suddenly risen to the surface like this. I still can't believe it. I am inclined to think that there must be some mistake, and that this bird who has been calling here is some different variety of Fink-Nottle. The chap I know wears horn-rimmed spectacles and has a face like a fish. How does that check up with your data?"

"The gentleman who came to the flat wore horn-rimmed spectacles, sir."

"And looked like something on a slab?"

"Possibly there was a certain suggestion of the piscine, sir."

"Then it must be Gussie, I suppose. But what on earth can have brought him up to London?"

"I am in a position to explain that, sir. Mr. Fink-Nottle confided to me his motive in visiting the metropolis. He came because the young lady is here."

"Young lady?"

"Yes, sir."

"You don't mean he's in love?"

"Yes, sir."

"Well, I'm dashed. I'm really dashed. I positively am dashed, Jeeves."

And I was too. I mean to say, a joke's a joke, but there are limits.

Then I found my mind turning to another aspect of this rummy affair. Conceding the fact that Gussie Fink-Nottle, against all the ruling of the form book, might have fallen in love, why should he have been haunting my flat like this? No doubt the occasion was one of those when a fellow needs a friend, but I couldn't see what had made him pick on me.

It wasn't as if he and I were in any way bosom. We had seen a lot of each other at one time, of course, but in the last two years I hadn't had so much as a post card from him.

I put all this to Jeeves:

"Odd, his coming to me. Still, if he did, he did. No argument about that. It must have been a nasty jar for the poor perisher when he found I wasn't here."

"No, sir. Mr. Fink-Nottle did not call to see you, sir."

"Pull yourself together, Jeeves. You've just told me that this is what he has been doing, and assiduously, at that."

"It was I with whom he was desirous of establishing communication, sir."

"You? But I didn't know you had ever met him."

"I had not had that pleasure until he called here, sir. But it appears that Mr. Sipperley, a fellow student with whom Mr. Fink-Nottle had been at the university, recommended him to place his affairs in my hands."

The mystery had conked. I saw all. As I dare say you know, Jeeves's reputation as a counsellor has long been established among the cognoscenti, and the first move of any of my little circle on discovering themselves in any form of soup is always to roll round and put the thing up to him. And when he's got A out of a bad spot, A puts B on to him. And then, when he has fixed up B, B sends C along. And so on, if you get my drift, and so forth.

That's how these big consulting practices like Jeeves's grow. Old Sippy, I knew, had been deeply impressed by the man's efforts on his behalf at the time when he was trying to get engaged to Elizabeth Moon, so it was not to be wondered at that he should have advised Gussie to apply. Pure routine, you might say.

"Oh, you're acting for him, are you?"

"Yes, sir."

"Now I follow. Now I understand. And what is Gussie's trouble?"

"Oddly enough, sir, precisely the same as that of Mr. Sipperley when I was enabled to be of assistance to him. No doubt you recall Mr. Sipperley's predicament, sir. Deeply attached to Miss Moon, he suffered from a rooted diffidence which made it impossible for him to speak."

I nodded.

"I remember. Yes, I recall the Sipperley case. He couldn't bring himself to the scratch. A marked coldness of the feet, was there not? I recollect you saying he was letting—what was it?—letting something do something. Cats entered into it, if I am not mistaken."

"Letting 'I dare not' wait upon 'I would', sir."

"That's right. But how about the cats?"

"Like the poor cat i' the adage, sir."

"Exactly. It beats me how you think up these things. And Gussie, you say, is in the same posish?"

"Yes, sir. Each time he endeavours to formulate a proposal of marriage, his courage fails him."

"And yet, if he wants this female to be his wife, he's got to say so, what? I mean, only civil to mention it."

"Precisely, sir."

I mused.

"Well, I suppose this was inevitable, Jeeves. I wouldn't have thought that this Fink-Nottle would ever have fallen a victim to the divine p, but, if he has, no wonder he finds the going sticky."

"Yes, sir."

"Look at the life he's led."

"Yes, sir."

"I don't suppose he has spoken to a girl for years. What a lesson this is to us, Jeeves, not to shut ourselves up in country houses and stare into glass tanks. You can't be the dominant male if you do that sort of thing. In this life, you can choose between two courses. You can either shut yourself up in a country house and stare into tanks, or you can be a dasher with the sex. You can't do both."

"No, sir."

I mused once more. Gussie and I, as I say, had rather lost touch, but all the same I was exercised about the poor fish, as I am about all my pals, close or distant, who find themselves treading upon Life's banana skins. It seemed to me that he was up against it.

I threw my mind back to the last time I had seen him. About two years ago, it had been. I had looked in at his place while on a motor trip, and he had put me right off my feed by bringing a couple of green things with legs to the luncheon table, crooning over them like a young mother and eventually losing one of them in the salad. That picture, rising before my eyes, didn't give me much confidence in the unfortunate goof's ability to woo and win, I must say. Especially if the girl he had earmarked was one of these tough modern thugs, all lipstick and cool, hard, sardonic eyes, as she probably was.

"Tell me, Jeeves," I said, wishing to know the worst, "what sort of a girl is this girl of Gussie's?"

"I have not met the young lady, sir. Mr. Fink-Nottle speaks highly of her attractions."

"Seemed to like her, did he?"

"Yes, sir."

"Did he mention her name? Perhaps I know her."

"She is a Miss Bassett, sir. Miss Madeline Bassett."

"What?"

"Yes, sir."

I was deeply intrigued.

"Egad, Jeeves! Fancy that. It's a small world, isn't it, what?"

"The young lady is an acquaintance of yours, sir?"

"I know her well. Your news has relieved my mind, Jeeves. It makes the whole thing begin to seem far more like a practical working proposition."

"Indeed, sir?"

"Absolutely. I confess that until you supplied this information I was feeling profoundly dubious about poor old Gussie's chances of inducing any spinster of any parish to join him in the saunter down the aisle. You will agree with me that he is not everybody's money."

"There may be something in what you say, sir."

"Cleopatra wouldn't have liked him."

"Possibly not, sir."

"And I doubt if he would go any too well with Tallulah Bankhead."

"No, sir."

"But when you tell me that the object of his affections is Miss Bassett, why, then, Jeeves, hope begins to dawn a bit. He's just the sort of chap a girl like Madeline Bassett might scoop in with relish."

This Bassett, I must explain, had been a fellow visitor of ours at Cannes; and as she and Angela had struck up one of those effervescent friendships which girls do strike up, I had seen quite a bit of her. Indeed, in my moodier moments it sometimes seemed to me that I could not move a step without stubbing my toe on the woman.

And what made it all so painful and distressing was that the more we met, the less did I seem able to find to say to her.

You know how it is with some girls. They seem to take the stuffing right out of you. I mean to say, there is something about their personality that paralyses the vocal cords and reduces the contents of the brain to cauliflower. It was like that with this Bassett and me; so much so that I have known occasions when for minutes at a stretch Bertram Wooster might have been observed fumbling with the tie, shuffling the feet, and behaving in all other respects in her presence like the complete dumb brick. When, therefore, she took her departure some two weeks before we did, you may readily imagine that, in Bertram's opinion, it was not a day too soon.

It was not her beauty, mark you, that thus numbed me. She was a pretty enough girl in a droopy, blonde, saucer-eyed way, but not the sort of breath-taker that takes the breath.

No, what caused this disintegration in a usually fairly fluent prattler with the sex was her whole mental attitude. I don't want to wrong anybody, so I won't go so far as to say that she actually wrote poetry, but her conversation, to my mind, was of a nature calculated to excite the liveliest suspicions. Well, I mean to say, when a girl suddenly asks you out of a blue sky if you don't sometimes feel that the stars are God's daisy-chain, you begin to think a bit.

As regards the fusing of her soul and mine, therefore, there was nothing doing. But with Gussie, the posish was entirely different. The thing that had stymied me—viz. that this girl was obviously all loaded down with ideals and sentiment and what not—was quite in order as far as he was concerned.

Gussie had always been one of those dreamy, soulful birds—you can't shut yourself up in the country and live only for newts, if you're not—and I could see no reason why, if he could somehow be induced to get the low, burning words off his chest, he and the Bassett shouldn't hit it off like ham and eggs.

"She's just the type for him," I said.

"I am most gratified to hear it, sir."

"And he's just the type for her. In fine, a good thing and one to be pushed along with the utmost energy. Strain every nerve, Jeeves."

"Very good, sir," replied the honest fellow. "I will attend to the matter at once."

Now up to this point, as you will doubtless agree, what you might call a perfect harmony had prevailed. Friendly gossip between employer and employed, and everything as sweet as a nut. But at this juncture, I regret to say, there was an unpleasant switch. The atmosphere suddenly changed, the storm clouds began to gather, and before we knew where we were, the jarring note had come bounding on the scene. I have known this to happen before in the Wooster home.

The first intimation I had that things were about to hot up was a pained and disapproving cough from the neighbourhood of the carpet. For, during the above exchanges, I should explain, while I, having dried the frame, had been dressing in a leisurely manner, donning here a sock, there a shoe, and gradually climbing into the vest, the shirt, the tie, and the knee-length, Jeeves had been down on the lower level, unpacking my effects.

He now rose, holding a white object. And at the sight of it, I realized that another of our domestic crises had arrived, another of those unfortunate clashes of will between two strong men, and that Bertram, unless he remembered his fighting ancestors and stood up for his rights, was about to be put upon.

I don't know if you were at Cannes this summer. If you were, you will recall that anybody with any pretensions to being the life and soul of the party was accustomed to attend binges at the Casino in the ordinary evening-wear trouserings topped to the north by a white mess-jacket with brass buttons. And ever since I had stepped aboard the Blue Train at Cannes station, I had been wondering on and off how mine would go with Jeeves.

In the matter of evening costume, you see, Jeeves is hidebound and reactionary. I had had trouble with him before about soft-bosomed shirts. And while these mess-jackets had, as I say, been all the rage—*tout ce qu'il y a de chic*—on the Côte d'Azur, I had never concealed it from myself, even when treading the measure at the Palm Beach Casino in the one I had hastened to buy, that there might be something of an upheaval about it on my return.

I prepared to be firm.

"Yes, Jeeves?" I said. And though my voice was suave, a close observer in a position to watch my eyes would have noticed a steely glint. Nobody has a greater respect for Jeeves's intellect than I have, but this disposition of his to dictate to the hand that fed him had got, I felt, to be checked. This mess-jacket was very near to my heart, and I jolly well intended to fight for it with all the vim of grand old Sieur de Wooster at the Battle of Agincourt.

"Yes, Jeeves?" I said. "Something on your mind, Jeeves?"

"I fear that you inadvertently left Cannes in the possession of a coat belonging to some other gentleman, sir."

I switched on the steely a bit more.

"No, Jeeves," I said, in a level tone, "the object under advisement is mine. I bought it out there."

"You wore it, sir?"

"Every night."

"But surely you are not proposing to wear it in England, sir?"

I saw that we had arrived at the nub.

"Yes, Jeeves."

"But, sir——"

"You were saying, Jeeves?"

"It is quite unsuitable, sir."

"I do not agree with you, Jeeves. I anticipate a great popular success for this jacket. It is my intention to spring it on the public tomorrow at Pongo Twistleton's birthday party, where I confidently expect it to be one long scream from start to finish. No argument, Jeeves. No discussion. Whatever fantastic objection you may have taken to it, I wear this jacket."

"Very good, sir."

He went on with his unpacking. I said no more on the subject. I had won the victory, and we Woosters do not triumph over a beaten foe. Presently, having completed my toilet, I bade the man a cheery farewell and in generous mood suggested that, as I was dining out, why didn't he take the evening off and go to some improving picture or something. Sort of olive branch, if you see what I mean.

He didn't seem to think much of it.

"Thank you, sir, I will remain in."

I surveyed him narrowly.

"Is this dudgeon, Jeeves?"

"No, sir, I am obliged to remain on the premises. Mr. Fink-Nottle informed me he would be calling to see me this evening."

"Oh, Gussie's coming, is he? Well, give him my love."

"Very good, sir."

"Yes, sir."

"And a whisky and soda, and so forth."

"Very good, sir."

"Right ho, Jeeves."

I then set off for the Drones.

At the Drones I ran into Pongo Twistleton, and he talked so much about his forthcoming merry-making of his, of which good reports had already reached me through my correspondents, that it was nearing eleven when I got home again.

And scarcely had I opened the door when I heard voices in the sitting-room, and scarcely had I entered the sitting-room when I found that these proceeded from Jeeves and what appeared at first sight to be the Devil.

A closer scrutiny informed me that it was Gussie Fink-Nottle, dressed as Mephistopheles.

-2-

"What-ho, Gussie," I said.

You couldn't have told it from my manner, but I was feeling more than a bit nonplussed. The spectacle before me was enough to nonplus anyone. I mean to say, this Fink-Nottle, as I remembered him, was the sort of shy, shrinking goop who might have been expected to shake like an aspen if invited to so much as a social Saturday afternoon at the vicarage. And yet here he was, if one could credit one's senses, about to take part in a fancy-dress ball, a form of entertainment notoriously a testing experience for the toughest.

And he was attending that fancy-dress ball, mark you—not, like every other well-bred Englishman, as a Pierrot, but as Mephistopheles—this involving, as I need scarcely stress, not only scarlet tights but a pretty frightful false beard.

Rummy, you'll admit. However, one masks one's feelings. I betrayed no vulgar astonishment, but, as I say, what-hoed with civil nonchalance.

He grinned through the fungus—rather sheepishly, I thought.

"Oh, hullo, Bertie."

"Long time since I saw you. Have a spot?"

"No, thanks. I must be off in a minute. I just came round to ask Jeeves how he thought I looked. How do you think I look, Bertie?"

Well, the answer to that, of course, was "perfectly foul". But we Woosters are men of tact and have a nice sense of the obligations of a host. We do not tell old friends beneath our roof-tree that they are an offence to the eyesight. I evaded the question.

"I hear you're in London," I said carelessly.

"Oh, yes."

"Must be years since you came up."

"Oh, yes."

"And now you're off for an evening's pleasure."

He shuddered a bit. He had, I noticed, a hunted air.

"Pleasure!"

"Aren't you looking forward to this rout or revel?"

"Oh, I suppose it'll be all right," he said, in a toneless voice. "Anyway, I ought to be off, I suppose. The thing starts round about eleven. I told my cab to wait.... Will you see if it's there, Jeeves?"

"Very good, sir."

There was something of a pause after the door had closed. A certain constraint. I mixed myself a beaker, while Gussie, a glutton for punishment, stared at himself in the mirror. Finally I decided that it would be best to let him know that I was abreast of his affairs. It might be that it would ease his mind to confide in a sympathetic man of experience. I have generally found, with those under the influence, that what they want more than anything is the listening ear.

"Well, Gussie, old leper," I said, "I've been hearing all about you."

"Eh?"

"This little trouble of yours. Jeeves has told me everything."

He didn't seem any too braced. It's always difficult to be sure, of course, when a chap has dug himself in behind a Mephistopheles beard, but I fancy he flushed a trifle.

"I wish Jeeves wouldn't go gassing all over the place. It was supposed to be confidential."

I could not permit this tone.

"Dishing up the dirt to the young master can scarcely be described as gassing all over the place," I said, with a touch of rebuke. "Anyway, there it is. I know all. And I should like to begin," I said, sinking my personal opinion that the female in question was a sloppy pest in my desire to buck and encourage, "by saying that Madeline Bassett is a charming girl. A winner, and just the sort for you."

"You don't know her?"

"Certainly I know her. What beats me is how you ever got in touch. Where did you meet?"

"She was staying at a place near mine in Lincolnshire the week before last."

"Yes, but even so. I didn't know you called on the neighbours."

"I don't. I met her out for a walk with her dog. The dog had got a thorn in its foot, and when she tried to take it out, it snapped at her. So, of course, I had to rally round."

"You extracted the thorn?"

"Yes."

"And fell in love at first sight?"

"Yes."

"Well, dash it, with a thing like that to give you a send-off, why didn't you cash in immediately?"

"I hadn't the nerve."

"What happened?"

"We talked for a bit."

"What about?"

"Oh, birds."

"Birds? What birds?"

"The birds that happened to be hanging round. And the scenery, and all that sort of thing. And she said she was going to London, and asked me to look her up if I was ever there."

"And even after that you didn't so much as press her hand?"

"Of course not."

Well, I mean, it looked as though there was no more to be said. If a chap is such a rabbit that he can't get action when he's handed the thing on a plate, his case would appear to be pretty hopeless. Nevertheless, I reminded myself that this non-starter and I had been at school together. One must make an effort for an old school friend.

"Ah, well," I said, "we must see what can be done. Things may brighten. At any rate, you will be glad to learn that I am behind you in this enterprise. You have Bertram Wooster in your corner, Gussie."

"Thanks, old man. And Jeeves, of course, which is the thing that really matters."

I don't mind admitting that I winced. He meant no harm, I suppose, but I'm bound to say that this tactless speech nettled me not a little. People are always nettling me like that. Giving me to understand, I mean to say, that in their opinion Bertram Wooster is a mere cipher and that the only member of the household with brains and resources is Jeeves.

It jars on me.

And tonight it jarred on me more than usual, because I was feeling pretty dashed fed with Jeeves. Over that matter of the mess jacket, I mean. True, I had forced him to climb down, quelling him, as described, with the quiet strength of my personality, but I was still a trifle shirty at his having brought the thing up at all. It seemed to me that what Jeeves wanted was the iron hand.

"And what is he doing about it?" I inquired stiffly.

"He's been giving the position of affairs a lot of thought."

"He has, has he?"

"It's on his advice that I'm going to this dance."

"Why?"

"She is going to be there. In fact, it was she who sent me the ticket of invitation. And Jeeves considered——"

"And why not as a Pierrot?" I said, taking up the point which had struck me before. "Why this break with a grand old tradition?"

"He particularly wanted me to go as Mephistopheles."

I started.

"He did, did he? He specifically recommended that definite costume?"

"Yes."

"Ha!"

"Eh?"

"Nothing. Just 'Ha!'"

And I'll tell you why I said "Ha!" Here was Jeeves making heavy weather about me wearing a perfectly ordinary white mess jacket, a garment not only *tout ce qu'il y a de chic*, but absolutely *de rigueur*, and in the same breath, as you might say, inciting Gussie Fink-Nottle to be a blot on the London scene in scarlet tights. Ironical, what? One looks askance at this sort of in-and-out running.

"What has he got against Pierrots?"

"I don't think he objects to Pierrots as Pierrots. But in my case he thought a Pierrot wouldn't be adequate."

"I don't follow that."

"He said that the costume of Pierrot, while pleasing to the eye, lacked the authority of the Mephistopheles costume."

"I still don't get it."

"Well, it's a matter of psychology, he said."

There was a time when a remark like that would have had me snookered. But long association with Jeeves has developed the

Wooster vocabulary considerably. Jeeves has always been a whale for the psychology of the individual, and I now follow him like a bloodhound when he snaps it out of the bag.

"Oh, psychology?"

"Yes. Jeeves is a great believer in the moral effect of clothes. He thinks I might be emboldened in a striking costume like this. He said a Pirate Chief would be just as good. In fact, a Pirate Chief was his first suggestion, but I objected to the boots."

I saw his point. There is enough sadness in life without having fellows like Gussie Fink-Nottle going about in sea boots.

"And are you emboldened?"

"Well, to be absolutely accurate, Bertie, old man, no."

A gust of compassion shook me. After all, though we had lost touch a bit of recent years, this man and I had once thrown inked darts at each other.

"Gussie," I said, "take an old friend's advice, and don't go within a mile of this binge."

"But it's my last chance of seeing her. She's off tomorrow to stay with some people in the country. Besides, you don't know."

"Don't know what?"

"That this idea of Jeeves's won't work. I feel a most frightful chump now, yes, but who can say whether that will not pass off when I get into a mob of other people in fancy dress. I had the same experience as a child, one year during the Christmas festivities. They dressed me up as a rabbit, and the shame was indescribable. Yet when I got to the party and found myself surrounded by scores of other children, many in costumes even ghastlier than my own, I perked up amazingly, joined freely in the revels, and was able to eat so hearty a supper that I was sick twice in the cab coming home. What I mean is, you can't tell in cold blood."

I weighed this. It was specious, of course.

"And you can't get away from it that, fundamentally, Jeeves's idea is sound. In a striking costume like Mephistopheles, I might quite easily pull off something pretty impressive. Colour does make a difference. Look at newts. During the courting season the male newt is brilliantly coloured. It helps him a lot."

"But you aren't a male newt."

"I wish I were. Do you know how a male newt proposes, Bertie?

46

He just stands in front of the female newt vibrating his tail and bending his body in a semi-circle. I could do that on my head. No, you wouldn't find me grousing if I were a male newt."

"But if you were a male newt, Madeline Bassett wouldn't look at you. Not with the eye of love, I mean."

"She would, if she were a female newt."

"But she isn't a female newt."

"No, but suppose she was."

"Well, if she was, you wouldn't be in love with her."

"Yes, I would, if I were a male newt."

A slight throbbing about the temples told me that this discussion had reached saturation point.

"Well, anyway," I said, "coming down to hard facts and cutting out all this visionary stuff about vibrating tails and what not, the salient point that emerges is that you are booked to appear at a fancy-dress ball. And I tell you out of my riper knowledge of fancy-dress balls, Gussie, that you won't enjoy yourself."

"It isn't a question of enjoying yourself."

"I wouldn't go."

"I must go. I keep telling you she's off to the country tomorrow."

I gave it up.

"So be it," I said. "Have it your own way.... Yes, Jeeves?"

"Mr. Fink-Nottle's cab, sir."

"Ah? The cab, eh?... Your cab, Gussie."

"Oh, the cab? Oh, right. Of course, yes, rather.... Thanks, Jeeves ... Well, so long, Bertie."

And giving me the sort of weak smile Roman gladiators used to give the Emperor before entering the arena, Gussie trickled off. And I turned to Jeeves. The moment had arrived for putting him in his place, and I was all for it.

It was a little difficult to know how to begin, of course. I mean to say, while firmly resolved to tick him off, I didn't want to gash his feelings too deeply. Even when displaying the iron hand, we Woosters like to keep the thing fairly matey.

However, on consideration, I saw that there was nothing to be gained by trying to lead up to it gently. It is never any use beating about the b.

"Jeeves," I said, "may I speak frankly?"

"Certainly, sir."

"What I have to say may wound you."

"Not at all, sir."

"Well, then, I have been having a chat with Mr. Fink-Nottle, and he has been telling me about this Mephistopheles scheme of yours."

"Yes, sir?"

"Now let me get it straight. If I follow your reasoning correctly, you think that, stimulated by being upholstered throughout in scarlet tights, Mr. Fink-Nottle, on encountering the adored object, will vibrate his tail and generally let himself go with a whoop."

"I am of opinion that he will lose much of his normal diffidence, sir."

"I don't agree with you, Jeeves."

"No, sir?"

"No. In fact, not to put too fine a point upon it, I consider that of all the dashed silly, drivelling ideas I ever heard in my puff this is the most blithering and futile. It won't work. Not a chance. All you have done is to subject Mr. Fink-Nottle to the nameless horrors of a fancy-dress ball for nothing. And this is not the first time this sort of thing has happened. To be quite candid, Jeeves, I have frequently noticed before now a tendency or disposition on your part to become—what's the word?"

"I could not say, sir."

"Eloquent? No, it's not eloquent. Elusive? No, it's not elusive. It's on the tip of my tongue. Begins with an 'e' and means being a jolly sight too clever."

"Elaborate, sir?"

"That is the exact word I was after. Too elaborate, Jeeves—that is what you are frequently prone to become. Your methods are not simple, not straightforward. You cloud the issue with a lot of fancy stuff that is not of the essence. All that Gussie needs is the elder-brotherly advice of a seasoned man of the world. So what I suggest is that from now onward you leave this case to me."

"Very good, sir."

"You lay off and devote yourself to your duties about the home."

"Very good, sir."

"I shall no doubt think of something quite simple and straightforward yet perfectly effective ere long. I will make a point of seeing Gussie tomorrow."

"Very good, sir."

"Right ho, Jeeves."

But on the morrow all those telegrams started coming in, and I confess that for twenty-four hours I didn't give the poor chap a thought, having problems of my own to contend with.

-3-

The first of the telegrams arrived shortly after noon, and Jeeves brought it in with the before-luncheon snifter. It was from my Aunt Dahlia, operating from Market Snodsbury, a small town of sorts a mile or two along the main road as you leave her country seat.

It ran as follows:

Come at once. Travers.

And when I say it puzzled me like the dickens, I am understating it; if anything. As mysterious a communication, I considered, as was ever flashed over the wires. I studied it in a profound reverie for the best part of two dry Martinis and a dividend. I read it backwards. I read it forwards. As a matter of fact, I have a sort of recollection of even smelling it. But it still baffled me.

Consider the facts, I mean. It was only a few hours since this aunt and I had parted, after being in constant association for nearly two months. And yet here she was—with my farewell kiss still lingering on her cheek, so to speak—pleading for another reunion. Bertram Wooster is not accustomed to this gluttonous appetite for his society. Ask anyone who knows me, and they will tell you that after two months of my company, what the normal person feels is that that will about do for the present. Indeed, I have known people who couldn't stick it out for more than a few days.

Before sitting down to the well-cooked, therefore, I sent this reply:

Perplexed. Explain. Bertie.

To this I received an answer during the after-luncheon sleep:

What on earth is there to be perplexed about, ass? Come at once. Travers.

Three cigarettes and a couple of turns about the room, and I had my response ready:

How do you mean come at once? Regards. Bertie.

I append the comeback:

I mean come at once, you maddening half-wit. What did you think I meant? Come at once or expect an aunt's curse first post tomorrow. Love. Travers.

I then dispatched the following message, wishing to get everything quite clear:

When you say "Come" do you mean "Come to Brinkley Court"? And when you say "At once" do you mean "At once"? Fogged. At a loss. All the best. Bertie.

I sent this one off on my way to the Drones, where I spent a restful afternoon throwing cards into a top-hat with some of the better element. Returning in the evening hush, I found the answer waiting for me:

Yes, yes, yes, yes, yes, yes, yes. It doesn't matter whether you understand or not. You just come at once, as I tell you, and for heaven's sake stop this back-chat. Do you think I am made of money that I can afford to send you telegrams every ten minutes. Stop being a fathead and come immediately. Love. Travers.

It was at this point that I felt the need of getting a second opinion. I pressed the bell.

"Jeeves," I said, "a V-shaped rumminess has manifested itself from the direction of Worcestershire. Read these," I said, handing him the papers in the case.

He scanned them.

"What do you make of it, Jeeves?"

"I think Mrs. Travers wishes you to come at once, sir."

"You gather that too, do you?"

"Yes, sir."

"I put the same construction on the thing. But why, Jeeves? Dash it all, she's just had nearly two months of me."

"Yes, sir."

"And many people consider the medium dose for an adult two

50

days."

"Yes, sir. I appreciate the point you raise. Nevertheless, Mrs. Travers appears very insistent. I think it would be well to acquiesce in her wishes."

"Pop down, you mean?"

"Yes, sir."

"Well, I certainly can't go at once. I've an important conference on at the Drones tonight. Pongo Twistleton's birthday party, you remember."

"Yes, sir."

There was a slight pause. We were both recalling the little unpleasantness that had arisen. I felt obliged to allude to it.

"You're all wrong about that mess jacket, Jeeves."

"These things are matters of opinion, sir."

"When I wore it at the Casino at Cannes, beautiful women nudged one another and whispered: 'Who is he?'"

"The code at Continental casinos is notoriously lax, sir."

"And when I described it to Pongo last night, he was fascinated."

"Indeed, sir?"

"So were all the rest of those present. One and all admitted that I had got hold of a good thing. Not a dissentient voice."

"Indeed, sir?"

"I am convinced that you will eventually learn to love this mess-jacket, Jeeves."

"I fear not, sir."

I gave it up. It is never any use trying to reason with Jeeves on these occasions. "Pig-headed" is the word that springs to the lips. One sighs and passes on.

"Well, anyway, returning to the agenda, I can't go down to Brinkley Court or anywhere else yet awhile. That's final. I'll tell you what, Jeeves. Give me form and pencil, and I'll wire her that I'll be with her some time next week or the week after. Dash it all, she ought to be able to hold out without me for a few days. It only requires will power."

"Yes, sir."

"Right ho, then. I'll wire 'Expect me tomorrow fortnight' or words to some such effect. That ought to meet the case. Then if you will toddle round the corner and send it off, that will be that."

"Very good, sir."

And so the long day wore on till it was time for me to dress for Pongo's party.

Pongo had assured me, while chatting of the affair on the previous night, that this birthday binge of his was to be on a scale calculated to stagger humanity, and I must say I have participated in less fruity functions. It was well after four when I got home, and by that time I was about ready to turn in. I can just remember groping for the bed and crawling into it, and it seemed to me that the lemon had scarcely touched the pillow before I was aroused by the sound of the door opening.

I was barely ticking over, but I contrived to raise an eyelid.

"Is that my tea, Jeeves?"

"No, sir. It is Mrs. Travers."

And a moment later there was a sound like a mighty rushing wind, and the relative had crossed the threshold at fifty m.p.h. under her own steam.

-4-

It has been well said of Bertram Wooster that, while no one views his flesh and blood with a keener and more remorselessly critical eye, he is nevertheless a man who delights in giving credit where credit is due. And if you have followed these memoirs of mine with the proper care, you will be aware that I have frequently had occasion to emphasise the fact that Aunt Dahlia is all right.

She is the one, if you remember, who married old Tom Travers *en secondes noces*, as I believe the expression is, the year Bluebottle won the Cambridgeshire, and once induced me to write an article on What the Well-Dressed Man is Wearing for that paper she runs— *Milady's Boudoir*. She is a large, genial soul, with whom it is a pleasure to hob-nob. In her spiritual make-up there is none of that subtle gosh-awfulness which renders such an exhibit as, say, my Aunt Agatha the curse of the Home Counties and a menace to one and all. I have the highest esteem for Aunt Dahlia, and have never wavered in my cordial appreciation of her humanity, sporting qualities and general good-eggishness.

This being so, you may conceive of my astonishment at finding her at my bedside at such an hour. I mean to say, I've stayed at her place many a time and oft, and she knows my habits. She is well aware that until I have had my cup of tea in the morning, I do not receive. This crashing in at a moment when she knew that solitude and repose were of the essence was scarcely, I could not but feel, the good old form.

Besides, what business had she being in London at all? That was what I asked myself. When a conscientious housewife has returned to her home after an absence of seven weeks, one does not expect her to start racing off again the day after her arrival. One feels that she ought to be sticking round, ministering to her husband, conferring with the cook, feeding the cat, combing and brushing the Pomeranian—in a word, staying put. I was more than a little bleary-eyed, but I endeavoured, as far as the fact that my eyelids were more or less glued together would permit, to give her an austere and censorious look.

She didn't seem to get it.

"Wake up, Bertie, you old ass!" she cried, in a voice that hit me between the eyebrows and went out at the back of my head.

If Aunt Dahlia has a fault, it is that she is apt to address a *vis-à-vis* as if he were somebody half a mile away whom she had observed riding over hounds. A throwback, no doubt, to the time when she counted the day lost that was not spent in chivvying some unfortunate fox over the countryside.

I gave her another of the austere and censorious, and this time it registered. All the effect it had, however, was to cause her to descend to personalities.

"Don't blink at me in that obscene way," she said. "I wonder, Bertie," she proceeded, gazing at me as I should imagine Gussie would have gazed at some newt that was not up to sample, "if you have the faintest conception how perfectly loathsome you look? A cross between an orgy scene in the movies and some low form of pond life. I suppose you were out on the tiles last night?"

"I attended a social function, yes," I said coldly. "Pongo Twistleton's birthday party. I couldn't let Pongo down. *Noblesse oblige.*"

"Well, get up and dress."

I felt I could not have heard her aright.

"Get up and dress?"

"Yes."

I turned on the pillow with a little moan, and at this juncture Jeeves entered with the vital oolong. I clutched at it like a drowning man at a straw hat. A deep sip or two, and I felt—I won't say restored, because a birthday party like Pongo Twistleton's isn't a thing you get restored after with a mere mouthful of tea, but sufficiently the old Bertram to be able to bend the mind on this awful thing which had come upon me.

And the more I bent same, the less could I grasp the trend of the scenario.

"What is this, Aunt Dahlia?" I inquired.

"It looks to me like tea," was her response. "But you know best. You're drinking it."

If I hadn't been afraid of spilling the healing brew, I have little doubt that I should have given an impatient gesture. I know I felt like it.

"Not the contents of this cup. All this. Your barging in and telling me to get up and dress, and all that rot."

"I've barged in, as you call it, because my telegrams seemed to produce no effect. And I told you to get up and dress because I want you to get up and dress. I've come to take you back with me. I like your crust, wiring that you would come next year or whenever it was. You're coming now. I've got a job for you."

"But I don't want a job."

"What you want, my lad, and what you're going to get are two very different things. There is man's work for you to do at Brinkley Court. Be ready to the last button in twenty minutes."

"But I can't possibly be ready to any buttons in twenty minutes. I'm feeling awful."

She seemed to consider.

"Yes," she said. "I suppose it's only humane to give you a day or two to recover. All right, then, I shall expect you on the thirtieth at the latest."

"But, dash it, what is all this? How do you mean, a job? Why a job? What sort of a job?"

"I'll tell you if you'll only stop talking for a minute. It's quite an easy, pleasant job. You will enjoy it. Have you ever heard of Market Snodsbury Grammar School?"

"Never."

"It's a grammar school at Market Snodsbury."

I told her a little frigidly that I had divined as much.

"Well, how was I to know that a man with a mind like yours would grasp it so quickly?" she protested. "All right, then. Market Snodsbury Grammar School is, as you have guessed, the grammar school at Market Snodsbury. I'm one of the governors."

"You mean one of the governesses."

"I don't mean one of the governesses. Listen, ass. There was a board of governors at Eton, wasn't there? Very well. So there is at Market Snodsbury Grammar School, and I'm a member of it. And they left the arrangements for the summer prize-giving to me. This prize-giving takes place on the last—or thirty-first—day of this month. Have you got that clear?"

I took another oz. of the life-saving and inclined my head. Even after a Pongo Twistleton birthday party, I was capable of grasping simple facts like these.

"I follow you, yes. I see the point you are trying to make, certainly. Market ... Snodsbury ... Grammar School ... Board of governors ... Prize-giving.... Quite. But what's it got to do with me?"

"You're going to give away the prizes."

I goggled. Her words did not appear to make sense. They seemed the mere aimless vapouring of an aunt who has been sitting out in the sun without a hat.

"Me?"

"You."

I goggled again.

"You don't mean me?"

"I mean you in person."

I goggled a third time.

"You're pulling my leg."

"I am not pulling your leg. Nothing would induce me to touch your beastly leg. The vicar was to have officiated, but when I got home I found a letter from him saying that he had strained a fetlock and must scratch his nomination. You can imagine the state I was in. I telephoned all over the place. Nobody would take it on. And then suddenly I thought of you."

I decided to check all this rot at the outset. Nobody is more eager to oblige deserving aunts than Bertram Wooster, but there are limits, and sharply defined limits, at that.

"So you think I'm going to strew prizes at this bally Dotheboys Hall of yours?"

"I do."

"And make a speech?"

"Exactly."

I laughed derisively.

"For goodness' sake, don't start gargling now. This is serious."

"I was laughing."

"Oh, were you? Well, I'm glad to see you taking it in this merry spirit."

"Derisively," I explained. "I won't do it. That's final. I simply will not do it."

"You will do it, young Bertie, or never darken my doors again. And you know what that means. No more of Anatole's dinners for you."

A strong shudder shook me. She was alluding to her *chef*, that superb artist. A monarch of his profession, unsurpassed—nay, unequalled—at dishing up the raw material so that it melted in the mouth of the ultimate consumer, Anatole had always been a magnet that drew me to Brinkley Court with my tongue hanging out. Many of my happiest moments had been those which I had spent champing this great man's roasts and ragouts, and the prospect of being barred from digging into them in the future was a numbing one.

"No, I say, dash it!"

"I thought that would rattle you. Greedy young pig."

"Greedy young pigs have nothing to do with it," I said with a touch of hauteur. "One is not a greedy young pig because one

56

appreciates the cooking of a genius."

"Well, I will say I like it myself," conceded the relative. "But not another bite of it do you get, if you refuse to do this simple, easy, pleasant job. No, not so much as another sniff. So put that in your twelve-inch cigarette-holder and smoke it."

I began to feel like some wild thing caught in a snare.

"But why do you want me? I mean, what am I? Ask yourself that."

"I often have."

"I mean to say, I'm not the type. You have to have some terrific nib to give away prizes. I seem to remember, when I was at school, it was generally a prime minister or somebody."

"Ah, but that was at Eton. At Market Snodsbury we aren't nearly so choosy. Anybody in spats impresses us."

"Why don't you get Uncle Tom?"

"Uncle Tom!"

"Well, why not? He's got spats."

"Bertie," she said, "I will tell you why not Uncle Tom. You remember me losing all that money at baccarat at Cannes? Well, very shortly I shall have to sidle up to Tom and break the news to him. If, right after that, I ask him to put on lavender gloves and a topper and distribute the prizes at Market Snodsbury Grammar School, there will be a divorce in the family. He would pin a note to the pincushion and be off like a rabbit. No, my lad, you're for it, so you may as well make the best of it."

"But, Aunt Dahlia, listen to reason. I assure you, you've got hold of the wrong man. I'm hopeless at a game like that. Ask Jeeves about the time I got lugged in to address a girls' school. I made the most colossal ass of myself."

"And I confidently anticipate that you will make an equally colossal ass of yourself on the thirty-first of this month. That's why I want you. The way I look at it is that, as the thing is bound to be a frost, anyway, one may as well get a hearty laugh out of it. I shall enjoy seeing you distribute those prizes, Bertie. Well, I won't keep you, as, no doubt, you want to do your Swedish exercises. I shall expect you in a day or two."

And with these heartless words she beetled off, leaving me a prey to the gloomiest emotions. What with the natural reaction after Pongo's party and this stunning blow, it is not too much to say that the soul was seared.

And I was still writhing in the depths, when the door opened and Jeeves appeared.

"Mr. Fink-Nottle to see you, sir," he announced.

-5-

I gave him one of my looks.

"Jeeves," I said, "I had scarcely expected this of you. You are aware that I was up to an advanced hour last night. You know that I have barely had my tea. You cannot be ignorant of the effect of that hearty voice of Aunt Dahlia's on a man with a headache. And yet you come bringing me Fink-Nottles. Is this a time for Fink or any other kind of Nottle?"

"But did you not give me to understand, sir, that you wished to see Mr. Fink-Nottle to advise him on his affairs?"

This, I admit, opened up a new line of thought. In the stress of my emotions, I had clean forgotten about having taken Gussie's interests in hand. It altered things. One can't give the raspberry to a client. I mean, you didn't find Sherlock Holmes refusing to see clients just because he had been out late the night before at Doctor Watson's birthday party. I could have wished that the man had selected some more suitable hour for approaching me, but as he appeared to be a sort of human lark, leaving his watery nest at daybreak, I supposed I had better give him an audience.

"True," I said. "All right. Bung him in."

"Very good, sir."

"But before doing so, bring me one of those pick-me-ups of yours."

"Very good, sir."

And presently he returned with the vital essence.

I have had occasion, I fancy, to speak before now of these pick-me-ups of Jeeves's and their effect on a fellow who is hanging to life by a thread on the morning after. What they consist of, I couldn't tell you. He says some kind of sauce, the yolk of a raw egg and a dash of red pepper, but nothing will convince me that the thing doesn't go much deeper than that. Be that as it may, however, the results of swallowing one are amazing.

For perhaps the split part of a second nothing happens. It is as though all Nature waited breathless. Then, suddenly, it is as if the Last Trump had sounded and Judgment Day set in with unusual severity.

Bonfires burst out in all in parts of the frame. The abdomen becomes heavily charged with molten lava. A great wind seems to blow through the world, and the subject is aware of something resembling a steam hammer striking the back of the head. During this phase, the ears ring loudly, the eyeballs rotate and there is a tingling about the brow.

And then, just as you are feeling that you ought to ring up your lawyer and see that your affairs are in order before it is too late, the whole situation seems to clarify. The wind drops. The ears cease to ring. Birds twitter. Brass bands start playing. The sun comes up over the horizon with a jerk.

And a moment later all you are conscious of is a great peace.

As I drained the glass now, new life seemed to burgeon within me. I remember Jeeves, who, however much he may go off the rails at times in the matter of dress clothes and in his advice to those in love, has always had a neat turn of phrase, once speaking of someone rising on stepping-stones of his dead self to higher things. It was that way with me now. I felt that the Bertram Wooster who lay propped up against the pillows had become a better, stronger, finer Bertram.

"Thank you, Jeeves," I said.

"Not at all, sir."

"That touched the exact spot. I am now able to cope with life's problems."

"I am gratified to hear it, sir."

"What madness not to have had one of those before tackling Aunt Dahlia! However, too late to worry about that now. Tell me of Gussie. How did he make out at the fancy-dress ball?"

"He did not arrive at the fancy-dress ball, sir."

I looked at him a bit austerely.

"Jeeves," I said, "I admit that after that pick-me-up of yours I feel better, but don't try me too high. Don't stand by my sick bed talking absolute rot. We shot Gussie into a cab and he started forth, headed for wherever this fancy-dress ball was. He must have arrived."

"No, sir. As I gather from Mr. Fink-Nottle, he entered the cab convinced in his mind that the entertainment to which he had been invited was to be held at No. 17, Suffolk Square, whereas the actual rendezvous was No. 71, Norfolk Terrace. These aberrations of memory are not uncommon with those who, like Mr. Fink-Nottle, belong essentially to what one might call the dreamer-type."

"One might also call it the fatheaded type."

"Yes, sir."

"Well?"

"On reaching No. 17, Suffolk Square, Mr. Fink-Nottle endeavoured to produce money to pay the fare."

"What stopped him?"

"The fact that he had no money, sir. He discovered that he had left it, together with his ticket of invitation, on the mantelpiece of his bedchamber in the house of his uncle, where he was residing. Bidding the cabman to wait, accordingly, he rang the door-bell, and when the butler appeared, requested him to pay the cab, adding that it was all right, as he was one of the guests invited to the dance. The butler then disclaimed all knowledge of a dance on the premises."

"And declined to unbelt?"

"Yes, sir."

"Upon which——"

"Mr. Fink-Nottle directed the cabman to drive him back to his uncle's residence."

"Well, why wasn't that the happy ending? All he had to do was go in, collect cash and ticket, and there he would have been, on velvet."

"I should have mentioned, sir, that Mr. Fink-Nottle had also left his latchkey on the mantelpiece of his bedchamber."

"He could have rung the bell."

"He did ring the bell, sir, for some fifteen minutes. At the expiration of that period he recalled that he had given permission to the caretaker—the house was officially closed and all the staff on holiday—to visit his sailor son at Portsmouth."

"Golly, Jeeves!"

"Yes, sir."

"These dreamer types do live, don't they?"

"Yes, sir."

"What happened then?"

"Mr. Fink-Nottle appears to have realized at this point that his position as regards the cabman had become equivocal. The figures on the clock had already reached a substantial sum, and he was not in a position to meet his obligations."

"He could have explained."

"You cannot explain to cabmen, sir. On endeavouring to do so, he found the fellow sceptical of his bona fides."

"I should have legged it."

"That is the policy which appears to have commended itself to Mr. Fink-Nottle. He darted rapidly away, and the cabman, endeavouring to detain him, snatched at his overcoat. Mr. Fink-Nottle contrived to extricate himself from the coat, and it would seem that his appearance in the masquerade costume beneath it came as something of a shock to the cabman. Mr. Fink-Nottle informs me that he heard a species of whistling gasp, and, looking round, observed the man crouching against the railings with his hands over his face. Mr. Fink-Nottle thinks he was praying. No doubt an uneducated, superstitious fellow, sir. Possibly a drinker."

"Well, if he hadn't been one before, I'll bet he started being one shortly afterwards. I expect he could scarcely wait for the pubs to open."

"Very possibly, in the circumstances he might have found a restorative agreeable, sir."

"And so, in the circumstances, might Gussie too, I should think. What on earth did he do after that? London late at night—or even in the daytime, for that matter—is no place for a man in scarlet tights."

"No, sir."

"He invites comment."

"Yes, sir."

"I can see the poor old bird ducking down side-streets, skulking in alley-ways, diving into dust-bins."

"I gathered from Mr. Fink-Nottle's remarks, sir, that something very much on those lines was what occurred. Eventually, after a trying night, he found his way to Mr. Sipperley's residence, where he was able to secure lodging and a change of costume in the morning."

I nestled against the pillows, the brow a bit drawn. It is all very well to try to do old school friends a spot of good, but I could not but feel that in espousing the cause of a lunkhead capable of mucking things up as Gussie had done, I had taken on a contract almost too big for human consumption. It seemed to me that what Gussie needed was not so much the advice of a seasoned man of the world as a padded cell in Colney Hatch and a couple of good keepers to see that he did not set the place on fire.

Indeed, for an instant I had half a mind to withdraw from the case and hand it back to Jeeves. But the pride of the Woosters restrained me. When we Woosters put our hands to the plough, we do not readily sheathe the sword. Besides, after that business of the mess-jacket, anything resembling weakness would have been fatal.

"I suppose you realize, Jeeves," I said, for though one dislikes to rub it in, these things have to be pointed out, "that all this was your fault?"

"Sir?"

"It's no good saying 'Sir?' You know it was. If you had not insisted on his going to that dance—a mad project, as I spotted from the first—this would not have happened."

"Yes, sir, but I confess I did not anticipate——"

"Always anticipate everything, Jeeves," I said, a little sternly. "It is the only way. Even if you had allowed him to wear a Pierrot costume, things would not have panned out as they did. A Pierrot costume has pockets. However," I went on more kindly, "we need not go into that now. If all this has shown you what comes of going about the place in scarlet tights, that is something gained. Gussie waits without, you say?"

"Yes, sir."

"Then shoot him in, and I will see what I can do for him."

-6-

Gussie, on arrival, proved to be still showing traces of his grim experience. The face was pale, the eyes gooseberry-like, the ears drooping, and the whole aspect that of a man who has passed through the furnace and been caught in the machinery. I hitched myself up a bit higher on the pillows and gazed at him narrowly. It was a moment, I could see, when first aid was required, and I prepared to get down to cases.

"Well, Gussie."

"Hullo, Bertie."

"What ho."

"What ho."

These civilities concluded, I felt that the moment had come to touch delicately on the past.

"I hear you've been through it a bit."

"Yes."

"Thanks to Jeeves."

"It wasn't Jeeves's fault."

"Entirely Jeeves's fault."

"I don't see that. I forgot my money and latchkey——"

"And now you'd better forget Jeeves. For you will be interested to hear, Gussie," I said, deeming it best to put him in touch with the position of affairs right away, "that he is no longer handling your little problem."

This seemed to slip it across him properly. The jaws fell, the ears drooped more limply. He had been looking like a dead fish. He now looked like a deader fish, one of last year's, cast up on some lonely beach and left there at the mercy of the wind and tides.

"What!"

"Yes."

"You don't mean that Jeeves isn't going to——"

"No."

"But, dash it——"

I was kind, but firm.

"You will be much better off without him. Surely your terrible experiences of that awful night have told you that Jeeves needs a rest. The keenest of thinkers strikes a bad patch occasionally. That is what has happened to Jeeves. I have seen it coming on for some time. He has lost his form. He wants his plugs decarbonized. No doubt this is a shock to you. I suppose you came here this morning to seek his advice?"

"Of course I did."

"On what point?"

"Madeline Bassett has gone to stay with these people in the country, and I want to know what he thinks I ought to do."

"Well, as I say, Jeeves is off the case."

"But, Bertie, dash it———"

"Jeeves," I said with a certain asperity, "is no longer on the case. I am now in sole charge."

"But what on earth can you do?"

I curbed my resentment. We Woosters are fair-minded. We can make allowances for men who have been parading London all night in scarlet tights.

"That," I said quietly, "we shall see. Sit down and let us confer. I am bound to say the thing seems quite simple to me. You say this girl has gone to visit friends in the country. It would appear obvious that you must go there too, and flock round her like a poultice. Elementary."

"But I can't plant myself on a lot of perfect strangers."

"Don't you know these people?"

"Of course I don't. I don't know anybody."

I pursed the lips. This did seem to complicate matters somewhat.

"All that I know is that their name is Travers, and it's a place called Brinkley Court down in Worcestershire."

I unpursed my lips.

"Gussie," I said, smiling paternally, "it was a lucky day for you when Bertram Wooster interested himself in your affairs. As I foresaw from the start, I can fix everything. This afternoon you shall go to Brinkley Court, an honoured guest."

He quivered like a *mousse*. I suppose it must always be rather a thrilling experience for the novice to watch me taking hold.

"But, Bertie, you don't mean you know these Traverses?"

"They are my Aunt Dahlia."

"My gosh!"

"You see now," I pointed out, "how lucky you were to get me behind you. You go to Jeeves, and what does he do? He dresses you up in scarlet tights and one of the foulest false beards of my experience, and sends you off to fancy-dress balls. Result, agony of spirit and no progress. I then take over and put you on the right lines. Could Jeeves have got you into Brinkley Court? Not a chance. Aunt Dahlia isn't his aunt. I merely mention these things."

"By Jove, Bertie, I don't know how to thank you."

"My dear chap!"

"But, I say."

"Now what?"

"What do I do when I get there?"

"If you knew Brinkley Court, you would not ask that question. In those romantic surroundings you can't miss. Great lovers through the ages have fixed up the preliminary formalities at Brinkley. The place is simply ill with atmosphere. You will stroll with the girl in the shady walks. You will sit with her on the shady lawns. You will row on the lake with her. And gradually you will find yourself working up to a point where——"

"By Jove, I believe you're right."

"Of course, I'm right. I've got engaged three times at Brinkley. No business resulted, but the fact remains. And I went there without the foggiest idea of indulging in the tender pash. I hadn't the slightest intention of proposing to anybody. Yet no sooner had I entered those romantic grounds than I found myself reaching out for the nearest girl in sight and slapping my soul down in front of her. It's something in the air."

"I see exactly what you mean. That's just what I want to be able to do—work up to it. And in London—curse the place—everything's in such a rush that you don't get a chance."

"Quite. You see a girl alone for about five minutes a day, and if you want to ask her to be your wife, you've got to charge into it as if you were trying to grab the gold ring on a merry-go-round."

"That's right. London rattles one. I shall be a different man altogether in the country. What a bit of luck this Travers woman turning out to be your aunt."

"I don't know what you mean, turning out to be my aunt. She has been my aunt all along."

"I mean, how extraordinary that it should be your aunt that Madeline's going to stay with."

"Not at all. She and my Cousin Angela are close friends. At Cannes she was with us all the time."

"Oh, you met Madeline at Cannes, did you? By Jove, Bertie," said the poor lizard devoutly, "I wish I could have seen her at Cannes. How wonderful she must have looked in beach pyjamas! Oh, Bertie———"

"Quite," I said, a little distantly. Even when restored by one of Jeeves's depth bombs, one doesn't want this sort of thing after a hard night. I touched the bell and, when Jeeves appeared, requested him to bring me telegraph form and pencil. I then wrote a well-worded communication to Aunt Dahlia, informing her that I was sending my friend, Augustus Fink-Nottle, down to Brinkley today to enjoy her hospitality, and handed it to Gussie.

"Push that in at the first post office you pass," I said. "She will find it waiting for her on her return."

Gussie popped along, flapping the telegram and looking like a close-up of Joan Crawford, and I turned to Jeeves and gave him a précis of my operations.

"Simple, you observe, Jeeves. Nothing elaborate."

"No, sir."

"Nothing far-fetched. Nothing strained or bizarre. Just Nature's remedy."

"Yes, sir."

"This is the attack as it should have been delivered. What do you call it when two people of opposite sexes are bunged together in close association in a secluded spot, meeting each other every day and seeing a lot of each other?"

"Is 'propinquity' the word you wish, sir?"

"It is. I stake everything on propinquity, Jeeves. Propinquity, in my opinion, is what will do the trick. At the moment, as you are aware, Gussie is a mere jelly when in the presence. But ask yourself how he will feel in a week or so, after he and she have been helping themselves to sausages out of the same dish day after day at the breakfast sideboard. Cutting the same ham, ladling out communal kidneys and bacon—why———"

I broke off abruptly. I had had one of my ideas.

"Golly, Jeeves!"

"Sir?"

"Here's an instance of how you have to think of everything. You heard me mention sausages, kidneys and bacon and ham."

"Yes, sir."

"Well, there must be nothing of that. Fatal. The wrong note entirely. Give me that telegraph form and pencil. I must warn Gussie without delay. What he's got to do is to create in this girl's mind the impression that he is pining away for love of her. This cannot be done by wolfing sausages."

"No, sir."

"Very well, then."

And, taking form and *p.*, I drafted the following:

Fink-Nottle

Brinkley Court,

Market Snodsbury

Worcestershire

Lay off the sausages. Avoid the ham. Bertie.

"Send that off, Jeeves, instanter."

"Very good, sir."

I sank back on the pillows.

"Well, Jeeves," I said, "you see how I am taking hold. You notice the grip I am getting on this case. No doubt you realize now that it would pay you to study my methods."

"No doubt, sir."

"And even now you aren't on to the full depths of the extraordinary sagacity I've shown. Do you know what brought Aunt Dahlia up here this morning? She came to tell me I'd got to distribute the prizes at some beastly seminary she's a governor of down at Market Snodsbury."

"Indeed, sir? I fear you will scarcely find that a congenial task."

"Ah, but I'm not going to do it. I'm going to shove it off on to Gussie."

"Sir?"

"I propose, Jeeves, to wire to Aunt Dahlia saying that I can't get down, and suggesting that she unleashes him on these young Borstal inmates of hers in my stead."

"But if Mr. Fink-Nottle should decline, sir?"

"Decline? Can you see him declining? Just conjure up the picture in your mind, Jeeves. Scene, the drawing-room at Brinkley; Gussie wedged into a corner, with Aunt Dahlia standing over him making hunting noises. I put it to you, Jeeves, can you see him declining?"

"Not readily, sir. I agree. Mrs. Travers is a forceful personality."

"He won't have a hope of declining. His only way out would be to slide off. And he can't slide off, because he wants to be with Miss Bassett. No, Gussie will have to toe the line, and I shall be saved from a job at which I confess the soul shuddered. Getting up on a platform and delivering a short, manly speech to a lot of foul school-kids! Golly, Jeeves. I've been through that sort of thing once, what? You remember that time at the girls' school?"

"Very vividly, sir."

"What an ass I made of myself!"

"Certainly I have seen you to better advantage, sir."

"I think you might bring me just one more of those dynamite specials of yours, Jeeves. This narrow squeak has made me come over all faint."

I suppose it must have taken Aunt Dahlia three hours or so to get back to Brinkley, because it wasn't till well after lunch that her telegram arrived. It read like a telegram that had been dispatched in a white-hot surge of emotion some two minutes after she had read mine.

As follows:

Am taking legal advice to ascertain whether strangling an idiot nephew counts as murder. If it doesn't look out for yourself. Consider your conduct frozen limit. What do you mean by planting your loathsome friends on me like this? Do you think Brinkley Court is a leper colony or what is it? Who is this Spink-Bottle? Love. Travers.

I had expected some such initial reaction. I replied in temperate vein:

Not Bottle. Nottle. Regards. Bertie.

Almost immediately after she had dispatched the above heart cry, Gussie must have arrived, for it wasn't twenty minutes later when I received the following:

Cipher telegram signed by you has reached me here. Runs "Lay off the sausages. Avoid the ham." Wire key immediately. Fink-Nottle.

I replied:

Also kidneys. Cheerio. Bertie.

I had staked all on Gussie making a favourable impression on his hostess, basing my confidence on the fact that he was one of those timid, obsequious, teacup-passing, thin-bread-and-butter-offering yes-men whom women of my Aunt Dahlia's type nearly always like at first sight. That I had not overrated my acumen was proved by her next in order, which, I was pleased to note, assayed a markedly larger percentage of the milk of human kindness.

As follows:

Well, this friend of yours has got here, and I must say that for a friend of yours he seems less sub-human than I had expected. A bit of a pop-eyed bleater, but on the whole clean and civil, and certainly most informative about newts. Am considering arranging series of lectures for him in neighbourhood. All the same I like your nerve using my house as a summer-hotel resort and shall have much to say to you on subject when you come down. Expect you thirtieth. Bring spats. Love. Travers.

To this I riposted:

On consulting engagement book find impossible come Brinkley Court. Deeply regret. Toodle-oo. Bertie.

Hers in reply stuck a sinister note:

Oh, so it's like that, is it? You and your engagement book, indeed. Deeply regret my foot. Let me tell you, my lad, that you will regret it a jolly sight more deeply if you don't come down. If you imagine for one moment that you are going to get out of distributing those prizes, you are very much mistaken. Deeply regret Brinkley Court hundred miles from London, as unable hit you with a brick. Love. Travers.

I then put my fortune to the test, to win or lose it all. It was not a moment for petty economies. I let myself go regardless of expense:

No, but dash it, listen. Honestly, you don't want me. Get Fink-Nottle distribute prizes. A born distributor, who will do you credit. Confidently anticipate Augustus Fink-Nottle as Master of Revels on thirty-first inst. would make genuine sensation. Do not miss this great chance, which may never occur again. Tinkerty-tonk. Bertie.

There was an hour of breathless suspense, and then the joyful tidings arrived:

Well, all right. Something in what you say, I suppose. Consider you treacherous worm and contemptible, spineless cowardly custard, but have booked Spink-Bottle. Stay where you are, then, and I hope you get run over by an omnibus. Love. Travers.

The relief, as you may well imagine, was stupendous. A great weight seemed to have rolled off my mind. It was as if somebody had been pouring Jeeves's pick-me-ups into me through a funnel. I sang as I dressed for dinner that night. At the Drones I was so gay and cheery that there were several complaints. And when I got home and turned into the old bed, I fell asleep like a little child within five minutes of inserting the person between the sheets. It seemed to me that the whole distressing affair might now be considered definitely closed.

Conceive my astonishment, therefore, when waking on the morrow and sitting up to dig into the morning tea-cup, I beheld on the tray another telegram.

My heart sank. Could Aunt Dahlia have slept on it and changed her mind? Could Gussie, unable to face the ordeal confronting him, have legged it during the night down a water-pipe? With these speculations racing through the bean, I tore open the envelope And as I noted contents I uttered a startled yip.

"Sir?" said Jeeves, pausing at the door.

I read the thing again. Yes, I had got the gist all right. No, I had not been deceived in the substance.

"Jeeves," I said, "do you know what?"

"No, sir."

"You know my cousin Angela?"

"Yes, sir."

"You know young Tuppy Glossop?"

"Yes, sir."

"They've broken off their engagement."

"I am sorry to hear that, sir."

"I have here a communication from Aunt Dahlia, specifically stating this. I wonder what the row was about."

70

"I could not say, sir."

"Of course you couldn't. Don't be an ass, Jeeves."

"No, sir."

I brooded. I was deeply moved.

"Well, this means that we shall have to go down to Brinkley today. Aunt Dahlia is obviously all of a twitter, and my place is by her side. You had better pack this morning, and catch that 12.45 train with the luggage. I have a lunch engagement, so will follow in the car."

"Very good, sir."

I brooded some more.

"I must say this has come as a great shock to me, Jeeves."

"No doubt, sir."

"A very great shock. Angela and Tuppy.... Tut, tut! Why, they seemed like the paper on the wall. Life is full of sadness, Jeeves."

"Yes, sir."

"Still, there it is."

"Undoubtedly, sir."

"Right ho, then. Switch on the bath."

"Very good, sir."

-7-

I meditated pretty freely as I drove down to Brinkley in the old two-seater that afternoon. The news of this rift or rupture of Angela's and Tuppy's had disturbed me greatly.

The projected match, you see, was one on which I had always looked with kindly approval. Too often, when a chap of your acquaintance is planning to marry a girl you know, you find yourself knitting the brow a bit and chewing the lower lip dubiously, feeling that he or she, or both, should be warned while there is yet time.

But I have never felt anything of this nature about Tuppy and Angela. Tuppy, when not making an ass of himself, is a soundish sort of egg. So is Angela a soundish sort of egg. And, as far as being in love was concerned, it had always seemed to me that you wouldn't have been far out in describing them as two hearts that beat as one.

True, they had had their little tiffs, notably on the occasion when Tuppy—with what he said was fearless honesty and I considered thorough goofiness—had told Angela that her new hat made her look like a Pekingese. But in every romance you have to budget for the occasional dust-up, and after that incident I had supposed that he had learned his lesson and that from then on life would be one grand, sweet song.

And now this wholly unforeseen severing of diplomatic relations had popped up through a trap.

I gave the thing the cream of the Wooster brain all the way down, but it continued to beat me what could have caused the outbreak of hostilities, and I bunged my foot sedulously on the accelerator in order to get to Aunt Dahlia with the greatest possible speed and learn the inside history straight from the horse's mouth. And what with all six cylinders hitting nicely, I made good time and found myself closeted with the relative shortly before the hour of the evening cocktail.

She seemed glad to see me. In fact, she actually said she was glad to see me—a statement no other aunt on the list would have committed herself to, the customary reaction of these near and dear ones to the spectacle of Bertram arriving for a visit being a sort of sick horror.

"Decent of you to rally round, Bertie," she said.

"My place was by your side, Aunt Dahlia," I responded.

I could see at a g. that the unfortunate affair had got in amongst her in no uncertain manner. Her usually cheerful map was clouded, and the genial smile conspic. by its a. I pressed her hand sympathetically, to indicate that my heart bled for her.

"Bad show this, my dear old flesh and blood," I said. "I'm afraid you've been having a sticky time. You must be worried."

She snorted emotionally. She looked like an aunt who has just bitten into a bad oyster.

"Worried is right. I haven't had a peaceful moment since I got back from Cannes. Ever since I put my foot across this blasted threshold," said Aunt Dahlia, returning for the nonce to the hearty *argot* of the hunting field, "everything's been at sixes and sevens. First there was that mix-up about the prize-giving."

She paused at this point and gave me a look. "I had been meaning to speak freely to you about your behaviour in that matter, Bertie," she said. "I had some good things all stored up. But, as you've rallied round like this, I suppose I shall have to let you off. And, anyway, it is probably all for the best that you evaded your obligations in that sickeningly craven way. I have an idea that this Spink-Bottle of yours is going to be good. If only he can keep off newts."

"Has he been talking about newts?"

"He has. Fixing me with a glittering eye, like the Ancient Mariner. But if that was the worst I had to bear, I wouldn't mind. What I'm worrying about is what Tom says when he starts talking."

"Uncle Tom?"

"I wish there was something else you could call him except 'Uncle Tom'," said Aunt Dahlia a little testily. "Every time you do it, I expect to see him turn black and start playing the banjo. Yes, Uncle Tom, if you must have it. I shall have to tell him soon about losing all that money at baccarat, and, when I do, he will go up like a rocket."

"Still, no doubt Time, the great healer———"

"Time, the great healer, be blowed. I've got to get a cheque for five hundred pounds out of him for *Milady's Boudoir* by August the third at the latest."

I was concerned. Apart from a nephew's natural interest in an aunt's refined weekly paper, I had always had a soft spot in my heart for *Milady's Boudoir* ever since I contributed that article to it on What the Well-Dressed Man is Wearing. Sentimental, possibly, but we old journalists do have these feelings.

"Is the *Boudoir* on the rocks?"

"It will be if Tom doesn't cough up. It needs help till it has turned the corner."

"But wasn't it turning the corner two years ago?"

"It was. And it's still at it. Till you've run a weekly paper for women, you don't know what corners are."

"And you think the chances of getting into uncle—into my uncle by marriage's ribs are slight?"

"I'll tell you, Bertie. Up till now, when these subsidies were required, I have always been able to come to Tom in the gay, confident spirit of an only child touching an indulgent father for chocolate cream. But he's just had a demand from the income-tax people for an additional fifty-eight pounds, one and threepence, and all he's been talking about since I got back has been ruin and the sinister trend of socialistic legislation and what will become of us all."

I could readily believe it. This Tom has a peculiarity I've noticed in other very oofy men. Nick him for the paltriest sum, and he lets out a squawk you can hear at Land's End. He has the stuff in gobs, but he hates giving up.

"If it wasn't for Anatole's cooking, I doubt if he would bother to carry on. Thank God for Anatole, I say."

I bowed my head reverently.

"Good old Anatole," I said.

"Amen," said Aunt Dahlia.

Then the look of holy ecstasy, which is always the result of letting the mind dwell, however briefly, on Anatole's cooking, died out of her face.

"But don't let me wander from the subject," she resumed. "I was telling you of the way hell's foundations have been quivering since I got home. First the prize-giving, then Tom, and now, on top of everything else, this infernal quarrel between Angela and young Glossop."

I nodded gravely. "I was frightfully sorry to hear of that. Terrible shock. What was the row about?"

"Sharks."

"Eh?"

"Sharks. Or, rather, one individual shark. The brute that went for the poor child when she was aquaplaning at Cannes. You remember Angela's shark?"

Certainly I remembered Angela's shark. A man of sensibility does not forget about a cousin nearly being chewed by monsters of the deep. The episode was still green in my memory.

In a nutshell, what had occurred was this: You know how you aquaplane. A motor-boat nips on ahead, trailing a rope. You stand on a board, holding the rope, and the boat tows you along. And every now and then you lose your grip on the rope and plunge into the sea and have to swim to your board again.

A silly process it has always seemed to me, though many find it diverting.

Well, on the occasion referred to, Angela had just regained her board after taking a toss, when a great beastly shark came along and cannoned into it, flinging her into the salty once more. It took her quite a bit of time to get on again and make the motor-boat chap realize what was up and haul her to safety, and during that interval you can readily picture her embarrassment.

According to Angela, the finny denizen kept snapping at her ankles virtually without cessation, so that by the time help arrived, she was feeling more like a salted almond at a public dinner than anything human. Very shaken the poor child had been, I recall, and had talked of nothing else for weeks.

"I remember the whole incident vividly," I said. "But how did that start the trouble?"

"She was telling him the story last night."

"Well?"

"Her eyes shining and her little hands clasped in girlish excitement."

"No doubt."

"And instead of giving her the understanding and sympathy to which she was entitled, what do you think this blasted Glossop did? He sat listening like a lump of dough, as if she had been talking about the weather, and when she had finished, he took his cigarette holder out of his mouth and said, 'I expect it was only a floating log'!"

"He didn't!"

"He did. And when Angela described how the thing had jumped and snapped at her, he took his cigarette holder out of his mouth again, and said, 'Ah! Probably a flatfish. Quite harmless. No doubt it was just trying to play.' Well, I mean! What would you have done if you had been Angela? She has pride, sensibility, all the natural feelings of a good woman. She told him he was an ass and a fool and an idiot, and didn't know what he was talking about."

I must say I saw the girl's viewpoint. It's only about once in a lifetime that anything sensational ever happens to one, and when it does, you don't want people taking all the colour out of it. I remember at school having to read that stuff where that chap, Othello, tells the girl what a hell of a time he'd been having among the cannibals and what not. Well, imagine his feelings if, after he had described some particularly sticky passage with a cannibal chief and was waiting for the awestruck "Oh-h! Not really?", she had said that the whole thing had no doubt been greatly exaggerated and that the man had probably really been a prominent local vegetarian.

Yes, I saw Angela's point of view.

"But don't tell me that when he saw how shirty she was about it, the chump didn't back down?"

"He didn't. He argued. And one thing led to another until, by easy stages, they had arrived at the point where she was saying that she didn't know if he was aware of it, but if he didn't knock off starchy foods and do exercises every morning, he would be getting as fat as a pig, and he was talking about this modern habit of girls putting make-up on their faces, of which he had always disapproved. This continued for a while, and then there was a loud pop and the air was full of mangled fragments of their engagement. I'm distracted about it. Thank goodness you've come, Bertie."

"Nothing could have kept me away," I replied, touched. "I felt you needed me."

"Yes."

"Quite."

"Or, rather," she said, "not you, of course, but Jeeves. The minute all this happened, I thought of him. The situation obviously cries out for Jeeves. If ever in the whole history of human affairs there was a moment when that lofty brain was required about the home, this is it."

I think, if I had been standing up, I would have staggered. In fact, I'm pretty sure I would. But it isn't so dashed easy to stagger when you're sitting in an arm-chair. Only my face, therefore, showed how deeply I had been stung by these words.

Until she spoke them, I had been all sweetness and light—the sympathetic nephew prepared to strain every nerve to do his bit. I now froze, and the face became hard and set.

"Jeeves!" I said, between clenched teeth.

"Oom beroofen," said Aunt Dahlia.

I saw that she had got the wrong angle.

"I was not sneezing. I was saying 'Jeeves!'"

"And well you may. What a man! I'm going to put the whole thing

76

up to him. There's nobody like Jeeves."

My frigidity became more marked.

"I venture to take issue with you, Aunt Dahlia."

"You take what?"

"Issue."

"You do, do you?"

"I emphatically do. Jeeves is hopeless."

"What?"

"Quite hopeless. He has lost his grip completely. Only a couple of days ago I was compelled to take him off a case because his handling of it was so footling. And, anyway, I resent this assumption, if assumption is the word I want, that Jeeves is the only fellow with brain. I object to the way everybody puts things up to him without consulting me and letting me have a stab at them first."

She seemed about to speak, but I checked her with a gesture.

"It is true that in the past I have sometimes seen fit to seek Jeeves's advice. It is possible that in the future I may seek it again. But I claim the right to have a pop at these problems, as they arise, in person, without having everybody behave as if Jeeves was the only onion in the hash. I sometimes feel that Jeeves, though admittedly not unsuccessful in the past, has been lucky rather than gifted."

"Have you and Jeeves had a row?"

"Nothing of the kind."

"You seem to have it in for him."

"Not at all."

And yet I must admit that there was a modicum of truth in what she said. I had been feeling pretty austere about the man all day, and I'll tell you why.

You remember that he caught that 12.45 train with the luggage, while I remained on in order to keep a luncheon engagement. Well, just before I started out to the tryst, I was pottering about the flat, and suddenly—I don't know what put the suspicion into my head, possibly the fellow's manner had been furtive—something seemed to whisper to me to go and have a look in the wardrobe.

And it was as I had suspected. There was the mess-jacket still on its hanger. The hound hadn't packed it.

Well, as anybody at the Drones will tell you, Bertram Wooster is a pretty hard chap to outgeneral. I shoved the thing in a brown-paper parcel and put it in the back of the car, and it was on a chair in the hall now. But that didn't alter the fact that Jeeves had attempted to do the dirty on me, and I suppose a certain what-d'you-call-it had crept into my manner during the above remarks.

"There has been no breach," I said. "You might describe it as a passing coolness, but no more. We did not happen to see eye to eye with regard to my white mess-jacket with the brass buttons and I was compelled to assert my personality. But——"

"Well, it doesn't matter, anyway. The thing that matters is that you are talking piffle, you poor fish. Jeeves lost his grip? Absurd. Why, I saw him for a moment when he arrived, and his eyes were absolutely glittering with intelligence. I said to myself 'Trust Jeeves,' and I intend to."

"You would be far better advised to let me see what I can accomplish, Aunt Dahlia."

"For heaven's sake, don't you start butting in. You'll only make matters worse."

"On the contrary, it may interest you to know that while driving here I concentrated deeply on this trouble of Angela's and was successful in formulating a plan, based on the psychology of the individual, which I am proposing to put into effect at an early moment."

"Oh, my God!"

"My knowledge of human nature tells me it will work."

"Bertie," said Aunt Dahlia, and her manner struck me as febrile, "lay off, lay off! For pity's sake, lay off. I know these plans of yours. I suppose you want to shove Angela into the lake and push young Glossop in after her to save her life, or something like that."

"Nothing of the kind."

"It's the sort of thing you would do."

"My scheme is far more subtle. Let me outline it for you."

"No, thanks."

"I say to myself——"

"But not to me."

"Do listen for a second."

"I won't."

"Right ho, then. I am dumb."

"And have been from a child."

I perceived that little good could result from continuing the discussion. I waved a hand and shrugged a shoulder.

"Very well, Aunt Dahlia," I said, with dignity, "if you don't want to be in on the ground floor, that is your affair. But you are missing an intellectual treat. And, anyway, no matter how much you may behave like the deaf adder of Scripture which, as you are doubtless aware, the more one piped, the less it danced, or words to that effect, I shall carry on as planned. I am extremely fond of Angela, and I shall spare no effort to bring the sunshine back into her heart."

"Bertie, you abysmal chump, I appeal to you once more. Will you please lay off? You'll only make things ten times as bad as they are already."

I remember reading in one of those historical novels once about a chap—a buck he would have been, no doubt, or a macaroni or some such bird as that—who, when people said the wrong thing, merely laughed down from lazy eyelids and flicked a speck of dust from the irreproachable Mechlin lace at his wrists. This was practically what I did now. At least, I straightened my tie and smiled one of those inscrutable smiles of mine. I then withdrew and went out for a saunter in the garden.

And the first chap I ran into was young Tuppy. His brow was furrowed, and he was moodily bunging stones at a flowerpot.

-8-

I think I have told you before about young Tuppy Glossop. He was the fellow, if you remember, who, callously ignoring the fact that we had been friends since boyhood, betted me one night at the Drones that I could swing myself across the swimming bath by the rings—a childish feat for one of my lissomeness—and then, having seen me well on the way, looped back the last ring, thus rendering it necessary for me to drop into the deep end in formal evening costume.

To say that I had not resented this foul deed, which seemed to me deserving of the title of the crime of the century, would be paltering with the truth. I had resented it profoundly, chafing not a little at the time and continuing to chafe for some weeks.

But you know how it is with these things. The wound heals. The agony abates.

I am not saying, mind you, that had the opportunity presented itself of dropping a wet sponge on Tuppy from some high spot or of putting an eel in his bed or finding some other form of self-expression of a like nature, I would not have embraced it eagerly; but that let me out. I mean to say, grievously injured though I had been, it gave me no pleasure to feel that the fellow's bally life was being ruined by the loss of a girl whom, despite all that had passed, I was convinced he still loved like the dickens.

On the contrary, I was heart and soul in favour of healing the breach and rendering everything hotsy-totsy once more between these two young sundered blighters. You will have gleaned that from my remarks to Aunt Dahlia, and if you had been present at this moment and had seen the kindly commiserating look I gave Tuppy, you would have gleaned it still more.

It was one of those searching, melting looks, and was accompanied by the hearty clasp of the right hand and the gentle laying of the left on the collar-bone.

"Well, Tuppy, old man," I said. "How are you, old man?"

My commiseration deepened as I spoke the words, for there had been no lighting up of the eye, no answering pressure of the palm, no sign whatever, in short, of any disposition on his part to do Spring dances at the sight of an old friend. The man seemed sandbagged. Melancholy, as I remember Jeeves saying once about Pongo Twistleton when he was trying to knock off smoking, had marked him for her own. Not that I was surprised, of course. In the circs., no doubt, a certain moodiness was only natural.

I released the hand, ceased to knead the shoulder, and, producing the old case, offered him a cigarette.

He took it dully.

"Are you here, Bertie?" he asked.

"Yes, I'm here."

"Just passing through, or come to stay?"

I thought for a moment. I might have told him that I had arrived at Brinkley Court with the express intention of bringing Angela and himself together once more, of knitting up the severed threads, and so on and so forth; and for perhaps half the time required for the lighting of a gasper I had almost decided to do so. Then, I reflected, better, on the whole, perhaps not. To broadcast the fact that I proposed to take him and Angela and play on them as on a couple of stringed instruments might have been injudicious. Chaps don't always like being played on as on a stringed instrument.

"It all depends," I said. "I may remain. I may push on. My plans are uncertain."

He nodded listlessly, rather in the manner of a man who did not give a damn what I did, and stood gazing out over the sunlit garden. In build and appearance, Tuppy somewhat resembles a bulldog, and his aspect now was that of one of these fine animals who has just been refused a slice of cake. It was not difficult for a man of my discernment to read what was in his mind, and it occasioned me no surprise, therefore, when his next words had to do with the subject marked with a cross on the agenda paper.

"You've heard of this business of mine, I suppose? Me and Angela?"

"I have, indeed, Tuppy, old man."

"We've bust up."

"I know. Some little friction, I gather, *in re* Angela's shark."

"Yes. I said it must have been a flatfish."

"So my informant told me."

"Who did you hear it from?"

"Aunt Dahlia."

"I suppose she cursed me properly?"

"Oh, no."

"Beyond referring to you in one passage as 'this blasted Glossop', she was, I thought, singularly temperate in her language for a woman who at one time hunted regularly with the Quorn. All the same, I could see, if you don't mind me saying so, old man, that she felt you might have behaved with a little more tact."

"Tact!"

81

"And I must admit I rather agreed with her. Was it nice, Tuppy, was it quite kind to take the bloom off Angela's shark like that? You must remember that Angela's shark is very dear to her. Could you not see what a sock on the jaw it would be for the poor child to hear it described by the man to whom she had given her heart as a flatfish?"

I saw that he was struggling with some powerful emotion.

"And what about my side of the thing?" he demanded, in a voice choked with feeling.

"Your side?"

"You don't suppose," said Tuppy, with rising vehemence, "that I would have exposed this dashed synthetic shark for the flatfish it undoubtedly was if there had not been causes that led up to it. What induced me to speak as I did was the fact that Angela, the little squirt, had just been most offensive, and I seized the opportunity to get a bit of my own back."

"Offensive?"

"Exceedingly offensive. Purely on the strength of my having let fall some casual remark—simply by way of saying something and keeping the conversation going—to the effect that I wondered what Anatole was going to give us for dinner, she said that I was too material and ought not always to be thinking of food. Material, my elbow! As a matter of fact, I'm particularly spiritual."

"Quite."

"I don't see any harm in wondering what Anatole was going to give us for dinner. Do you?"

"Of course not. A mere ordinary tribute of respect to a great artist."

"Exactly."

"All the same——"

"Well?"

"I was only going to say that it seems a pity that the frail craft of love should come a stinker like this when a few manly words of contrition——"

He stared at me.

"You aren't suggesting that I should climb down?"

"It would be the fine, big thing, old egg."

"I wouldn't dream of climbing down."

"But, Tuppy——"

"No. I wouldn't do it."

"But you love her, don't you?"

This touched the spot. He quivered noticeably, and his mouth twisted. Quite the tortured soul.

"I'm not saying I don't love the little blighter," he said, obviously moved. "I love her passionately. But that doesn't alter the fact that I consider that what she needs most in this world is a swift kick in the pants."

A Wooster could scarcely pass this. "Tuppy, old man!"

"It's no good saying 'Tuppy, old man'."

"Well, I do say 'Tuppy, old man'. Your tone shocks me. One raises the eyebrows. Where is the fine, old, chivalrous spirit of the Glossops."

"That's all right about the fine, old, chivalrous spirit of the Glossops. Where is the sweet, gentle, womanly spirit of the Angelas? Telling a fellow he was getting a double chin!"

"Did she do that?"

"She did."

"Oh, well, girls will be girls. Forget it, Tuppy. Go to her and make it up."

He shook his head.

"No. It is too late. Remarks have been passed about my tummy which it is impossible to overlook."

"But, Tummy—Tuppy, I mean—be fair. You once told her her new hat made her look like a Pekingese."

"It did make her look like a Pekingese. That was not vulgar abuse. It was sound, constructive criticism, with no motive behind it but the kindly desire to keep her from making an exhibition of herself in public. Wantonly to accuse a man of puffing when he goes up a flight of stairs is something very different."

I began to see that the situation would require all my address and ingenuity. If the wedding bells were ever to ring out in the little church of Market Snodsbury, Bertram had plainly got to put in some shrewdish work. I had gathered, during my conversation with Aunt Dahlia, that there had been a certain amount of frank speech between the two contracting parties, but I had not realized till now that matters had gone so far.

The pathos of the thing gave me the pip. Tuppy had admitted in so many words that love still animated the Glossop bosom, and I was convinced that, even after all that occurred, Angela had not ceased to love him. At the moment, no doubt, she might be wishing that she could hit him with a bottle, but deep down in her I was prepared to bet that there still lingered all the old affection and tenderness. Only injured pride was keeping these two apart, and I felt that if Tuppy would make the first move, all would be well.

I had another whack at it.

"She's broken-hearted about this rift, Tuppy."

"How do you know? Have you seen her?"

"No, but I'll bet she is."

"She doesn't look it."

"Wearing the mask, no doubt. Jeeves does that when I assert my authority."

"She wrinkles her nose at me as if I were a drain that had got out of order."

"Merely the mask. I feel convinced she loves you still, and that a kindly word from you is all that is required."

I could see that this had moved him. He plainly wavered. He did a sort of twiddly on the turf with his foot. And, when he spoke, one spotted the tremolo in the voice:

"You really think that?"

"Absolutely."

"H'm."

"If you were to go to her——"

He shook his head.

"I can't do that. It would be fatal. Bing, instantly, would go my prestige. I know girls. Grovel, and the best of them get uppish." He mused. "The only way to work the thing would be by tipping her off in some indirect way that I am prepared to open negotiations. Should I sigh a bit when we meet, do you think?"

"She would think you were puffing."

"That's true."

I lit another cigarette and gave my mind to the matter. And first crack out of the box, as is so often the way with the Woosters, I got an idea. I remembered the counsel I had given Gussie in the matter of the sausages and ham.

"I've got it, Tuppy. There is one infallible method of indicating to a girl that you love her, and it works just as well when you've had a row and want to make it up. Don't eat any dinner tonight. You can see how impressive that would be. She knows how devoted you are to food."

He started violently.

"I am not devoted to food!"

"No, no."

"I am not devoted to food at all."

"Quite. All I meant——"

"This rot about me being devoted to food," said Tuppy warmly, "has got to stop. I am young and healthy and have a good appetite, but that's not the same as being devoted to food. I admire Anatole as a master of his craft, and am always willing to consider anything he may put before me, but when you say I am devoted to food——"

"Quite, quite. All I meant was that if she sees you push away your dinner untasted, she will realize that your heart is aching, and will probably be the first to suggest blowing the all clear."

Tuppy was frowning thoughtfully.

"Push my dinner away, eh?"

"Yes."

"Push away a dinner cooked by Anatole?"

"Yes."

"Push it away untasted?"

"Yes."

"Let us get this straight. Tonight, at dinner, when the butler offers me a *ris de veau à la financiere*, or whatever it may be, hot from Anatole's hands, you wish me to push it away untasted?"

"Yes."

He chewed his lip. One could sense the struggle going on within. And then suddenly a sort of glow came into his face. The old martyrs probably used to look like that.

"All right."

"You'll do it?"

"I will."

"Fine."

"Of course, it will be agony."

I pointed out the silver lining.

"Only for the moment. You could slip down tonight, after everyone is in bed, and raid the larder."

He brightened.

"That's right. I could, couldn't I?"

"I expect there would be something cold there."

"There is something cold there," said Tuppy, with growing cheerfulness. "A steak-and-kidney pie. We had it for lunch today. One of Anatole's ripest. The thing I admire about that man," said Tuppy reverently, "the thing that I admire so enormously about Anatole is that, though a Frenchman, he does not, like so many of these *chefs*, confine himself exclusively to French dishes, but is always willing and ready to weigh in with some good old simple English fare such as this steak-and-kidney pie to which I have alluded. A masterly pie, Bertie, and it wasn't more than half finished. It will do me nicely."

"And at dinner you will push, as arranged?"

"Absolutely as arranged."

"Fine."

"It's an excellent idea. One of Jeeves's best. You can tell him from me, when you see him, that I'm much obliged."

The cigarette fell from my fingers. It was as though somebody had slapped Bertram Wooster across the face with a wet dish-rag.

"You aren't suggesting that you think this scheme I have been sketching out is Jeeves's?"

"Of course it is. It's no good trying to kid me, Bertie. You wouldn't have thought of a wheeze like that in a million years."

There was a pause. I drew myself up to my full height; then, seeing that he wasn't looking at me, lowered myself again.

"Come, Glossop," I said coldly, "we had better be going. It is time we were dressing for dinner."

-9-

Tuppy's fatheaded words were still rankling in my bosom as I

86

went up to my room. They continued rankling as I shed the form-fitting, and had not ceased to rankle when, clad in the old dressing-gown, I made my way along the corridor to the *salle de bain.*

It is not too much to say that I was piqued to the tonsils.

I mean to say, one does not court praise. The adulation of the multitude means very little to one. But, all the same, when one has taken the trouble to whack out a highly juicy scheme to benefit an in-the-soup friend in his hour of travail, it's pretty foul to find him giving the credit to one's personal attendant, particularly if that personal attendant is a man who goes about the place not packing mess-jackets.

But after I had been splashing about in the porcelain for a bit, composure began to return. I have always found that in moments of heart-bowed-downness there is nothing that calms the bruised spirit like a good go at the soap and water. I don't say I actually sang in the tub, but there were times when it was a mere spin of the coin whether I would do so or not.

The spiritual anguish induced by that tactless speech had become noticeably lessened.

The discovery of a toy duck in the soap dish, presumably the property of some former juvenile visitor, contributed not a little to this new and happier frame of mind. What with one thing and another, I hadn't played with toy ducks in my bath for years, and I found the novel experience most invigorating. For the benefit of those interested, I may mention that if you shove the thing under the surface with the sponge and then let it go, it shoots out of the water in a manner calculated to divert the most careworn. Ten minutes of this and I was enabled to return to the bedchamber much more the old merry Bertram.

Jeeves was there, laying out the dinner disguise. He greeted the young master with his customary suavity.

"Good evening, sir."

I responded in the same affable key.

"Good evening, Jeeves."

"I trust you had a pleasant drive, sir."

"Very pleasant, thank you, Jeeves. Hand me a sock or two, will you?"

He did so, and I commenced to don,

"Well, Jeeves," I said, reaching for the underlinen, "here we are again at Brinkley Court in the county of Worcestershire."

"Yes, sir."

"A nice mess things seem to have gone and got themselves into in this rustic joint."

"Yes, sir."

"The rift between Tuppy Glossop and my cousin Angela would appear to be serious."

"Yes, sir. Opinion in the servants' hall is inclined to take a grave view of the situation."

"And the thought that springs to your mind, no doubt, is that I shall have my work cut out to fix things up?"

"Yes, sir."

"You are wrong, Jeeves. I have the thing well in hand."

"You surprise me, sir."

"I thought I should. Yes, Jeeves, I pondered on the matter most of the way down here, and with the happiest results. I have just been in conference with Mr. Glossop, and everything is taped out."

"Indeed, sir? Might I inquire——"

"You know my methods, Jeeves. Apply them. Have you," I asked, slipping into the shirt and starting to adjust the cravat, "been gnawing on the thing at all?"

"Oh, yes, sir. I have always been much attached to Miss Angela, and I felt that it would afford me great pleasure were I to be able to be of service to her."

"A laudable sentiment. But I suppose you drew blank?"

"No, sir. I was rewarded with an idea."

"What was it?"

"It occurred to me that a reconciliation might be effected between Mr. Glossop and Miss Angela by appealing to that instinct which prompts gentlemen in time of peril to hasten to the rescue of——"

I had to let go of the cravat in order to raise a hand. I was shocked.

"Don't tell me you were contemplating descending to that old he-saved-her-from-drowning gag? I am surprised, Jeeves. Surprised and pained. When I was discussing the matter with Aunt Dahlia on my arrival, she said in a sniffy sort of way that she supposed I was going to shove my Cousin Angela into the lake and push Tuppy in to haul her out, and I let her see pretty clearly that I considered the suggestion an insult to my intelligence. And now, if your words have the meaning I read into them, you are mooting precisely the same drivelling scheme. Really, Jeeves!"

"No, sir. Not that. But the thought did cross my mind, as I walked in the grounds and passed the building where the fire-bell hangs, that a sudden alarm of fire in the night might result in Mr. Glossop endeavouring to assist Miss Angela to safety."

I shivered.

"Rotten, Jeeves."

"Well, sir——"

"No good. Not a bit like it."

"I fancy, sir——"

"No, Jeeves. No more. Enough has been said. Let us drop the subj."

I finished tying the tie in silence. My emotions were too deep for speech. I knew, of course, that this man had for the time being lost his grip, but I had never suspected that he had gone absolutely to pieces like this. Remembering some of the swift ones he had pulled in the past, I shrank with horror from the spectacle of his present ineptitude. Or is it ineptness? I mean this frightful disposition of his to stick straws in his hair and talk like a perfect ass. It was the old, old story, I supposed. A man's brain whizzes along for years exceeding the speed limit, and something suddenly goes wrong with the steering-gear and it skids and comes a smeller in the ditch.

"A bit elaborate," I said, trying to put the thing in as kindly a light as possible. "Your old failing. You can see that it's a bit elaborate?"

"Possibly the plan I suggested might be considered open to that criticism, sir, but *faute de mieux*——"

"I don't get you, Jeeves."

"A French expression, sir, signifying 'for want of anything better'."

A moment before, I had been feeling for this wreck of a once fine thinker nothing but a gentle pity. These words jarred the Wooster pride, inducing asperity.

"I understand perfectly well what *faute de mieux* means, Jeeves. I did not recently spend two months among our Gallic neighbours for nothing. Besides, I remember that one from school. What caused my bewilderment was that you should be employing the expression, well knowing that there is no bally *faute de mieux* about it at all. Where do you get that *faute-de-mieux* stuff? Didn't I tell you I had everything taped out?"

"Yes, sir, but——"

"What do you mean—but?"

"Well, sir——"

"Push on, Jeeves. I am ready, even anxious, to hear your views."

"Well, sir, if I may take the liberty of reminding you of it, your plans in the past have not always been uniformly successful."

There was a silence—rather a throbbing one—during which I put on my waistcoat in a marked manner. Not till I had got the buckle at the back satisfactorily adjusted did I speak.

"It is true, Jeeves," I said formally, "that once or twice in the past I may have missed the bus. This, however, I attribute purely to bad luck."

"Indeed, sir?"

"On the present occasion I shall not fail, and I'll tell you why I shall not fail. Because my scheme is rooted in human nature."

"Indeed, sir?"

"It is simple. Not elaborate. And, furthermore, based on the psychology of the individual."

"Indeed, sir?"

"Jeeves," I said, "don't keep saying 'Indeed, sir?' No doubt nothing is further from your mind than to convey such a suggestion, but you have a way of stressing the 'in' and then coming down with a thud on the 'deed' which makes it virtually tantamount to 'Oh, yeah?' Correct this, Jeeves."

"Very good, sir."

"I tell you I have everything nicely lined up. Would you care to hear what steps I have taken?"

"Very much, sir."

"Then listen. Tonight at dinner I have recommended Tuppy to lay off the food."

"Sir?"

"Tut, Jeeves, surely you can follow the idea, even though it is one that would never have occurred to yourself. Have you forgotten that telegram I sent to Gussie Fink-Nottle, steering him away from the sausages and ham? This is the same thing. Pushing the food away untasted is a universally recognized sign of love. It cannot fail to bring home the gravy. You must see that?"

"Well, sir——"

I frowned.

"I don't want to seem always to be criticizing your methods of voice production, Jeeves," I said, "but I must inform you that that 'Well, sir' of yours is in many respects fully as unpleasant as your 'Indeed, sir?' Like the latter, it seems to be tinged with a definite scepticism. It suggests a lack of faith in my vision. The impression I retain after hearing you shoot it at me a couple of times is that you consider me to be talking through the back of my neck, and that only a feudal sense of what is fitting restrains you from substituting for it the words 'Says you!'"

"Oh, no, sir."

"Well, that's what it sounds like. Why don't you think this scheme will work?"

"I fear Miss Angela will merely attribute Mr. Glossop's abstinence to indigestion, sir."

I hadn't thought of that, and I must confess it shook me for a moment. Then I recovered myself. I saw what was at the bottom of all this. Mortified by the consciousness of his own ineptness—or ineptitude—the fellow was simply trying to hamper and obstruct. I decided to knock the stuffing out of him without further preamble.

"Oh?" I said. "You do, do you? Well, be that as it may, it doesn't alter the fact that you've put out the wrong coat. Be so good, Jeeves," I said, indicating with a gesture the gent's ordinary dinner jacket or *smoking*, as we call it on the Côte d'Azur, which was suspended from the hanger on the knob of the wardrobe, "as to shove that bally black thing in the cupboard and bring out my white mess-jacket with the brass buttons."

He looked at me in a meaning manner. And when I say a meaning manner, I mean there was a respectful but at the same time uppish glint in his eye and a sort of muscular spasm flickered across his face which wasn't quite a quiet smile and yet wasn't quite not a quiet smile. Also the soft cough.

"I regret to say, sir, that I inadvertently omitted to pack the garment to which you refer."

The vision of that parcel in the hall seemed to rise before my eyes, and I exchanged a merry wink with it. I may even have hummed a bar or two. I'm not quite sure.

"I know you did, Jeeves," I said, laughing down from lazy eyelids and nicking a speck of dust from the irreproachable Mechlin lace at my wrists. "But I didn't. You will find it on a chair in the hall in a brown-paper parcel."

The information that his low manoeuvres had been rendered null and void and that the thing was on the strength after all, must have been the nastiest of jars, but there was no play of expression on his finely chiselled to indicate it. There very seldom is on Jeeves's f-c. In moments of discomfort, as I had told Tuppy, he wears a mask, preserving throughout the quiet stolidity of a stuffed moose.

"You might just slide down and fetch it, will you?"

"Very good, sir."

"Right ho, Jeeves."

And presently I was sauntering towards the drawing-room with me good old j. nestling snugly abaft the shoulder blades.

And Dahlia was in the drawing-room. She glanced up at my entrance.

"Hullo, eyesore," she said. "What do you think you're made up as?"

I did not get the purport.

"The jacket, you mean?" I queried, groping.

"I do. You look like one of the chorus of male guests at Abernethy Towers in Act 2 of a touring musical comedy."

"You do not admire this jacket?"

"I do not."

"You did at Cannes."

"Well, this isn't Cannes."

"But, dash it——"

"Oh, never mind. Let it go. If you want to give my butler a laugh, what does it matter? What does anything matter now?"

There was a death-where-is-thy-sting-fullness about her manner which I found distasteful. It isn't often that I score off Jeeves in the devastating fashion just described, and when I do I like to see happy, smiling faces about me.

"Tails up, Aunt Dahlia," I urged buoyantly.

"Tails up be dashed," was her sombre response. "I've just been talking to Tom."

"Telling him?"

"No, listening to him. I haven't had the nerve to tell him yet."

"Is he still upset about that income-tax money?"

"Upset is right. He says that Civilisation is in the melting-pot and that all thinking men can read the writing on the wall."

"What wall?"

"Old Testament, ass. Belshazzar's feast."

"Oh, that, yes. I've often wondered how that gag was worked. With mirrors, I expect."

"I wish I could use mirrors to break it to Tom about this baccarat business."

I had a word of comfort to offer here. I had been turning the thing over in my mind since our last meeting, and I thought I saw where she had got twisted. Where she made her error, it seemed to me, was in feeling she had got to tell Uncle Tom. To my way of thinking, the matter was one on which it would be better to continue to exercise a quiet reserve.

"I don't see why you need mention that you lost that money at baccarat."

"What do you suggest, then? Letting *Milady's Boudoir* join Civilisation in the melting-pot. Because that is what it will infallibly do unless I get a cheque by next week. The printers have been showing a nasty spirit for months."

"You don't follow. Listen. It's an understood thing, I take it, that Uncle Tom foots the *Boudoir* bills. If the bally sheet has been turning the corner for two years, he must have got used to forking out by this time. Well, simply ask him for the money to pay the printers."

"I did. Just before I went to Cannes."

"Wouldn't he give it to you?"

93

"Certainly he gave it to me. He brassed up like an officer and a gentleman. That was the money I lost at baccarat."

"Oh? I didn't know that."

"There isn't much you do know."

A nephew's love made me overlook the slur.

"Tut!" I said.

"What did you say?"

"I said 'Tut!'"

"Say it once again, and I'll biff you where you stand. I've enough to endure without being tutted at."

"Quite."

"Any tutting that's required, I'll attend to myself. And the same applies to clicking the tongue, if you were thinking of doing that."

"Far from it."

"Good."

I stood awhile in thought. I was concerned to the core. My heart, if you remember, had already bled once for Aunt Dahlia this evening. It now bled again. I knew how deeply attached she was to this paper of hers. Seeing it go down the drain would be for her like watching a loved child sink for the third time in some pond or mere.

And there was no question that, unless carefully prepared for the touch, Uncle Tom would see a hundred *Milady's Boudoirs* go phut rather than take the rap.

Then I saw how the thing could be handled. This aunt, I perceived, must fall into line with my other clients. Tuppy Glossop was knocking off dinner to melt Angela. Gussie Fink-Nottle was knocking off dinner to impress the Bassett. Aunt Dahlia must knock off dinner to soften Uncle Tom. For the beauty of this scheme of mine was that there was no limit to the number of entrants. Come one, come all, the more the merrier, and satisfaction guaranteed in every case.

"I've got it," I said. "There is only one course to pursue. Eat less meat."

She looked at me in a pleading sort of way. I wouldn't swear that her eyes were wet with unshed tears, but I rather think they were, certainly she clasped her hands in piteous appeal.

"Must you drivel, Bertie? Won't you stop it just this once? Just for tonight, to please Aunt Dahlia?"

"I'm not drivelling."

"I dare say that to a man of your high standards it doesn't come under the head of drivel, but——"

I saw what had happened. I hadn't made myself quite clear.

"It's all right," I said. "Have no misgivings. This is the real Tabasco. When I said 'Eat less meat', what I meant was that you must refuse your oats at dinner tonight. Just sit there, looking blistered, and wave away each course as it comes with a weary gesture of resignation. You see what will happen. Uncle Tom will notice your loss of appetite, and I am prepared to bet that at the conclusion of the meal he will come to you and say 'Dahlia, darling'—I take it he calls you 'Dahlia'—'Dahlia darling,' he will say, 'I noticed at dinner tonight that you were a bit off your feed. Is anything the matter, Dahlia, darling?' 'Why, yes, Tom, darling,' you will reply. 'It is kind of you to ask, darling. The fact is, darling, I am terribly worried.' 'My darling,' he will say——"

Aunt Dahlia interrupted at this point to observe that these Traverses seemed to be a pretty soppy couple of blighters, to judge by their dialogue. She also wished to know when I was going to get to the point.

I gave her a look.

"'My darling,' he will say tenderly, 'is there anything I can do?' To which your reply will be that there jolly well is—viz. reach for his cheque-book and start writing."

I was watching her closely as I spoke, and was pleased to note respect suddenly dawn in her eyes.

"But, Bertie, this is positively bright."

"I told you Jeeves wasn't the only fellow with brain."

"I believe it would work."

"It's bound to work. I've recommended it to Tuppy."

"Young Glossop?"

"In order to soften Angela."

"Splendid!"

"And to Gussie Fink-Nottle, who wants to make a hit with the Bassett."

"Well, well, well! What a busy little brain it is."

"Always working, Aunt Dahlia, always working."

"You're not the chump I took you for, Bertie."

"When did you ever take me for a chump?"

"Oh, some time last summer. I forget what gave me the idea. Yes, Bertie, this scheme is bright. I suppose, as a matter of fact, Jeeves suggested it."

"Jeeves did not suggest it. I resent these implications. Jeeves had nothing to do with it whatsoever."

"Well, all right, no need to get excited about it. Yes, I think it will work. Tom's devoted to me."

"Who wouldn't be?"

"I'll do it."

And then the rest of the party trickled in, and we toddled down to dinner.

Conditions being as they were at Brinkley Court—I mean to say, the place being loaded down above the Plimsoll mark with aching hearts and standing room only as regarded tortured souls—I hadn't expected the evening meal to be particularly effervescent. Nor was it. Silent. Sombre. The whole thing more than a bit like Christmas dinner on Devil's Island.

I was glad when it was over.

What with having, on top of her other troubles, to rein herself back from the trough, Aunt Dahlia was a total loss as far as anything in the shape of brilliant badinage was concerned. The fact that he was fifty quid in the red and expecting Civilisation to take a toss at any moment had caused Uncle Tom, who always looked a bit like a pterodactyl with a secret sorrow, to take on a deeper melancholy. The Bassett was a silent bread crumbler. Angela might have been hewn from the living rock. Tuppy had the air of a condemned murderer refusing to make the usual hearty breakfast before tooling off to the execution shed.

And as for Gussie Fink-Nottle, many an experienced undertaker would have been deceived by his appearance and started embalming him on sight.

This was the first glimpse I had had of Gussie since we parted at my flat, and I must say his demeanour disappointed me. I had been expecting something a great deal more sparkling.

At my flat, on the occasion alluded to, he had, if you recall, practically given me a signed guarantee that all he needed to touch him off was a rural setting. Yet in this aspect now I could detect no indication whatsoever that he was about to round into mid-season form. He still looked like a cat in an adage, and it did not take me long to realise that my very first act on escaping from this morgue must be to draw him aside and give him a pep talk.

If ever a chap wanted the clarion note, it looked as if it was this Fink-Nottle.

In the general exodus of mourners, however, I lost sight of him, and, owing to the fact that Aunt Dahlia roped me in for a game of backgammon, it was not immediately that I was able to institute a search. But after we had been playing for a while, the butler came in and asked her if she would speak to Anatole, so I managed to get away. And some ten minutes later, having failed to find scent in the house, I started to throw out the drag-net through the grounds, and flushed him in the rose garden.

He was smelling a rose at the moment in a limp sort of way, but removed the beak as I approached.

"Well, Gussie," I said.

I had beamed genially upon him as I spoke, such being my customary policy on meeting an old pal; but instead of beaming back genially, he gave me a most unpleasant look. His attitude perplexed me. It was as if he were not glad to see Bertram. For a moment he stood letting this unpleasant look play upon me, as it were, and then he spoke.

"You and your 'Well, Gussie'!"

He said this between clenched teeth, always an unmatey thing to do, and I found myself more fogged than ever.

"How do you mean—me and my 'Well, Gussie'?"

"I like your nerve, coming bounding about the place, saying 'Well, Gussie.' That's about all the 'Well, Gussie' I shall require from you, Wooster. And it's no good looking like that. You know what I mean. That damned prize-giving! It was a dastardly act to crawl out as you did and shove it off on to me. I will not mince my words. It was the act of a hound and a stinker."

Now, though, as I have shown, I had devoted most of the time on the journey down to meditating upon the case of Angela and Tuppy, I had not neglected to give a thought or two to what I was going to say when I encountered Gussie. I had foreseen that there might be some little temporary unpleasantness when we met, and when a difficult interview is in the offing Bertram Wooster likes to have his story ready.

So now I was able to reply with a manly, disarming frankness. The sudden introduction of the topic had given me a bit of a jolt, it is true, for in the stress of recent happenings I had rather let that prize-giving business slide to the back of my mind; but I had speedily recovered and, as I say, was able to reply with a manly d.f.

"But, my dear chap," I said, "I took it for granted that you would understand that that was all part of my schemes."

He said something about my schemes which I did not catch.

"Absolutely. 'Crawling out' is entirely the wrong way to put it. You don't suppose I didn't want to distribute those prizes, do you? Left to myself, there is nothing I would find a greater treat. But I saw that the square, generous thing to do was to step aside and let you take it on, so I did so. I felt that your need was greater than mine. You don't mean to say you aren't looking forward to it?"

He uttered a coarse expression which I wouldn't have thought he would have known. It just shows that you can bury yourself in the country and still somehow acquire a vocabulary. No doubt one picks up things from the neighbours—the vicar, the local doctor, the man who brings the milk, and so on.

"But, dash it," I said, "can't you see what this is going to do for you? It will send your stock up with a jump. There you will be, up on that platform, a romantic, impressive figure, the star of the whole proceedings, the what-d'you-call-it of all eyes. Madeline Bassett will be all over you. She will see you in a totally new light."

"She will, will she?"

"Certainly she will. Augustus Fink-Nottle, the newts' friend, she knows. She is acquainted with Augustus Fink-Nottle, the dogs' chiropodist. But Augustus Fink-Nottle, the orator—that'll knock her sideways, or I know nothing of the female heart. Girls go potty over a public man. If ever anyone did anyone else a kindness, it was I when I gave this extraordinary attractive assignment to you."

He seemed impressed by my eloquence. Couldn't have helped

himself, of course. The fire faded from behind his horn-rimmed spectacles, and in its place appeared the old fish-like goggle.

"'Myes," he said meditatively. "Have you ever made a speech, Bertie?"

"Dozens of times. It's pie. Nothing to it. Why, I once addressed a girls' school."

"You weren't nervous?"

"Not a bit."

"How did you go?"

"They hung on my lips. I held them in the hollow of my hand."

"They didn't throw eggs, or anything?"

"Not a thing."

He expelled a deep breath, and for a space stood staring in silence at a passing slug.

"Well," he said, at length, "it may be all right. Possibly I am letting the thing prey on my mind too much. I may be wrong in supposing it the fate that is worse than death. But I'll tell you this much: the prospect of that prize-giving on the thirty-first of this month has been turning my existence into a nightmare. I haven't been able to sleep or think or eat ... By the way, that reminds me. You never explained that cipher telegram about the sausages and ham."

"It wasn't a cipher telegram. I wanted you to go light on the food, so that she would realize you were in love."

He laughed hollowly.

"I see. Well, I've been doing that, all right."

"Yes, I was noticing at dinner. Splendid."

"I don't see what's splendid about it. It's not going to get me anywhere. I shall never be able to ask her to marry me. I couldn't find nerve to do that if I lived on wafer biscuits for the rest of my life."

"But, dash it, Gussie. In these romantic surroundings. I should have thought the whispering trees alone——"

"I don't care what you would have thought. I can't do it."

"Oh, come!"

"I can't. She seems so aloof, so remote."

"She doesn't."

"Yes, she does. Especially when you see her sideways. Have you seen her sideways, Bertie? That cold, pure profile. It just takes all the heart out of one."

"It doesn't."

"I tell you it does. I catch sight of it, and the words freeze on my lips."

He spoke with a sort of dull despair, and so manifest was his lack of ginger and the spirit that wins to success that for an instant, I confess, I felt a bit stymied. It seemed hopeless to go on trying to steam up such a human jellyfish. Then I saw the way. With that extraordinary quickness of mine, I realized exactly what must be done if this Fink-Nottle was to be enabled to push his nose past the judges' box.

"She must be softened up," I said.

"Be what?"

"Softened up. Sweetened. Worked on. Preliminary spadework must be put in. Here, Gussie, is the procedure I propose to adopt: I shall now return to the house and lug this Bassett out for a stroll. I shall talk to her of hearts that yearn, intimating that there is one actually on the premises. I shall pitch it strong, sparing no effort. You, meanwhile, will lurk on the outskirts, and in about a quarter of an hour you will come along and carry on from there. By that time, her emotions having been stirred, you ought to be able to do the rest on your head. It will be like leaping on to a moving bus."

I remember when I was a kid at school having to learn a poem of sorts about a fellow named Pig-something—a sculptor he would have been, no doubt—who made a statue of a girl, and what should happen one morning but that the bally thing suddenly came to life. A pretty nasty shock for the chap, of course, but the point I'm working round to is that there were a couple of lines that went, if I remember correctly:

She starts. She moves. She seems to feel The stir of life along her keel.

And what I'm driving at is that you couldn't get a better description of what happened to Gussie as I spoke these heartening words. His brow cleared, his eyes brightened, he lost that fishy look, and he gazed at the slug, which was still on the long, long trail with something approaching bonhomie. A marked improvement.

"I see what you mean. You will sort of pave the way, as it were."

"That's right. Spadework."

"It's a terrific idea, Bertie. It will make all the difference."

"Quite. But don't forget that after that it will be up to you. You will have to haul up your slacks and give her the old oil, or my efforts will have been in vain."

Something of his former Gawd-help-us-ness seemed to return to him. He gasped a bit.

"That's true. What the dickens shall I say?"

I restrained my impatience with an effort. The man had been at school with me.

"Dash it, there are hundreds of things you can say. Talk about the sunset."

"The sunset?"

"Certainly. Half the married men you meet began by talking about the sunset."

"But what can I say about the sunset?"

"Well, Jeeves got off a good one the other day. I met him airing the dog in the park one evening, and he said, 'Now fades the glimmering landscape on the sight, sir, and all the air a solemn stillness holds.' You might use that."

"What sort of landscape?"

"Glimmering. *G* for 'gastritis,' *l* for 'lizard'——"

"Oh, glimmering? Yes, that's not bad. Glimmering landscape ... solemn stillness.... Yes, I call that pretty good."

"You could then say that you have often thought that the stars are God's daisy chain."

"But I haven't."

"I dare say not. But she has. Hand her that one, and I don't see how she can help feeling that you're a twin soul."

"God's daisy chain?"

"God's daisy chain. And then you go on about how twilight always makes you sad. I know you're going to say it doesn't, but on this occasion it has jolly well got to."

"Why?"

"That's just what she will ask, and you will then have got her going. Because you will reply that it is because yours is such a lonely life. It wouldn't be a bad idea to give her a brief description of a typical home evening at your Lincolnshire residence, showing how you pace the meadows with a heavy tread."

"I generally sit indoors and listen to the wireless."

"No, you don't. You pace the meadows with a heavy tread, wishing that you had someone to love you. And then you speak of the day when she came into your life."

"Like a fairy princess."

"Absolutely," I said with approval. I hadn't expected such a hot one from such a quarter. "Like a fairy princess. Nice work, Gussie."

"And then?"

"Well, after that it's easy. You say you have something you want to say to her, and then you snap into it. I don't see how it can fail. If I were you, I should do it in this rose garden. It is well established that there is no sounder move than to steer the adored object into rose gardens in the gloaming. And you had better have a couple of quick ones first."

"Quick ones?"

"Snifters."

"Drinks, do you mean? But I don't drink."

"What?"

"I've never touched a drop in my life."

This made me a bit dubious, I must confess. On these occasions it is generally conceded that a moderate skinful is of the essence.

However, if the facts were as he had stated, I supposed there was nothing to be done about it.

"Well, you'll have to make out as best you can on ginger pop."

"I always drink orange juice."

"Orange juice, then. Tell me, Gussie, to settle a bet, do you really like that muck?"

"Very much."

"Then there is no more to be said. Now, let's just have a run through, to see that you've got the lay-out straight. Start off with the glimmering landscape."

"Stars God's daisy chain."

"Twilight makes you feel sad."

"Because mine lonely life."

"Describe life."

"Talk about the day I met her."

"Add fairy-princess gag. Say there's something you want to say to her. Heave a couple of sighs. Grab her hand. And give her the works. Right."

And confident that he had grasped the scenario and that everything might now be expected to proceed through the proper channels, I picked up the feet and hastened back to the house.

It was not until I had reached the drawing-room and was enabled to take a square look at the Bassett that I found the debonair gaiety with which I had embarked on this affair beginning to wane a trifle. Beholding her at close range like this, I suddenly became cognisant of what I was in for. The thought of strolling with this rummy specimen undeniably gave me a most unpleasant sinking feeling. I could not but remember how often, when in her company at Cannes, I had gazed dumbly at her, wishing that some kindly motorist in a racing car would ease the situation by coming along and ramming her amidships. As I have already made abundantly clear, this girl was not one of my most congenial buddies.

However, a Wooster's word is his bond. Woosters may quail, but they do not edge out. Only the keenest ear could have detected the tremor in the voice as I asked her if she would care to come out for half an hour.

"Lovely evening," I said.

"Yes, lovely, isn't it?"

"Lovely. Reminds me of Cannes."

"How lovely the evenings were there!"

"Lovely," I said.

"Lovely," said the Bassett.

"Lovely," I agreed.

That completed the weather and news bulletin for the French Riviera. Another minute, and we were out in the great open spaces, she cooing a bit about the scenery, and self replying, "Oh, rather, quite," and wondering how best to approach the matter in hand.

-10-

How different it all would have been, I could not but reflect, if this girl had been the sort of girl one chirrups cheerily to over the telephone and takes for spins in the old two-seater. In that case, I would simply have said, "Listen," and she would have said, "What?" and I would have said, "You know Gussie Fink-Nottle," and she would have said, "Yes," and I would have said, "He loves you," and she would have said either, "What, that mutt? Well, thank heaven for one good laugh today," or else, in more passionate vein, "Hot dog! Tell me more."

I mean to say, in either event the whole thing over and done with in under a minute.

But with the Bassett something less snappy and a good deal more glutinous was obviously indicated. What with all this daylight-saving stuff, we had hit the great open spaces at a moment when twilight had not yet begun to cheese it in favour of the shades of night. There was a fag-end of sunset still functioning. Stars were beginning to peep out, bats were fooling round, the garden was full of the aroma of those niffy white flowers which only start to put in their heavy work at the end of the day—in short, the glimmering landscape was fading on the sight and all the air held a solemn stillness, and it was plain that this was having the worst effect on her. Her eyes were enlarged, and her whole map a good deal too suggestive of the soul's awakening for comfort.

Her aspect was that of a girl who was expecting something fairly fruity from Bertram.

In these circs., conversation inevitably flagged a bit. I am never at my best when the situation seems to call for a certain soupiness, and I've heard other members of the Drones say the same thing about themselves. I remember Pongo Twistleton telling me that he was out in a gondola with a girl by moonlight once, and the only time he spoke was to tell her that old story about the chap who was so good at swimming that they made him a traffic cop in Venice.

Fell rather flat, he assured me, and it wasn't much later when the girl said she thought it was getting a little chilly and how about pushing back to the hotel.

So now, as I say, the talk rather hung fire. It had been all very well for me to promise Gussie that I would cut loose to this girl about aching hearts, but you want a cue for that sort of thing. And when, toddling along, we reached the edge of the lake and she finally spoke, conceive my chagrin when I discovered that what she was talking about was stars.

Not a bit of good to me.

"Oh, look," she said. She was a confirmed Oh-looker. I had noticed this at Cannes, where she had drawn my attention in this manner on various occasions to such diverse objects as a French actress, a Provençal filling station, the sunset over the Estorels, Michael Arlen, a man selling coloured spectacles, the deep velvet blue of the Mediterranean, and the late mayor of New York in a striped one-piece bathing suit. "Oh, look at that sweet little star up there all by itself."

I saw the one she meant, a little chap operating in a detached sort of way above a spinney.

"Yes," I said.

"I wonder if it feels lonely."

"Oh, I shouldn't think so."

"A fairy must have been crying."

"Eh?"

"Don't you remember? 'Every time a fairy sheds a tear, a wee bit star is born in the Milky Way.' Have you ever thought that, Mr. Wooster?"

I never had. Most improbable, I considered, and it didn't seem to me to check up with her statement that the stars were God's daisy chain. I mean, you can't have it both ways.

However, I was in no mood to dissect and criticize. I saw that I had been wrong in supposing that the stars were not germane to the issue. Quite a decent cue they had provided, and I leaped on it Promptly: "Talking of shedding tears——"

But she was now on the subject of rabbits, several of which were messing about in the park to our right.

"Oh, look. The little bunnies!"

"Talking of shedding tears——"

"Don't you love this time of the evening, Mr. Wooster, when the sun has gone to bed and all the bunnies come out to have their little suppers? When I was a child, I used to think that rabbits were gnomes, and that if I held my breath and stayed quite still, I should see the fairy queen."

Indicating with a reserved gesture that this was just the sort of loony thing I should have expected her to think as a child, I returned to the point.

"Talking of shedding tears," I said firmly, "it may interest you to know that there is an aching heart in Brinkley Court."

This held her. She cheesed the rabbit theme. Her face, which had been aglow with what I supposed was a pretty animation, clouded. She unshipped a sigh that sounded like the wind going out of a rubber duck.

"Ah, yes. Life is very sad, isn't it?"

"It is for some people. This aching heart, for instance."

"Those wistful eyes of hers! Drenched irises. And they used to dance like elves of delight. And all through a foolish misunderstanding about a shark. What a tragedy misunderstandings are. That pretty romance broken and over just because Mr. Glossop would insist that it was a flatfish."

I saw that she had got the wires crossed.

"I'm not talking about Angela."

"But her heart is aching."

"I know it's aching. But so is somebody else's."

She looked at me, perplexed.

"Somebody else? Mr. Glossop's, you mean?"

"No, I don't."

"Mrs. Travers's?"

The exquisite code of politeness of the Woosters prevented me clipping her one on the ear-hole, but I would have given a shilling to be able to do it. There seemed to me something deliberately fat-headed in the way she persisted in missing the gist.

"No, not Aunt Dahlia's, either."

"I'm sure she is dreadfully upset."

"Quite. But this heart I'm talking about isn't aching because of Tuppy's row with Angela. It's aching for a different reason altogether. I mean to say—dash it, you know why hearts ache!"

She seemed to shimmy a bit. Her voice, when she spoke, was whispery: "You mean—for love?"

"Absolutely. Right on the bull's-eye. For love."

"Oh, Mr. Wooster!"

"I take it you believe in love at first sight?"

"I do, indeed."

"Well, that's what happened to this aching heart. It fell in love at first sight, and ever since it's been eating itself out, as I believe the expression is."

There was a silence. She had turned away and was watching a duck out on the lake. It was tucking into weeds, a thing I've never been able to understand anyone wanting to do. Though I suppose, if you face it squarely, they're no worse than spinach. She stood drinking it in for a bit, and then it suddenly stood on its head and disappeared, and this seemed to break the spell.

"Oh, Mr. Wooster!" she said again, and from the tone of her voice, I could see that I had got her going.

"For you, I mean to say," I proceeded, starting to put in the fancy touches. I dare say you have noticed on these occasions that the difficulty is to plant the main idea, to get the general outline of the thing well fixed. The rest is mere detail work. I don't say I became glib at this juncture, but I certainly became a dashed glibber than I had been.

"It's having the dickens of a time. Can't eat, can't sleep—all for love of you. And what makes it all so particularly rotten is that it—this aching heart—can't bring itself up to the scratch and tell you the position of affairs, because your profile has gone and given it cold feet. Just as it is about to speak, it catches sight of you sideways, and words fail it. Silly, of course, but there it is."

I heard her give a gulp, and I saw that her eyes had become moistish. Drenched irises, if you care to put it that way.

"Lend you a handkerchief?"

"No, thank you. I'm quite all right."

It was more than I could say for myself. My efforts had left me weak. I don't know if you suffer in the same way, but with me the act of talking anything in the nature of real mashed potatoes always induces a sort of prickly sensation and a hideous feeling of shame, together with a marked starting of the pores.

I remember at my Aunt Agatha's place in Hertfordshire once

being put on the spot and forced to enact the role of King Edward III saying goodbye to that girl of his, Fair Rosamund, at some sort of pageant in aid of the Distressed Daughters of the Clergy. It involved some rather warmish medieval dialogue, I recall, racy of the days when they called a spade a spade, and by the time the whistle blew, I'll bet no Daughter of the Clergy was half as distressed as I was. Not a dry stitch.

My reaction now was very similar. It was a highly liquid Bertram who, hearing his *vis-à-vis* give a couple of hiccups and start to speak bent an attentive ear.

"Please don't say any more, Mr. Wooster."

Well, I wasn't going to, of course.

"I understand."

I was glad to hear this.

"Yes, I understand. I won't be so silly as to pretend not to know what you mean. I suspected this at Cannes, when you used to stand and stare at me without speaking a word, but with whole volumes in your eyes."

If Angela's shark had bitten me in the leg, I couldn't have leaped more convulsively. So tensely had I been concentrating on Gussie's interests that it hadn't so much as crossed my mind that another and an unfortunate construction could be placed on those words of mine. The persp., already bedewing my brow, became a regular Niagara.

My whole fate hung upon a woman's word. I mean to say, I couldn't back out. If a girl thinks a man is proposing to her, and on that understanding books him up, he can't explain to her that she has got hold of entirely the wrong end of the stick and that he hadn't the smallest intention of suggesting anything of the kind. He must simply let it ride. And the thought of being engaged to a girl who talked openly about fairies being born because stars blew their noses, or whatever it was, frankly appalled me.

She was carrying on with her remarks, and as I listened I clenched my fists till I shouldn't wonder if the knuckles didn't stand out white under the strain. It seemed as if she would never get to the nub.

"Yes, all through those days at Cannes I could see what you were trying to say. A girl always knows. And then you followed me down here, and there was that same dumb, yearning look in your eyes when we met this evening. And then you were so insistent that I should come out and walk with you in the twilight. And now you stammer out those halting words. No, this does not come as a surprise. But I am sorry——"

The word was like one of Jeeves's pick-me-ups. Just as if a glassful of meat sauce, red pepper, and the yolk of an egg—though, as I say, I am convinced that these are not the sole ingredients—had been shot into me, I expanded like some lovely flower blossoming in the sunshine. It was all right, after all. My guardian angel had not been asleep at the switch.

"—but I am afraid it is impossible."

She paused.

"Impossible," she repeated.

I had been so busy feeling saved from the scaffold that I didn't get on to it for a moment that an early reply was desired.

"Oh, right ho," I said hastily.

"I'm sorry."

"Quite all right."

"Sorrier than I can say."

"Don't give it another thought."

"We can still be friends."

"Oh, rather."

"Then shall we just say no more about it; keep what has happened as a tender little secret between ourselves?"

"Absolutely."

"We will. Like something lovely and fragrant laid away in lavender."

"In lavender—right."

There was a longish pause. She was gazing at me in a divinely pitying sort of way, much as if I had been a snail she had happened accidentally to bring her short French vamp down on, and I longed to tell her that it was all right, and that Bertram, so far from being the victim of despair, had never felt fizzier in his life. But, of course, one can't do that sort of thing. I simply said nothing, and stood there looking brave.

"I wish I could," she murmured.

"Could?" I said, for my attensh had been wandering.

"Feel towards you as you would like me to feel."

"Oh, ah."

"But I can't. I'm sorry."

"Absolutely O.K. Faults on both sides, no doubt."

"Because I am fond of you, Mr.—no, I think I must call you Bertie. May I?"

"Oh, rather."

"Because we are real friends."

"Quite."

"I do like you, Bertie. And if things were different—I wonder——"

"Eh?"

"After all, we are real friends.... We have this common memory.... You have a right to know.... I don't want you to think——Life is such a muddle, isn't it?"

To many men, no doubt, these broken utterances would have appeared mere drooling and would have been dismissed as such. But the Woosters are quicker-witted than the ordinary and can read between the lines. I suddenly divined what it was that she was trying to get off the chest.

"You mean there's someone else?"

She nodded.

"You're in love with some other bloke?"

She nodded.

"Engaged, what?"

This time she shook the pumpkin.

"No, not engaged."

Well, that was something, of course. Nevertheless, from the way she spoke, it certainly looked as if poor old Gussie might as well scratch his name off the entry list, and I didn't at all like the prospect of having to break the bad news to him. I had studied the man closely, and it was my conviction that this would about be his finish.

Gussie, you see, wasn't like some of my pals—the name of Bingo Little is one that springs to the lips—who, if turned down by a girl, would simply say, "Well, bung-oh!" and toddle off quite happily to find another. He was so manifestly a bird who, having failed to score in the first chukker, would turn the thing up and spend the rest of his life brooding over his newts and growing long grey whiskers, like one of those chaps you read about in novels, who live in the great white house you can just see over there through the trees and shut themselves off from the world and have pained faces.

"I'm afraid he doesn't care for me in that way. At least, he has said nothing. You understand that I am only telling you this because——"

"Oh, rather."

"It's odd that you should have asked me if I believed in love at first sight." She half closed her eyes. "'Who ever loved that loved not at first sight?'" she said in a rummy voice that brought back to me—I don't know why—the picture of my Aunt Agatha, as Boadicea, reciting at that pageant I was speaking of. "It's a silly little story. I was staying with some friends in the country, and I had gone for a walk with my dog, and the poor wee mite got a nasty thorn in his little foot and I didn't know what to do. And then suddenly this man came along——"

Harking back once again to that pageant, in sketching out for you my emotions on that occasion, I showed you only the darker side of the picture. There was, I should now mention, a splendid aftermath when, having climbed out of my suit of chain mail and sneaked off to the local pub, I entered the saloon bar and requested mine host to start pouring. A moment later, a tankard of their special home-brewed was in my hand, and the ecstasy of that first gollup is still green in my memory. The recollection of the agony through which I had passed was just what was needed to make it perfect.

It was the same now. When I realized, listening to her words, that she must be referring to Gussie—I mean to say, there couldn't have been a whole platoon of men taking thorns out of her dog that day; the animal wasn't a pin-cushion—and became aware that Gussie, who an instant before had, to all appearances, gone so far back in the betting as not to be worth a quotation, was the big winner after all, a positive thrill permeated the frame and there escaped my lips a "Wow!" so crisp and hearty that the Bassett leaped a liberal inch and a half from terra firma.

"I beg your pardon?" she said.

I waved a jaunty hand.

"Nothing," I said. "Nothing. Just remembered there's a letter I have to write tonight without fail. If you don't mind, I think I'll be going in. Here," I said, "comes Gussie Fink-Nottle. He will look after you."

And, as I spoke, Gussie came sidling out from behind a tree.

I passed away and left them to it. As regards these two, everything was beyond a question absolutely in order. All Gussie had to do was keep his head down and not press. Already, I felt, as I legged it back to the house, the happy ending must have begun to function. I mean to say, when you leave a girl and a man, each of whom has admitted in set terms that she and he loves him and her, in close juxtaposition in the twilight, there doesn't seem much more to do but start pricing fish slices.

Something attempted, something done, seemed to me to have earned two-penn'orth of wassail in the smoking-room.

I proceeded thither.

-11-

The makings were neatly laid out on a side-table, and to pour into a glass an inch or so of the raw spirit and shoosh some soda-water on top of it was with me the work of a moment. This done, I retired to an arm-chair and put my feet up, sipping the mixture with carefree enjoyment, rather like Caesar having one in his tent the day he overcame the Nervii.

As I let the mind dwell on what must even now be taking place in that peaceful garden, I felt bucked and uplifted. Though never for an instant faltering in my opinion that Augustus Fink-Nottle was Nature's final word in cloth-headed guffins, I liked the man, wished him well, and could not have felt more deeply involved in the success of his wooing if I, and not he, had been under the ether.

The thought that by this time he might quite easily have completed the preliminary *pourparlers* and be deep in an informal discussion of honeymoon plans was very pleasant to me.

Of course, considering the sort of girl Madeline Bassett was—stars and rabbits and all that, I mean—you might say that a sober sadness would have been more fitting. But in these matters you have got to realize that tastes differ. The impulse of right-thinking men might be to run a mile when they saw the Bassett, but for some reason she appealed to the deeps in Gussie, so that was that.

I had reached this point in my meditations, when I was aroused by the sound of the door opening. Somebody came in and started moving like a leopard toward the side-table and, lowering the feet, I perceived that it was Tuppy Glossop.

The sight of him gave me a momentary twinge of remorse, reminding me, as it did, that in the excitement of getting Gussie fixed up I had rather forgotten about this other client. It is often that way when you're trying to run two cases at once.

However, Gussie now being off my mind, I was prepared to devote my whole attention to the Glossop problem.

I had been much pleased by the way he had carried out the task assigned him at the dinner-table. No easy one, I can assure you, for the browsing and sluicing had been of the highest quality, and there had been one dish in particular—I allude to the *nonnettes de poulet Agnès Sorel*—which might well have broken down the most iron resolution. But he had passed it up like a professional fasting man, and I was proud of him.

"Oh, hullo, Tuppy," I said, "I wanted to see you."

He turned, snifter in hand, and it was easy to see that his privations had tried him sorely. He was looking like a wolf on the steppes of Russia which has seen its peasant shin up a high tree.

"Yes?" he said, rather unpleasantly. "Well, here I am."

"Well?"

"How do you mean——well?"

"Make your report."

"What report?"

"Have you nothing to tell me about Angela?"

"Only that she's a blister."

I was concerned.

"Hasn't she come clustering round you yet?"

"She has not."

"Very odd."

"Why odd?"

"She must have noted your lack of appetite."

113

He barked raspingly, as if he were having trouble with the tonsils of the soul.

"Lack of appetite! I'm as hollow as the Grand Canyon."

"Courage, Tuppy! Think of Gandhi."

"What about Gandhi?"

"He hasn't had a square meal for years."

"Nor have I. Or I could swear I hadn't. Gandhi, my left foot."

I saw that it might be best to let the Gandhi *motif* slide. I went back to where we had started.

"She's probably looking for you now."

"Who is? Angela?"

"Yes. She must have noticed your supreme sacrifice."

"I don't suppose she noticed it at all, the little fathead. I'll bet it didn't register in any way whatsoever."

"Come, Tuppy," I urged, "this is morbid. Don't take this gloomy view. She must at least have spotted that you refused those *nonnettes de poulet Agnès Sorel.* It was a sensational renunciation and stuck out like a sore thumb. And the *cèpes à la Rossini*——"

A hoarse cry broke from his twisted lips:

"Will you stop it, Bertie! Do you think I am made of marble? Isn't it bad enough to have sat watching one of Anatole's supremest dinners flit by, course after course, without having you making a song about it? Don't remind me of those *nonnettes.* I can't stand it."

I endeavoured to hearten and console.

"Be brave, Tuppy. Fix your thoughts on that cold steak-and-kidney pie in the larder. As the Good Book says, it cometh in the morning."

"Yes, in the morning. And it's now about half-past nine at night. You would bring that pie up, wouldn't you? Just when I was trying to keep my mind off it."

I saw what he meant. Hours must pass before he could dig into that pie. I dropped the subject, and we sat for a pretty good time in silence. Then he rose and began to pace the room in an overwrought sort of way, like a zoo lion who has heard the dinner-gong go and is hoping the keeper won't forget him in the general distribution. I averted my gaze tactfully, but I could hear him kicking chairs and things. It was plain that the man's soul was in travail and his blood pressure high.

Presently he returned to his seat, and I saw that he was looking at me intently. There was that about his demeanour that led me to think that he had something to communicate.

Nor was I wrong. He tapped me significantly on the knee and spoke:

"Bertie."

"Hullo?"

"Shall I tell you something?"

"Certainly, old bird," I said cordially. "I was just beginning to feel that the scene could do with a bit more dialogue."

"This business of Angela and me."

"Yes?"

"I've been putting in a lot of solid thinking about it."

"Oh, yes?"

"I have analysed the situation pitilessly, and one thing stands out as clear as dammit. There has been dirty work afoot."

"I don't get you."

"All right. Let me review the facts. Up to the time she went to Cannes Angela loved me. She was all over me. I was the blue-eyed boy in every sense of the term. You'll admit that?"

"Indisputably."

"And directly she came back we had this bust-up."

"Quite."

"About nothing."

"Oh, dash it, old man, nothing? You were a bit tactless, what, about her shark."

"I was frank and candid about her shark. And that's my point. Do you seriously believe that a trifling disagreement about sharks would make a girl hand a man his hat, if her heart were really his?"

"Certainly."

It beats me why he couldn't see it. But then poor old Tuppy has never been very hot on the finer shades. He's one of those large, tough, football-playing blokes who lack the more delicate sensibilities, as I've heard Jeeves call them. Excellent at blocking a punt or walking across an opponent's face in cleated boots, but not so good when it comes to understanding the highly-strung female temperament. It simply wouldn't occur to him that a girl might be prepared to give up her life's happiness rather than waive her shark.

"Rot! It was just a pretext."

"What was?"

"This shark business. She wanted to get rid of me, and grabbed at the first excuse."

"No, no."

"I tell you she did."

"But what on earth would she want to get rid of you for?"

"Exactly. That's the very question I asked myself. And here's the answer: Because she has fallen in love with somebody else. It sticks out a mile. There's no other possible solution. She goes to Cannes all for me, she comes back all off me. Obviously during those two months, she must have transferred her affections to some foul blister she met out there."

"No, no."

"Don't keep saying 'No, no'. She must have done. Well, I'll tell you one thing, and you can take this as official. If ever I find this slimy, slithery snake in the grass, he had better make all the necessary arrangements at his favourite nursing-home without delay, because I am going to be very rough with him. I propose, if and when found, to take him by his beastly neck, shake him till he froths, and pull him inside out and make him swallow himself."

With which words he biffed off; and I, having given him a minute or two to get out of the way, rose and made for the drawing-room. The tendency of females to roost in drawing-rooms after dinner being well marked, I expected to find Angela there. It was my intention to have a word with Angela.

To Tuppy's theory that some insinuating bird had stolen the girl's heart from him at Cannes I had given, as I have indicated, little credence, considering it the mere unbalanced apple sauce of a bereaved man. It was, of course, the shark, and nothing but the shark, that had caused love's young dream to go temporarily off the boil, and I was convinced that a word or two with the cousin at this juncture would set everything right.

For, frankly, I thought it incredible that a girl of her natural sweetness and tender-heartedness should not have been moved to her foundations by what she had seen at dinner that night. Even

Seppings, Aunt Dahlia's butler, a cold, unemotional man, had gasped and practically reeled when Tuppy waved aside those *nonnettes de poulet Agnès Sorel*, while the footman, standing by with the potatoes, had stared like one seeing a vision. I simply refused to consider the possibility of the significance of the thing having been lost on a nice girl like Angela. I fully expected to find her in the drawing-room with her heart bleeding freely, all ripe for an immediate reconciliation.

In the drawing-room, however, when I entered, only Aunt Dahlia met the eye. It seemed to me that she gave me rather a jaundiced look as I hove in sight, but this, having so recently beheld Tuppy in his agony, I attributed to the fact that she, like him, had been going light on the menu. You can't expect an empty aunt to beam like a full aunt.

"Oh, it's you, is it?" she said.

Well, it was, of course.

"Where's Angela?" I asked.

"Gone to bed."

"Already?"

"She said she had a headache."

"H'm."

I wasn't so sure that I liked the sound of that so much. A girl who has observed the sundered lover sensationally off his feed does not go to bed with headaches if love has been reborn in her heart. She sticks around and gives him the swift, remorseful glance from beneath the drooping eyelashes and generally endeavours to convey to him that, if he wants to get together across a round table and try to find a formula, she is all for it too. Yes, I am bound to say I found that going-to-bed stuff a bit disquieting.

"Gone to bed, eh?" I murmured musingly.

"What did you want her for?"

"I thought she might like a stroll and a chat."

"Are you going for a stroll?" said Aunt Dahlia, with a sudden show of interest. "Where?"

"Oh, hither and thither."

"Then I wonder if you would mind doing something for me."

"Give it a name."

117

"It won't take you long. You know that path that runs past the greenhouses into the kitchen garden. If you go along it, you come to a pond."

"That's right."

"Well, will you get a good, stout piece of rope or cord and go down that path till you come to the pond——"

"To the pond. Right."

"——and look about you till you find a nice, heavy stone. Or a fairly large brick would do."

"I see," I said, though I didn't, being still fogged. "Stone or brick. Yes. And then?"

"Then," said the relative, "I want you, like a good boy, to fasten the rope to the brick and tie it around your damned neck and jump into the pond and drown yourself. In a few days I will send and have you fished up and buried because I shall need to dance on your grave."

I was more fogged than ever. And not only fogged—wounded and resentful. I remember reading a book where a girl "suddenly fled from the room, afraid to stay for fear dreadful things would come tumbling from her lips; determined that she would not remain another day in this house to be insulted and misunderstood." I felt much about the same.

Then I reminded myself that one has got to make allowances for a woman with only about half a spoonful of soup inside her, and I checked the red-hot crack that rose to the lips.

"What," I said gently, "is this all about? You seem pipped with Bertram."

"Pipped!"

"Noticeably pipped. Why this ill-concealed animus?"

A sudden flame shot from her eyes, singeing my hair.

"Who was the ass, who was the chump, who was the dithering idiot who talked me, against my better judgment, into going without my dinner? I might have guessed——"

I saw that I had divined correctly the cause of her strange mood.

"It's all right. Aunt Dahlia. I know just how you're feeling. A bit on the hollow side, what? But the agony will pass. If I were you, I'd sneak down and raid the larder after the household have gone to bed. I am told there's a pretty good steak-and-kidney pie there which will repay inspection. Have faith, Aunt Dahlia," I urged. "Pretty soon Uncle Tom will be along, full of sympathy and anxious inquiries."

"Will he? Do you know where he is now?"

"I haven't seen him."

"He is in the study with his face buried in his hands, muttering about civilization and melting pots."

"Eh? Why?"

"Because it has just been my painful duty to inform him that Anatole has given notice."

I own that I reeled.

"What?"

"Given notice. As the result of that drivelling scheme of yours. What did you expect a sensitive, temperamental French cook to do, if you went about urging everybody to refuse all food? I hear that when the first two courses came back to the kitchen practically untouched, his feelings were so hurt that he cried like a child. And when the rest of the dinner followed, he came to the conclusion that the whole thing was a studied and calculated insult, and decided to hand in his portfolio."

"Golly!"

"You may well say 'Golly!' Anatole, God's gift to the gastric juices, gone like the dew off the petal of a rose, all through your idiocy. Perhaps you understand now why I want you to go and jump in that pond. I might have known that some hideous disaster would strike this house like a thunderbolt if once you wriggled your way into it and started trying to be clever."

Harsh words, of course, as from aunt to nephew, but I bore her no resentment. No doubt, if you looked at it from a certain angle, Bertram might be considered to have made something of a floater.

"I am sorry."

"What's the good of being sorry?"

"I acted for what I deemed the best."

"Another time try acting for the worst. Then we may possibly escape with a mere flesh wound."

"Uncle Tom's not feeling too bucked about it all, you say?"

"He's groaning like a lost soul. And any chance I ever had of getting that money out of him has gone."

I stroked the chin thoughtfully. There was, I had to admit, reason in what she said. None knew better than I how terrible a blow the passing of Anatole would be to Uncle Tom.

I have stated earlier in this chronicle that this curious object of the seashore with whom Aunt Dahlia has linked her lot is a bloke who habitually looks like a pterodactyl that has suffered, and the reason he does so is that all those years he spent in making millions in the Far East put his digestion on the blink, and the only cook that has ever been discovered capable of pushing food into him without starting something like Old Home Week in Moscow under the third waistcoat button is this uniquely gifted Anatole. Deprived of Anatole's services, all he was likely to give the wife of his b. was a dirty look. Yes, unquestionably, things seemed to have struck a somewhat rocky patch, and I must admit that I found myself, at moment of going to press, a little destitute of constructive ideas.

Confident, however, that these would come ere long, I kept the stiff upper lip.

"Bad," I conceded. "Quite bad, beyond a doubt. Certainly a nasty jar for one and all. But have no fear, Aunt Dahlia, I will fix everything."

I have alluded earlier to the difficulty of staggering when you're sitting down, showing that it is a feat of which I, personally, am not capable. Aunt Dahlia, to my amazement, now did it apparently without an effort. She was well wedged into a deep arm-chair, but, nevertheless, she staggered like billy-o. A sort of spasm of horror and apprehension contorted her face.

"If you dare to try any more of your lunatic schemes——"

I saw that it would be fruitless to try to reason with her. Quite plainly, she was not in the vein. Contenting myself, accordingly, with a gesture of loving sympathy, I left the room. Whether she did or did not throw a handsomely bound volume of the Works of Alfred, Lord Tennyson, at me, I am not in a position to say. I had seen it lying on the table beside her, and as I closed the door I remember receiving the impression that some blunt instrument had crashed against the woodwork, but I was feeling too pre-occupied to note and observe.

I blame myself for not having taken into consideration the possible effects of a sudden abstinence on the part of virtually the whole strength of the company on one of Anatole's impulsive Provençal temperament. These Gauls, I should have remembered, can't take it. Their tendency to fly off the handle at the slightest provocation is well known. No doubt the man had put his whole soul into those *nonnettes de poulet,* and to see them come homing back to him must have gashed him like a knife.

However, spilt milk blows nobody any good, and it is useless to dwell upon it. The task now confronting Bertram was to put matters right, and I was pacing the lawn, pondering to this end, when I suddenly heard a groan so lost-soulish that I thought it must have proceeded from Uncle Tom, escaped from captivity and come to groan in the garden.

Looking about me, however, I could discern no uncles. Puzzled, I was about to resume my meditations, when the sound came again. And peering into the shadows I observed a dim form seated on one of the rustic benches which so liberally dotted this pleasance and another dim form standing beside same. A second and more penetrating glance and I had assembled the facts.

These dim forms were, in the order named, Gussie Fink-Nottle and Jeeves. And what Gussie was doing, groaning all over the place like this, was more than I could understand.

Because, I mean to say, there was no possibility of error. He wasn't singing. As I approached, he gave an encore, and it was beyond question a groan. Moreover, I could now see him clearly, and his whole aspect was definitely sand-bagged.

"Good evening, sir," said Jeeves. "Mr. Fink-Nottle is not feeling well."

Nor was I. Gussie had begun to make a low, bubbling noise, and I could no longer disguise it from myself that something must have gone seriously wrong with the works. I mean, I know marriage is a pretty solemn business and the realization that he is in for it frequently churns a chap up a bit, but I had never come across a case of a newly-engaged man taking it on the chin so completely as this.

Gussie looked up. His eye was dull. He clutched the thatch.

"Goodbye, Bertie," he said, rising.

I seemed to spot an error.

"You mean 'Hullo,' don't you?"

"No, I don't. I mean goodbye. I'm off."

"Off where?"

"To the kitchen garden. To drown myself."

"Don't be an ass."

"I'm not an ass.... Am I an ass, Jeeves?"

"Possibly a little injudicious, sir."

"Drowning myself, you mean?"

"Yes, sir."

"You think, on the whole, not drown myself?"

"I should not advocate it, sir."

"Very well, Jeeves. I accept your ruling. After all, it would be unpleasant for Mrs. Travers to find a swollen body floating in her pond."

"Yes, sir."

"And she has been very kind to me."

"Yes, sir."

"And you have been very kind to me, Jeeves."

"Thank you, sir."

"So have you, Bertie. Very kind. Everybody has been very kind to me. Very, very kind. Very kind indeed. I have no complaints to make. All right, I'll go for a walk instead."

I followed him with bulging eyes as he tottered off into the dark.

"Jeeves," I said, and I am free to admit that in my emotion I bleated like a lamb drawing itself to the attention of the parent sheep, "what the dickens is all this?"

"Mr. Fink-Nottle is not quite himself, sir. He has passed through a trying experience."

I endeavoured to put together a brief synopsis of previous events.

"I left him out here with Miss Bassett."

"Yes, sir."

"I had softened her up."

"Yes, sir."

"He knew exactly what he had to do. I had coached him thoroughly in lines and business."

"Yes, sir. So Mr. Fink-Nottle informed me."

"Well, then——"

"I regret to say, sir, that there was a slight hitch."

"You mean, something went wrong?"

"Yes, sir."

I could not fathom. The brain seemed to be tottering on its throne.

"But how could anything go wrong? She loves him, Jeeves."

"Indeed, sir?"

"She definitely told me so. All he had to do was propose."

"Yes sir."

"Well, didn't he?"

"No, sir."

"Then what the dickens did he talk about?"

"Newts, sir."

"Newts?"

"Yes, sir."

"Newts?"

"Yes, sir."

"But why did he want to talk about newts?"

"He did not want to talk about newts, sir. As I gather from Mr. Fink-Nottle, nothing could have been more alien to his plans."

I simply couldn't grasp the trend.

"But you can't force a man to talk about newts."

"Mr. Fink-Nottle was the victim of a sudden unfortunate spasm of nervousness, sir. Upon finding himself alone with the young lady, he admits to having lost his morale. In such circumstances, gentlemen frequently talk at random, saying the first thing that chances to enter their heads. This, in Mr. Fink-Nottle's case, would seem to have been the newt, its treatment in sickness and in health."

The scales fell from my eyes. I understood. I had had the same sort of thing happen to me in moments of crisis. I remember once detaining a dentist with the drill at one of my lower bicuspids and holding him up for nearly ten minutes with a story about a Scotchman, an Irishman, and a Jew. Purely automatic. The more he tried to jab, the more I said "Hoots, mon," "Begorrah," and "Oy, oy". When one loses one's nerve, one simply babbles.

I could put myself in Gussie's place. I could envisage the scene. There he and the Bassett were, alone together in the evening stillness.

No doubt, as I had advised, he had shot the works about sunsets and fairy princesses, and so forth, and then had arrived at the point where he had to say that bit about having something to say to her. At this, I take it, she lowered her eyes and said, "Oh, yes?"

He then, I should imagine, said it was something very important; to which her response would, one assumes, have been something on the lines of "Really?" or "Indeed?" or possibly just the sharp intake of the breath. And then their eyes met, just as mine met the dentist's, and something suddenly seemed to catch him in the pit of the stomach and everything went black and he heard his voice starting to drool about newts. Yes, I could follow the psychology.

Nevertheless, I found myself blaming Gussie. On discovering that he was stressing the newt note in this manner, he ought, of course, to have tuned out, even if it had meant sitting there saying nothing. No matter how much of a twitter he was in, he should have had sense enough to see that he was throwing a spanner into the works. No girl, when she has been led to expect that a man is about to pour forth his soul in a fervour of passion, likes to find him suddenly shelving the whole topic in favour of an address on aquatic Salamandridae.

"Bad, Jeeves."

"Yes, sir."

"And how long did this nuisance continue?"

"For some not inconsiderable time, I gather, sir. According to Mr. Fink-Nottle, he supplied Miss Bassett with very full and complete information not only with respect to the common newt, but also the crested and palmated varieties. He described to her how newts, during the breeding season, live in the water, subsisting upon tadpoles, insect larvae, and crustaceans; how, later, they make their way to the land and eat slugs and worms; and how the newly born newt has three pairs of long, plumlike, external gills. And he was just observing that newts differ from salamanders in the shape of the tail, which is compressed, and that a marked sexual dimorphism prevails in most species, when the young lady rose and said that she thought she would go back to the house."

"And then——"

"She went, sir."

I stood musing. More and more, it was beginning to be borne in upon me what a particularly difficult chap Gussie was to help. He seemed to so marked an extent to lack snap and finish. With infinite toil, you manoeuvred him into a position where all he had to do was charge ahead, and he didn't charge ahead, but went off sideways, missing the objective completely.

"Difficult, Jeeves."

"Yes, sir."

In happier circs., of course, I would have canvassed his views on the matter. But after what had occurred in connection with that mess-jacket, my lips were sealed.

"Well, I must think it over."

"Yes, sir."

"Burnish the brain a bit and endeavour to find the way out."

"Yes, sir."

"Well, good night, Jeeves."

"Good night, sir."

He shimmered off, leaving a pensive Bertram Wooster standing motionless in the shadows. It seemed to me that it was hard to know what to do for the best.

-12-

I don't know if it has happened to you at all, but a thing I've noticed with myself is that, when I'm confronted by a problem which seems for the moment to stump and baffle, a good sleep will often bring the solution in the morning.

It was so on the present occasion.

The nibs who study these matters claim, I believe, that this has got something to do with the subconscious mind, and very possibly they may be right. I wouldn't have said off-hand that I had a subconscious mind, but I suppose I must without knowing it, and no doubt it was there, sweating away diligently at the old stand, all the while the corporeal Wooster was getting his eight hours.

For directly I opened my eyes on the morrow, I saw daylight. Well, I don't mean that exactly, because naturally I did. What I mean is that I found I had the thing all mapped out. The good old subconscious m. had delivered the goods, and I perceived exactly what steps must be taken in order to put Augustus Fink-Nottle among the practising Romeos.

I should like you, if you can spare me a moment of your valuable time, to throw your mind back to that conversation he and I had had in the garden on the previous evening. Not the glimmering landscape bit, I don't mean that, but the concluding passages of it. Having done so, you will recall that when he informed me that he never touched alcoholic liquor, I shook the head a bit, feeling that this must inevitably weaken him as a force where proposing to girls was concerned.

And events had shown that my fears were well founded.

Put to the test, with nothing but orange juice inside him, he had proved a complete bust. In a situation calling for words of molten passion of a nature calculated to go through Madeline Bassett like a red-hot gimlet through half a pound of butter, he had said not a syllable that could bring a blush to the cheek of modesty, merely delivering a well-phrased but, in the circumstances, quite misplaced lecture on newts.

A romantic girl is not to be won by such tactics. Obviously, before attempting to proceed further, Augustus Fink-Nottle must be induced to throw off the shackling inhibitions of the past and fuel up. It must be a primed, confident Fink-Nottle who squared up to the Bassett for Round No. 2.

Only so could the *Morning Post* make its ten bob, or whatever it is, for printing the announcement of the forthcoming nuptials.

Having arrived at this conclusion I found the rest easy, and by the time Jeeves brought me my tea I had evolved a plan complete in every detail. This I was about to place before him—indeed, I had got as far as the preliminary "I say, Jeeves"—when we were interrupted by the arrival of Tuppy.

He came listlessly into the room, and I was pained to observe that a night's rest had effected no improvement in the unhappy wreck's appearance. Indeed, I should have said, if anything, that he was looking rather more moth-eaten than when I had seen him last. If you can visualize a bulldog which has just been kicked in the ribs and had its dinner sneaked by the cat, you will have Hildebrand Glossop as he now stood before me.

"Stap my vitals, Tuppy, old corpse," I said, concerned, "you're looking pretty blue round the rims."

Jeeves slid from the presence in that tactful, eel-like way of his, and I motioned the remains to take a seat.

"What's the matter?" I said.

He came to anchor on the bed, and for awhile sat picking at the coverlet in silence.

"I've been through hell, Bertie."

"Through where?"

"Hell."

"Oh, hell? And what took you there?"

Once more he became silent, staring before him with sombre eyes. Following his gaze, I saw that he was looking at an enlarged photograph of my Uncle Tom in some sort of Masonic uniform which stood on the mantelpiece. I've tried to reason with Aunt Dahlia about this photograph for years, placing before her two alternative suggestions: (a) To burn the beastly thing; or (b) if she must preserve it, to shove me in another room when I come to stay. But she declines to accede. She says it's good for me. A useful discipline, she maintains, teaching me that there is a darker side to life and that we were not put into this world for pleasure only.

"Turn it to the wall, if it hurts you, Tuppy," I said gently.

"Eh?"

"That photograph of Uncle Tom as the bandmaster."

"I didn't come here to talk about photographs. I came for sympathy."

"And you shall have it. What's the trouble? Worrying about Angela, I suppose? Well, have no fear. I have another well-laid plan for encompassing that young shrimp. I'll guarantee that she will be weeping on your neck before yonder sun has set."

He barked sharply.

"A fat chance!"

"Tup, Tushy!"

"Eh?"

"I mean 'Tush, Tuppy.' I tell you I will do it. I was just going to describe this plan of mine to Jeeves when you came in. Care to hear it?"

"I don't want to hear any of your beastly plans. Plans are no good. She's gone and fallen in love with this other bloke, and now hates my gizzard."

"Rot."

"It isn't rot."

"I tell you, Tuppy, as one who can read the female heart, that this Angela loves you still."

"Well, it didn't look much like it in the larder last night."

"Oh, you went to the larder last night?"

"I did."

"And Angela was there?"

"She was. And your aunt. Also your uncle."

I saw that I should require foot-notes. All this was new stuff to me. I had stayed at Brinkley Court quite a lot in my time, but I had no idea the larder was such a social vortex. More like a snack bar on a race-course than anything else, it seemed to have become.

"Tell me the whole story in your own words," I said, "omitting no detail, however apparently slight, for one never knows how important the most trivial detail may be."

He inspected the photograph for a moment with growing gloom.

"All right," he said. "This is what happened. You know my views about that steak-and-kidney pie."

"Quite."

"Well, round about one a.m. I thought the time was ripe. I stole from my room and went downstairs. The pie seemed to beckon me."

I nodded. I knew how pies do.

"I got to the larder. I fished it out. I set it on the table. I found knife and fork. I collected salt, mustard, and pepper. There were some cold potatoes. I added those. And I was about to pitch in when I heard a sound behind me, and there was your aunt at the door. In a blue-and-yellow dressing gown."

"Embarrassing."

"Most."

"I suppose you didn't know where to look."

"I looked at Angela."

"She came in with my aunt?"

128

"No. With your uncle, a minute or two later. He was wearing mauve pyjamas and carried a pistol. Have you ever seen your uncle in pyjamas and a pistol?"

"Never."

"You haven't missed much."

"Tell me, Tuppy," I asked, for I was anxious to ascertain this, "about Angela. Was there any momentary softening in her gaze as she fixed it on you?"

"She didn't fix it on me. She fixed it on the pie."

"Did she say anything?"

"Not right away. Your uncle was the first to speak. He said to your aunt, 'God bless my soul, Dahlia, what are you doing here?' To which she replied, 'Well, if it comes to that, my merry somnambulist, what are you?' Your uncle then said that he thought there must be burglars in the house, as he had heard noises."

I nodded again. I could follow the trend. Ever since the scullery window was found open the year Shining Light was disqualified in the Cesarewitch for boring, Uncle Tom has had a marked complex about burglars. I can still recall my emotions when, paying my first visit after he had bars put on all the windows and attempting to thrust the head out in order to get a sniff of country air, I nearly fractured my skull on a sort of iron grille, as worn by the tougher kinds of mediaeval prison.

"'What sort of noises?' said your aunt. 'Funny noises,' said your uncle. Whereupon Angela—with a nasty, steely tinkle in her voice, the little buzzard—observed, 'I expect it was Mr. Glossop eating.' And then she did give me a look. It was the sort of wondering, revolted look a very spiritual woman would give a fat man gulping soup in a restaurant. The kind of look that makes a fellow feel he's forty-six round the waist and has great rolls of superfluous flesh pouring down over the back of his collar. And, still speaking in the same unpleasant tone, she added, 'I ought to have told you, father, that Mr. Glossop always likes to have a good meal three or four times during the night. It helps to keep him going till breakfast. He has the most amazing appetite. See, he has practically finished a large steak-and-kidney pie already'."

129

As he spoke these words, a feverish animation swept over Tuppy. His eyes glittered with a strange light, and he thumped the bed violently with his fist, nearly catching me a juicy one on the leg.

"That was what hurt, Bertie. That was what stung. I hadn't so much as started on that pie. But that's a woman all over."

"The eternal feminine."

"She continued her remarks. 'You've no idea,' she said, 'how Mr. Glossop loves food. He just lives for it. He always eats six or seven meals a day, and then starts in again after bedtime. I think it's rather wonderful.' Your aunt seemed interested, and said it reminded her of a boa constrictor. Angela said, didn't she mean a python? And then they argued as to which of the two it was. Your uncle, meanwhile, poking about with that damned pistol of his till human life wasn't safe in the vicinity. And the pie lying there on the table, and me unable to touch it. You begin to understand why I said I had been through hell."

"Quite. Can't have been at all pleasant."

"Presently your aunt and Angela settled their discussion, deciding that Angela was right and that it was a python that I reminded them of. And shortly after that we all pushed back to bed, Angela warning me in a motherly voice not to take the stairs too quickly. After seven or eight solid meals, she said, a man of my build ought to be very careful, because of the danger of apoplectic fits. She said it was the same with dogs. When they became very fat and overfed, you had to see that they didn't hurry upstairs, as it made them puff and pant, and that was bad for their hearts. She asked your aunt if she remembered the late spaniel, Ambrose; and your aunt said, 'Poor old Ambrose, you couldn't keep him away from the garbage pail'; and Angela said, 'Exactly, so do please be careful, Mr. Glossop.' And you tell me she loves me still!"

I did my best to encourage.

"Girlish banter, what?"

"Girlish banter be dashed. She's right off me. Once her ideal, I am now less than the dust beneath her chariot wheels. She became infatuated with this chap, whoever he was, at Cannes, and now she can't stand the sight of me."

I raised my eyebrows.

"My dear Tuppy, you are not showing your usual good sense in this Angela-chap-at-Cannes matter. If you will forgive me saying so, you have got an *idée fixe.*"

"A what?"

"An *idée fixe.* You know. One of those things fellows get. Like Uncle Tom's delusion that everybody who is known even slightly to the police is lurking in the garden, waiting for a chance to break into the house. You keep talking about this chap at Cannes, and there never was a chap at Cannes, and I'll tell you why I'm so sure about this. During those two months on the Riviera, it so happens that Angela and I were practically inseparable. If there had been somebody nosing round her, I should have spotted it in a second."

He started. I could see that this had impressed him.

"Oh, she was with you all the time at Cannes, was she?"

"I don't suppose she said two words to anybody else, except, of course, idle conv. at the crowded dinner table or a chance remark in a throng at the Casino."

"I see. You mean that anything in the shape of mixed bathing and moonlight strolls she conducted solely in your company?"

"That's right. It was quite a joke in the hotel."

"You must have enjoyed that."

"Oh, rather. I've always been devoted to Angela."

"Oh, yes?"

"When we were kids, she used to call herself my little sweetheart."

"She did?"

"Absolutely."

"I see."

He sat plunged in thought, while I, glad to have set his mind at rest, proceeded with my tea. And presently there came the banging of a gong from the hall below, and he started like a war horse at the sound of the bugle.

"Breakfast!" he said, and was off to a flying start, leaving me to brood and ponder. And the more I brooded and pondered, the more did it seem to me that everything now looked pretty smooth. Tuppy, I could see, despite that painful scene in the larder, still loved Angela with all the old fervour.

This meant that I could rely on that plan to which I had referred

131

to bring home the bacon. And as I had found the way to straighten out the Gussie-Bassett difficulty, there seemed nothing more to worry about.

It was with an uplifted heart that I addressed Jeeves as he came in to remove the tea tray.

-13-

"Jeeves," I said.

"Sir?"

"I've just been having a chat with young Tuppy, Jeeves. Did you happen to notice that he wasn't looking very roguish this morning?"

"Yes, sir. It seemed to me that Mr. Glossop's face was sicklied o'er with the pale cast of thought."

"Quite. He met my cousin Angela in the larder last night, and a rather painful interview ensued."

"I am sorry, sir."

"Not half so sorry as he was. She found him closeted with a steak-and-kidney pie, and appears to have been a bit caustic about fat men who lived for food alone."

"Most disturbing, sir."

"Very. In fact, many people would say that things had gone so far between these two nothing now could bridge the chasm. A girl who could make cracks about human pythons who ate nine or ten meals a day and ought to be careful not to hurry upstairs because of the danger of apoplectic fits is a girl, many people would say, in whose heart love is dead. Wouldn't people say that, Jeeves?"

"Undeniably, sir."

"They would be wrong."

"You think so, sir?"

"I am convinced of it. I know these females. You can't go by what they say."

"You feel that Miss Angela's strictures should not be taken too much *au pied de la lettre*, sir?"

"Eh?"

"In English, we should say 'literally'."

"Literally. That's exactly what I mean. You know what girls are. A

132

tiff occurs, and they shoot their heads off. But underneath it all the old love still remains. Am I correct?"

"Quite correct, sir. The poet Scott——"

"Right ho, Jeeves."

"Very good, sir."

"And in order to bring that old love whizzing to the surface once more, all that is required is the proper treatment."

"By 'proper treatment,' sir, you mean——"

"Clever handling, Jeeves. A spot of the good old snaky work. I see what must be done to jerk my Cousin Angela back to normalcy. I'll tell you, shall I?"

"If you would be so kind, sir."

I lit a cigarette, and eyed him keenly through the smoke. He waited respectfully for me to unleash the words of wisdom. I must say for Jeeves that—till, as he is so apt to do, he starts shoving his oar in and cavilling and obstructing—he makes a very good audience. I don't know if he is actually agog, but he looks agog, and that's the great thing.

"Suppose you were strolling through the illimitable jungle, Jeeves, and happened to meet a tiger cub."

"The contingency is a remote one, sir."

"Never mind. Let us suppose it."

"Very good, sir."

"Let us now suppose that you sloshed that tiger cub, and let us suppose further that word reached its mother that it was being put upon. What would you expect the attitude of that mother to be? In what frame of mind do you consider that that tigress would approach you?"

"I should anticipate a certain show of annoyance, sir."

"And rightly. Due to what is known as the maternal instinct, what?"

"Yes, sir."

"Very good, Jeeves. We will now suppose that there has recently been some little coolness between this tiger cub and this tigress. For some days, let us say, they have not been on speaking terms. Do you think that that would make any difference to the vim with which the latter would leap to the former's aid?"

"No, sir."

"Exactly. Here, then, in brief, is my plan, Jeeves. I am going to draw my Cousin Angela aside to a secluded spot and roast Tuppy properly."

"Roast, sir?"

"Knock. Slam. Tick-off. Abuse. Denounce. I shall be very terse about Tuppy, giving it as my opinion that in all essentials he is more like a wart hog than an ex-member of a fine old English public school. What will ensue? Hearing him attacked, my Cousin Angela's womanly heart will be as sick as mud. The maternal tigress in her will awake. No matter what differences they may have had, she will remember only that he is the man she loves, and will leap to his defence. And from that to falling into his arms and burying the dead past will be but a step. How do you react to that?"

"The idea is an ingenious one, sir."

"We Woosters are ingenious, Jeeves, exceedingly ingenious."

"Yes, sir."

"As a matter of fact, I am not speaking without a knowledge of the form book. I have tested this theory."

"Indeed, sir?"

"Yes, in person. And it works. I was standing on the Eden rock at Antibes last month, idly watching the bathers disport themselves in the water, and a girl I knew slightly pointed at a male diver and asked me if I didn't think his legs were about the silliest-looking pair of props ever issued to human being. I replied that I did, indeed, and for the space of perhaps two minutes was extraordinarily witty and satirical about this bird's underpinning. At the end of that period, I suddenly felt as if I had been caught up in the tail of a cyclone.

"Beginning with a *critique* of my own limbs, which she said, justly enough, were nothing to write home about, this girl went on to dissect my manners, morals, intellect, general physique, and method of eating asparagus with such acerbity that by the time she had finished the best you could say of Bertram was that, so far as was known, he had never actually committed murder or set fire to an orphan asylum. Subsequent investigation proved that she was engaged to the fellow with the legs and had had a slight disagreement with him the evening before on the subject of whether she should or should not have made an original call of two spades, having seven, but without the ace. That night I saw them dining together with every indication of relish, their differences made up and the lovelight once more in their eyes. That shows you, Jeeves."

"Yes, sir."

"I expect precisely similar results from my Cousin Angela when I start roasting Tuppy. By lunchtime, I should imagine, the engagement will be on again and the diamond-and-platinum ring glittering as of yore on her third finger. Or is it the fourth?"

"Scarcely by luncheon time, sir. Miss Angela's maid informs me that Miss Angela drove off in her car early this morning with the intention of spending the day with friends in the vicinity."

"Well, within half an hour of whatever time she comes back, then. These are mere straws, Jeeves. Do not let us chop them."

"No, sir."

"The point is that, as far as Tuppy and Angela are concerned, we may say with confidence that everything will shortly be hotsy-totsy once more. And what an agreeable thought that is, Jeeves."

"Very true, sir."

"If there is one thing that gives me the pip, it is two loving hearts being estranged."

"I can readily appreciate the fact, sir."

I placed the stub of my gasper in the ash tray and lit another, to indicate that that completed Chap. I.

"Right ho, then. So much for the western front. We now turn to the eastern."

"Sir?"

"I speak in parables, Jeeves. What I mean is, we now approach the matter of Gussie and Miss Bassett."

"Yes, sir."

"Here, Jeeves, more direct methods are required. In handling the case of Augustus Fink-Nottle, we must keep always in mind the fact that we are dealing with a poop."

"A sensitive plant would, perhaps, be a kinder expression, sir."

"No, Jeeves, a poop. And with poops one has to employ the strong, forceful, straightforward policy. Psychology doesn't get you anywhere. You, if I may remind you without wounding your feelings, fell into the error of mucking about with psychology in connection with this Fink-Nottle, and the result was a wash-out. You attempted to push him over the line by rigging him out in a Mephistopheles costume and sending him off to a fancy-dress ball, your view being that scarlet tights would embolden him. Futile."

"The matter was never actually put to the test, sir."

"No. Because he didn't get to the ball. And that strengthens my argument. A man who can set out in a cab for a fancy-dress ball and not get there is manifestly a poop of no common order. I don't think I have ever known anybody else who was such a dashed silly ass that he couldn't even get to a fancy-dress ball. Have you, Jeeves?"

"No, sir."

"But don't forget this, because it is the point I wish, above all, to make: Even if Gussie had got to that ball; even if those scarlet tights, taken in conjunction with his horn-rimmed spectacles, hadn't given the girl a fit of some kind; even if she had rallied from the shock and he had been able to dance and generally hobnob with her; even then your efforts would have been fruitless, because, Mephistopheles costume or no Mephistopheles costume, Augustus Fink-Nottle would never have been able to summon up the courage to ask her to be his. All that would have resulted would have been that she would have got that lecture on newts a few days earlier. And why, Jeeves? Shall I tell you why?"

"Yes, sir."

"Because he would have been attempting the hopeless task of trying to do the thing on orange juice."

"Sir?"

"Gussie is an orange-juice addict. He drinks nothing else."

"I was not aware of that, sir."

"I have it from his own lips. Whether from some hereditary taint, or because he promised his mother he wouldn't, or simply because he doesn't like the taste of the stuff, Gussie Fink-Nottle has never in the whole course of his career pushed so much as the simplest gin and tonic over the larynx. And he expects—this poop expects, Jeeves— this wabbling, shrinking, diffident rabbit in human shape expects under these conditions to propose to the girl he loves. One hardly knows whether to smile or weep, what?"

"You consider total abstinence a handicap to a gentleman who wishes to make a proposal of marriage, sir?"

The question amazed me.

"Why, dash it," I said, astounded, "you must know it is. Use your intelligence, Jeeves. Reflect what proposing means. It means that a decent, self-respecting chap has got to listen to himself saying things which, if spoken on the silver screen, would cause him to dash to the box-office and demand his money back. Let him attempt to do it on orange juice, and what ensues? Shame seals his lips, or, if it doesn't do that, makes him lose his morale and start to babble. Gussie, for example, as we have seen, babbles of syncopated newts."

"Palmated newts, sir."

"Palmated or syncopated, it doesn't matter which. The point is that he babbles and is going to babble again, if he has another try at it. Unless—and this is where I want you to follow me very closely, Jeeves—unless steps are taken at once through the proper channels. Only active measures, promptly applied, can provide this poor, pusillanimous poop with the proper pep. And that is why, Jeeves, I intend tomorrow to secure a bottle of gin and lace his luncheon orange juice with it liberally."

"Sir?"

I clicked the tongue.

"I have already had occasion, Jeeves," I said rebukingly, "to comment on the way you say 'Well, sir' and 'Indeed, sir?' I take this opportunity of informing you that I object equally strongly to your 'Sir?' pure and simple. The word seems to suggest that in your opinion I have made a statement or mooted a scheme so bizarre that your brain reels at it. In the present instance, there is absolutely nothing to say 'Sir?' about. The plan I have put forward is entirely reasonable and icily logical, and should excite no sirring whatsoever. Or don't you think so?"

"Well, sir——"

"Jeeves!"

"I beg your pardon, sir. The expression escaped me inadvertently. What I intended to say, since you press me, was that the action which you propose does seem to me somewhat injudicious."

"Injudicious? I don't follow you, Jeeves."

"A certain amount of risk would enter into it, in my opinion, sir. It is not always a simple matter to gauge the effect of alcohol on a subject unaccustomed to such stimulant. I have known it to have distressing results in the case of parrots."

"Parrots?"

"I was thinking of an incident of my earlier life, sir, before I entered your employment. I was in the service of the late Lord Brancaster at the time, a gentleman who owned a parrot to which he was greatly devoted, and one day the bird chanced to be lethargic, and his lordship, with the kindly intention of restoring it to its customary animation, offered it a portion of seed cake steeped in the '84 port. The bird accepted the morsel gratefully and consumed it with every indication of satisfaction. Almost immediately afterwards, however, its manner became markedly feverish. Having bitten his lordship in the thumb and sung part of a sea-chanty, it fell to the bottom of the cage and remained there for a considerable period of time with its legs in the air, unable to move. I merely mention this, sir, in order to——"

I put my finger on the flaw. I had spotted it all along.

"But Gussie isn't a parrot."

"No, sir, but——"

"It is high time, in my opinion, that this question of what young Gussie really is was threshed out and cleared up. He seems to think he is a male newt, and you now appear to suggest that he is a parrot. The truth of the matter being that he is just a plain, ordinary poop and needs a snootful as badly as ever man did. So no more discussion, Jeeves. My mind is made up. There is only one way of handling this difficult case, and that is the way I have outlined."

"Very good, sir."

"Right ho, Jeeves. So much for that, then. Now here's something else: You noticed that I said I was going to put this project through tomorrow, and no doubt you wondered why I said tomorrow. Why did I, Jeeves?"

"Because you feel that if it were done when 'tis done, then 'twere well it were done quickly, sir?"

"Partly, Jeeves, but not altogether. My chief reason for fixing the date as specified is that tomorrow, though you have doubtless forgotten, is the day of the distribution of prizes at Market Snodsbury Grammar School, at which, as you know, Gussie is to be the male star and master of the revels. So you see we shall, by lacing that juice, not only embolden him to propose to Miss Bassett, but also put him so into shape that he will hold that Market Snodsbury audience spellbound."

"In fact, you will be killing two birds with one stone, sir."

"Exactly. A very neat way of putting it. And now here is a minor point. On second thoughts, I think the best plan will be for you, not me, to lace the juice."

"Sir?"

"Jeeves!"

"I beg your pardon, sir."

"And I'll tell you why that will be the best plan. Because you are in a position to obtain ready access to the stuff. It is served to Gussie daily, I have noticed, in an individual jug. This jug will presumably be lying about the kitchen or somewhere before lunch tomorrow. It will be the simplest of tasks for you to slip a few fingers of gin in it."

"No doubt, sir, but——"

"Don't say 'but,' Jeeves."

"I fear, sir——"

"'I fear, sir' is just as bad."

"What I am endeavouring to say, sir, is that I am sorry, but I am afraid I must enter an unequivocal *nolle prosequi*."

"Do what?"

"The expression is a legal one, sir, signifying the resolve not to proceed with a matter. In other words, eager though I am to carry out your instructions, sir, as a general rule, on this occasion I must respectfully decline to co-operate."

"You won't do it, you mean?"

"Precisely, sir."

I was stunned. I began to understand how a general must feel when he has ordered a regiment to charge and has been told that it isn't in the mood.

"Jeeves," I said, "I had not expected this of you."

"No, sir?"

"No, indeed. Naturally, I realize that lacing Gussie's orange juice is not one of those regular duties for which you receive the monthly stipend, and if you care to stand on the strict letter of the contract, I suppose there is nothing to be done about it. But you will permit me to observe that this is scarcely the feudal spirit."

"I am sorry, sir."

"It is quite all right, Jeeves, quite all right. I am not angry, only a little hurt."

"Very good, sir."

"Right ho, Jeeves."

-14-

Investigation proved that the friends Angela had gone to spend the day with were some stately-home owners of the name of Stretchley-Budd, hanging out in a joint called Kingham Manor, about eight miles distant in the direction of Pershore. I didn't know these birds, but their fascination must have been considerable, for she tore herself away from them only just in time to get back and dress for dinner. It was, accordingly, not until coffee had been consumed that I was able to get matters moving. I found her in the drawing-room and at once proceeded to put things in train.

It was with very different feelings from those which had animated the bosom when approaching the Bassett twenty-four hours before in the same manner in this same drawing-room that I headed for where she sat. As I had told Tuppy, I have always been devoted to Angela, and there is nothing I like better than a ramble in her company.

And I could see by the look of her now how sorely in need she was of my aid and comfort.

Frankly, I was shocked by the unfortunate young prune's appearance. At Cannes she had been a happy, smiling English girl of the best type, full of beans and buck. Her face now was pale and drawn, like that of a hockey centre-forward at a girls' school who, in addition to getting a fruity one on the shin, has just been penalized for "sticks". In any normal gathering, her demeanour would have excited instant remark, but the standard of gloom at Brinkley Court had become so high that it passed unnoticed. Indeed, I shouldn't wonder if Uncle Tom, crouched in his corner waiting for the end, didn't think she was looking indecently cheerful.

I got down to the agenda in my debonair way.

"What ho, Angela, old girl."

"Hullo, Bertie, darling."

"Glad you're back at last. I missed you."

"Did you, darling?"

"I did, indeed. Care to come for a saunter?"

"I'd love it."

"Fine. I have much to say to you that is not for the public ear."

I think at this moment poor old Tuppy must have got a sudden touch of cramp. He had been sitting hard by, staring at the ceiling, and he now gave a sharp leap like a gaffed salmon and upset a small table containing a vase, a bowl of potpourri, two china dogs, and a copy of Omar Khayyám bound in limp leather.

Aunt Dahlia uttered a startled hunting cry. Uncle Tom, who probably imagined from the noise that this was civilization crashing at last, helped things along by breaking a coffee-cup.

Tuppy said he was sorry. Aunt Dahlia, with a deathbed groan, said it didn't matter. And Angela, having stared haughtily for a moment like a princess of the old régime confronted by some notable example of gaucherie on the part of some particularly foul member of the underworld, accompanied me across the threshold. And presently I had deposited her and self on one of the rustic benches in the garden, and was ready to snap into the business of the evening.

I considered it best, however, before doing so, to ease things along with a little informal chitchat. You don't want to rush a delicate job like the one I had in hand. And so for a while we spoke of neutral topics. She said that what had kept her so long at the Stretchley-Budds was that Hilda Stretchley-Budd had made her stop on and help with the arrangements for their servants' ball tomorrow night, a task which she couldn't very well decline, as all the Brinkley Court domestic staff were to be present. I said that a jolly night's revelry might be just what was needed to cheer Anatole up and take his mind off things. To which she replied that Anatole wasn't going. On being urged to do so by Aunt Dahlia, she said, he had merely shaken his head sadly and gone on talking of returning to Provence, where he was appreciated.

It was after the sombre silence induced by this statement that Angela said the grass was wet and she thought she would go in.

This, of course, was entirely foreign to my policy.

"No, don't do that. I haven't had a chance to talk to you since you arrived."

"I shall ruin my shoes."

"Put your feet up on my lap."

"All right. And you can tickle my ankles."

"Quite."

Matters were accordingly arranged on these lines, and for some minutes we continued chatting in desultory fashion. Then the conversation petered out. I made a few observations *in re* the scenic effects, featuring the twilight hush, the peeping stars, and the soft glimmer of the waters of the lake, and she said yes. Something rustled in the bushes in front of us, and I advanced the theory that it was possibly a weasel, and she said it might be. But it was plain that the girl was distraite, and I considered it best to waste no more time.

"Well, old thing," I said, "I've heard all about your little dust-up So those wedding bells are not going to ring out, what?"

"No."

"Definitely over, is it?"

"Yes."

"Well, if you want my opinion, I think that's a bit of goose for you, Angela, old girl. I think you're extremely well out of it. It's a mystery to me how you stood this Glossop so long. Take him for all in all, he ranks very low down among the wines and spirits. A washout, I should describe him as. A frightful oik, and a mass of side to boot. I'd pity the girl who was linked for life to a bargee like Tuppy Glossop."

And I emitted a hard laugh—one of the sneering kind.

"I always thought you were such friends," said Angela.

I let go another hard one, with a bit more top spin on it than the first time:

"Friends? Absolutely not. One was civil, of course, when one met the fellow, but it would be absurd to say one was a friend of his. A club acquaintance, and a mere one at that. And then one was at school with the man."

"At Eton?"

"Good heavens, no. We wouldn't have a fellow like that at Eton. At a kid's school before I went there. A grubby little brute he was, I recollect. Covered with ink and mire generally, washing only on alternate Thursdays. In short, a notable outsider, shunned by all."

I paused. I was more than a bit perturbed. Apart from the agony of having to talk in this fashion of one who, except when he was looping back rings and causing me to plunge into swimming baths in correct evening costume, had always been a very dear and esteemed crony, I didn't seem to be getting anywhere. Business was not resulting. Staring into the bushes without a yip, she appeared to be bearing these slurs and innuendos of mine with an easy calm.

I had another pop at it:

"'Uncouth' about sums it up. I doubt if I've ever seen an uncouther kid than this Glossop. Ask anyone who knew him in those days to describe him in a word, and the word they will use is 'uncouth'. And he's just the same today. It's the old story. The boy is the father of the man."

She appeared not to have heard.

"The boy," I repeated, not wishing her to miss that one, "is the father of the man."

"What are you talking about?"

"I'm talking about this Glossop."

"I thought you said something about somebody's father."

"I said the boy was the father of the man."

"What boy?"

"The boy Glossop."

"He hasn't got a father."

"I never said he had. I said he was the father of the boy—or, rather, of the man."

"What man?"

I saw that the conversation had reached a point where, unless care was taken, we should be muddled.

"The point I am trying to make," I said, "is that the boy Glossop is the father of the man Glossop. In other words, each loathsome fault and blemish that led the boy Glossop to be frowned upon by his fellows is present in the man Glossop, and causes him—I am speaking now of the man Glossop—to be a hissing and a byword at places like the Drones, where a certain standard of decency is demanded from the inmates. Ask anyone at the Drones, and they will tell you that it was a black day for the dear old club when this chap Glossop somehow wriggled into the list of members. Here you will find a man who dislikes his face; there one who could stand his face if it wasn't for his habits. But the universal consensus of opinion is that the fellow is a bounder and a tick, and that the moment he showed signs of wanting to get into the place he should have been met with a firm *nolle prosequi* and heartily blackballed."

I had to pause again here, partly in order to take in a spot of breath, and partly to wrestle with the almost physical torture of saying these frightful things about poor old Tuppy.

"There are some chaps," I resumed, forcing myself once more to the nauseous task, "who, in spite of looking as if they had slept in their clothes, can get by quite nicely because they are amiable and suave. There are others who, for all that they excite adverse comment by being fat and uncouth, find themselves on the credit side of the ledger owing to their wit and sparkling humour. But this Glossop, I regret to say, falls into neither class. In addition to looking like one of those things that come out of hollow trees, he is universally admitted to be a dumb brick of the first water. No soul. No conversation. In short, any girl who, having been rash enough to get engaged to him, has managed at the eleventh hour to slide out is justly entitled to consider herself dashed lucky."

I paused once more, and cocked an eye at Angela to see how the treatment was taking. All the while I had been speaking, she had sat gazing silently into the bushes, but it seemed to me incredible that she should not now turn on me like a tigress, according to specifications. It beat me why she hadn't done it already. It seemed to me that a mere tithe of what I had said, if said to a tigress about a tiger of which she was fond, would have made her—the tigress, I mean—hit the ceiling.

And the next moment you could have knocked me down with a toothpick.

"Yes," she said, nodding thoughtfully, "you're quite right."

"Eh?"

"That's exactly what I've been thinking myself."

"What!"

"'Dumb brick.' It just describes him. One of the six silliest asses in England, I should think he must be."

I did not speak. I was endeavouring to adjust the faculties, which were in urgent need of a bit of first-aid treatment.

I mean to say, all this had come as a complete surprise. In formulating the well-laid plan which I had just been putting into effect, the one contingency I had not budgeted for was that she might adhere to the sentiments which I expressed. I had braced myself for a gush of stormy emotion. I was expecting the tearful ticking off, the girlish recriminations and all the rest of the bag of tricks along those lines.

But this cordial agreement with my remarks I had not foreseen, and it gave me what you might call pause for thought.

She proceeded to develop her theme, speaking in ringing, enthusiastic tones, as if she loved the topic. Jeeves could tell you the word I want. I think it's "ecstatic", unless that's the sort of rash you get on your face and have to use ointment for. But if that is the right word, then that's what her manner was as she ventilated the subject of poor old Tuppy. If you had been able to go simply by the sound of her voice, she might have been a court poet cutting loose about an Oriental monarch, or Gussie Fink-Nottle describing his last consignment of newts.

"It's so nice, Bertie, talking to somebody who really takes a sensible view about this man Glossop. Mother says he's a good chap, which is simply absurd. Anybody can see that he's absolutely impossible. He's conceited and opinionative and argues all the time, even when he knows perfectly well that he's talking through his hat, and he smokes too much and eats too much and drinks too much, and I don't like the colour of his hair. Not that he'll have any hair in a year or two, because he's pretty thin on the top already, and before he knows where he is he'll be as bald as an egg, and he's the last man who can afford to go bald. And I think it's simply disgusting, the way he gorges all the time. Do you know, I found him in the larder at one o'clock this morning, absolutely wallowing in a steak-and-kidney pie? There was hardly any of it left. And you remember what an enormous dinner he had. Quite disgusting, I call it. But I can't stop out here all night, talking about men who aren't worth wasting a word on and haven't even enough sense to tell sharks from flatfish. I'm going in."

And gathering about her slim shoulders the shawl which she had put on as a protection against the evening dew, she buzzed off, leaving me alone in the silent night.

Well, as a matter of fact, not absolutely alone, because a few moments later there was a sort of upheaval in the bushes in front of me, and Tuppy emerged.

-15-

I gave him the eye. The evening had begun to draw in a bit by now and the visibility, in consequence, was not so hot, but there still remained ample light to enable me to see him clearly. And what I saw convinced me that I should be a lot easier in my mind with a stout rustic bench between us. I rose, accordingly, modelling my style on that of a rocketing pheasant, and proceeded to deposit myself on the other side of the object named.

My prompt agility was not without its effect. He seemed somewhat taken aback. He came to a halt, and, for about the space of time required to allow a bead of persp. to trickle from the top of the brow to the tip of the nose, stood gazing at me in silence.

"So!" he said at length, and it came as a complete surprise to me that fellows ever really do say "So!" I had always thought it was just a thing you read in books. Like "Quotha!" I mean to say, or "Odds bodikins!" or even "Eh, ba goom!"

Still, there it was. Quaint or not quaint, bizarre or not bizarre, he had said "So!" and it was up to me to cope with the situation on those lines.

It would have been a duller man than Bertram Wooster who had failed to note that the dear old chap was a bit steamed up. Whether his eyes were actually shooting forth flame, I couldn't tell you, but there appeared to me to be a distinct incandescence. For the rest, his fists were clenched, his ears quivering, and the muscles of his jaw rotating rhythmically, as if he were making an early supper off something.

His hair was full of twigs, and there was a beetle hanging to the side of his head which would have interested Gussie Fink-Nottle. To this, however, I paid scant attention. There is a time for studying beetles and a time for not studying beetles.

"So!" he said again.

Now, those who know Bertram Wooster best will tell you that he is always at his shrewdest and most level-headed in moments of peril. Who was it who, when gripped by the arm of the law on boat-race night not so many years ago and hauled off to Vine Street police station, assumed in a flash the identity of Eustace H. Plimsoll, of The Laburnums, Alleyn Road, West Dulwich, thus saving the grand old name of Wooster from being dragged in the mire and avoiding wide publicity of the wrong sort? Who was it ...

But I need not labour the point. My record speaks for itself. Three times pinched, but never once sentenced under the correct label. Ask anyone at the Drones about this.

So now, in a situation threatening to become every moment more scaly, I did not lose my head. I preserved the old sang-froid. Smiling a genial and affectionate smile, and hoping that it wasn't too dark for it to register, I spoke with a jolly cordiality:

"Why, hallo, Tuppy. You here?"

He said, yes, he was here.

"Been here long?"

"I have."

"Fine. I wanted to see you."

"Well, here I am. Come out from behind that bench."

"No, thanks, old man. I like leaning on it. It seems to rest the spine."

"In about two seconds," said Tuppy, "I'm going to kick your spine up through the top of your head."

I raised the eyebrows. Not much good, of course, in that light, but it seemed to help the general composition.

"Is this Hildebrand Glossop speaking?" I said.

He replied that it was, adding that if I wanted to make sure I might move a few feet over in his direction. He also called me an opprobrious name.

I raised the eyebrows again.

"Come, come, Tuppy, don't let us let this little chat become acrid. Is 'acrid' the word I want?"

"I couldn't say," he replied, beginning to sidle round the bench.

I saw that anything I might wish to say must be said quickly. Already he had sidled some six feet. And though, by dint of sidling, too, I had managed to keep the bench between us, who could predict how long this happy state of affairs would last?

I came to the point, therefore.

"I think I know what's on your mind, Tuppy," I said. "If you were in those bushes during my conversation with the recent Angela, I dare say you heard what I was saying about you."

"I did."

"I see. Well, we won't go into the ethics of the thing. Eavesdropping, some people might call it, and I can imagine stern critics drawing in the breath to some extent. Considering it—I don't want to hurt your feelings, Tuppy—but considering it un-English. A bit un-English, Tuppy, old man, you must admit."

"I'm Scotch."

"Really?" I said. "I never knew that before. Rummy how you don't suspect a man of being Scotch unless he's Mac-something and says 'Och, aye' and things like that. I wonder," I went on, feeling that an academic discussion on some neutral topic might ease the tension, "if you can tell me something that has puzzled me a good deal. What exactly is it that they put into haggis? I've often wondered about that."

From the fact that his only response to the question was to leap over the bench and make a grab at me, I gathered that his mind was not on haggis.

"However," I said, leaping over the bench in my turn, "that is a side issue. If, to come back to it, you were in those bushes and heard what I was saying about you———"

He began to move round the bench in a nor'-nor'-easterly direction. I followed his example, setting a course sou'-sou'-west.

148

"No doubt you were surprised at the way I was talking."

"Not a bit."

"What? Did nothing strike you as odd in the tone of my remarks?"

"It was just the sort of stuff I should have expected a treacherous, sneaking hound like you to say."

"My dear chap," I protested, "this is not your usual form. A bit slow in the uptake, surely? I should have thought you would have spotted right away that it was all part of a well-laid plan."

"I'll get you in a jiffy," said Tuppy, recovering his balance after a swift clutch at my neck. And so probable did this seem that I delayed no longer, but hastened to place all the facts before him.

Speaking rapidly and keeping moving, I related my emotions on receipt of Aunt Dahlia's telegram, my instant rush to the scene of the disaster, my meditations in the car, and the eventual framing of this well-laid plan of mine. I spoke clearly and well, and it was with considerable concern, consequently, that I heard him observe— between clenched teeth, which made it worse—that he didn't believe a damned word of it.

"But, Tuppy," I said, "why not? To me the thing rings true to the last drop. What makes you sceptical? Confide in me, Tuppy."

He halted and stood taking a breather. Tuppy, pungently though Angela might have argued to the contrary, isn't really fat. During the winter months you will find him constantly booting the football with merry shouts, and in the summer the tennis racket is seldom out of his hand.

But at the recently concluded evening meal, feeling, no doubt, that after that painful scene in the larder there was nothing to be gained by further abstinence, he had rather let himself go and, as it were, made up leeway; and after really immersing himself in one of Anatole's dinners, a man of his sturdy build tends to lose elasticity a bit. During the exposition of my plans for his happiness a certain animation had crept into this round-and-round-the mulberry-bush jamboree of ours—so much so, indeed, that for the last few minutes we might have been a rather oversized greyhound and a somewhat slimmer electric hare doing their stuff on a circular track for the entertainment of the many-headed.

This, it appeared, had taken it out of him a bit, and I was not displeased. I was feeling the strain myself, and welcomed a lull.

"It absolutely beats me why you don't believe it," I said. "You know we've been pals for years. You must be aware that, except at the moment when you caused me to do a nose dive into the Drones' swimming bath, an incident which I long since decided to put out of my mind and let the dead past bury its dead about, if you follow what I mean—except on that one occasion, as I say, I have always regarded you with the utmost esteem. Why, then, if not for the motives I have outlined, should I knock you to Angela? Answer me that. Be very careful."

"What do you mean, be very careful?"

Well, as a matter of fact, I didn't quite know myself. It was what the magistrate had said to me on the occasion when I stood in the dock as Eustace Plimsoll, of The Laburnums: and as it had impressed me a good deal at the time, I just bunged it in now by way of giving the conversation a tone.

"All right. Never mind about being careful, then. Just answer me that question. Why, if I had not your interests sincerely at heart, should I have ticked you off, as stated?"

A sharp spasm shook him from base to apex. The beetle, which, during the recent exchanges, had been clinging to his head, hoping for the best, gave it up at this and resigned office. It shot off and was swallowed in the night.

"Ah!" I said. "Your beetle," I explained. "No doubt you were unaware of it, but all this while there has been a beetle of sorts parked on the side of your head. You have now dislodged it."

He snorted.

"Beetles!"

"Not beetles. One beetle only."

"I like your crust!" cried Tuppy, vibrating like one of Gussie's newts during the courting season. "Talking of beetles, when all the time you know you're a treacherous, sneaking hound."

It was a debatable point, of course, why treacherous, sneaking hounds should be considered ineligible to talk about beetles, and I dare say a good cross-examining counsel would have made quite a lot of it.

But I let it go.

"That's the second time you've called me that. And," I said firmly, "I insist on an explanation. I have told you that I acted throughout from the best and kindliest motives in roasting you to Angela. It cut me to the quick to have to speak like that, and only the recollection of our lifelong friendship would have made me do it. And now you say you don't believe me and call me names for which I am not sure I couldn't have you up before a beak and jury and mulct you in very substantial damages. I should have to consult my solicitor, of course, but it would surprise me very much if an action did not lie. Be reasonable, Tuppy. Suggest another motive I could have had. Just one."

"I will. Do you think I don't know? You're in love with Angela yourself."

"What?"

"And you knocked me in order to poison her mind against me and finally remove me from your path."

I had never heard anything so absolutely loopy in my life. Why, dash it, I've known Angela since she was so high. You don't fall in love with close relations you've known since they were so high. Besides, isn't there something in the book of rules about a man may not marry his cousin? Or am I thinking of grandmothers?

"Tuppy, my dear old ass," I cried, "this is pure banana oil! You've come unscrewed."

"Oh, yes?"

"Me in love with Angela? Ha-ha!"

"You can't get out of it with ha-ha's. She called you 'darling'."

"I know. And I disapproved. This habit of the younger g. of scattering 'darlings' about like birdseed is one that I deprecate. Lax, is how I should describe it."

"You tickled her ankles."

"In a purely cousinly spirit. It didn't mean a thing. Why, dash it, you must know that in the deeper and truer sense I wouldn't touch Angela with a barge pole."

"Oh? And why not? Not good enough for you?"

"You misunderstand me," I hastened to reply. "When I say I wouldn't touch Angela with a barge pole, I intend merely to convey that my feelings towards her are those of distant, though cordial, esteem. In other words, you may rest assured that between this young prune and myself there never has been and never could be any sentiment warmer and stronger than that of ordinary friendship."

"I believe it was you who tipped her off that I was in the larder last night, so that she could find me there with that pie, thus damaging my prestige."

"My dear Tuppy! A Wooster?" I was shocked. "You think a Wooster would do that?"

He breathed heavily.

"Listen," he said. "It's no good your standing there arguing. You can't get away from the facts. Somebody stole her from me at Cannes. You told me yourself that she was with you all the time at Cannes and hardly saw anybody else. You gloated over the mixed bathing, and those moonlight walks you had together———"

"Not gloated. Just mentioned them."

"So now you understand why, as soon as I can get you clear of this damned bench, I am going to tear you limb from limb. Why they have these bally benches in gardens," said Tuppy discontentedly, "is more than I can see. They only get in the way."

He ceased, and, grabbing out, missed me by a hair's breadth.

It was a moment for swift thinking, and it is at such moments, as I have already indicated, that Bertram Wooster is at his best. I suddenly remembered the recent misunderstanding with the Bassett, and with a flash of clear vision saw that this was where it was going to come in handy.

"You've got it all wrong, Tuppy," I said, moving to the left. "True, I saw a lot of Angela, but my dealings with her were on a basis from start to finish of the purest and most wholesome camaraderie. I can prove it. During that sojourn in Cannes my affections were engaged elsewhere."

"What?"

"Engaged elsewhere. My affections. During that sojourn."

I had struck the right note. He stopped sidling. His clutching hand fell to his side.

"Is that true?"

"Quite official."

"Who was she?"

"My dear Tuppy, does one bandy a woman's name?"

"One does if one doesn't want one's ruddy head pulled off."

I saw that it was a special case.

"Madeline Bassett," I said.

"Who?"

"Madeline Bassett."

He seemed stunned.

"You stand there and tell me you were in love with that Bassett disaster?"

"I wouldn't call her 'that Bassett disaster', Tuppy. Not respectful."

"Dash being respectful. I want the facts. You deliberately assert that you loved that weird Gawd-help-us?"

"I don't see why you should call her a weird Gawd-help-us, either. A very charming and beautiful girl. Odd in some of her views perhaps—one does not quite see eye to eye with her in the matter of stars and rabbits—but not a weird Gawd-help-us."

"Anyway, you stick to it that you were in love with her?"

"I do."

"It sounds thin to me, Wooster, very thin."

I saw that it would be necessary to apply the finishing touch.

"I must ask you to treat this as entirely confidential, Glossop, but I may as well inform you that it is not twenty-four hours since she turned me down."

"Turned you down?"

"Like a bedspread. In this very garden."

"Twenty-four hours?"

"Call it twenty-five. So you will readily see that I can't be the chap, if any, who stole Angela from you at Cannes."

And I was on the brink of adding that I wouldn't touch Angela with a barge pole, when I remembered I had said it already and it hadn't gone frightfully well. I desisted, therefore.

My manly frankness seemed to be producing good results. The homicidal glare was dying out of Tuppy's eyes. He had the aspect of a hired assassin who had paused to think things over.

"I see," he said, at length. "All right, then. Sorry you were troubled."

153

"Don't mention it, old man," I responded courteously.

For the first time since the bushes had begun to pour forth Glossops, Bertram Wooster could be said to have breathed freely. I don't say I actually came out from behind the bench, but I did let go of it, and with something of the relief which those three chaps in the Old Testament must have experienced after sliding out of the burning fiery furnace, I even groped tentatively for my cigarette case.

The next moment a sudden snort made me take my fingers off it as if it had bitten me. I was distressed to note in the old friend a return of the recent frenzy.

"What the hell did you mean by telling her that I used to be covered with ink when I was a kid?"

"My dear Tuppy——"

"I was almost finickingly careful about my personal cleanliness as a boy. You could have eaten your dinner off me."

"Quite. But——"

"And all that stuff about having no soul. I'm crawling with soul. And being looked on as an outsider at the Drones——"

"But, my dear old chap, I explained that. It was all part of my ruse or scheme."

"It was, was it? Well, in future do me a favour and leave me out of your foul ruses."

"Just as you say, old boy."

"All right, then. That's understood."

He relapsed into silence, standing with folded arms, staring before him rather like a strong, silent man in a novel when he's just been given the bird by the girl and is thinking of looking in at the Rocky Mountains and bumping off a few bears. His manifest pippedness excited my compash, and I ventured a kindly word.

"I don't suppose you know what *au pied de la lettre* means, Tuppy, but that's how I don't think you ought to take all that stuff Angela was saying just now too much."

He seemed interested.

"What the devil," he asked, "are you talking about?"

I saw that I should have to make myself clearer.

"Don't take all that guff of hers too literally, old man. You know what girls are like."

"I do," he said, with another snort that came straight up from his insteps. "And I wish I'd never met one."

"I mean to say, it's obvious that she must have spotted you in those bushes and was simply talking to score off you. There you were, I mean, if you follow the psychology, and she saw you, and in that impulsive way girls have, she seized the opportunity of ribbing you a bit—just told you a few home truths, I mean to say."

"Home truths?"

"That's right."

He snorted once more, causing me to feel rather like royalty receiving a twenty-one gun salute from the fleet. I can't remember ever having met a better right-and-left-hand snorter.

"What do you mean, 'home truths'? I'm not fat."

"No, no."

"And what's wrong with the colour of my hair?"

"Quite in order, Tuppy, old man. The hair, I mean."

"And I'm not a bit thin on the top.... What the dickens are you grinning about?"

"Not grinning. Just smiling slightly. I was conjuring up a sort of vision, if you know what I mean, of you as seen through Angela's eyes. Fat in the middle and thin on the top. Rather funny."

"You think it funny, do you?"

"Not a bit."

"You'd better not."

"Quite."

It seemed to me that the conversation was becoming difficult again. I wished it could be terminated. And so it was. For at this moment something came shimmering through the laurels in the quiet evenfall, and I perceived that it was Angela.

She was looking sweet and saintlike, and she had a plate of sandwiches in her hand. Ham, I was to discover later.

"If you see Mr. Glossop anywhere, Bertie," she said, her eyes resting dreamily on Tuppy's facade, "I wish you would give him these. I'm so afraid he may be hungry, poor fellow. It's nearly ten o'clock, and he hasn't eaten a morsel since dinner. I'll just leave them on this bench."

She pushed off, and it seemed to me that I might as well go with her. Nothing to keep me here, I mean. We moved towards the house, and presently from behind us there sounded in the night the splintering crash of a well-kicked plate of ham sandwiches, accompanied by the muffled oaths of a strong man in his wrath.

"How still and peaceful everything is," said Angela.

-16-

Sunshine was gilding the grounds of Brinkley Court and the ear detected a marked twittering of birds in the ivy outside the window when I woke next morning to a new day. But there was no corresponding sunshine in Bertram Wooster's soul and no answering twitter in his heart as he sat up in bed, sipping his cup of strengthening tea. It could not be denied that to Bertram, reviewing the happenings of the previous night, the Tuppy-Angela situation seemed more or less to have slipped a cog. With every desire to look for the silver lining, I could but feel that the rift between these two haughty spirits had now reached such impressive proportions that the task of bridging same would be beyond even my powers.

I am a shrewd observer, and there had been something in Tuppy's manner as he booted that plate of ham sandwiches that seemed to tell me that he would not lightly forgive.

In these circs., I deemed it best to shelve their problem for the nonce and turn the mind to the matter of Gussie, which presented a brighter picture.

With regard to Gussie, everything was in train. Jeeves's morbid scruples about lacing the chap's orange juice had put me to a good deal of trouble, but I had surmounted every obstacle in the old Wooster way. I had secured an abundance of the necessary spirit, and it was now lying in its flask in the drawer of the dressing-table. I had also ascertained that the jug, duly filled, would be standing on a shelf in the butler's pantry round about the hour of one. To remove it from that shelf, sneak it up to my room, and return it, laced, in good time for the midday meal would be a task calling, no doubt, for address, but in no sense an exacting one.

It was with something of the emotions of one preparing a treat for a deserving child that I finished my tea and rolled over for that extra spot of sleep which just makes all the difference when there is man's work to be done and the brain must be kept clear for it.

And when I came downstairs an hour or so later, I knew how right I had been to formulate this scheme for Gussie's bucking up. I ran into him on the lawn, and I could see at a glance that if ever there was a man who needed a snappy stimulant, it was he. All nature, as I have indicated, was smiling, but not Augustus Fink-Nottle. He was walking round in circles, muttering something about not proposing to detain us long, but on this auspicious occasion feeling compelled to say a few words.

"Ah, Gussie," I said, arresting him as he was about to start another lap. "A lovely morning, is it not?"

Even if I had not been aware of it already, I could have divined from the abruptness with which he damned the lovely morning that he was not in merry mood. I addressed myself to the task of bringing the roses back to his cheeks.

"I've got good news for you, Gussie."

He looked at me with a sudden sharp interest.

"Has Market Snodsbury Grammar School burned down?"

"Not that I know of."

"Have mumps broken out? Is the place closed on account of measles?"

"No, no."

"Then what do you mean you've got good news?"

I endeavoured to soothe.

"You mustn't take it so hard, Gussie. Why worry about a laughably simple job like distributing prizes at a school?"

"Laughably simple, eh? Do you realize I've been sweating for days and haven't been able to think of a thing to say yet, except that I won't detain them long. You bet I won't detain them long. I've been timing my speech, and it lasts five seconds. What the devil am I to say, Bertie? What do you say when you're distributing prizes?"

I considered. Once, at my private school, I had won a prize for Scripture knowledge, so I suppose I ought to have been full of inside stuff. But memory eluded me.

Then something emerged from the mists.

"You say the race is not always to the swift."

"Why?"

"Well, it's a good gag. It generally gets a hand."

"I mean, why isn't it? Why isn't the race to the swift?"

"Ah, there you have me. But the nibs say it isn't."

"But what does it mean?"

"I take it it's supposed to console the chaps who haven't won prizes."

"What's the good of that to me? I'm not worrying about them. It's the ones that have won prizes that I'm worrying about, the little blighters who will come up on the platform. Suppose they make faces at me."

"They won't."

"How do you know they won't? It's probably the first thing they'll think of. And even if they don't—Bertie, shall I tell you something?"

"What?"

"I've a good mind to take that tip of yours and have a drink."

I smiled. He little knew, about summed up what I was thinking.

"Oh, you'll be all right," I said.

He became fevered again.

"How do you know I'll be all right? I'm sure to blow up in my lines."

"Tush!"

"Or drop a prize."

"Tut!"

"Or something. I can feel it in my bones. As sure as I'm standing here, something is going to happen this afternoon which will make everybody laugh themselves sick at me. I can hear them now. Like hyenas.... Bertie!"

"Hullo?"

"Do you remember that kids' school we went to before Eton?"

"Quite. It was there I won my Scripture prize."

"Never mind about your Scripture prize. I'm not talking about your Scripture prize. Do you recollect the Bosher incident?"

I did, indeed. It was one of the high spots of my youth.

"Major-General Sir Wilfred Bosher came to distribute the prizes at that school," proceeded Gussie in a dull, toneless voice. "He dropped a book. He stooped to pick it up. And, as he stooped, his trousers split up the back."

"How we roared!"

Gussie's face twisted.

"We did, little swine that we were. Instead of remaining silent and exhibiting a decent sympathy for a gallant officer at a peculiarly embarrassing moment, we howled and yelled with mirth. I loudest of any. That is what will happen to me this afternoon, Bertie. It will be a judgment on me for laughing like that at Major-General Sir Wilfred Bosher."

"No, no, Gussie, old man. Your trousers won't split."

"How do you know they won't? Better men than I have split their trousers. General Bosher was a D.S.O., with a fine record of service on the north-western frontier of India, and his trousers split. I shall be a mockery and a scorn. I know it. And you, fully cognizant of what I am in for, come babbling about good news. What news could possibly be good to me at this moment except the information that bubonic plague had broken out among the scholars of Market Snodsbury Grammar School, and that they were all confined to their beds with spots?"

The moment had come for me to speak. I laid a hand gently on his shoulder. He brushed it off. I laid it on again. He brushed it off once more. I was endeavouring to lay it on for the third time, when he moved aside and desired, with a certain petulance, to be informed if I thought I was a ruddy osteopath.

I found his manner trying, but one has to make allowances. I was telling myself that I should be seeing a very different Gussie after lunch.

"When I said I had good news, old man, I meant about Madeline Bassett."

The febrile gleam died out of his eyes, to be replaced by a look of infinite sadness.

"You can't have good news about her. I've dished myself there completely."

"Not at all. I am convinced that if you take another whack at her, all will be well."

And, keeping it snappy, I related what had passed between the

Bassett and myself on the previous night.

"So all you have to do is play a return date, and you cannot fail to swing the voting. You are her dream man."

He shook his head.

"No."

"What?"

"No use."

"What do you mean?"

"Not a bit of good trying."

"But I tell you she said in so many words——"

"It doesn't make any difference. She may have loved me once. Last night will have killed all that."

"Of course it won't."

"It will. She despises me now."

"Not a bit of it. She knows you simply got cold feet."

"And I should get cold feet if I tried again. It's no good, Bertie. I'm hopeless, and there's an end of it. Fate made me the sort of chap who can't say 'bo' to a goose."

"It isn't a question of saying 'bo' to a goose. The point doesn't arise at all. It is simply a matter of——"

"I know, I know. But it's no good. I can't do it. The whole thing is off. I am not going to risk a repetition of last night's fiasco. You talk in a light way of taking another whack at her, but you don't know what it means. You have not been through the experience of starting to ask the girl you love to marry you and then suddenly finding yourself talking about the plumlike external gills of the newly-born newt. It's not a thing you can do twice. No, I accept my destiny. It's all over. And now, Bertie, like a good chap, shove off. I want to compose my speech. I can't compose my speech with you mucking around. If you are going to continue to muck around, at least give me a couple of stories. The little hell hounds are sure to expect a story or two."

"Do you know the one about——"

"No good. I don't want any of your off-colour stuff from the Drones' smoking-room. I need something clean. Something that will be a help to them in their after lives. Not that I care a damn about their after lives, except that I hope they'll all choke."

"I heard a story the other day. I can't quite remember it, but it was about a chap who snored and disturbed the neighbours, and it ended, 'It was his adenoids that adenoid them.'"

He made a weary gesture.

"You expect me to work that in, do you, into a speech to be delivered to an audience of boys, every one of whom is probably riddled with adenoids? Damn it, they'd rush the platform. Leave me, Bertie. Push off. That's all I ask you to do. Push off.... Ladies and gentlemen," said Gussie, in a low, soliloquizing sort of way, "I do not propose to detain this auspicious occasion long——"

It was a thoughtful Wooster who walked away and left him at it. More than ever I was congratulating myself on having had the sterling good sense to make all my arrangements so that I could press a button and set things moving at an instant's notice.

Until now, you see, I had rather entertained a sort of hope that when I had revealed to him the Bassett's mental attitude, Nature would have done the rest, bracing him up to such an extent that artificial stimulants would not be required. Because, naturally, a chap doesn't want to have to sprint about country houses lugging jugs of orange juice, unless it is absolutely essential.

But now I saw that I must carry on as planned. The total absence of pep, ginger, and the right spirit which the man had displayed during these conversational exchanges convinced me that the strongest measures would be necessary. Immediately upon leaving him, therefore, I proceeded to the pantry, waited till the butler had removed himself elsewhere, and nipped in and secured the vital jug. A few moments later, after a wary passage of the stairs, I was in my room. And the first thing I saw there was Jeeves, fooling about with trousers.

He gave the jug a look which—wrongly, as it was to turn out—I diagnosed as censorious. I drew myself up a bit. I intended to have no rot from the fellow.

"Yes, Jeeves?"

"Sir?"

"You have the air of one about to make a remark, Jeeves."

"Oh, no, sir. I note that you are in possession of Mr. Fink-Nottle's orange juice. I was merely about to observe that in my opinion it would be injudicious to add spirit to it."

"That is a remark, Jeeves, and it is precisely———"

"Because I have already attended to the matter, sir."

"What?"

"Yes, sir. I decided, after all, to acquiesce in your wishes."

I stared at the man, astounded. I was deeply moved. Well, I mean, wouldn't any chap who had been going about thinking that the old feudal spirit was dead and then suddenly found it wasn't have been deeply moved?

"Jeeves," I said, "I am touched."

"Thank you, sir."

"Touched and gratified."

"Thank you very much, sir."

"But what caused this change of heart?"

"I chanced to encounter Mr. Fink-Nottle in the garden, sir, while you were still in bed, and we had a brief conversation."

"And you came away feeling that he needed a bracer?"

"Very much so, sir. His attitude struck me as defeatist."

I nodded.

"I felt the same. 'Defeatist' sums it up to a nicety. Did you tell him his attitude struck you as defeatist?"

"Yes, sir."

"But it didn't do any good?"

"No, sir."

"Very well, then, Jeeves. We must act. How much gin did you put in the jug?"

"A liberal tumblerful, sir."

"Would that be a normal dose for an adult defeatist, do you think?"

"I fancy it should prove adequate, sir."

"I wonder. We must not spoil the ship for a ha'porth of tar. I think I'll add just another fluid ounce or so."

"I would not advocate it, sir. In the case of Lord Brancaster's parrot———"

"You are falling into your old error, Jeeves, of thinking that Gussie is a parrot. Fight against this. I shall add the oz."

"Very good, sir."

"And, by the way, Jeeves, Mr. Fink-Nottle is in the market for bright, clean stories to use in his speech. Do you know any?"

"I know a story about two Irishmen, sir."

"Pat and Mike?"

"Yes, sir."

"Who were walking along Broadway?"

"Yes, sir."

"Just what he wants. Any more?"

"No, sir."

"Well, every little helps. You had better go and tell it to him."

"Very good, sir."

He passed from the room, and I unscrewed the flask and tilted into the jug a generous modicum of its contents. And scarcely had I done so, when there came to my ears the sound of footsteps without. I had only just time to shove the jug behind the photograph of Uncle Tom on the mantelpiece before the door opened and in came Gussie, curveting like a circus horse.

"What-ho, Bertie," he said. "What-ho, what-ho, what-ho, and again what-ho. What a beautiful world this is, Bertie. One of the nicest I ever met."

I stared at him, speechless. We Woosters are as quick as lightning, and I saw at once that something had happened.

I mean to say, I told you about him walking round in circles. I recorded what passed between us on the lawn. And if I portrayed the scene with anything like adequate skill, the picture you will have retained of this Fink-Nottle will have been that of a nervous wreck, sagging at the knees, green about the gills, and picking feverishly at the lapels of his coat in an ecstasy of craven fear. In a word, defeatist. Gussie, during that interview, had, in fine, exhibited all the earmarks of one licked to a custard.

Vastly different was the Gussie who stood before me now. Self-confidence seemed to ooze from the fellow's every pore. His face was flushed, there was a jovial light in his eyes, the lips were parted in a swashbuckling smile. And when with a genial hand he sloshed me on the back before I could sidestep, it was as if I had been kicked by a mule.

"Well, Bertie," he proceeded, as blithely as a linnet without a thing on his mind, "you will be glad to hear that you were right. Your theory has been tested and proved correct. I feel like a fighting cock."

My brain ceased to reel. I saw all.

"Have you been having a drink?"

"I have. As you advised. Unpleasant stuff. Like medicine. Burns your throat, too, and makes one as thirsty as the dickens. How anyone can mop it up, as you do, for pleasure, beats me. Still, I would be the last to deny that it tunes up the system. I could bite a tiger."

"What did you have?"

"Whisky. At least, that was the label on the decanter, and I have no reason to suppose that a woman like your aunt—staunch, true-blue, British—would deliberately deceive the public. If she labels her decanters Whisky, then I consider that we know where we are."

"A whisky and soda, eh? You couldn't have done better."

"Soda?" said Gussie thoughtfully. "I knew there was something I had forgotten."

"Didn't you put any soda in it?"

"It never occurred to me. I just nipped into the dining-room and drank out of the decanter."

"How much?"

"Oh, about ten swallows. Twelve, maybe. Or fourteen. Say sixteen medium-sized gulps. Gosh, I'm thirsty."

He moved over to the wash-stand and drank deeply out of the water bottle. I cast a covert glance at Uncle Tom's photograph behind his back. For the first time since it had come into my life, I was glad that it was so large. It hid its secret well. If Gussie had caught sight of that jug of orange juice, he would unquestionably have been on to it like a knife.

"Well, I'm glad you're feeling braced," I said.

He moved buoyantly from the wash-hand stand, and endeavoured to slosh me on the back again. Foiled by my nimble footwork, he staggered to the bed and sat down upon it.

"Braced? Did I say I could bite a tiger?"

"You did."

"Make it two tigers. I could chew holes in a steel door. What an ass you must have thought me out there in the garden. I see now you were laughing in your sleeve."

"No, no."

"Yes," insisted Gussie. "That very sleeve," he said, pointing. "And I don't blame you. I can't imagine why I made all that fuss about a potty job like distributing prizes at a rotten little country grammar school. Can you imagine, Bertie?"

"Exactly. Nor can I imagine. There's simply nothing to it. I just shin up on the platform, drop a few gracious words, hand the little blighters their prizes, and hop down again, admired by all. Not a suggestion of split trousers from start to finish. I mean, why should anybody split his trousers? I can't imagine. Can you imagine?"

"No."

"Nor can I imagine. I shall be a riot. I know just the sort of stuff that's needed—simple, manly, optimistic stuff straight from the shoulder. This shoulder," said Gussie, tapping. "Why I was so nervous this morning I can't imagine. For anything simpler than distributing a few footling books to a bunch of grimy-faced kids I can't imagine. Still, for some reason I can't imagine, I was feeling a little nervous, but now I feel fine, Bertie—fine, fine, fine—and I say this to you as an old friend. Because that's what you are, old man, when all the smoke has cleared away—an old friend. I don't think I've ever met an older friend. How long have you been an old friend of mine, Bertie?"

"Oh, years and years."

"Imagine! Though, of course, there must have been a time when you were a new friend.... Hullo, the luncheon gong. Come on, old friend."

And, rising from the bed like a performing flea, he made for the door.

I followed rather pensively. What had occurred was, of course, so much velvet, as you might say. I mean, I had wanted a braced Fink-Nottle— indeed, all my plans had had a braced Fink-Nottle as their end and aim —but I found myself wondering a little whether the Fink-Nottle now sliding down the banister wasn't, perhaps, a shade too braced. His demeanour seemed to me that of a man who might quite easily throw bread about at lunch.

Fortunately, however, the settled gloom of those round him exercised a restraining effect upon him at the table. It would have needed a far more plastered man to have been rollicking at such a gathering. I had told the Bassett that there were aching hearts in Brinkley Court, and it now looked probable that there would shortly be aching tummies. Anatole, I learned, had retired to his bed with a fit of the vapours, and the meal now before us had been cooked by the kitchen maid—as C3 a performer as ever wielded a skillet.

This, coming on top of their other troubles, induced in the company a pretty unanimous silence—a solemn stillness, as you might say—which even Gussie did not seem prepared to break. Except, therefore, for one short snatch of song on his part, nothing untoward marked the occasion, and presently we rose, with instructions from Aunt Dahlia to put on festal raiment and be at Market Snodsbury not later than 3.30. This leaving me ample time to smoke a gasper or two in a shady bower beside the lake, I did so, repairing to my room round about the hour of three.

Jeeves was on the job, adding the final polish to the old topper, and I was about to apprise him of the latest developments in the matter of Gussie, when he forestalled me by observing that the latter had only just concluded an agreeable visit to the Wooster bedchamber.

"I found Mr. Fink-Nottle seated here when I arrived to lay out your clothes, sir."

"Indeed, Jeeves? Gussie was in here, was he?"

"Yes, sir. He left only a few moments ago. He is driving to the school with Mr. and Mrs. Travers in the large car."

"Did you give him your story of the two Irishmen?"

"Yes, sir. He laughed heartily."

"Good. Had you any other contributions for him?"

"I ventured to suggest that he might mention to the young gentlemen that education is a drawing out, not a putting in. The late Lord Brancaster was much addicted to presenting prizes at schools, and he invariably employed this dictum."

"And how did he react to that?"

"He laughed heartily, sir."

"This surprised you, no doubt? This practically incessant merriment, I mean."

"Yes, sir."

"You thought it odd in one who, when you last saw him, was well up in Group A of the defeatists."

"Yes, sir."

"There is a ready explanation, Jeeves. Since you last saw him, Gussie has been on a bender. He's as tight as an owl."

"Indeed, sir?"

"Absolutely. His nerve cracked under the strain, and he sneaked into the dining-room and started mopping the stuff up like a vacuum cleaner. Whisky would seem to be what he filled the radiator with. I gather that he used up most of the decanter. Golly, Jeeves, it's lucky he didn't get at that laced orange juice on top of that, what?"

"Extremely, sir."

I eyed the jug. Uncle Tom's photograph had fallen into the fender, and it was standing there right out in the open, where Gussie couldn't have helped seeing it. Mercifully, it was empty now.

"It was a most prudent act on your part, if I may say so, sir, to dispose of the orange juice."

I stared at the man.

"What? Didn't you?"

"No, sir."

"Jeeves, let us get this clear. Was it not you who threw away that o.j.?"

"No, sir. I assumed, when I entered the room and found the pitcher empty, that you had done so."

We looked at each other, awed. Two minds with but a single thought.

"I very much fear, sir———"

"So do I, Jeeves."

"It would seem almost certain———"

"Quite certain. Weigh the facts. Sift the evidence. The jug was standing on the mantelpiece, for all eyes to behold. Gussie had been complaining of thirst. You found him in here, laughing heartily. I think that there can be little doubt, Jeeves, that the entire contents of that jug are at this moment reposing on top of the existing cargo in that already brilliantly lit man's interior. Disturbing, Jeeves."

"Most disturbing, sir."

"Let us face the position, forcing ourselves to be calm. You inserted in that jug—shall we say a tumblerful of the right stuff?"

"Fully a tumblerful, sir."

"And I added of my plenty about the same amount."

"Yes, sir."

"And in two shakes of a duck's tail Gussie, with all that lapping about inside him, will be distributing the prizes at Market Snodsbury Grammar School before an audience of all that is fairest and most refined in the county."

"Yes, sir."

"It seems to me, Jeeves, that the ceremony may be one fraught with considerable interest."

"Yes, sir."

"What, in your opinion, will the harvest be?"

"One finds it difficult to hazard a conjecture, sir."

"You mean imagination boggles?"

"Yes, sir."

I inspected my imagination. He was right. It boggled.

-17-

"And yet, Jeeves," I said, twiddling a thoughtful steering wheel, "there is always the bright side."

Some twenty minutes had elapsed, and having picked the honest fellow up outside the front door, I was driving in the two-seater to the picturesque town of Market Snodsbury. Since we had parted—he to go to his lair and fetch his hat, I to remain in my room and complete the formal costume—I had been doing some close thinking.

The results of this I now proceeded to hand on to him.

"However dark the prospect may be, Jeeves, however murkily the storm clouds may seem to gather, a keen eye can usually discern the blue bird. It is bad, no doubt, that Gussie should be going, some ten minutes from now, to distribute prizes in a state of advanced intoxication, but we must never forget that these things cut both ways."

"You imply, sir———"

"Precisely. I am thinking of him in his capacity of wooer. All this ought to have put him in rare shape for offering his hand in marriage. I shall be vastly surprised if it won't turn him into a sort of caveman. Have you ever seen James Cagney in the movies?"

"Yes, sir."

"Something on those lines."

I heard him cough, and sniped him with a sideways glance. He was wearing that informative look of his.

"Then you have not heard, sir?"

"Eh?"

"You are not aware that a marriage has been arranged and will shortly take place between Mr. Fink-Nottle and Miss Bassett?"

"What?"

"Yes, sir."

"When did this happen?"

"Shortly after Mr. Fink-Nottle had left your room, sir."

"Ah! In the post-orange-juice era?"

"Yes, sir."

"But are you sure of your facts? How do you know?"

"My informant was Mr. Fink-Nottle himself, sir. He appeared anxious to confide in me. His story was somewhat incoherent, but I had no difficulty in apprehending its substance. Prefacing his remarks with the statement that this was a beautiful world, he laughed heartily and said that he had become formally engaged."

"No details?"

"No, sir."

"But one can picture the scene."

"Yes, sir."

"I mean, imagination doesn't boggle."

"No, sir."

And it didn't. I could see exactly what must have happened. Insert a liberal dose of mixed spirits in a normally abstemious man, and he becomes a force. He does not stand around, twiddling his fingers and stammering. He acts. I had no doubt that Gussie must have reached for the Bassett and clasped her to him like a stevedore handling a sack of coals. And one could readily envisage the effect of that sort of thing on a girl of romantic mind.

"Well, well, well, Jeeves."

"Yes, sir."

"This is splendid news."

"Yes, sir."

"You see now how right I was."

"Yes, sir."

"It must have been rather an eye-opener for you, watching me handle this case."

"Yes, sir."

"The simple, direct method never fails."

"No, sir."

"Whereas the elaborate does."

"Yes, sir."

"Right ho, Jeeves."

We had arrived at the main entrance of Market Snodsbury Grammar School. I parked the car, and went in, well content. True, the Tuppy-Angela problem still remained unsolved and Aunt Dahlia's five hundred quid seemed as far off as ever, but it was gratifying to feel that good old Gussie's troubles were over, at any rate.

The Grammar School at Market Snodsbury had, I understood, been built somewhere in the year 1416, and, as with so many of these ancient foundations, there still seemed to brood over its Great Hall, where the afternoon's festivities were to take place, not a little of the fug of the centuries. It was the hottest day of the summer, and though somebody had opened a tentative window or two, the atmosphere remained distinctive and individual.

In this hall the youth of Market Snodsbury had been eating its daily lunch for a matter of five hundred years, and the flavour lingered. The air was sort of heavy and languorous, if you know what I mean, with the scent of Young England and boiled beef and carrots.

Aunt Dahlia, who was sitting with a bevy of the local nibs in the second row, sighted me as I entered and waved to me to join her, but I was too smart for that. I wedged myself in among the standees at the back, leaning up against a chap who, from the aroma, might have been a corn chandler or something on that order. The essence of strategy on these occasions is to be as near the door as possible.

The hall was gaily decorated with flags and coloured paper, and the eye was further refreshed by the spectacle of a mixed drove of boys, parents, and what not, the former running a good deal to shiny faces and Eton collars, the latter stressing the black-satin note rather when female, and looking as if their coats were too tight, if male. And presently there was some applause—sporadic, Jeeves has since told me it was—and I saw Gussie being steered by a bearded bloke in a gown to a seat in the middle of the platform.

And I confess that as I beheld him and felt that there but for the grace of God went Bertram Wooster, a shudder ran through the frame. It all reminded me so vividly of the time I had addressed that girls' school.

Of course, looking at it dispassionately, you may say that for horror and peril there is no comparison between an almost human audience like the one before me and a mob of small girls with pigtails down their backs, and this, I concede, is true. Nevertheless, the spectacle was enough to make me feel like a fellow watching a pal going over Niagara Falls in a barrel, and the thought of what I had escaped caused everything for a moment to go black and swim before my eyes.

When I was able to see clearly once more, I perceived that Gussie was now seated. He had his hands on his knees, with his elbows out at right angles, like a nigger minstrel of the old school about to ask Mr. Bones why a chicken crosses the road, and he was staring before him with a smile so fixed and pebble-beached that I should have thought that anybody could have guessed that there sat one in whom the old familiar juice was plashing up against the back of the front teeth.

In fact, I saw Aunt Dahlia, who, having assisted at so many hunting dinners in her time, is second to none as a judge of the symptoms, give a start and gaze long and earnestly. And she was just saying something to Uncle Tom on her left when the bearded bloke stepped to the footlights and started making a speech. From the fact that he spoke as if he had a hot potato in his mouth without getting the raspberry from the lads in the ringside seats, I deduced that he must be the head master.

With his arrival in the spotlight, a sort of perspiring resignation seemed to settle on the audience. Personally, I snuggled up against the chandler and let my attention wander. The speech was on the subject of the doings of the school during the past term, and this part of a prize-giving is always apt rather to fail to grip the visiting stranger. I mean, you know how it is. You're told that J.B. Brewster has won an Exhibition for Classics at Cat's, Cambridge, and you feel that it's one of those stories where you can't see how funny it is unless you really know the fellow. And the same applies to G. Bullett being awarded the Lady Jane Wix Scholarship at the Birmingham College of Veterinary Science.

In fact, I and the corn chandler, who was looking a bit fagged I thought, as if he had had a hard morning chandling the corn, were beginning to doze lightly when things suddenly brisked up, bringing Gussie into the picture for the first time.

"Today," said the bearded bloke, "we are all happy to welcome as the guest of the afternoon Mr. Fitz-Wattle——"

At the beginning of the address, Gussie had subsided into a sort of daydream, with his mouth hanging open. About half-way through, faint signs of life had begun to show. And for the last few minutes he had been trying to cross one leg over the other and failing and having another shot and failing again. But only now did he exhibit any real animation. He sat up with a jerk.

"Fink-Nottle," he said, opening his eyes.

"Fitz-Nottle."

"Fink-Nottle."

"I should say Fink-Nottle."

"Of course you should, you silly ass," said Gussie genially. "All right, get on with it."

And closing his eyes, he began trying to cross his legs again.

I could see that this little spot of friction had rattled the bearded bloke a bit. He stood for a moment fumbling at the fungus with a hesitating hand. But they make these head masters of tough stuff. The weakness passed. He came back nicely and carried on.

"We are all happy, I say, to welcome as the guest of the afternoon Mr. Fink-Nottle, who has kindly consented to award the prizes. This task, as you know, is one that should have devolved upon that well-beloved and vigorous member of our board of governors, the Rev. William Plomer, and we are all, I am sure, very sorry that illness at the last moment should have prevented him from being here today. But, if I may borrow a familiar metaphor from the—if I may employ a homely metaphor familiar to you all—what we lose on the swings we gain on the roundabouts."

He paused, and beamed rather freely, to show that this was comedy. I could have told the man it was no use. Not a ripple. The corn chandler leaned against me and muttered "Whoddidesay?" but that was all.

It's always a nasty jar to wait for the laugh and find that the gag hasn't got across. The bearded bloke was visibly discomposed. At that, however, I think he would have got by, had he not, at this juncture, unfortunately stirred Gussie up again.

"In other words, though deprived of Mr. Plomer, we have with us this afternoon Mr. Fink-Nottle. I am sure that Mr. Fink-Nottle's name is one that needs no introduction to you. It is, I venture to assert, a name that is familiar to us all."

"Not to you," said Gussie.

And the next moment I saw what Jeeves had meant when he had described him as laughing heartily. "Heartily" was absolutely the *mot juste*. It sounded like a gas explosion.

"You didn't seem to know it so dashed well, what, what?" said Gussie. And, reminded apparently by the word "what" of the word "Wattle," he repeated the latter some sixteen times with a rising inflection.

"Wattle, Wattle, Wattle," he concluded. "Right-ho. Push on."

But the bearded bloke had shot his bolt. He stood there, licked at last; and, watching him closely, I could see that he was now at the crossroads. I could spot what he was thinking as clearly as if he had confided it to my personal ear. He wanted to sit down and call it a day, I mean, but the thought that gave him pause was that, if he did, he must then either uncork Gussie or take the Fink-Nottle speech as read and get straight on to the actual prize-giving.

It was a dashed tricky thing, of course, to have to decide on the spur of the moment. I was reading in the paper the other day about those birds who are trying to split the atom, the nub being that they haven't the foggiest as to what will happen if they do. It may be all right. On the other hand, it may not be all right. And pretty silly a chap would feel, no doubt, if, having split the atom, he suddenly found the house going up in smoke and himself torn limb from limb.

So with the bearded bloke. Whether he was abreast of the inside facts in Gussie's case, I don't know, but it was obvious to him by this time that he had run into something pretty hot. Trial gallops had shown that Gussie had his own way of doing things. Those interruptions had been enough to prove to the perspicacious that here, seated on the platform at the big binge of the season, was one who, if pushed forward to make a speech, might let himself go in a rather epoch-making manner.

On the other hand, chain him up and put a green-baize cloth over him, and where were you? The proceeding would be over about half an hour too soon.

It was, as I say, a difficult problem to have to solve, and, left to himself, I don't know what conclusion he would have come to. Personally, I think he would have played it safe. As it happened, however, the thing was taken out of his hands, for at this moment, Gussie, having stretched his arms and yawned a bit, switched on that pebble-beached smile again and tacked down to the edge of the platform.

"Speech," he said affably.

He then stood with his thumbs in the armholes of his waistcoat, waiting for the applause to die down.

It was some time before this happened, for he had got a very fine hand indeed. I suppose it wasn't often that the boys of Market Snodsbury Grammar School came across a man public-spirited enough to call their head master a silly ass, and they showed their appreciation in no uncertain manner. Gussie may have been one over the eight, but as far as the majority of those present were concerned he was sitting on top of the world.

"Boys," said Gussie, "I mean ladies and gentlemen and boys, I do not detain you long, but I suppose on this occasion to feel compelled to say a few auspicious words; Ladies—and boys and gentlemen—we have all listened with interest to the remarks of our friend here who forgot to shave this morning—I don't know his name, but then he didn't know mine—Fitz-Wattle, I mean, absolutely absurd—which squares things up a bit—and we are all sorry that the Reverend Whatever-he-was-called should be dying of adenoids, but after all, here today, gone tomorrow, and all flesh is as grass, and what not, but that wasn't what I wanted to say. What I wanted to say was this—and I say it confidently—without fear of contradiction—I say, in short, I am happy to be here on this auspicious occasion and I take much pleasure in kindly awarding the prizes, consisting of the handsome books you see laid out on that table. As Shakespeare says, there are sermons in books, stones in the running brooks, or, rather, the other way about, and there you have it in a nutshell."

It went well, and I wasn't surprised. I couldn't quite follow some of it, but anybody could see that it was real ripe stuff, and I was amazed that even the course of treatment he had been taking could have rendered so normally tongue-tied a dumb brick as Gussie capable of it.

It just shows, what any member of Parliament will tell you, that if you want real oratory, the preliminary noggin is essential. Unless pie-eyed, you cannot hope to grip.

"Gentlemen," said Gussie, "I mean ladies and gentlemen and, of course, boys, what a beautiful world this is. A beautiful world, full of happiness on every side. Let me tell you a little story. Two Irishmen, Pat and Mike, were walking along Broadway, and one said to the other, 'Begorrah, the race is not always to the swift,' and the other replied, 'Faith and begob, education is a drawing out, not a putting in.'"

I must say it seemed to me the rottenest story I had ever heard, and I was surprised that Jeeves should have considered it worth while shoving into a speech. However, when I taxed him with this later, he said that Gussie had altered the plot a good deal, and I dare say that accounts for it.

At any rate, that was the *conte* as Gussie told it, and when I say that it got a very fair laugh, you will understand what a popular favourite he had become with the multitude. There might be a bearded bloke or so on the platform and a small section in the second row who were wishing the speaker would conclude his remarks and resume his seat, but the audience as a whole was for him solidly.

There was applause, and a voice cried: "Hear, hear!"

"Yes," said Gussie, "it is a beautiful world. The sky is blue, the birds are singing, there is optimism everywhere. And why not, boys and ladies and gentlemen? I'm happy, you're happy, we're all happy, even the meanest Irishman that walks along Broadway. Though, as I say, there were two of them—Pat and Mike, one drawing out, the other putting in. I should like you boys, taking the time from me, to give three cheers for this beautiful world. All together now."

Presently the dust settled down and the plaster stopped falling from the ceiling, and he went on.

"People who say it isn't a beautiful world don't know what they are talking about. Driving here in the car today to award the kind prizes, I was reluctantly compelled to tick off my host on this very point. Old Tom Travers. You will see him sitting there in the second row next to the large lady in beige."

He pointed helpfully, and the hundred or so Market Snods-buryians who craned their necks in the direction indicated were able to observe Uncle Tom blushing prettily.

"I ticked him off properly, the poor fish. He expressed the opinion that the world was in a deplorable state. I said, 'Don't talk rot, old Tom Travers.' 'I am not accustomed to talk rot,' he said. 'Then, for a beginner,' I said, 'you do it dashed well.' And I think you will admit, boys and ladies and gentlemen, that that was telling him."

The audience seemed to agree with him. The point went big. The voice that had said, "Hear, hear" said "Hear, hear" again, and my corn chandler hammered the floor vigorously with a large-size walking stick.

"Well, boys," resumed Gussie, having shot his cuffs and smirked horribly, "this is the end of the summer term, and many of you, no doubt, are leaving the school. And I don't blame you, because there's a frost in here you could cut with a knife. You are going out into the great world. Soon many of you will be walking along Broadway. And what I want to impress upon you is that, however much you may suffer from adenoids, you must all use every effort to prevent yourselves becoming pessimists and talking rot like old Tom Travers. There in the second row. The fellow with a face rather like a walnut."

He paused to allow those wishing to do so to refresh themselves with another look at Uncle Tom, and I found myself musing in some little perplexity. Long association with the members of the Drones has put me pretty well in touch with the various ways in which an overdose of the blushful Hippocrene can take the individual, but I had never seen anyone react quite as Gussie was doing.

There was a snap about his work which I had never witnessed before, even in Barmy Fotheringay-Phipps on New Year's Eve.

Jeeves, when I discussed the matter with him later, said it was something to do with inhibitions, if I caught the word correctly, and the suppression of, I think he said, the ego. What he meant, I gathered, was that, owing to the fact that Gussie had just completed a five years' stretch of blameless seclusion among the newts, all the goofiness which ought to have been spread out thin over those five years and had been bottled up during that period came to the surface on this occasion in a lump—or, if you prefer to put it that way, like a tidal wave.

There may be something in this. Jeeves generally knows.

Anyway, be that as it may, I was dashed glad I had had the shrewdness to keep out of that second row. It might be unworthy of the prestige of a Wooster to squash in among the proletariat in the standing-room-only section, but at least, I felt, I was out of the danger zone. So thoroughly had Gussie got it up his nose by now that it seemed to me that had he sighted me he might have become personal about even an old school friend.

"If there's one thing in the world I can't stand," proceeded Gussie, "it's a pessimist. Be optimists, boys. You all know the difference between an optimist and a pessimist. An optimist is a man who— well, take the case of two Irishmen walking along Broadway. One is an optimist and one is a pessimist, just as one's name is Pat and the other's Mike.... Why, hullo, Bertie; I didn't know you were here."

Too late, I endeavoured to go to earth behind the chandler, only to discover that there was no chandler there. Some appointment, suddenly remembered—possibly a promise to his wife that he would be home to tea—had caused him to ooze away while my attention was elsewhere, leaving me right out in the open.

Between me and Gussie, who was now pointing in an offensive manner, there was nothing but a sea of interested faces looking up at me.

"Now, there," boomed Gussie, continuing to point, "is an instance of what I mean. Boys and ladies and gentlemen, take a good look at that object standing up there at the back—morning coat, trousers as worn, quiet grey tie, and carnation in buttonhole—you can't miss him. Bertie Wooster, that is, and as foul a pessimist as ever bit a tiger. I tell you I despise that man. And why do I despise him? Because, boys and ladies and gentlemen, he is a pessimist. His attitude is defeatist. When I told him I was going to address you this afternoon, he tried to dissuade me. And do you know why he tried to dissuade me? Because he said my trousers would split up the back."

The cheers that greeted this were the loudest yet. Anything about splitting trousers went straight to the simple hearts of the young scholars of Market Snodsbury Grammar School. Two in the row in front of me turned purple, and a small lad with freckles seated beside them asked me for my autograph.

"Let me tell you a story about Bertie Wooster."

A Wooster can stand a good deal, but he cannot stand having his name bandied in a public place. Picking my feet up softly, I was in the very process of executing a quiet sneak for the door, when I perceived that the bearded bloke had at last decided to apply the closure.

Why he hadn't done so before is beyond me. Spell-bound, I take it. And, of course, when a chap is going like a breeze with the public, as Gussie had been, it's not so dashed easy to chip in. However, the prospect of hearing another of Gussie's anecdotes seemed to have done the trick. Rising rather as I had risen from my bench at the beginning of that painful scene with Tuppy in the twilight, he made a leap for the table, snatched up a book and came bearing down on the speaker.

He touched Gussie on the arm, and Gussie, turning sharply and seeing a large bloke with a beard apparently about to bean him with a book, sprang back in an attitude of self-defence.

"Perhaps, as time is getting on, Mr. Fink-Nottle, we had better——"

"Oh, ah," said Gussie, getting the trend. He relaxed. "The prizes, eh? Of course, yes. Right-ho. Yes, might as well be shoving along with it. What's this one?"

"Spelling and dictation—P.K. Purvis," announced the bearded bloke.

"Spelling and dictation—P.K. Purvis," echoed Gussie, as if he were calling coals. "Forward, P.K. Purvis."

Now that the whistle had been blown on his speech, it seemed to me that there was no longer any need for the strategic retreat which I had been planning. I had no wish to tear myself away unless I had to. I mean, I had told Jeeves that this binge would be fraught with interest, and it was fraught with interest. There was a fascination about Gussie's methods which gripped and made one reluctant to pass the thing up provided personal innuendoes were steered clear of. I decided, accordingly, to remain, and presently there was a musical squeaking and P.K. Purvis climbed the platform.

The spelling-and-dictation champ was about three foot six in his squeaking shoes, with a pink face and sandy hair. Gussie patted his hair. He seemed to have taken an immediate fancy to the lad.

"You P.K. Purvis?"

"Sir, yes, sir."

"It's a beautiful world, P.K. Purvis."

"Sir, yes, sir."

"Ah, you've noticed it, have you? Good. You married, by any chance?"

"Sir, no, sir."

"Get married, P.K. Purvis," said Gussie earnestly. "It's the only life ... Well, here's your book. Looks rather bilge to me from a glance at the title page, but, such as it is, here you are."

P.K. Purvis squeaked off amidst sporadic applause, but one could not fail to note that the sporadic was followed by a rather strained silence. It was evident that Gussie was striking something of a new note in Market Snodsbury scholastic circles. Looks were exchanged between parent and parent. The bearded bloke had the air of one who has drained the bitter cup. As for Aunt Dahlia, her demeanour now told only too clearly that her last doubts had been resolved and her verdict was in. I saw her whisper to the Bassett, who sat on her right, and the Bassett nodded sadly and looked like a fairy about to shed a tear and add another star to the Milky Way.

Gussie, after the departure of P.K. Purvis, had fallen into a sort of daydream and was standing with his mouth open and his hands in his pockets. Becoming abruptly aware that a fat kid in knickerbockers was at his elbow, he started violently.

"Hullo!" he said, visibly shaken. "Who are you?"

"This," said the bearded bloke, "is R.V. Smethurst."

"What's he doing here?" asked Gussie suspiciously.

"You are presenting him with the drawing prize, Mr. Fink-Nottle."

This apparently struck Gussie as a reasonable explanation. His face cleared.

"That's right, too," he said.... "Well, here it is, cocky. You off?" he said, as the kid prepared to withdraw.

"Sir, yes, sir."

"Wait, R.V. Smethurst. Not so fast. Before you go, there is a question I wish to ask you."

But the beard bloke's aim now seemed to be to rush the ceremonies a bit. He hustled R.V. Smethurst off stage rather like a chucker-out in a pub regretfully ejecting an old and respected customer, and starting paging G.G. Simmons. A moment later the latter was up and coming, and conceive my emotion when it was announced that the subject on which he had clicked was Scripture knowledge. One of us, I mean to say.

G.G. Simmons was an unpleasant, perky-looking stripling, mostly front teeth and spectacles, but I gave him a big hand. We Scripture-knowledge sharks stick together.

Gussie, I was sorry to see, didn't like him. There was in his manner, as he regarded G.G. Simmons, none of the chumminess which had marked it during his interview with P.K. Purvis or, in a somewhat lesser degree, with R.V. Smethurst. He was cold and distant.

"Well, G.G. Simmons."

"Sir, yes, sir."

"What do you mean—sir, yes, sir? Dashed silly thing to say. So you've won the Scripture-knowledge prize, have you?"

"Sir, yes, sir."

"Yes," said Gussie, "you look just the sort of little tick who would. And yet," he said, pausing and eyeing the child keenly, "how are we to know that this has all been open and above board? Let me test you, G.G. Simmons. What was What's-His-Name—the chap who begat Thingummy? Can you answer me that, Simmons?"

"Sir, no, sir."

Gussie turned to the bearded bloke.

"Fishy," he said. "Very fishy. This boy appears to be totally lacking in Scripture knowledge."

The bearded bloke passed a hand across his forehead.

"I can assure you, Mr. Fink-Nottle, that every care was taken to ensure a correct marking and that Simmons outdistanced his competitors by a wide margin."

"Well, if you say so," said Gussie doubtfully. "All right, G.G. Simmons, take your prize."

"Sir, thank you, sir."

"But let me tell you that there's nothing to stick on side about in winning a prize for Scripture knowledge. Bertie Wooster——"

I don't know when I've had a nastier shock. I had been going on the assumption that, now that they had stopped him making his speech, Gussie's fangs had been drawn, as you might say. To duck my head down and resume my edging toward the door was with me the work of a moment.

"Bertie Wooster won the Scripture-knowledge prize at a kids' school we were at together, and you know what he's like. But, of course, Bertie frankly cheated. He succeeded in scrounging that Scripture-knowledge trophy over the heads of better men by means of some of the rawest and most brazen swindling methods ever witnessed even at a school where such things were common. If that man's pockets, as he entered the examination-room, were not stuffed to bursting-point with lists of the kings of Judah——"

I heard no more. A moment later I was out in God's air, fumbling with a fevered foot at the self-starter of the old car.

The engine raced. The clutch slid into position. I tooted and drove off.

My ganglions were still vibrating as I ran the car into the stables of Brinkley Court, and it was a much shaken Bertram who tottered up to his room to change into something loose. Having donned flannels, I lay down on the bed for a bit, and I suppose I must have dozed off, for the next thing I remember is finding Jeeves at my side.

I sat up. "My tea, Jeeves?"

"No, sir. It is nearly dinner-time."

The mists cleared away.

"I must have been asleep."

"Yes, sir."

"Nature taking its toll of the exhausted frame."

"Yes, sir."

"And enough to make it."

"Yes, sir."

"And now it's nearly dinner-time, you say? All right. I am in no mood for dinner, but I suppose you had better lay out the clothes."

"It will not be necessary, sir. The company will not be dressing tonight. A cold collation has been set out in the dining-room."

"Why's that?"

"It was Mrs. Travers's wish that this should be done in order to minimize the work for the staff, who are attending a dance at Sir Percival Stretchley-Budd's residence tonight."

"Of course, yes. I remember. My Cousin Angela told me. Tonight's the night, what? You going, Jeeves?"

"No, sir. I am not very fond of this form of entertainment in the rural districts, sir."

"I know what you mean. These country binges are all the same. A piano, one fiddle, and a floor like sandpaper. Is Anatole going? Angela hinted not."

"Miss Angela was correct, sir. Monsieur Anatole is in bed."

"Temperamental blighters, these Frenchmen."

"Yes, sir."

There was a pause.

"Well, Jeeves," I said, "it was certainly one of those afternoons, what?"

"Yes, sir."

"I cannot recall one more packed with incident. And I left before the finish."

"Yes, sir. I observed your departure."

"You couldn't blame me for withdrawing."

"No, sir. Mr. Fink-Nottle had undoubtedly become embarrassingly personal."

"Was there much more of it after I went?"

"No, sir. The proceedings terminated very shortly. Mr. Fink-Nottle's remarks with reference to Master G.G. Simmons brought about an early closure."

"But he had finished his remarks about G.G. Simmons."

"Only temporarily, sir. He resumed them immediately after your departure. If you recollect, sir, he had already proclaimed himself suspicious of Master Simmons's bona fides, and he now proceeded to deliver a violent verbal attack upon the young gentleman, asserting that it was impossible for him to have won the Scripture-knowledge prize without systematic cheating on an impressive scale. He went so far as to suggest that Master Simmons was well known to the police."

"Golly, Jeeves!"

"Yes, sir. The words did create a considerable sensation. The reaction of those present to this accusation I should describe as mixed. The young students appeared pleased and applauded vigorously, but Master Simmons's mother rose from her seat and addressed Mr. Fink-Nottle in terms of strong protest."

"Did Gussie seem taken aback? Did he recede from his position?"

"No, sir. He said that he could see it all now, and hinted at a guilty liaison between Master Simmons's mother and the head master, accusing the latter of having cooked the marks, as his expression was, in order to gain favour with the former."

"You don't mean that?"

"Yes, sir."

"Egad, Jeeves! And then——"

"They sang the national anthem, sir."

"Surely not?"

"Yes, sir."

"At a moment like that?"

"Yes, sir."

"Well, you were there and you know, of course, but I should have thought the last thing Gussie and this woman would have done in the circs. would have been to start singing duets."

"You misunderstand me, sir. It was the entire company who sang. The head master turned to the organist and said something to him in a low tone. Upon which the latter began to play the national anthem, and the proceedings terminated."

"I see. About time, too."

"Yes, sir. Mrs. Simmons's attitude had become unquestionably menacing."

I pondered. What I had heard was, of course, of a nature to excite pity and terror, not to mention alarm and despondency, and it would be paltering with the truth to say that I was pleased about it. On the other hand, it was all over now, and it seemed to me that the thing to do was not to mourn over the past but to fix the mind on the bright future. I mean to say, Gussie might have lowered the existing Worcestershire record for goofiness and definitely forfeited all chance of becoming Market Snodsbury's favourite son, but you couldn't get away from the fact that he had proposed to Madeline Bassett, and you had to admit that she had accepted him.

I put this to Jeeves.

"A frightful exhibition," I said, "and one which will very possibly ring down history's pages. But we must not forget, Jeeves, that Gussie, though now doubtless looked upon in the neighbourhood as the world's worst freak, is all right otherwise."

"No, sir."

I did not get quite this.

"When you say 'No, sir,' do you mean 'Yes, sir'?"

"No, sir. I mean 'No, sir.'"

"He is not all right otherwise?"

"No, sir."

"But he's betrothed."

"No longer, sir. Miss Bassett has severed the engagement."

"You don't mean that?"

"Yes, sir."

I wonder if you have noticed a rather peculiar thing about this chronicle. I allude to the fact that at one time or another practically everybody playing a part in it has had occasion to bury his or her face in his or her hands. I have participated in some pretty glutinous affairs in my time, but I think that never before or since have I been mixed up with such a solid body of brow clutchers.

Uncle Tom did it, if you remember. So did Gussie. So did Tuppy. So, probably, though I have no data, did Anatole, and I wouldn't put it past the Bassett. And Aunt Dahlia, I have no doubt, would have done it, too, but for the risk of disarranging the carefully fixed coiffure.

Well, what I am trying to say is that at this juncture I did it myself. Up went the hands and down went the head, and in another jiffy I was clutching as energetically as the best of them.

And it was while I was still massaging the coconut and wondering what the next move was that something barged up against the door like the delivery of a ton of coals.

"I think this may very possibly be Mr. Fink-Nottle himself, sir," said Jeeves.

His intuition, however, had led him astray. It was not Gussie but Tuppy. He came in and stood breathing asthmatically. It was plain that he was deeply stirred.

-18-

I eyed him narrowly. I didn't like his looks. Mark you, I don't say I ever had, much, because Nature, when planning this sterling fellow, shoved in a lot more lower jaw than was absolutely necessary and made the eyes a bit too keen and piercing for one who was neither an Empire builder nor a traffic policeman. But on the present occasion, in addition to offending the aesthetic sense, this Glossop seemed to me to be wearing a distinct air of menace, and I found myself wishing that Jeeves wasn't always so dashed tactful. I mean, it's all very well to remove yourself like an eel sliding into mud when the employer has a visitor, but there are moments—and it looked to me as if this was going to be one of them—when the truer tact is to stick round and stand ready to lend a hand in the free-for-all.

For Jeeves was no longer with us. I hadn't seen him go, and I hadn't heard him go, but he had gone. As far as the eye could reach, one noted nobody but Tuppy. And in Tuppy's demeanour, as I say, there was a certain something that tended to disquiet. He looked to me very much like a man who had come to reopen that matter of my tickling Angela's ankles.

However, his opening remark told me that I had been alarming myself unduly. It was of a pacific nature, and came as a great relief.

"Bertie," he said, "I owe you an apology. I have come to make it."

My relief on hearing these words, containing as they did no reference of any sort to tickled ankles, was, as I say, great. But I don't think it was any greater than my surprise. Months had passed since that painful episode at the Drones, and until now he hadn't given a sign of remorse and contrition. Indeed, word had reached me through private sources that he frequently told the story at dinners and other gatherings and, when doing so, laughed his silly head off.

I found it hard to understand, accordingly, what could have caused him to abase himself at this later date. Presumably he had been given the elbow by his better self, but why?

Still, there it was.

"My dear chap," I said, gentlemanly to the gills, "don't mention it."

"What's the sense of saying, 'Don't mention it'? I have mentioned it."

"I mean, don't mention it any more. Don't give the matter another thought. We all of us forget ourselves sometimes and do things which, in our calmer moments, we regret. No doubt you were a bit tight at the time."

"What the devil do you think you're talking about?"

I didn't like his tone. Brusque.

"Correct me if I am wrong," I said, with a certain stiffness, "but I assumed that you were apologizing for your foul conduct in looping back the last ring that night in the Drones, causing me to plunge into the swimming b. in the full soup and fish."

"Ass! Not that, at all."

"Then what?"

"This Bassett business."

"What Bassett business?"

"Bertie," said Tuppy, "when you told me last night that you were in love with Madeline Bassett, I gave you the impression that I believed you, but I didn't. The thing seemed too incredible. However, since then I have made inquiries, and the facts appear to square with your statement. I have now come to apologize for doubting you."

"Made inquiries?"

"I asked her if you had proposed to her, and she said, yes, you had."

"Tuppy! You didn't?"

"I did."

"Have you no delicacy, no proper feeling?"

"No."

"Oh? Well, right-ho, of course, but I think you ought to have."

"Delicacy be dashed. I wanted to be certain that it was not you who stole Angela from me. I now know it wasn't."

So long as he knew that, I didn't so much mind him having no delicacy.

"Ah," I said. "Well, that's fine. Hold that thought."

"I have found out who it was."

"What?"

He stood brooding for a moment. His eyes were smouldering with a dull fire. His jaw stuck out like the back of Jeeves's head.

"Bertie," he said, "do you remember what I swore I would do to the chap who stole Angela from me?"

"As nearly as I recall, you planned to pull him inside out——"

"——and make him swallow himself. Correct. The programme still holds good."

"But, Tuppy, I keep assuring you, as a competent eyewitness, that nobody snitched Angela from you during that Cannes trip."

"No. But they did after she got back."

"What?"

"Don't keep saying, 'What?' You heard."

"But she hasn't seen anybody since she got back."

"Oh, no? How about that newt bloke?"

"Gussie?"

"Precisely. The serpent Fink-Nottle."

This seemed to me absolute gibbering.

"But Gussie loves the Bassett."

"You can't all love this blighted Bassett. What astonishes me is that anyone can do it. He loves Angela, I tell you. And she loves him."

"But Angela handed you your hat before Gussie ever got here."

"No, she didn't. Couple of hours after."

187

"He couldn't have fallen in love with her in a couple of hours."

"Why not? I fell in love with her in a couple of minutes. I worshipped her immediately we met, the popeyed little excrescence."

"But, dash it——"

"Don't argue, Bertie. The facts are all docketed. She loves this newt-nuzzling blister."

"Quite absurd, laddie—quite absurd."

"Oh?" He ground a heel into the carpet—a thing I've often read about, but had never seen done before. "Then perhaps you will explain how it is that she happens to come to be engaged to him?"

You could have knocked me down with a f.

"Engaged to him?"

"She told me herself."

"She was kidding you."

"She was not kidding me. Shortly after the conclusion of this afternoon's binge at Market Snodsbury Grammar School he asked her to marry him, and she appears to have right-hoed without a murmur."

"There must be some mistake."

"There was. The snake Fink-Nottle made it, and by now I bet he realizes it. I've been chasing him since 5.30."

"Chasing him?"

"All over the place. I want to pull his head off."

"I see. Quite."

"You haven't seen him, by any chance?"

"No."

"Well, if you do, say goodbye to him quickly and put in your order for lilies.... Oh, Jeeves."

"Sir?"

I hadn't heard the door open, but the man was on the spot once more. My private belief, as I think I have mentioned before, is that Jeeves doesn't have to open doors. He's like one of those birds in India who bung their astral bodies about—the chaps, I mean, who having gone into thin air in Bombay, reassemble the parts and appear two minutes later in Calcutta. Only some such theory will account for the fact that he's not there one moment and is there the next. He just seems to float from Spot A to Spot B like some form of gas.

"Have you seen Mr. Fink-Nottle, Jeeves?"

"No, sir."

"I'm going to murder him."

"Very good, sir."

Tuppy withdrew, banging the door behind him, and I put Jeeves abreast.

"Jeeves," I said, "do you know what? Mr. Fink-Nottle is engaged to my Cousin Angela."

"Indeed, sir?"

"Well, how about it? Do you grasp the psychology? Does it make sense? Only a few hours ago he was engaged to Miss Bassett."

"Gentlemen who have been discarded by one young lady are often apt to attach themselves without delay to another, sir. It is what is known as a gesture."

I began to grasp.

"I see what you mean. Defiant stuff."

"Yes, sir."

"A sort of 'Oh, right-ho, please yourself, but if you don't want me, there are plenty who do.'"

"Precisely, sir. My Cousin George——"

"Never mind about your Cousin George, Jeeves."

"Very good, sir."

"Keep him for the long winter evenings, what?"

"Just as you wish, sir."

"And, anyway, I bet your Cousin George wasn't a shrinking, non-goose-bo-ing jellyfish like Gussie. That is what astounds me, Jeeves—that it should be Gussie who has been putting in all this heavy gesture-making stuff."

"You must remember, sir, that Mr. Fink-Nottle is in a somewhat inflamed cerebral condition."

"That's true. A bit above par at the moment, as it were?"

"Exactly, sir."

"Well, I'll tell you one thing—he'll be in a jolly sight more inflamed cerebral condition if Tuppy gets hold of him.... What's the time?"

"Just on eight o'clock, sir."

"Then Tuppy has been chasing him for two hours and a half. We

189

must save the unfortunate blighter, Jeeves."

"Yes, sir."

"A human life is a human life, what?"

"Exceedingly true, sir."

"The first thing, then, is to find him. After that we can discuss plans and schemes. Go forth, Jeeves, and scour the neighbourhood."

"It will not be necessary, sir. If you will glance behind you, you will see Mr. Fink-Nottle coming out from beneath your bed."

And, by Jove, he was absolutely right.

There was Gussie, emerging as stated. He was covered with fluff and looked like a tortoise popping forth for a bit of a breather.

"Gussie!" I said.

"Jeeves," said Gussie.

"Sir?" said Jeeves.

"Is that door locked, Jeeves?"

"No, sir, but I will attend to the matter immediately."

Gussie sat down on the bed, and I thought for a moment that he was going to be in the mode by burying his face in his hands. However, he merely brushed a dead spider from his brow.

"Have you locked the door, Jeeves?"

"Yes, sir."

"Because you can never tell that that ghastly Glossop may not take it into his head to come——"

The word "back" froze on his lips. He hadn't got any further than a *b*-ish sound, when the handle of the door began to twist and rattle. He sprang from the bed, and for an instant stood looking exactly like a picture my Aunt Agatha has in her dining-room—The Stag at Bay—Landseer. Then he made a dive for the cupboard and was inside it before one really got on to it that he had started leaping. I have seen fellows late for the 9.15 move less nippily.

I shot a glance at Jeeves. He allowed his right eyebrow to flicker slightly, which is as near as he ever gets to a display of the emotions.

"Hullo?" I yipped.

"Let me in, blast you!" responded Tuppy's voice from without. "Who locked this door?"

I consulted Jeeves once more in the language of the eyebrow. He raised one of his. I raised one of mine. He raised his other. I raised my other. Then we both raised both. Finally, there seeming no other

190

policy to pursue, I flung wide the gates and Tuppy came shooting in.

"Now what?" I said, as nonchalantly as I could manage.

"Why was the door locked?" demanded Tuppy.

I was in pretty good eyebrow-raising form by now, so I gave him a touch of it.

"Is one to have no privacy, Glossop?" I said coldly. "I instructed Jeeves to lock the door because I was about to disrobe."

"A likely story!" said Tuppy, and I'm not sure he didn't add "Forsooth!" "You needn't try to make me believe that you're afraid people are going to run excursion trains to see you in your underwear. You locked that door because you've got the snake Fink-Nottle concealed in here. I suspected it the moment I'd left, and I decided to come back and investigate. I'm going to search this room from end to end. I believe he's in that cupboard.... What's in this cupboard?"

"Just clothes," I said, having another stab at the nonchalant, though extremely dubious as to whether it would come off. "The usual wardrobe of the English gentleman paying a country-house visit."

"You're lying!"

Well, I wouldn't have been if he had only waited a minute before speaking, because the words were hardly out of his mouth before Gussie was out of the cupboard. I have commented on the speed with which he had gone in. It was as nothing to the speed with which he emerged. There was a sort of whir and blur, and he was no longer with us.

I think Tuppy was surprised. In fact, I'm sure he was. Despite the confidence with which he had stated his view that the cupboard contained Fink-Nottles, it plainly disconcerted him to have the chap fizzing out at him like this. He gargled sharply, and jumped back about five feet. The next moment, however, he had recovered his poise and was galloping down the corridor in pursuit. It only needed Aunt Dahlia after them, shouting "Yoicks!" or whatever is customary on these occasions, to complete the resemblance to a brisk run with the Quorn.

I sank into a handy chair. I am not a man whom it is easy to discourage, but it seemed to me that things had at last begun to get too complex for Bertram.

"Jeeves," I said, "all this is a bit thick."

"Yes, sir."

"The head rather swims."

"Yes, sir."

"I think you had better leave me, Jeeves. I shall need to devote the very closest thought to the situation which has arisen."

"Very good, sir."

The door closed. I lit a cigarette and began to ponder.

-19-

Most chaps in my position, I imagine, would have pondered all the rest of the evening without getting a bite, but we Woosters have an uncanny knack of going straight to the heart of things, and I don't suppose it was much more than ten minutes after I had started pondering before I saw what had to be done.

What was needed to straighten matters out, I perceived, was a heart-to- heart talk with Angela. She had caused all the trouble by her mutton- headed behaviour in saying "Yes" instead of "No" when Gussie, in the grip of mixed drinks and cerebral excitement, had suggested teaming up. She must obviously be properly ticked off and made to return him to store. A quarter of an hour later, I had tracked her down to the summer-house in which she was taking a cooler and was seating myself by her side.

"Angela," I said, and if my voice was stern, well, whose wouldn't have been, "this is all perfect drivel."

She seemed to come out of a reverie. She looked at me inquiringly.

"I'm sorry, Bertie, I didn't hear. What were you talking drivel about?"

"I was not talking drivel."

"Oh, sorry, I thought you said you were."

"Is it likely that I would come out here in order to talk drivel?"

"Very likely."

I thought it best to haul off and approach the matter from another angle.

"I've just been seeing Tuppy."

"Oh?"

"And Gussie Fink-Nottle."

"Oh, yes?"

"It appears that you have gone and got engaged to the latter."

"Quite right."

"Well, that's what I meant when I said it was all perfect drivel. You can't possibly love a chap like Gussie."

"Why not?"

"You simply can't."

Well, I mean to say, of course she couldn't. Nobody could love a freak like Gussie except a similar freak like the Bassett. The shot wasn't on the board. A splendid chap, of course, in many ways— courteous, amiable, and just the fellow to tell you what to do till the doctor came, if you had a sick newt on your hands—but quite obviously not of Mendelssohn's March timber. I have no doubt that you could have flung bricks by the hour in England's most densely populated districts without endangering the safety of a single girl capable of becoming Mrs. Augustus Fink-Nottle without an anaesthetic.

I put this to her, and she was forced to admit the justice of it.

"All right, then. Perhaps I don't."

"Then what," I said keenly, "did you want to go and get engaged to him for, you unreasonable young fathead?"

"I thought it would be fun."

"Fun!"

"And so it has been. I've had a lot of fun out of it. You should have seen Tuppy's face when I told him."

A sudden bright light shone upon me.

"Ha! A gesture!"

"What?"

"You got engaged to Gussie just to score off Tuppy?"

"I did."

"Well, then, that was what I was saying. It was a gesture."

"Yes, I suppose you could call it that."

193

"And I'll tell you something else I'll call it—viz. a dashed low trick. I'm surprised at you, young Angela."

"I don't see why."

I curled the lip about half an inch. "Being a female, you wouldn't. You gentler sexes are like that. You pull off the rawest stuff without a pang. You pride yourselves on it. Look at Jael, the wife of Heber."

"Where did you ever hear of Jael, the wife of Heber?"

"Possibly you are not aware that I once won a Scripture-knowledge prize at school?"

"Oh, yes. I remember Augustus mentioning it in his speech."

"Quite," I said, a little hurriedly. I had no wish to be reminded of Augustus's speech. "Well, as I say, look at Jael, the wife of Heber. Dug spikes into the guest's coconut while he was asleep, and then went swanking about the place like a Girl Guide. No wonder they say, 'Oh, woman, woman!'"

"Who?"

"The chaps who do. Coo, what a sex! But you aren't proposing to keep this up, of course?"

"Keep what up?"

"This rot of being engaged to Gussie."

"I certainly am."

"Just to make Tuppy look silly."

"Do you think he looks silly?"

"I do."

"So he ought to."

I began to get the idea that I wasn't making real headway. I remember when I won that Scripture-knowledge prize, having to go into the facts about Balaam's ass. I can't quite recall what they were, but I still retain a sort of general impression of something digging its feet in and putting its ears back and refusing to co-operate; and it seemed to me that this was what Angela was doing now. She and Balaam's ass were, so to speak, sisters under the skin. There's a word beginning with r——"re" something——"recal" something—No, it's gone. But what I am driving at is that is what this Angela was showing herself.

"Silly young geezer," I said.

She pinkened.

"I'm not a silly young geezer."

194

"You are a silly young geezer. And, what's more, you know it."

"I don't know anything of the kind."

"Here you are, wrecking Tuppy's life, wrecking Gussie's life, all for the sake of a cheap score."

"Well, it's no business of yours."

I sat on this promptly:

"No business of mine when I see two lives I used to go to school with wrecked? Ha! Besides, you know you're potty about Tuppy."

"I'm not!"

"Is that so? If I had a quid for every time I've seen you gaze at him with the lovelight in your eyes——"

She gazed at me, but without the lovelight.

"Oh, for goodness sake, go away and boil your head, Bertie!"

I drew myself up.

"That," I replied, with dignity, "is just what I am going to go away and boil. At least, I mean, I shall now leave you. I have said my say."

"Good."

"But permit me to add——"

"I won't."

"Very good," I said coldly. "In that case, tinkerty tonk."

And I meant it to sting.

"Moody" and "discouraged" were about the two adjectives you would have selected to describe me as I left the summer-house. It would be idle to deny that I had expected better results from this little chat.

I was surprised at Angela. Odd how you never realize that every girl is at heart a vicious specimen until something goes wrong with her love affair. This cousin and I had been meeting freely since the days when I wore sailor suits and she hadn't any front teeth, yet only now was I beginning to get on to her hidden depths. A simple, jolly, kindly young pimple she had always struck me as—the sort you could more or less rely on not to hurt a fly. But here she was now laughing heartlessly—at least, I seemed to remember hearing her laugh heartlessly—like something cold and callous out of a sophisticated talkie, and fairly spitting on her hands in her determination to bring Tuppy's grey hairs in sorrow to the grave.

I've said it before, and I'll say it again—girls are rummy. Old Pop Kipling never said a truer word than when he made that crack about the f. of the s. being more d. than the m.

It seemed to me in the circs. that there was but one thing to do—that is head for the dining-room and take a slash at the cold collation of which Jeeves had spoken. I felt in urgent need of sustenance, for the recent interview had pulled me down a bit. There is no gainsaying the fact that this naked-emotion stuff reduces a chap's vitality and puts him in the vein for a good whack at the beef and ham.

To the dining-room, accordingly, I repaired, and had barely crossed the threshold when I perceived Aunt Dahlia at the sideboard, tucking into salmon mayonnaise.

The spectacle drew from me a quick "Oh, ah," for I was somewhat embarrassed. The last time this relative and I had enjoyed a *tête-à-tête*, it will be remembered, she had sketched out plans for drowning me in the kitchen-garden pond, and I was not quite sure what my present standing with her was.

I was relieved to find her in genial mood. Nothing could have exceeded the cordiality with which she waved her fork.

"Hallo, Bertie, you old ass," was her very matey greeting. "I thought I shouldn't find you far away from the food. Try some of this salmon. Excellent."

"Anatole's?" I queried.

"No. He's still in bed. But the kitchen maid has struck an inspired streak. It suddenly seems to have come home to her that she isn't catering for a covey of buzzards in the Sahara Desert, and she has put out something quite fit for human consumption. There is good in the girl, after all, and I hope she enjoys herself at the dance."

I ladled out a portion of salmon, and we fell into pleasant conversation, chatting of this servants' ball at the Stretchley-Budds and speculating idly, I recall, as to what Seppings, the butler, would look like, doing the rumba.

It was not till I had cleaned up the first platter and was embarking on a second that the subject of Gussie came up. Considering what had passed at Market Snodsbury that afternoon, it was one which I had been expecting her to touch on earlier. When she did touch on it, I could see that she had not yet been informed of Angela's engagement.

196

"I say, Bertie," she said, meditatively chewing fruit salad. "This Spink-Bottle."

"Nottle."

"Bottle," insisted the aunt firmly. "After that exhibition of his this afternoon, Bottle, and nothing but Bottle, is how I shall always think of him. However, what I was going to say was that, if you see him, I wish you would tell him that he has made an old woman very, very happy. Except for the time when the curate tripped over a loose shoelace and fell down the pulpit steps, I don't think I have ever had a more wonderful moment than when good old Bottle suddenly started ticking Tom off from the platform. In fact, I thought his whole performance in the most perfect taste."

I could not but demur.

"Those references to myself——"

"Those were what I liked next best. I thought they were fine. Is it true that you cheated when you won that Scripture-knowledge prize?"

"Certainly not. My victory was the outcome of the most strenuous and unremitting efforts."

"And how about this pessimism we hear of? Are you a pessimist, Bertie?"

I could have told her that what was occurring in this house was rapidly making me one, but I said no, I wasn't.

"That's right. Never be a pessimist. Everything is for the best in this best of all possible worlds. It's a long lane that has no turning. It's always darkest before the dawn. Have patience and all will come right. The sun will shine, although the day's a grey one.... Try some of this salad."

I followed her advice, but even as I plied the spoon my thoughts were elsewhere. I was perplexed. It may have been the fact that I had recently been hobnobbing with so many bowed-down hearts that made this cheeriness of hers seem so bizarre, but bizarre was certainly what I found it.

"I thought you might have been a trifle peeved," I said.

"Peeved?"

"By Gussie's manoeuvres on the platform this afternoon. I

confess that I had rather expected the tapping foot and the drawn brow."

"Nonsense. What was there to be peeved about? I took the whole thing as a great compliment, proud to feel that any drink from my cellars could have produced such a majestic jag. It restores one's faith in post-war whisky. Besides, I couldn't be peeved at anything tonight. I am like a little child clapping its hands and dancing in the sunshine. For though it has been some time getting a move on, Bertie, the sun has at last broken through the clouds. Ring out those joy bells. Anatole has withdrawn his notice."

"What? Oh, very hearty congratulations."

"Thanks. Yes, I worked on him like a beaver after I got back this afternoon, and finally, vowing he would ne'er consent, he consented. He stays on, praises be, and the way I look at it now is that God's in His heaven and all's right with——"

She broke off. The door had opened, and we were plus a butler.

"Hullo, Seppings," said Aunt Dahlia. "I thought you had gone."

"Not yet, madam."

"Well, I hope you will all have a good time."

"Thank you, madam."

"Was there something you wanted to see me about?"

"Yes, madam. It is with reference to Monsieur Anatole. Is it by your wish, madam, that Mr. Fink-Nottle is making faces at Monsieur Anatole through the skylight of his bedroom?"

-20-

There was one of those long silences. Pregnant, I believe, is what they're generally called. Aunt looked at butler. Butler looked at aunt. I looked at both of them. An eerie stillness seemed to envelop the room like a linseed poultice. I happened to be biting on a slice of apple in my fruit salad at the moment, and it sounded as if Carnera had jumped off the top of the Eiffel Tower on to a cucumber frame.

Aunt Dahlia steadied herself against the sideboard, and spoke in a low, husky voice:

"Faces?"

"Yes, madam."

"Through the skylight?"

"Yes, madam."

"You mean he's sitting on the roof?"

"Yes, madam. It has upset Monsieur Anatole very much."

I suppose it was that word "upset" that touched Aunt Dahlia off. Experience had taught her what happened when Anatole got upset. I had always known her as a woman who was quite active on her pins, but I had never suspected her of being capable of the magnificent burst of speed which she now showed. Pausing merely to get a rich hunting-field expletive off her chest, she was out of the room and making for the stairs before I could swallow a sliver of—I think—banana. And feeling, as I had felt when I got that telegram of hers about Angela and Tuppy, that my place was by her side, I put down my plate and hastened after her, Seppings following at a loping gallop.

I say that my place was by her side, but it was not so dashed easy to get there, for she was setting a cracking pace. At the top of the first flight she must have led by a matter of half a dozen lengths, and was still shaking off my challenge when she rounded into the second. At the next landing, however, the gruelling going appeared to tell on her, for she slackened off a trifle and showed symptoms of roaring, and by the time we were in the straight we were running practically neck and neck. Our entry into Anatole's room was as close a finish as you could have wished to see.

Result:

1. *Aunt Dahlia.*

2. *Bertram.*

3. *Seppings.*

Won by a short head. Half a staircase separated second and third.

The first thing that met the eye on entering was Anatole. This wizard of the cooking-stove is a tubby little man with a moustache of the outsize or soup-strainer type, and you can generally take a line through it as to the state of his emotions. When all is well, it turns up at the ends like a sergeant-major's. When the soul is bruised, it droops.

It was drooping now, striking a sinister note. And if any shadow

199

of doubt had remained as to how he was feeling, the way he was carrying on would have dispelled it. He was standing by the bed in pink pyjamas, waving his fists at the skylight. Through the glass, Gussie was staring down. His eyes were bulging and his mouth was open, giving him so striking a resemblance to some rare fish in an aquarium that one's primary impulse was to offer him an ant's egg.

Watching this fist-waving cook and this goggling guest, I must say that my sympathies were completely with the former. I considered him thoroughly justified in waving all the fists he wanted to.

Review the facts, I mean to say. There he had been, lying in bed, thinking idly of whatever French cooks do think about when in bed, and he had suddenly become aware of that frightful face at the window. A thing to jar the most phlegmatic. I know I should hate to be lying in bed and have Gussie popping up like that. A chap's bedroom—you can't get away from it—is his castle, and he has every right to look askance if gargoyles come glaring in at him.

While I stood musing thus, Aunt Dahlia, in her practical way, was coming straight to the point:

"What's all this?"

Anatole did a sort of Swedish exercise, starting at the base of the spine, carrying on through the shoulder-blades and finishing up among the back hair.

Then he told her.

In the chats I have had with this wonder man, I have always found his English fluent, but a bit on the mixed side. If you remember, he was with Mrs. Bingo Little for a time before coming to Brinkley, and no doubt he picked up a good deal from Bingo. Before that, he had been a couple of years with an American family at Nice and had studied under their chauffeur, one of the Maloneys of Brooklyn. So, what with Bingo and what with Maloney, he is, as I say, fluent but a bit mixed.

He spoke, in part, as follows:

"Hot dog! You ask me what is it? Listen. Make some attention a little. Me, I have hit the hay, but I do not sleep so good, and presently I wake and up I look, and there is one who make faces against me through the dashed window. Is that a pretty affair? Is that convenient? If you think I like it, you jolly well mistake yourself. I am so mad as a wet hen. And why not? I am somebody, isn't it? This is a bedroom, what-what, not a house for some apes? Then for what do blighters sit on my window so cool as a few cucumbers, making some faces?"

"Quite," I said. Dashed reasonable, was my verdict.

He threw another look up at Gussie, and did Exercise 2—the one where you clutch the moustache, give it a tug and then start catching flies.

"Wait yet a little. I am not finish. I say I see this type on my window, making a few faces. But what then? Does he buzz off when I shout a cry, and leave me peaceable? Not on your life. He remain planted there, not giving any damns, and sit regarding me like a cat watching a duck. He make faces against me and again he make faces against me, and the more I command that he should get to hell out of here, the more he do not get to hell out of here. He cry something towards me, and I demand what is his desire, but he do not explain. Oh, no, that arrives never. He does but shrug his head. What damn silliness! Is this amusing for me? You think I like it? I am not content with such folly. I think the poor mutt's loony. *Je me fiche de ce type infect. C'est idiot de faire comme ça l'oiseau.... Allez-vous-en, louffier....* Tell the boob to go away. He is mad as some March hatters."

I must say I thought he was making out a jolly good case, and evidently Aunt Dahlia felt the same. She laid a quivering hand on his shoulder.

"I will, Monsieur Anatole, I will," she said, and I couldn't have believed that robust voice capable of sinking to such an absolute coo. More like a turtle dove calling to its mate than anything else. "It's quite all right."

She had said the wrong thing. He did Exercise 3.

"All right? *Nom d'un nom d'un nom!* The hell you say it's all right! Of what use to pull stuff like that? Wait one half-moment. Not yet quite so quick, my old sport. It is by no means all right. See yet again a little. It is some very different dishes of fish. I can take a few smooths with a rough, it is true, but I do not find it agreeable when one play larks against me on my windows. That cannot do. A nice thing, no. I am a serious man. I do not wish a few larks on my windows. I enjoy larks on my windows worse as any. It is very little all right. If such rannygazoo is to arrive, I do not remain any longer in this house no more. I buzz off and do not stay planted."

Sinister words, I had to admit, and I was not surprised that Aunt Dahlia, hearing them, should have uttered a cry like the wail of a master of hounds seeing a fox shot. Anatole had begun to wave his fists again at Gussie, and she now joined him. Seppings, who was puffing respectfully in the background, didn't actually wave his fists, but he gave Gussie a pretty austere look. It was plain to the thoughtful observer that this Fink-Nottle, in getting on to that skylight, had done a mistaken thing. He couldn't have been more unpopular in the home of G.G. Simmons.

"Go away, you crazy loon!" cried Aunt Dahlia, in that ringing voice of hers which had once caused nervous members of the Quorn to lose stirrups and take tosses from the saddle.

Gussie's reply was to waggle his eyebrows. I could read the message he was trying to convey.

"I think he means," I said—reasonable old Bertram, always trying to throw oil on the troubled w's——"that if he does he will fall down the side of the house and break his neck."

"Well, why not?" said Aunt Dahlia.

I could see her point, of course, but it seemed to me that there might be a nearer solution. This skylight happened to be the only window in the house which Uncle Tom had not festooned with his bally bars. I suppose he felt that if a burglar had the nerve to climb up as far as this, he deserved what was coming to him.

"If you opened the skylight, he could jump in."

The idea got across.

"Seppings, how does this skylight open?"

"With a pole, madam."

"Then get a pole. Get two poles. Ten."

And presently Gussie was mixing with the company, Like one of those chaps you read about in the papers, the wretched man seemed deeply conscious of his position.

I must say Aunt Dahlia's bearing and demeanour did nothing to assist toward a restored composure. Of the amiability which she had exhibited when discussing this unhappy chump's activities with me over the fruit salad, no trace remained, and I was not surprised that speech more or less froze on the Fink-Nottle lips. It isn't often that Aunt Dahlia, normally as genial a bird as ever encouraged a gaggle of hounds to get their noses down to it, lets her angry passions rise, but when she does, strong men climb trees and pull them up after them.

"Well?" she said.

In answer to this, all that Gussie could produce was a sort of strangled hiccough.

"Well?"

Aunt Dahlia's face grew darker. Hunting, if indulged in regularly over a period of years, is a pastime that seldom fails to lend a fairly deepish tinge to the patient's complexion, and her best friends could not have denied that even at normal times the relative's map tended a little toward the crushed strawberry. But never had I seen it take on so pronounced a richness as now. She looked like a tomato struggling for self-expression.

"Well?"

Gussie tried hard. And for a moment it seemed as if something was going to come through. But in the end it turned out nothing more than a sort of death-rattle.

"Oh, take him away, Bertie, and put ice on his head," said Aunt Dahlia, giving the thing up. And she turned to tackle what looked like the rather man's size job of soothing Anatole, who was now carrying on a muttered conversation with himself in a rapid sort of way.

Seeming to feel that the situation was one to which he could not do justice in Bingo-cum-Maloney Anglo-American, he had fallen back on his native tongue. Words like "*marmiton de Domange,*" "*pignouf,*" "*hurluberlu*" and "*roustisseur*" were fluttering from him like bats out of a barn. Lost on me, of course, because, though I sweated a bit at the Gallic language during that Cannes visit, I'm still more or less in the Esker-vous-avez stage. I regretted this, for they sounded good.

I assisted Gussie down the stairs. A cooler thinker than Aunt Dahlia, I had already guessed the hidden springs and motives which had led him to the roof. Where she had seen only a cockeyed reveller indulging himself in a drunken prank or whimsy, I had spotted the hunted fawn.

"Was Tuppy after you?" I asked sympathetically.

What I believe is called a *frisson* shook him.

"He nearly got me on the top landing. I shinned out through a passage window and scrambled along a sort of ledge."

"That baffled him, what?"

"Yes. But then I found I had stuck. The roof sloped down in all directions. I couldn't go back. I had to go on, crawling along this ledge. And then I found myself looking down the skylight. Who was that chap?"

"That was Anatole, Aunt Dahlia's chef."

"French?"

"To the core."

"That explains why I couldn't make him understand. What asses these Frenchmen are. They don't seem able to grasp the simplest thing. You'd have thought if a chap saw a chap on a skylight, the chap would realize the chap wanted to be let in. But no, he just stood there."

"Waving a few fists."

"Yes. Silly idiot. Still, here I am."

"Here you are, yes—for the moment."

"Eh?"

"I was thinking that Tuppy is probably lurking somewhere."

He leaped like a lamb in springtime.

"What shall I do?"

I considered this.

"Sneak back to your room and barricade the door. That is the manly policy."

"Suppose that's where he's lurking?"

"In that case, move elsewhere."

But on arrival at the room, it transpired that Tuppy, if anywhere, was infesting some other portion of the house. Gussie shot in, and I heard the key turn. And feeling that there was no more that I could do in that quarter, I returned to the dining-room for further fruit salad and a quiet think. And I had barely filled my plate when the door opened and Aunt Dahlia came in. She sank into a chair, looking a bit shopworn.

"Give me a drink, Bertie."

"What sort?"

"Any sort, so long as it's strong."

Approach Bertram Wooster along these lines, and you catch him at his best. St. Bernard dogs doing the square thing by Alpine travellers could not have bustled about more assiduously. I filled the order, and for some moments nothing was to be heard but the sloshing sound of an aunt restoring her tissues.

"Shove it down, Aunt Dahlia," I said sympathetically. "These things take it out of one, don't they? You've had a toughish time, no doubt, soothing Anatole," I proceeded, helping myself to anchovy paste on toast. "Everything pretty smooth now, I trust?"

She gazed at me in a long, lingering sort of way, her brow wrinkled as if in thought.

"Attila," she said at length. "That's the name. Attila, the Hun."

"Eh?"

"I was trying to think who you reminded me of. Somebody who went about strewing ruin and desolation and breaking up homes which, until he came along, had been happy and peaceful. Attila is the man. It's amazing." she said, drinking me in once more. "To look at you, one would think you were just an ordinary sort of amiable idiot—certifiable, perhaps, but quite harmless. Yet, in reality, you are worse a scourge than the Black Death. I tell you, Bertie, when I contemplate you I seem to come up against all the underlying sorrow and horror of life with such a thud that I feel as if I had walked into a lamp post."

Pained and surprised, I would have spoken, but the stuff I had thought was anchovy paste had turned out to be something far more gooey and adhesive. It seemed to wrap itself round the tongue and impede utterance like a gag. And while I was still endeavouring to clear the vocal cords for action, she went on:

"Do you realize what you started when you sent that Spink-Bottle man down here? As regards his getting blotto and turning the prize-giving ceremonies at Market Snodsbury Grammar School into a sort of two-reel comic film, I will say nothing, for frankly I enjoyed it. But when he comes leering at Anatole through skylights, just after I had with infinite pains and tact induced him to withdraw his notice, and makes him so temperamental that he won't hear of staying on after tomorrow——"

The paste stuff gave way. I was able to speak:

"What?"

"Yes, Anatole goes tomorrow, and I suppose poor old Tom will have indigestion for the rest of his life. And that is not all. I have just seen Angela, and she tells me she is engaged to this Bottle."

"Temporarily, yes," I had to admit.

"Temporarily be blowed. She's definitely engaged to him and talks with a sort of hideous coolness of getting married in October. So there it is. If the prophet Job were to walk into the room at this moment, I could sit swapping hard-luck stories with him till bedtime. Not that Job was in my class."

"He had boils."

"Well, what are boils?"

"Dashed painful, I understand."

"Nonsense. I'd take all the boils on the market in exchange for my troubles. Can't you realize the position? I've lost the best cook to England. My husband, poor soul, will probably die of dyspepsia. And my only daughter, for whom I had dreamed such a wonderful future, is engaged to be married to an inebriated newt fancier. And you talk about boils!"

I corrected her on a small point:

"I don't absolutely talk about boils. I merely mentioned that Job had them. Yes, I agree with you, Aunt Dahlia, that things are not looking too oojah-cum-spiff at the moment, but be of good cheer. A Wooster is seldom baffled for more than the nonce."

"You rather expect to be coming along shortly with another of your schemes?"

"At any minute."

She sighed resignedly.

"I thought as much. Well, it needed but this. I don't see how things could possibly be worse than they are, but no doubt you will succeed in making them so. Your genius and insight will find the way. Carry on, Bertie. Yes, carry on. I am past caring now. I shall even find a faint interest in seeing into what darker and profounder abysses of hell you can plunge this home. Go to it, lad.... What's that stuff you're eating?"

"I find it a little difficult to classify. Some sort of paste on toast.

Rather like glue flavoured with beef extract."

"Gimme," said Aunt Dahlia listlessly.

"Be careful how you chew," I advised. "It sticketh closer than a brother.... Yes, Jeeves?"

The man had materialized on the carpet. Absolutely noiseless, as usual.

"A note for you, sir."

"A note for me, Jeeves?"

"A note for you, sir."

"From whom, Jeeves?"

"From Miss Bassett, sir."

"From whom, Jeeves?"

"From Miss Bassett, sir."

"From Miss Bassett, Jeeves?"

"From Miss Bassett, sir."

At this point, Aunt Dahlia, who had taken one nibble at her whatever-it-was-on-toast and laid it down, begged us—a little fretfully, I thought—for heaven's sake to cut out the cross-talk vaudeville stuff, as she had enough to bear already without having to listen to us doing our imitation of the Two Macs. Always willing to oblige, I dismissed Jeeves with a nod, and he flickered for a moment and was gone. Many a spectre would have been less slippy.

"But what," I mused, toying with the envelope, "can this female be writing to me about?"

"Why not open the damn thing and see?"

"A very excellent idea," I said, and did so.

"And if you are interested in my movements," proceeded Aunt Dahlia, heading for the door, "I propose to go to my room, do some Yogi deep breathing, and try to forget."

"Quite," I said absently, skimming p. l. And then, as I turned over, a sharp howl broke from my lips, causing Aunt Dahlia to shy like a startled mustang.

"Don't do it!" she exclaimed, quivering in every limb.

"Yes, but dash it——"

"What a pest you are, you miserable object," she sighed. "I remember years ago, when you were in your cradle, being left alone with you one day and you nearly swallowed your rubber comforter and started turning purple. And I, ass that I was, took it out and saved your life. Let me tell you, young Bertie, it will go very hard with you if you ever swallow a rubber comforter again when only I am by to aid."

"But, dash it!" I cried. "Do you know what's happened? Madeline Bassett says she's going to marry me!"

"I hope it keeps fine for you," said the relative, and passed from the room looking like something out of an Edgar Allan Poe story.

-21-

I don't suppose I was looking so dashed unlike something out of an Edgar Allan Poe story myself, for, as you can readily imagine, the news item which I have just recorded had got in amongst me properly. If the Bassett, in the belief that the Wooster heart had long been hers and was waiting ready to be scooped in on demand, had decided to take up her option, I should, as a man of honour and sensibility, have no choice but to come across and kick in. The matter was obviously not one that could be straightened out with a curt *nolle prosequi*. All the evidence, therefore, seemed to point to the fact that the doom had come upon me and, what was more, had come to stay.

And yet, though it would be idle to pretend that my grip on the situation was quite the grip I would have liked it to be, I did not despair of arriving at a solution. A lesser man, caught in this awful snare, would no doubt have thrown in the towel at once and ceased to struggle; but the whole point about the Woosters is that they are not lesser men.

By way of a start, I read the note again. Not that I had any hope that a second perusal would enable me to place a different construction on its contents, but it helped to fill in while the brain was limbering up. I then, to assist thought, had another go at the fruit salad, and in addition ate a slice of sponge cake. And it was as I passed on to the cheese that the machinery started working. I saw what had to be done.

To the question which had been exercising the mind—viz., can

Bertram cope?—I was now able to reply with a confident "Absolutely."

The great wheeze on these occasions of dirty work at the crossroads is not to lose your head but to keep cool and try to find the ringleaders. Once find the ringleaders, and you know where you are.

The ringleader here was plainly the Bassett. It was she who had started the whole imbroglio by chucking Gussie, and it was clear that before anything could be done to solve and clarify, she must be induced to revise her views and take him on again. This would put Angela back into circulation, and that would cause Tuppy to simmer down a bit, and then we could begin to get somewhere.

I decided that as soon as I had had another morsel of cheese I would seek this Bassett out and be pretty eloquent.

And at this moment in she came. I might have foreseen that she would be turning up shortly. I mean to say, hearts may ache, but if they know that there is a cold collation set out in the dining-room, they are pretty sure to come popping in sooner or later.

Her eyes, as she entered the room, were fixed on the salmon mayonnaise, and she would no doubt have made a bee-line for it and started getting hers, had I not, in the emotion of seeing her, dropped a glass of the best with which I was endeavouring to bring about a calmer frame of mind. The noise caused her to turn, and for an instant embarrassment supervened. A slight flush mantled the cheek, and the eyes popped a bit.

"Oh!" she said.

I have always found that there is nothing that helps to ease you over one of these awkward moments like a spot of stage business. Find something to do with your hands, and it's half the battle. I grabbed a plate and hastened forward.

"A touch of salmon?"

"Thank you."

"With a suspicion of salad?"

"If you please."

"And to drink? Name the poison."

"I think I would like a little orange juice."

She gave a gulp. Not at the orange juice, I don't mean, because she hadn't got it yet, but at all the tender associations those two words provoked. It was as if someone had mentioned spaghetti to the relict of an Italian organ-grinder. Her face flushed a deeper shade, she registered anguish, and I saw that it was no longer within the sphere of practical politics to try to confine the conversation to neutral topics like cold boiled salmon.

So did she, I imagine, for when I, as a preliminary to getting down to brass tacks, said "Er," she said "Er," too, simultaneously, the brace of "Ers" clashing in mid-air.

"I'm sorry."

"I beg your pardon."

"You were saying———"

"You were saying———"

"No, please go on."

"Oh, right-ho."

I straightened the tie, my habit when in this girl's society, and had at it:

"With reference to yours of even date———"

She flushed again, and took a rather strained forkful of salmon.

"You got my note?"

"Yes, I got your note."

"I gave it to Jeeves to give it to you."

"Yes, he gave it to me. That's how I got it."

There was another silence. And as she was plainly shrinking from talking turkey, I was reluctantly compelled to do so. I mean, somebody had got to. Too dashed silly, a male and female in our position simply standing eating salmon and cheese at one another without a word.

"Yes, I got it all right."

"I see. You got it."

"Yes, I got it. I've just been reading it. And what I was rather wanting to ask you, if we happened to run into each other, was— well, what about it?"

"What about it?"

"That's what I say: What about it?"

"But it was quite clear."

"Oh, quite. Perfectly clear. Very well expressed and all that. But—

I mean—Well, I mean, deeply sensible of the honour, and so forth—but—— Well, dash it!"

She had polished off her salmon, and now put the plate down.

"Fruit salad?"

"No, thank you."

"Spot of pie?"

"No, thanks."

"One of those glue things on toast?"

"No, thank you."

She took a cheese straw. I found a cold egg which I had overlooked. Then I said "I mean to say" just as she said "I think I know", and there was another collision.

"I beg your pardon."

"I'm sorry."

"Do go on."

"No, you go on."

I waved my cold egg courteously, to indicate that she had the floor, and she started again:

"I think I know what you are trying to say. You are surprised."

"Yes."

"You are thinking of——"

"Exactly."

"—Mr. Fink-Nottle."

"The very man."

"You find what I have done hard to understand."

"Absolutely."

"I don't wonder."

"I do."

"And yet it is quite simple."

She took another cheese straw. She seemed to like cheese straws.

"Quite simple, really. I want to make you happy."

"Dashed decent of you."

"I am going to devote the rest of my life to making you happy."

"A very matey scheme."

"I can at least do that. But—may I be quite frank with you, Bertie?"

"Oh, rather."

"Then I must tell you this. I am fond of you. I will marry you. I will do my best to make you a good wife. But my affection for you can never be the flamelike passion I felt for Augustus."

"Just the very point I was working round to. There, as you say, is the snag. Why not chuck the whole idea of hitching up with me? Wash it out altogether. I mean, if you love old Gussie——"

"No longer."

"Oh, come."

"No. What happened this afternoon has killed my love. A smear of ugliness has been drawn across a thing of beauty, and I can never feel towards him as I did."

I saw what she meant, of course. Gussie had bunged his heart at her feet; she had picked it up, and, almost immediately after doing so, had discovered that he had been stewed to the eyebrows all the time. The shock must have been severe. No girl likes to feel that a chap has got to be thoroughly plastered before he can ask her to marry him. It wounds the pride.

Nevertheless, I persevered.

"But have you considered," I said, "that you may have got a wrong line on Gussie's performance this afternoon? Admitted that all the evidence points to a more sinister theory, what price him simply having got a touch of the sun? Chaps do get touches of the sun, you know, especially when the weather's hot."

She looked at me, and I saw that she was putting in a bit of the old drenched-irises stuff.

"It was like you to say that, Bertie. I respect you for it."

"Oh, no."

"Yes. You have a splendid, chivalrous soul."

"Not a bit."

"Yes, you have. You remind me of Cyrano."

"Who?"

"Cyrano de Bergerac."

"The chap with the nose?"

"Yes."

I can't say I was any too pleased. I felt the old beak furtively. It was a bit on the prominent side, perhaps, but, dash it, not in the Cyrano class. It began to look as if the next thing this girl would do would be to compare me to Schnozzle Durante.

"He loved, but pleaded another's cause."

"Oh, I see what you mean now."

"I like you for that, Bertie. It was fine of you—fine and big. But it is no use. There are things which kill love. I can never forget Augustus, but my love for him is dead. I will be your wife."

Well, one has to be civil.

"Right ho," I said. "Thanks awfully."

Then the dialogue sort of poofed out once more, and we stood eating cheese straws and cold eggs respectively in silence. There seemed to exist some little uncertainty as to what the next move was.

Fortunately, before embarrassment could do much more supervening, Angela came in, and this broke up the meeting. Then Bassett announced our engagement, and Angela kissed her and said she hoped she would be very, very happy, and the Bassett kissed her and said she hoped she would be very, very happy with Gussie, and Angela said she was sure she would, because Augustus was such a dear, and the Bassett kissed her again, and Angela kissed her again and, in a word, the whole thing got so bally feminine that I was glad to edge away.

I would have been glad to do so, of course, in any case, for if ever there was a moment when it was up to Bertram to think, and think hard, this moment was that moment.

It was, it seemed to me, the end. Not even on the occasion, some years earlier, when I had inadvertently become betrothed to Tuppy's frightful Cousin Honoria, had I experienced a deeper sense of being waist high in the gumbo and about to sink without trace. I wandered out into the garden, smoking a tortured gasper, with the iron well embedded in the soul. And I had fallen into a sort of trance, trying to picture what it would be like having the Bassett on the premises for the rest of my life and at the same time, if you follow me, trying not to picture what it would be like, when I charged into something which might have been a tree, but was not—being, in point of fact, Jeeves.

"I beg your pardon, sir," he said. "I should have moved to one side."

I did not reply. I stood looking at him in silence. For the sight of him had opened up a new line of thought.

This Jeeves, now, I reflected. I had formed the opinion that he had lost his grip and was no longer the force he had been, but was it not possible, I asked myself, that I might be mistaken? Start him off exploring avenues and might he not discover one through which I would be enabled to sneak off to safety, leaving no hard feelings behind? I found myself answering that it was quite on the cards that he might.

After all, his head still bulged out at the back as of old. One noted in the eyes the same intelligent glitter.

Mind you, after what had passed between us in the matter of that white mess-jacket with the brass buttons, I was not prepared absolutely to hand over to the man. I would, of course, merely take him into consultation. But, recalling some of his earlier triumphs—the Sipperley Case, the Episode of My Aunt Agatha and the Dog McIntosh, and the smoothly handled Affair of Uncle George and The Barmaid's Niece were a few that sprang to my mind—I felt justified at least in offering him the opportunity of coming to the aid of the young master in his hour of peril.

But before proceeding further, there was one thing that had got to be understood between us, and understood clearly.

"Jeeves," I said, "a word with you."

"Sir?"

"I am up against it a bit, Jeeves."

"I am sorry to hear that, sir. Can I be of any assistance?"

"Quite possibly you can, if you have not lost your grip. Tell me frankly, Jeeves, are you in pretty good shape mentally?"

"Yes, sir."

"Still eating plenty of fish?"

"Yes, sir."

"Then it may be all right. But there is just one point before I begin. In the past, when you have contrived to extricate self or some pal from some little difficulty, you have frequently shown a disposition to take advantage of my gratitude to gain some private end. Those purple socks, for instance. Also the plus fours and the Old Etonian spats. Choosing your moment with subtle cunning, you came to me when I was weakened by relief and got me to get rid of them. And what I am saying now is that if you are successful on the present occasion there must be no rot of that description about that mess-jacket of mine."

"Very good, sir."

"You will not come to me when all is over and ask me to jettison the jacket?"

"Certainly not, sir."

"On that understanding then, I will carry on. Jeeves, I'm engaged."

"I hope you will be very happy, sir."

"Don't be an ass. I'm engaged to Miss Bassett."

"Indeed, sir? I was not aware——"

"Nor was I. It came as a complete surprise. However, there it is. The official intimation was in that note you brought me."

"Odd, sir."

"What is?"

"Odd, sir, that the contents of that note should have been as you describe. It seemed to me that Miss Bassett, when she handed me the communication, was far from being in a happy frame of mind."

"She is far from being in a happy frame of mind. You don't suppose she really wants to marry me, do you? Pshaw, Jeeves! Can't you see that this is simply another of those bally gestures which are rapidly rendering Brinkley Court a hell for man and beast? Dash all gestures, is my view."

"Yes, sir."

"Well, what's to be done?"

"You feel that Miss Bassett, despite what has occurred, still retains a fondness for Mr. Fink-Nottle, sir?"

"She's pining for him."

"In that case, sir, surely the best plan would be to bring about a reconciliation between them."

"How? You see. You stand silent and twiddle the fingers. You are stumped."

"No, sir. If I twiddled my fingers, it was merely to assist thought."

"Then continue twiddling."

"It will not be necessary, sir."

"You don't mean you've got a bite already?"

215

"Yes, sir."

"You astound me, Jeeves. Let's have it."

"The device which I have in mind is one that I have already mentioned to you, sir."

"When did you ever mention any device to me?"

"If you will throw your mind back to the evening of our arrival, sir. You were good enough to inquire of me if I had any plan to put forward with a view to bringing Miss Angela and Mr. Glossop together, and I ventured to suggest——"

"Good Lord! Not the old fire-alarm thing?"

"Precisely, sir."

"You're still sticking to that?"

"Yes, sir."

It shows how much the ghastly blow I had received had shaken me when I say that, instead of dismissing the proposal with a curt "Tchah!" or anything like that, I found myself speculating as to whether there might not be something in it, after all.

When he had first mooted this fire-alarm scheme of his, I had sat upon it, if you remember, with the maximum of promptitude and vigour. "Rotten" was the adjective I had employed to describe it, and you may recall that I mused a bit sadly, considering the idea conclusive proof of the general breakdown of a once fine mind. But now it somehow began to look as if it might have possibilities. The fact of the matter was that I had about reached the stage where I was prepared to try anything once, however goofy.

"Just run through that wheeze again, Jeeves," I said thoughtfully. "I remember thinking it cuckoo, but it may be that I missed some of the finer shades."

"Your criticism of it at the time, sir, was that it was too elaborate, but I do not think it is so in reality. As I see it, sir, the occupants of the house, hearing the fire bell ring, will suppose that a conflagration has broken out."

I nodded. One could follow the train of thought.

"Yes, that seems reasonable."

"Whereupon Mr. Glossop will hasten to save Miss Angela, while Mr. Fink-Nottle performs the same office for Miss Bassett."

"Is that based on psychology?"

"Yes, sir. Possibly you may recollect that it was an axiom of the

216

late Sir Arthur Conan Doyle's fictional detective, Sherlock Holmes, that the instinct of everyone, upon an alarm of fire, is to save the object dearest to them."

"It seems to me that there is a grave danger of seeing Tuppy come out carrying a steak-and-kidney pie, but resume, Jeeves, resume. You think that this would clean everything up?"

"The relations of the two young couples could scarcely continue distant after such an occurrence, sir."

"Perhaps you're right. But, dash it, if we go ringing fire bells in the night watches, shan't we scare half the domestic staff into fits? There is one of the housemaids—Jane, I believe—who already skips like the high hills if I so much as come on her unexpectedly round a corner."

"A neurotic girl, sir, I agree. I have noticed her. But by acting promptly we should avoid such a contingency. The entire staff, with the exception of Monsieur Anatole, will be at the ball at Kingham Manor tonight."

"Of course. That just shows the condition this thing has reduced me to. Forget my own name next. Well, then, let's just try to envisage. Bong goes the bell. Gussie rushes and grabs the Bassett.... Wait. Why shouldn't she simply walk downstairs?"

"You are overlooking the effect of sudden alarm on the feminine temperament, sir."

"That's true."

"Miss Bassett's impulse, I would imagine, sir, would be to leap from her window."

"Well, that's worse. We don't want her spread out in a sort of *purée* on the lawn. It seems to me that the flaw in this scheme of yours, Jeeves, is that it's going to litter the garden with mangled corpses."

"No, sir. You will recall that Mr. Travers's fear of burglars has caused him to have stout bars fixed to all the windows."

"Of course, yes. Well, it sounds all right," I said, though still a bit doubtfully. "Quite possibly it may come off. But I have a feeling that it will slip up somewhere. However, I am in no position to cavil at even a 100 to 1 shot. I will adopt this policy of yours, Jeeves, though, as I say, with misgivings. At what hour would you suggest bonging the bell?"

"Not before midnight, sir."

"That is to say, some time after midnight."

"Yes, sir."

"Right-ho, then. At 12.30 on the dot, I will bong."

"Very good, sir."

-22-

I Don't know why it is, but there's something about the rural districts after dark that always has a rummy effect on me. In London I can stay out till all hours and come home with the milk without a tremor, but put me in the garden of a country house after the strength of the company has gone to roost and the place is shut up, and a sort of goose-fleshy feeling steals over me. The night wind stirs the tree-tops, twigs crack, bushes rustle, and before I know where I am, the morale has gone phut and I'm expecting the family ghost to come sneaking up behind me, making groaning noises. Dashed unpleasant, the whole thing, and if you think it improves matters to know that you are shortly about to ring the loudest fire bell in England and start an all-hands-to-the-pumps panic in that quiet, darkened house, you err.

I knew all about the Brinkley Court fire bell. The dickens of a row it makes. Uncle Tom, in addition to not liking burglars, is a bloke who has always objected to the idea of being cooked in his sleep, so when he bought the place he saw to it that the fire bell should be something that might give you heart failure, but which you couldn't possibly mistake for the drowsy chirping of a sparrow in the ivy.

When I was a kid and spent my holidays at Brinkley, we used to have fire drills after closing time, and many is the night I've had it jerk me out of the dreamless like the Last Trump.

I confess that the recollection of what this bell could do when it buckled down to it gave me pause as I stood that night at 12.30 p.m. prompt beside the outhouse where it was located. The sight of the rope against the whitewashed wall and the thought of the bloodsome uproar which was about to smash the peace of the night into hash served to deepen that rummy feeling to which I have alluded.

Moreover, now that I had had time to meditate upon it, I was more than ever defeatist about this scheme of Jeeves's.

Jeeves seemed to take it for granted that Gussie and Tuppy, faced with a hideous fate, would have no thought beyond saving the Bassett and Angela.

I could not bring myself to share his sunny confidence.

I mean to say, I know how moments when they're faced with a hideous fate affect chaps. I remember Freddie Widgeon, one of the most chivalrous birds in the Drones, telling me how there was an alarm of fire once at a seaside hotel where he was staying and, so far from rushing about saving women, he was down the escape within ten seconds of the kick-off, his mind concerned with but one thing— viz., the personal well-being of F. Widgeon.

As far as any idea of doing the delicately nurtured a bit of good went, he tells me, he was prepared to stand underneath and catch them in blankets, but no more.

Why, then, should this not be so with Augustus Fink-Nottle and Hildebrand Glossop?

Such were my thoughts as I stood toying with the rope, and I believe I should have turned the whole thing up, had it not been that at this juncture there floated into my mind a picture of the Bassett hearing that bell for the first time. Coming as a wholly new experience, it would probably startle her into a decline.

And so agreeable was this reflection that I waited no longer, but seized the rope, braced the feet and snapped into it.

Well, as I say, I hadn't been expecting that bell to hush things up to any great extent. Nor did it. The last time I had heard it, I had been in my room on the other side of the house, and even so it had hoiked me out of bed as if something had exploded under me. Standing close to it like this, I got the full force and meaning of the thing, and I've never heard anything like it in my puff.

I rather enjoy a bit of noise, as a general rule. I remember Cats-meat Potter-Pirbright bringing a police rattle into the Drones one night and loosing it off behind my chair, and I just lay back and closed my eyes with a pleasant smile, like someone in a box at the opera. And the same applies to the time when my Aunt Agatha's son, young Thos., put a match to the parcel of Guy Fawkes Day fireworks to see what would happen.

But the Brinkley Court fire bell was too much for me. I gave about half a dozen tugs, and then, feeling that enough was enough, sauntered round to the front lawn to ascertain what solid results had been achieved.

Brinkley Court had given of its best. A glance told me that we were playing to capacity. The eye, roving to and fro, noted here Uncle Tom in a purple dressing gown, there Aunt Dahlia in the old blue and yellow. It also fell upon Anatole, Tuppy, Gussie, Angela, the Bassett and Jeeves, in the order named. There they all were, present and correct.

But—and this was what caused me immediate concern—I could detect no sign whatever that there had been any rescue work going on.

What I had been hoping, of course, was to see Tuppy bending solicitously over Angela in one corner, while Gussie fanned the Bassett with a towel in the other. Instead of which, the Bassett was one of the group which included Aunt Dahlia and Uncle Tom and seemed to be busy trying to make Anatole see the bright side, while Angela and Gussie were, respectively, leaning against the sundial with a peeved look and sitting on the grass rubbing a barked shin. Tuppy was walking up and down the path, all by himself.

A disturbing picture, you will admit. It was with a rather imperious gesture that I summoned Jeeves to my side.

"Well, Jeeves?"

"Sir?"

I eyed him sternly. "Sir?" forsooth!

"It's no good saying 'Sir?' Jeeves. Look round you. See for yourself. Your scheme has proved a bust."

"Certainly it would appear that matters have not arranged themselves quite as we anticipated, sir."

"We?"

"As I had anticipated, sir."

"That's more like it. Didn't I tell you it would be a flop?"

"I remember that you did seem dubious, sir."

"Dubious is no word for it, Jeeves. I hadn't a scrap of faith in the idea from the start. When you first mooted it, I said it was rotten, and

I was right. I'm not blaming you, Jeeves. It is not your fault that you have sprained your brain. But after this—forgive me if I hurt your feelings, Jeeves——I shall know better than to allow you to handle any but the simplest and most elementary problems. It is best to be candid about this, don't you think? Kindest to be frank and straightforward?"

"Certainly, sir."

"I mean, the surgeon's knife, what?"

"Precisely, sir."

"I consider——"

"If you will pardon me for interrupting you, sir, I fancy Mrs. Travers is endeavouring to attract your attention."

And at this moment a ringing "Hoy!" which could have proceeded only from the relative in question, assured me that his view was correct.

"Just step this way a moment, Attila, if you don't mind," boomed that well-known—and under certain conditions, well-loved—voice, and I moved over.

I was not feeling unmixedly at my ease. For the first time it was beginning to steal upon me that I had not prepared a really good story in support of my questionable behaviour in ringing fire bells at such an hour, and I have known Aunt Dahlia to express herself with a hearty freedom upon far smaller provocation.

She exhibited, however, no signs of violence. More a sort of frozen calm, if you know what I mean. You could see that she was a woman who had suffered.

"Well, Bertie, dear," she said, "here we all are."

"Quite," I replied guardedly.

"Nobody missing, is there?"

"I don't think so."

"Splendid. So much healthier for us out in the open like this than frowsting in bed. I had just dropped off when you did your bell-ringing act. For it was you, my sweet child, who rang that bell, was it not?"

"I did ring the bell, yes."

"Any particular reason, or just a whim?"

"I thought there was a fire."

"What gave you that impression, dear?"

"I thought I saw flames."

"Where, darling? Tell Aunt Dahlia."

"In one of the windows."

"I see. So we have all been dragged out of bed and scared rigid because you have been seeing things."

Here Uncle Tom made a noise like a cork coming out of a bottle, and Anatole, whose moustache had hit a new low, said something about "some apes" and, if I am not mistaken, a "*rogommier*"— whatever that is.

"I admit I was mistaken. I am sorry."

"Don't apologize, ducky. Can't you see how pleased we all are? What were you doing out here, anyway?"

"Just taking a stroll."

"I see. And are you proposing to continue your stroll?"

"No, I think I'll go in now."

"That's fine. Because I was thinking of going in, too, and I don't believe I could sleep knowing you were out here giving rein to that powerful imagination of yours. The next thing that would happen would be that you would think you saw a pink elephant sitting on the drawing-room window-sill and start throwing bricks at it.... Well, come on, Tom, the entertainment seems to be over.... But wait. The newt king wishes a word with us.... Yes, Mr. Fink-Nottle?"

Gussie, as he joined our little group, seemed upset about something.

"I say!"

"Say on, Augustus."

"I say, what are we going to do?"

"Speaking for myself, I intend to return to bed."

"But the door's shut."

"What door?"

"The front door. Somebody must have shut it."

"Then I shall open it."

"But it won't open."

"Then I shall try another door."

"But all the other doors are shut."

"What? Who shut them?"

"I don't know."

I advanced a theory!

"The wind?"

Aunt Dahlia's eyes met mine.

"Don't try me too high," she begged. "Not now, precious." And, indeed, even as I spoke, it did strike me that the night was pretty still.

Uncle Tom said we must get in through a window. Aunt Dahlia sighed a bit.

"How? Could Lloyd George do it, could Winston do it, could Baldwin do it? No. Not since you had those bars of yours put on."

"Well, well, well. God bless my soul, ring the bell, then."

"The fire bell?"

"The door bell."

"To what end, Thomas? There's nobody in the house. The servants are all at Kingham."

"But, confound it all, we can't stop out here all night."

"Can't we? You just watch us. There is nothing—literally nothing—which a country house party can't do with Attila here operating on the premises. Seppings presumably took the back-door key with him. We must just amuse ourselves till he comes back."

Tuppy made a suggestion:

"Why not take out one of the cars and drive over to Kingham and get the key from Seppings?"

It went well. No question about that. For the first time, a smile lit up Aunt Dahlia's drawn face. Uncle Tom grunted approvingly. Anatole said something in Provençal that sounded complimentary. And I thought I detected even on Angela's map a slight softening.

"A very excellent idea," said Aunt Dahlia. "One of the best. Nip round to the garage at once."

After Tuppy had gone, some extremely flattering things were said about his intelligence and resource, and there was a disposition to draw rather invidious comparisons between him and Bertram. Painful for me, of course, but the ordeal didn't last long, for it couldn't have been more than five minutes before he was with us again.

Tuppy seemed perturbed.

"I say, it's all off."

"Why?"

"The garage is locked."

"Unlock it."

"I haven't the key."

"Shout, then, and wake Waterbury."

"Who's Waterbury?"

"The chauffeur, ass. He sleeps over the garage."

"But he's gone to the dance at Kingham."

It was the final wallop. Until this moment, Aunt Dahlia had been able to preserve her frozen calm. The dam now burst. The years rolled away from her, and she was once more the Dahlia Wooster of the old yoicks-and-tantivy days—the emotional, free-speaking girl who had so often risen in her stirrups to yell derogatory personalities at people who were heading hounds.

"Curse all dancing chauffeurs! What on earth does a chauffeur want to dance for? I mistrusted that man from the start. Something told me he was a dancer. Well, this finishes it. We're out here till breakfast-time. If those blasted servants come back before eight o'clock, I shall be vastly surprised. You won't get Seppings away from a dance till you throw him out. I know him. The jazz'll go to his head, and he'll stand clapping and demanding encores till his hands blister. Damn all dancing butlers! What is Brinkley Court? A respectable English country house or a crimson dancing school? One might as well be living in the middle of the Russian Ballet. Well, all right. If we must stay out here, we must. We shall all be frozen stiff, except"— here she directed at me not one of her friendliest glances——"except dear old Attila, who is, I observe, well and warmly clad. We will resign ourselves to the prospect of freezing to death like the Babes in the Wood, merely expressing a dying wish that our old pal Attila will see that we are covered with leaves. No doubt he will also toll that fire bell of his as a mark of respect—And what might you want, my good man?"

She broke off, and stood glaring at Jeeves. During the latter portion of her address, he had been standing by in a respectful manner, endeavouring to catch the speaker's eye.

"If I might make a suggestion, madam."

I am not saying that in the course of our long association I have always found myself able to view Jeeves with approval. There are aspects of his character which have frequently caused coldnesses to arise between us. He is one of those fellows who, if you give them a thingummy, take a what-d'you-call-it. His work is often raw, and he has been known to allude to me as "mentally negligible". More than once, as I have shown, it has been my painful task to squelch in him a tendency to get uppish and treat the young master as a serf or peon.

These are grave defects.

But one thing I have never failed to hand the man. He is magnetic. There is about him something that seems to soothe and hypnotize. To the best of my knowledge, he has never encountered a charging rhinoceros, but should this contingency occur, I have no doubt that the animal, meeting his eye, would check itself in mid-stride, roll over and lie purring with its legs in the air.

At any rate he calmed down Aunt Dahlia, the nearest thing to a charging rhinoceros, in under five seconds. He just stood there looking respectful, and though I didn't time the thing—not having a stop-watch on me—I should say it wasn't more than three seconds and a quarter before her whole manner underwent an astounding change for the better. She melted before one's eyes.

"Jeeves! You haven't got an idea?"

"Yes, madam."

"That great brain of yours has really clicked as ever in the hour of need?"

"Yes, madam."

"Jeeves," said Aunt Dahlia in a shaking voice, "I am sorry I spoke so abruptly. I was not myself. I might have known that you would not come simply trying to make conversation. Tell us this idea of yours, Jeeves. Join our little group of thinkers and let us hear what you have to say. Make yourself at home, Jeeves, and give us the good word. Can you really get us out of this mess?"

"Yes, madam, if one of the gentlemen would be willing to ride a bicycle."

"A bicycle?"

"There is a bicycle in the gardener's shed in the kitchen garden, madam. Possibly one of the gentlemen might feel disposed to ride over to Kingham Manor and procure the back-door key from Mr.

225

Seppings."

"Splendid, Jeeves!"

"Thank you, madam."

"Wonderful!"

"Thank you, madam."

"Attila!" said Aunt Dahlia, turning and speaking in a quiet, authoritative manner.

I had been expecting it. From the very moment those ill-judged words had passed the fellow's lips, I had had a presentiment that a determined effort would be made to elect me as the goat, and I braced myself to resist and obstruct.

And as I was about to do so, while I was in the very act of summoning up all my eloquence to protest that I didn't know how to ride a bike and couldn't possibly learn in the brief time at my disposal, I'm dashed if the man didn't go and nip me in the bud.

"Yes, madam, Mr. Wooster would perform the task admirably. He is an expert cyclist. He has often boasted to me of his triumphs on the wheel."

I hadn't. I hadn't done anything of the sort. It's simply monstrous how one's words get twisted. All I had ever done was to mention to him—casually, just as an interesting item of information, one day in New York when we were watching the six-day bicycle race—that at the age of fourteen, while spending my holidays with a vicar of sorts who had been told off to teach me Latin, I had won the Choir Boys' Handicap at the local school treat.

A different thing from boasting of one's triumphs on the wheel.

I mean, he was a man of the world and must have known that the form of school treats is never of the hottest. And, if I'm not mistaken, I had specifically told him that on the occasion referred to I had received half a lap start and that Willie Punting, the odds-on favourite to whom the race was expected to be a gift, had been forced to retire, owing to having pinched his elder brother's machine without asking the elder brother, and the elder brother coming along just as the pistol went and giving him one on the side of the head and taking it away from him, thus rendering him a scratched-at-the-post non-starter. Yet, from the way he talked, you would have thought I was one of those chaps in sweaters with medals all over them, whose photographs bob up from time to time in the illustrated press on the occasion of their having ridden from Hyde Park Corner to Glasgow in three seconds under the hour, or whatever it is.

And as if this were not bad enough, Tuppy had to shove his oar in.

"That's right," said Tuppy. "Bertie has always been a great cyclist. I remember at Oxford he used to take all his clothes off on bump-supper nights and ride around the quad, singing comic songs. Jolly fast he used to go too."

"Then he can go jolly fast now," said Aunt Dahlia with animation. "He can't go too fast for me. He may also sing comic songs, if he likes.... And if you wish to take your clothes off, Bertie, my lamb, by all means do so. But whether clothed or in the nude, whether singing comic songs or not singing comic songs, get a move on."

I found speech:

"But I haven't ridden for years."

"Then it's high time you began again."

"I've probably forgotten how to ride."

"You'll soon get the knack after you've taken a toss or two. Trial and error. The only way."

"But it's miles to Kingham."

"So the sooner you're off, the better."

"But——"

"Bertie, dear."

"But, dash it——"

"Bertie, darling."

"Yes, but dash it——"

"Bertie, my sweet."

And so it was arranged. Presently I was moving sombrely off through the darkness, Jeeves at my side, Aunt Dahlia calling after me something about trying to imagine myself the man who brought the good news from Ghent to Aix. The first I had heard of the chap.

"So, Jeeves," I said, as we reached the shed, and my voice was cold and bitter, "this is what your great scheme has accomplished! Tuppy, Angela, Gussie and the Bassett not on speaking terms, and self faced with an eight-mile ride——"

"Nine, I believe, sir."

227

"—a nine-mile ride, and another nine-mile ride back."

"I am sorry, sir."

"No good being sorry now. Where is this foul bone-shaker?"

"I will bring it out, sir."

He did so. I eyed it sourly.

"Where's the lamp?"

"I fear there is no lamp, sir."

"No lamp?"

"No, sir."

"But I may come a fearful stinker without a lamp. Suppose I barge into something."

I broke off and eyed him frigidly.

"You smile, Jeeves. The thought amuses you?"

"I beg your pardon, sir. I was thinking of a tale my Uncle Cyril used to tell me as a child. An absurd little story, sir, though I confess that I have always found it droll. According to my Uncle Cyril, two men named Nicholls and Jackson set out to ride to Brighton on a tandem bicycle, and were so unfortunate as to come into collision with a brewer's van. And when the rescue party arrived on the scene of the accident, it was discovered that they had been hurled together with such force that it was impossible to sort them out at all adequately. The keenest eye could not discern which portion of the fragments was Nicholls and which Jackson. So they collected as much as they could, and called it Nixon. I remember laughing very much at that story when I was a child, sir."

I had to pause a moment to master my feelings.

"You did, eh?"

"Yes, sir."

"You thought it funny?"

"Yes, sir."

"And your Uncle Cyril thought it funny?"

"Yes, sir."

"Golly, what a family! Next time you meet your Uncle Cyril, Jeeves, you can tell him from me that his sense of humour is morbid and unpleasant."

"He is dead, sir."

"Thank heaven for that.... Well, give me the blasted machine."

"Very good, sir."

"Are the tyres inflated?"

"Yes, sir."

"The nuts firm, the brakes in order, the sprockets running true with the differential gear?"

"Yes, sir."

"Right ho, Jeeves."

In Tuppy's statement that, when at the University of Oxford, I had been known to ride a bicycle in the nude about the quadrangle of our mutual college, there had been, I cannot deny, a certain amount of substance. Correct, however, though his facts were, so far as they went, he had not told all. What he had omitted to mention was that I had invariably been well oiled at the time, and when in that condition a chap is capable of feats at which in cooler moments his reason would rebel.

Stimulated by the juice, I believe, men have even been known to ride alligators.

As I started now to pedal out into the great world, I was icily sober, and the old skill, in consequence, had deserted me entirely. I found myself wobbling badly, and all the stories I had ever heard of nasty bicycle accidents came back to me with a rush, headed by Jeeves's Uncle Cyril's cheery little anecdote about Nicholls and Jackson.

Pounding wearily through the darkness, I found myself at a loss to fathom the mentality of men like Jeeves's Uncle Cyril. What on earth he could see funny in a disaster which had apparently involved the complete extinction of a human creature—or, at any rate, of half a human creature and half another human creature—was more than I could understand. To me, the thing was one of the most poignant tragedies that had ever been brought to my attention, and I have no doubt that I should have continued to brood over it for quite a time, had my thoughts not been diverted by the sudden necessity of zigzagging sharply in order to avoid a pig in the fairway.

For a moment it looked like being real Nicholls-and-Jackson stuff, but, fortunately, a quick zig on my part, coinciding with an adroit zag on the part of the pig, enabled me to win through, and I continued my ride safe, but with the heart fluttering like a captive bird.

The effect of this narrow squeak upon me was to shake the nerve to the utmost. The fact that pigs were abroad in the night seemed to bring home to me the perilous nature of my enterprise. It set me thinking of all the other things that could happen to a man out and about on a velocipede without a lamp after lighting-up time. In particular, I recalled the statement of a pal of mine that in certain sections of the rural districts goats were accustomed to stray across the road to the extent of their chains, thereby forming about as sound a booby trap as one could well wish.

He mentioned, I remember, the case of a friend of his whose machine got entangled with a goat chain and who was dragged seven miles—like skijoring in Switzerland—so that he was never the same man again. And there was one chap who ran into an elephant, left over from a travelling circus.

Indeed, taking it for all in all, it seemed to me that, with the possible exception of being bitten by sharks, there was virtually no front-page disaster that could not happen to a fellow, once he had allowed his dear ones to override his better judgment and shove him out into the great unknown on a push-bike, and I am not ashamed to confess that, taking it by and large, the amount of quailing I did from this point on was pretty considerable.

However, in respect to goats and elephants, I must say things panned out unexpectedly well.

Oddly enough, I encountered neither. But when you have said that you have said everything, for in every other way the conditions could scarcely have been fouler.

Apart from the ceaseless anxiety of having to keep an eye skinned for elephants, I found myself much depressed by barking dogs, and once I received a most unpleasant shock when, alighting to consult a signpost, I saw sitting on top of it an owl that looked exactly like my Aunt Agatha. So agitated, indeed, had my frame of mind become by this time that I thought at first it was Aunt Agatha, and only when reason and reflection told me how alien to her habits it would be to climb signposts and sit on them, could I pull myself together and overcome the weakness.

In short, what with all this mental disturbance added to the more purely physical anguish in the billowy portions and the calves and ankles, the Bertram Wooster who eventually toppled off at the door of Kingham Manor was a very different Bertram from the gay and insouciant *boulevardier* of Bond Street and Piccadilly.

Even to one unaware of the inside facts, it would have been evident that Kingham Manor was throwing its weight about a bit tonight. Lights shone in the windows, music was in the air, and as I drew nearer my ear detected the sibilant shuffling of the feet of butlers, footmen, chauffeurs, parlourmaids, housemaids, tweenies and, I have no doubt, cooks, who were busily treading the measure. I suppose you couldn't sum it up much better than by saying that there was a sound of revelry by night.

The orgy was taking place in one of the ground-floor rooms which had French windows opening on to the drive, and it was to these French windows that I now made my way. An orchestra was playing something with a good deal of zip to it, and under happier conditions I dare say my feet would have started twitching in time to the melody. But I had sterner work before me than to stand hoofing it by myself on gravel drives.

I wanted that back-door key, and I wanted it instanter.

Scanning the throng within, I found it difficult for a while to spot Seppings. Presently, however, he hove in view, doing fearfully lissom things in mid-floor. I "Hi-Seppings!"-ed a couple of times, but his mind was too much on his job to be diverted, and it was only when the swirl of the dance had brought him within prodding distance of my forefinger that a quick one to the lower ribs enabled me to claim his attention.

The unexpected buffet caused him to trip over his partner's feet, and it was with marked austerity that he turned. As he recognized Bertram, however, coldness melted, to be replaced by astonishment.

"Mr. Wooster!"

I was in no mood for bandying words.

"Less of the 'Mr. Wooster' and more back-door keys," I said curtly. "Give me the key of the back door, Seppings."

He did not seem to grasp the gist.

"The key of the back door, sir?"

"Precisely. The Brinkley Court back-door key."

"But it is at the Court, sir."

I clicked the tongue, annoyed.

"Don't be frivolous, my dear old butler," I said. "I haven't ridden nine miles on a push-bike to listen to you trying to be funny. You've got it in your trousers pocket."

"No, sir. I left it with Mr. Jeeves."

"You did—what?"

"Yes, sir. Before I came away. Mr. Jeeves said that he wished to walk in the garden before retiring for the night. He was to place the key on the kitchen window-sill."

I stared at the man dumbly. His eye was clear, his hand steady. He had none of the appearance of a butler who has had a couple.

"You mean that all this while the key has been in Jeeves's possession?"??

"Yes, sir."

I could speak no more. Emotion had overmastered my voice. I was at a loss and not abreast; but of one thing, it seemed to me, there could be no doubt. For some reason, not to be fathomed now, but most certainly to be gone well into as soon as I had pushed this infernal sewing-machine of mine over those nine miles of lonely, country road and got within striking distance of him, Jeeves had been doing the dirty. Knowing that at any given moment he could have solved the whole situation, he had kept Aunt Dahlia and others roosting out on the front lawn *en déshabille* and, worse still, had stood calmly by and watched his young employer set out on a wholly unnecessary eighteen-mile bicycle ride.

I could scarcely believe such a thing of him. Of his Uncle Cyril, yes. With that distorted sense of humour of his, Uncle Cyril might quite conceivably have been capable of such conduct. But that it should be Jeeves—

I leaped into the saddle and, stifling the cry of agony which rose to the lips as the bruised person touched the hard leather, set out on the homeward journey.

-23-

I remember Jeeves saying on one occasion—I forgot how the subject had arisen—he may simply have thrown the observation out, as he does sometimes, for me to take or leave—that hell hath no fury like a woman scorned. And until tonight I had always felt that there was a lot in it. I had never scorned a woman myself, but Pongo Twistleton once scorned an aunt of his, flatly refusing to meet her son Gerald at Paddington and give him lunch and see him off to school at Waterloo, and he never heard the end of it. Letters were written, he tells me, which had to be seen to be believed. Also two very strong telegrams and a bitter picture post card with a view of the Little Chilbury War Memorial on it.

Until tonight, therefore, as I say, I had never questioned the accuracy of the statement. Scorned women first and the rest nowhere, was how it had always seemed to me.

But tonight I revised my views. If you want to know what hell can really do in the way of furies, look for the chap who has been hornswoggled into taking a long and unnecessary bicycle ride in the dark without a lamp.

Mark that word "unnecessary". That was the part of it that really jabbed the iron into the soul. I mean, if it was a case of riding to the doctor's to save the child with croup, or going off to the local pub to fetch supplies in the event of the cellar having run dry, no one would leap to the handlebars more readily than I. Young Lochinvar, absolutely. But this business of being put through it merely to gratify one's personal attendant's diseased sense of the amusing was a bit too thick, and I chafed from start to finish.

So, what I mean to say, although the providence which watches over good men saw to it that I was enabled to complete the homeward journey unscathed except in the billowy portions, removing from my path all goats, elephants, and even owls that looked like my Aunt Agatha, it was a frowning and jaundiced Bertram who finally came to anchor at the Brinkley Court front door. And when I saw a dark figure emerging from the porch to meet me, I prepared to let myself go and uncork all that was fizzing in the mind.

"Jeeves!" I said.

"It is I, Bertie."

The voice which spoke sounded like warm treacle, and even if I had not recognized it immediately as that of the Bassett, I should have known that it did not proceed from the man I was yearning to confront. For this figure before me was wearing a simple tweed dress and had employed my first name in its remarks. And Jeeves, whatever his moral defects, would never go about in skirts calling me Bertie.

The last person, of course, whom I would have wished to meet after a long evening in the saddle, but I vouchsafed a courteous "What ho!"

There was a pause, during which I massaged the calves. Mine, of course, I mean.

"You got in, then?" I said, in allusion to the change of costume.

"Oh, yes. About a quarter of an hour after you left Jeeves went searching about and found the back-door key on the kitchen window-sill."

"Ha!"

"What?"

"Nothing."

"I thought you said something."

"No, nothing."

And I continued to do so. For at this juncture, as had so often happened when this girl and I were closeted, the conversation once more went blue on us. The night breeze whispered, but not the Bassett. A bird twittered, but not so much as a chirp escaped Bertram. It was perfectly amazing, the way her mere presence seemed to wipe speech from my lips—and mine, for that matter, from hers. It began to look as if our married life together would be rather like twenty years among the Trappist monks.

"Seen Jeeves anywhere?" I asked, eventually coming through.

"Yes, in the dining-room."

"The dining-room?"

"Waiting on everybody. They are having eggs and bacon and champagne.... What did you say?"

I had said nothing—merely snorted. There was something about the thought of these people carelessly revelling at a time when, for all they knew, I was probably being dragged about the countryside by goats or chewed by elephants, that struck home at me like a poisoned dart. It was the sort of thing you read about as having happened just before the French Revolution—the haughty nobles in their castles callously digging in and quaffing while the unfortunate blighters outside were suffering frightful privations.

The voice of the Bassett cut in on these mordant reflections:

"Bertie."

"Hullo!"

Silence.

"Hullo!" I said again.

No response. Whole thing rather like one of those telephone conversations where you sit at your end of the wire saying: "Hullo! Hullo!" unaware that the party of the second part has gone off to tea.

Eventually, however, she came to the surface again:

"Bertie, I have something to say to you."

"What?"

"I have something to say to you."

"I know. I said 'What?'"

"Oh, I thought you didn't hear what I said."

"Yes, I heard what you said, all right, but not what you were going to say."

"Oh, I see."

"Right-ho."

So that was straightened out. Nevertheless, instead of proceeding she took time off once more. She stood twisting the fingers and scratching the gravel with her foot. When finally she spoke, it was to deliver an impressive boost:

"Bertie, do you read Tennyson?"

"Not if I can help."

"You remind me so much of those Knights of the Round Table in the 'Idylls of the King'."

Of course I had heard of them—Lancelot, Galahad and all that lot, but I didn't see where the resemblance came in. It seemed to me that she must be thinking of a couple of other fellows.

"How do you mean?"

"You have such a great heart, such a fine soul. You are so generous, so unselfish, so chivalrous. I have always felt that about you—that you are one of the few really chivalrous men I have ever met."

Well, dashed difficult, of course, to know what to say when

235

someone is giving you the old oil on a scale like that. I muttered an "Oh, yes?" or something on those lines, and rubbed the billowy portions in some embarrassment. And there was another silence, broken only by a sharp howl as I rubbed a bit too hard.

"Bertie."

"Hullo?"

I heard her give a sort of gulp.

"Bertie, will you be chivalrous now?"

"Rather. Only too pleased. How do you mean?"

"I am going to try you to the utmost. I am going to test you as few men have ever been tested. I am going——"

I didn't like the sound of this.

"Well," I said doubtfully, "always glad to oblige, you know, but I've just had the dickens of a bicycle ride, and I'm a bit stiff and sore, especially in the—as I say, a bit stiff and sore. If it's anything to be fetched from upstairs——"

"No, no, you don't understand."

"I don't, quite, no."

"Oh, it's so difficult.... How can I say it?... Can't you guess?"

"No. I'm dashed if I can."

"Bertie—let me go!"

"But I haven't got hold of you."

"Release me!"

"Re——"

And then I suddenly got it. I suppose it was fatigue that had made me so slow to apprehend the nub.

"What?"

I staggered, and the left pedal came up and caught me on the shin. But such was the ecstasy in the soul that I didn't utter a cry.

"Release you?"

"Yes."

I didn't want any confusion on the point.

"You mean you want to call it all off? You're going to hitch up with Gussie, after all?"

"Only if you are fine and big enough to consent."

"Oh, I am."

"I gave you my promise."

"Dash promises."

"Then you really——"

"Absolutely."

"Oh, Bertie!"

She seemed to sway like a sapling. It is saplings that sway, I believe.

"A very parfait knight!" I heard her murmur, and there not being much to say after that, I excused myself on the ground that I had got about two pecks of dust down my back and would like to go and get my maid to put me into something loose.

"You go back to Gussie," I said, "and tell him that all is well."

She gave a sort of hiccup and, darting forward, kissed me on the forehead. Unpleasant, of course, but, as Anatole would say, I can take a few smooths with a rough. The next moment she was legging it for the dining-room, while I, having bunged the bicycle into a bush, made for the stairs.

I need not dwell upon my buckedness. It can be readily imagined. Talk about chaps with the noose round their necks and the hangman about to let her go and somebody galloping up on a foaming horse, waving the reprieve—not in it. Absolutely not in it at all. I don't know that I can give you a better idea of the state of my feelings than by saying that as I started to cross the hall I was conscious of so profound a benevolence toward all created things that I found myself thinking kindly thoughts even of Jeeves.

I was about to mount the stairs when a sudden "What ho!" from my rear caused me to turn. Tuppy was standing in the hall. He had apparently been down to the cellar for reinforcements, for there were a couple of bottles under his arm.

"Hullo, Bertie," he said. "You back?" He laughed amusedly. "You look like the Wreck of the Hesperus. Get run over by a steam-roller or something?"

At any other time I might have found his coarse badinage hard to bear. But such was my uplifted mood that I waved it aside and slipped him the good news.

"Tuppy, old man, the Bassett's going to marry Gussie Fink-Nottle."

"Tough luck on both of them, what?"

"But don't you understand? Don't you see what this means? It means that Angela is once more out of pawn, and you have only to play your cards properly——"

He bellowed rollickingly. I saw now that he was in the pink. As a matter of fact, I had noticed something of the sort directly I met him, but had attributed it to alcoholic stimulant.

"Good Lord! You're right behind the times, Bertie. Only to be expected, of course, if you will go riding bicycles half the night. Angela and I made it up hours ago."

"What?"

"Certainly. Nothing but a passing tiff. All you need in these matters is a little give and take, a bit of reasonableness on both sides. We got together and talked things over. She withdrew my double chin. I conceded her shark. Perfectly simple. All done in a couple of minutes."

"But——"

"Sorry, Bertie. Can't stop chatting with you all night. There is a rather impressive beano in progress in the dining-room, and they are waiting for supplies."

Endorsement was given to this statement by a sudden shout from the apartment named. I recognized—as who would not—Aunt Dahlia's voice:

"Glossop!"

"Hullo?"

"Hurry up with that stuff."

"Coming, coming."

"Well, come, then. Yoicks! Hard for-rard!"

"Tallyho, not to mention tantivy. Your aunt," said Tuppy, "is a bit above herself. I don't know all the facts of the case, but it appears that Anatole gave notice and has now consented to stay on, and also your uncle has given her a cheque for that paper of hers. I didn't get the details, but she is much braced. See you later. I must rush."

To say that Bertram was now definitely nonplussed would be but to state the simple truth. I could make nothing of this. I had left Brinkley Court a stricken home, with hearts bleeding wherever you looked, and I had returned to find it a sort of earthly paradise. It baffled me.

I bathed bewilderedly. The toy duck was still in the soap-dish, but

I was too preoccupied to give it a thought. Still at a loss, I returned to my room, and there was Jeeves. And it is proof of my fogged condish that my first words to him were words not of reproach and stern recrimination but of inquiry:

"I say, Jeeves!"

"Good evening, sir. I was informed that you had returned. I trust you had an enjoyable ride."

At any other moment, a crack like that would have woken the fiend in Bertram Wooster. I barely noticed it. I was intent on getting to the bottom of this mystery.

"But I say, Jeeves, what?"

"Sir?"

"What does all this mean?"

"You refer, sir——"

"Of course I refer. You know what I'm talking about. What has been happening here since I left? The place is positively stiff with happy endings."

"Yes, sir. I am glad to say that my efforts have been rewarded."

"What do you mean, your efforts? You aren't going to try to make out that that rotten fire bell scheme of yours had anything to do with it?"

"Yes, sir."

"Don't be an ass, Jeeves. It flopped."

"Not altogether, sir. I fear, sir, that I was not entirely frank with regard to my suggestion of ringing the fire bell. I had not really anticipated that it would in itself produce the desired results. I had intended it merely as a preliminary to what I might describe as the real business of the evening."

"You gibber, Jeeves."

"No, sir. It was essential that the ladies and gentlemen should be brought from the house, in order that, once out of doors, I could ensure that they remained there for the necessary period of time."

"How do you mean?"

"My plan was based on psychology, sir."

"How?"

"It is a recognized fact, sir, that there is nothing that so satisfactorily unites individuals who have been so unfortunate as to quarrel amongst themselves as a strong mutual dislike for some definite person. In my own family, if I may give a homely illustration, it was a generally accepted axiom that in times of domestic disagreement it was necessary only to invite my Aunt Annie for a visit to heal all breaches between the other members of the household. In the mutual animosity excited by Aunt Annie, those who had become estranged were reconciled almost immediately. Remembering this, it occurred to me that were you, sir, to be established as the person responsible for the ladies and gentlemen being forced to spend the night in the garden, everybody would take so strong a dislike to you that in this common sympathy they would sooner or later come together."

I would have spoken, but he continued:

"And such proved to be the case. All, as you see, sir, is now well. After your departure on the bicycle, the various estranged parties agreed so heartily in their abuse of you that the ice, if I may use the expression, was broken, and it was not long before Mr. Glossop was walking beneath the trees with Miss Angela, telling her anecdotes of your career at the university in exchange for hers regarding your childhood; while Mr. Fink-Nottle, leaning against the sundial, held Miss Bassett enthralled with stories of your schooldays. Mrs. Travers, meanwhile, was telling Monsieur Anatole———"

I found speech.

"Oh?" I said. "I see. And now, I suppose, as the result of this dashed psychology of yours, Aunt Dahlia is so sore with me that it will be years before I can dare to show my face here again—years, Jeeves, during which, night after night, Anatole will be cooking those dinners of his———"

"No, sir. It was to prevent any such contingency that I suggested that you should bicycle to Kingham Manor. When I informed the ladies and gentlemen that I had found the key, and it was borne in upon them that you were having that long ride for nothing, their animosity vanished immediately, to be replaced by cordial amusement. There was much laughter."

"There was, eh?"

"Yes, sir. I fear you may possibly have to submit to a certain amount of good-natured chaff, but nothing more. All, if I may say so, is forgiven, sir."

"Oh?"

"Yes, sir."

I mused awhile.

"You certainly seem to have fixed things."

"Yes, sir."

"Tuppy and Angela are once more betrothed. Also Gussie and the Bassett; Uncle Tom appears to have coughed up that money for *Milady's Boudoir*. And Anatole is staying on."

"Yes, sir."

"I suppose you might say that all's well that ends well."

"Very apt, sir."

I mused again.

"All the same, your methods are a bit rough, Jeeves."

"One cannot make an omelette without breaking eggs, sir."

I started.

"Omelette! Do you think you could get me one?"

"Certainly, sir."

"Together with half a bot. of something?"

"Undoubtedly, sir."

"Do so, Jeeves, and with all speed."

I climbed into bed and sank back against the pillows. I must say that my generous wrath had ebbed a bit. I was aching the whole length of my body, particularly toward the middle, but against this you had to set the fact that I was no longer engaged to Madeline Bassett. In a good cause one is prepared to suffer. Yes, looking at the thing from every angle, I saw that Jeeves had done well, and it was with an approving beam that I welcomed him as he returned with the needful.

He did not check up with this beam. A bit grave, he seemed to me to be looking, and I probed the matter with a kindly query:

"Something on your mind, Jeeves?"

"Yes, sir. I should have mentioned it earlier, but in the evening's disturbance it escaped my memory, I fear I have been remiss, sir."

"Yes, Jeeves?" I said, champing contentedly.

"In the matter of your mess-jacket, sir."

241

A nameless fear shot through me, causing me to swallow a mouthful of omelette the wrong way.

"I am sorry to say, sir, that while I was ironing it this afternoon I was careless enough to leave the hot instrument upon it. I very much fear that it will be impossible for you to wear it again, sir."

One of those old pregnant silences filled the room.

"I am extremely sorry, sir."

For a moment, I confess, that generous wrath of mine came bounding back, hitching up its muscles and snorting a bit through the nose, but, as we say on the Riviera, *à quoi sert-il?* There was nothing to be gained by g.w. now.

We Woosters can bite the bullet. I nodded moodily and speared another slab of omelette.

"Right ho, Jeeves."

"Very good, sir."

MY MAN JEEVES, BY P. G. WODEHOUSE

CONTENTS

LEAVE IT TO JEEVES

Jeeves—my man, you know—is really a most extraordinary chap. So capable. Honestly, I shouldn't know what to do without him. On broader lines he's like those chappies who sit peering sadly over the marble battlements at the Pennsylvania Station in the place marked "Inquiries." You know the Johnnies I mean. You go up to them and say: "When's the next train for Melonsquashville, Tennessee?" and they reply, without stopping to think, "Two-forty-three, track ten, change at San Francisco." And they're right every time. Well, Jeeves gives you just the same impression of omniscience.

As an instance of what I mean, I remember meeting Monty Byng in Bond Street one morning, looking the last word in a grey check suit, and I felt I should never be happy till I had one like it. I dug the address of the tailors out of him, and had them working on the thing inside the hour.

"Jeeves," I said that evening. "I'm getting a check suit like that one of Mr. Byng's."

"Injudicious, sir," he said firmly. "It will not become you."

"What absolute rot! It's the soundest thing I've struck for years."

"Unsuitable for you, sir."

Well, the long and the short of it was that the confounded thing came home, and I put it on, and when I caught sight of myself in the glass I nearly swooned. Jeeves was perfectly right. I looked a cross between a music-hall comedian and a cheap bookie. Yet Monty had looked fine in absolutely the same stuff. These things are just Life's mysteries, and that's all there is to it.

But it isn't only that Jeeves's judgment about clothes is infallible, though, of course, that's really the main thing. The man knows

245

everything. There was the matter of that tip on the "Lincolnshire." I forget now how I got it, but it had the aspect of being the real, red-hot tabasco.

"Jeeves," I said, for I'm fond of the man, and like to do him a good turn when I can, "if you want to make a bit of money have something on Wonderchild for the 'Lincolnshire.'"

He shook his head.

"I'd rather not, sir."

"But it's the straight goods. I'm going to put my shirt on him."

"I do not recommend it, sir. The animal is not intended to win. Second place is what the stable is after."

Perfect piffle, I thought, of course. How the deuce could Jeeves know anything about it? Still, you know what happened. Wonderchild led till he was breathing on the wire, and then Banana Fritter came along and nosed him out. I went straight home and rang for Jeeves.

"After this," I said, "not another step for me without your advice. From now on consider yourself the brains of the establishment."

"Very good, sir. I shall endeavour to give satisfaction."

And he has, by Jove! I'm a bit short on brain myself; the old bean would appear to have been constructed more for ornament than for use, don't you know; but give me five minutes to talk the thing over with Jeeves, and I'm game to advise any one about anything. And that's why, when Bruce Corcoran came to me with his troubles, my first act was to ring the bell and put it up to the lad with the bulging forehead.

"Leave it to Jeeves," I said.

I first got to know Corky when I came to New York. He was a pal of my cousin Gussie, who was in with a lot of people down Washington Square way. I don't know if I ever told you about it, but the reason why I left England was because I was sent over by my Aunt Agatha to try to stop young Gussie marrying a girl on the vaudeville stage, and I got the whole thing so mixed up that I decided that it would be a sound scheme for me to stop on in America for a bit instead of going back and having long cosy chats about the thing with aunt. So I sent Jeeves out to find a decent apartment, and settled down for a bit of exile. I'm bound to say that New York's a topping place to be exiled in. Everybody was awfully good to me, and there seemed to be plenty of things going on, and I'm a wealthy bird, so everything was fine. Chappies introduced me to other chappies, and so on and so forth, and it wasn't long before I knew squads of the right sort, some who rolled in dollars in houses up by the Park, and others who lived with the gas turned down mostly around Washington Square—artists and writers and so forth. Brainy coves.

Corky was one of the artists. A portrait-painter, he called himself, but he hadn't painted any portraits. He was sitting on the side-lines with a blanket over his shoulders, waiting for a chance to get into the game. You see, the catch about portrait-painting—I've looked into the thing a bit—is that you can't start painting portraits till people come along and ask you to, and they won't come and ask you to until you've painted a lot first. This makes it kind of difficult for a chappie. Corky managed to get along by drawing an occasional picture for the comic papers—he had rather a gift for funny stuff when he got a good idea—and doing bedsteads and chairs and things for the advertisements. His principal source of income, however, was derived from biting the ear of a rich uncle—one Alexander Worple, who was in the jute business. I'm a bit foggy as to what jute is, but it's apparently something the populace is pretty keen on, for Mr. Worple had made quite an indecently large stack out of it.

Now, a great many fellows think that having a rich uncle is a pretty soft snap: but, according to Corky, such is not the case. Corky's uncle was a robust sort of cove, who looked like living for ever. He was fifty-one, and it seemed as if he might go to par. It was not this, however, that distressed poor old Corky, for he was not bigoted and had no objection to the man going on living. What Corky kicked at was the way the above Worple used to harry him.

Corky's uncle, you see, didn't want him to be an artist. He didn't think he had any talent in that direction. He was always urging him to chuck Art and go into the jute business and start at the bottom and work his way up. Jute had apparently become a sort of obsession with him. He seemed to attach almost a spiritual importance to it. And what Corky said was that, while he didn't know what they did at the bottom of the jute business, instinct told him that it was something too beastly for words. Corky, moreover, believed in his future as an artist. Some day, he said, he was going to make a hit.

Meanwhile, by using the utmost tact and persuasiveness, he was inducing his uncle to cough up very grudgingly a small quarterly allowance.

He wouldn't have got this if his uncle hadn't had a hobby. Mr. Worple was peculiar in this respect. As a rule, from what I've observed, the American captain of industry doesn't do anything out of business hours. When he has put the cat out and locked up the office for the night, he just relapses into a state of coma from which he emerges only to start being a captain of industry again. But Mr. Worple in his spare time was what is known as an ornithologist. He had written a book called *American Birds*, and was writing another, to be called *More American Birds*. When he had finished that, the presumption was that he would begin a third, and keep on till the supply of American birds gave out. Corky used to go to him about once every three months and let him talk about American birds. Apparently you could do what you liked with old Worple if you gave him his head first on his pet subject, so these little chats used to make Corky's allowance all right for the time being. But it was pretty rotten for the poor chap. There was the frightful suspense, you see, and, apart from that, birds, except when broiled and in the society of a cold bottle, bored him stiff.

To complete the character-study of Mr. Worple, he was a man of extremely uncertain temper, and his general tendency was to think that Corky was a poor chump and that whatever step he took in any direction on his own account, was just another proof of his innate idiocy. I should imagine Jeeves feels very much the same about me.

So when Corky trickled into my apartment one afternoon, shooing a girl in front of him, and said, "Bertie, I want you to meet my fiancée, Miss Singer," the aspect of the matter which hit me first was precisely the one which he had come to consult me about. The very first words I spoke were, "Corky, how about your uncle?"

The poor chap gave one of those mirthless laughs. He was looking anxious and worried, like a man who has done the murder all right but can't think what the deuce to do with the body.

"We're so scared, Mr. Wooster," said the girl. "We were hoping that you might suggest a way of breaking it to him."

Muriel Singer was one of those very quiet, appealing girls who have a way of looking at you with their big eyes as if they thought you were the greatest thing on earth and wondered that you hadn't got on to it yet yourself. She sat there in a sort of shrinking way, looking at me as if she were saying to herself, "Oh, I do hope this great strong man isn't going to hurt me." She gave a fellow a protective kind of feeling, made him want to stroke her hand and say, "There, there, little one!" or words to that effect. She made me feel that there was nothing I wouldn't do for her. She was rather like one of those innocent-tasting American drinks which creep imperceptibly into your system so that, before you know what you're doing, you're starting out to reform the world by force if necessary and pausing on your way to tell the large man in the corner that, if he looks at you like that, you will knock his head off. What I mean is, she made me feel alert and dashing, like a jolly old knight-errant or something of that kind. I felt that I was with her in this thing to the limit.

"I don't see why your uncle shouldn't be most awfully bucked," I said to Corky. "He will think Miss Singer the ideal wife for you."

Corky declined to cheer up.

"You don't know him. Even if he did like Muriel he wouldn't admit it. That's the sort of pig-headed guy he is. It would be a matter of principle with him to kick. All he would consider would be that I had gone and taken an important step without asking his advice, and he would raise Cain automatically. He's always done it."

I strained the old bean to meet this emergency.

"You want to work it so that he makes Miss Singer's acquaintance without knowing that you know her. Then you come along——"

"But how can I work it that way?"

I saw his point. That was the catch.

"There's only one thing to do," I said.

"What's that?"

"Leave it to Jeeves."

And I rang the bell.

"Sir?" said Jeeves, kind of manifesting himself. One of the rummy things about Jeeves is that, unless you watch like a hawk, you very seldom see him come into a room. He's like one of those weird chappies in India who dissolve themselves into thin air and nip through space in a sort of disembodied way and assemble the parts again just where they want them. I've got a cousin who's what they call a Theosophist, and he says he's often nearly worked the thing himself, but couldn't quite bring it off, probably owing to having fed in his boyhood on the flesh of animals slain in anger and pie.

The moment I saw the man standing there, registering respectful attention, a weight seemed to roll off my mind. I felt like a lost child who spots his father in the offing. There was something about him that gave me confidence.

Jeeves is a tallish man, with one of those dark, shrewd faces. His eye gleams with the light of pure intelligence.

"Jeeves, we want your advice."

"Very good, sir."

I boiled down Corky's painful case into a few well-chosen words.

"So you see what it amount to, Jeeves. We want you to suggest some way by which Mr. Worple can make Miss Singer's acquaintance without getting on to the fact that Mr. Corcoran already knows her. Understand?"

"Perfectly, sir."

"Well, try to think of something."

"I have thought of something already, sir."

"You have!"

"The scheme I would suggest cannot fail of success, but it has what may seem to you a drawback, sir, in that it requires a certain financial outlay."

"He means," I translated to Corky, "that he has got a pippin of an idea, but it's going to cost a bit."

Naturally the poor chap's face dropped, for this seemed to dish the whole thing. But I was still under the influence of the girl's melting gaze, and I saw that this was where I started in as a knight-errant.

"You can count on me for all that sort of thing, Corky," I said. "Only too glad. Carry on, Jeeves."

"I would suggest, sir, that Mr. Corcoran take advantage of Mr. Worple's attachment to ornithology."

"How on earth did you know that he was fond of birds?"

"It is the way these New York apartments are constructed, sir. Quite unlike our London houses. The partitions between the rooms are of the flimsiest nature. With no wish to overhear, I have sometimes heard Mr. Corcoran expressing himself with a generous strength on the subject I have mentioned."

"Oh! Well?"

"Why should not the young lady write a small volume, to be entitled—let us say—*The Children's Book of American Birds*, and dedicate it to Mr. Worple! A limited edition could be published at your expense, sir, and a great deal of the book would, of course, be given over to eulogistic remarks concerning Mr. Worple's own larger treatise on the same subject. I should recommend the dispatching of a presentation copy to Mr. Worple, immediately on publication, accompanied by a letter in which the young lady asks to be allowed to make the acquaintance of one to whom she owes so much. This would, I fancy, produce the desired result, but as I say, the expense involved would be considerable."

I felt like the proprietor of a performing dog on the vaudeville stage when the tyke has just pulled off his trick without a hitch. I had betted on Jeeves all along, and I had known that he wouldn't let me down. It beats me sometimes why a man with his genius is satisfied to hang around pressing my clothes and whatnot. If I had half Jeeves's brain, I should have a stab, at being Prime Minister or something.

"Jeeves," I said, "that is absolutely ripping! One of your very best efforts."

"Thank you, sir."

The girl made an objection.

"But I'm sure I couldn't write a book about anything. I can't even write good letters."

"Muriel's talents," said Corky, with a little cough "lie more in the direction of the drama, Bertie. I didn't mention it before, but one of our reasons for being a trifle nervous as to how Uncle Alexander will receive the news is that Muriel is in the chorus of that show *Choose your Exit* at the Manhattan. It's absurdly unreasonable, but we both feel that that fact might increase Uncle Alexander's natural tendency to kick like a steer."

I saw what he meant. Goodness knows there was fuss enough in our family when I tried to marry into musical comedy a few years ago. And the recollection of my Aunt Agatha's attitude in the matter of Gussie and the vaudeville girl was still fresh in my mind. I don't know why it is—one of these psychology sharps could explain it, I suppose—but uncles and aunts, as a class, are always dead against the drama, legitimate or otherwise. They don't seem able to stick it at any price.

But Jeeves had a solution, of course.

"I fancy it would be a simple matter, sir, to find some impecunious author who would be glad to do the actual composition of the volume for a small fee. It is only necessary that the young lady's name should appear on the title page."

"That's true," said Corky. "Sam Patterson would do it for a hundred dollars. He writes a novelette, three short stories, and ten thousand words of a serial for one of the all-fiction magazines under different names every month. A little thing like this would be nothing to him. I'll get after him right away."

"Fine!"

"Will that be all, sir?" said Jeeves. "Very good, sir. Thank you, sir."

I always used to think that publishers had to be devilish intelligent fellows, loaded down with the grey matter; but I've got their number now. All a publisher has to do is to write cheques at intervals, while a lot of deserving and industrious chappies rally round and do the real work. I know, because I've been one myself. I simply sat tight in the old apartment with a fountain-pen, and in due season a topping, shiny book came along.

I happened to be down at Corky's place when the first copies of *The Children's Book of American Birds* bobbed up. Muriel Singer was there, and we were talking of things in general when there was a bang at the door and the parcel was delivered.

It was certainly some book. It had a red cover with a fowl of some species on it, and underneath the girl's name in gold letters. I opened a copy at random.

"Often of a spring morning," it said at the top of page twenty-one, "as you wander through the fields, you will hear the sweet-toned, carelessly flowing warble of the purple finch linnet. When you are older you must read all about him in Mr. Alexander Worple's wonderful book—*American Birds*."

You see. A boost for the uncle right away. And only a few pages later there he was in the limelight again in connection with the yellow-billed cuckoo. It was great stuff. The more I read, the more I admired the chap who had written it and Jeeves's genius in putting us on to the wheeze. I didn't see how the uncle could fail to drop. You can't call a chap the world's greatest authority on the yellow-billed cuckoo without rousing a certain disposition towards chumminess in him.

"It's a cert!" I said.

"An absolute cinch!" said Corky.

And a day or two later he meandered up the Avenue to my apartment to tell me that all was well. The uncle had written Muriel a letter so dripping with the milk of human kindness that if he hadn't known Mr. Worple's handwriting Corky would have refused to believe him the author of it. Any time it suited Miss Singer to call, said the uncle, he would be delighted to make her acquaintance.

Shortly after this I had to go out of town. Divers sound sportsmen had invited me to pay visits to their country places, and it wasn't for several months that I settled down in the city again. I had been wondering a lot, of course, about Corky, whether it all turned out right, and so forth, and my first evening in New York, happening to pop into a quiet sort of little restaurant which I go to when I don't feel inclined for the bright lights, I found Muriel Singer there, sitting by herself at a table near the door. Corky, I took it, was out telephoning. I went up and passed the time of day.

"Well, well, well, what?" I said.

"Why, Mr. Wooster! How do you do?"

"Corky around?"

"I beg your pardon?"

"You're waiting for Corky, aren't you?"

"Oh, I didn't understand. No, I'm not waiting for him."

It seemed to roe that there was a sort of something in her voice, a kind of thingummy, you know.

"I say, you haven't had a row with Corky, have you?"

"A row?"

"A spat, don't you know—little misunderstanding—faults on both sides—er—and all that sort of thing."

253

"Why, whatever makes you think that?"

"Oh, well, as it were, what? What I mean is—I thought you usually dined with him before you went to the theatre."

"I've left the stage now."

Suddenly the whole thing dawned on me. I had forgotten what a long time I had been away.

"Why, of course, I see now! You're married!"

"Yes."

"How perfectly topping! I wish you all kinds of happiness."

"Thank you, so much. Oh Alexander," she said, looking past me, "this is a friend of mine—Mr. Wooster."

I spun round. A chappie with a lot of stiff grey hair and a red sort of healthy face was standing there. Rather a formidable Johnnie, he looked, though quite peaceful at the moment.

"I want you to meet my husband, Mr. Wooster. Mr. Wooster is a friend of Bruce's, Alexander."

The old boy grasped my hand warmly, and that was all that kept me from hitting the floor in a heap. The place was rocking. Absolutely.

"So you know my nephew, Mr. Wooster," I heard him say. "I wish you would try to knock a little sense into him and make him quit this playing at painting. But I have an idea that he is steadying down. I noticed it first that night he came to dinner with us, my dear, to be introduced to you. He seemed altogether quieter and more serious. Something seemed to have sobered him. Perhaps you will give us the pleasure of your company at dinner to-night, Mr. Wooster? Or have you dined?"

I said I had. What I needed then was air, not dinner. I felt that I wanted to get into the open and think this thing out.

When I reached my apartment I heard Jeeves moving about in his lair. I called him.

"Jeeves," I said, "now is the time for all good men to come to the aid of the party. A stiff b.-and-s. first of all, and then I've a bit of news for you."

He came back with a tray and a long glass.

"Better have one yourself, Jeeves. You'll need it."

"Later on, perhaps, thank you, sir."

"All right. Please yourself. But you're going to get a shock. You remember my friend, Mr. Corcoran?"

"Yes, sir."

"And the girl who was to slide gracefully into his uncle's esteem by writing the book on birds?"

"Perfectly, sir."

"Well, she's slid. She's married the uncle."

He took it without blinking. You can't rattle Jeeves.

"That was always a development to be feared, sir."

"You don't mean to tell me that you were expecting it?"

"It crossed my mind as a possibility."

"Did it, by Jove! Well, I think, you might have warned us!"

"I hardly liked to take the liberty, sir."

Of course, as I saw after I had had a bite to eat and was in a calmer frame of mind, what had happened wasn't my fault, if you come down to it. I couldn't be expected to foresee that the scheme, in itself a cracker-jack, would skid into the ditch as it had done; but all the same I'm bound to admit that I didn't relish the idea of meeting Corky again until time, the great healer, had been able to get in a bit of soothing work. I cut Washington Square out absolutely for the next few months. I gave it the complete miss-in-baulk. And then, just when I was beginning to think I might safely pop down in that direction and gather up the dropped threads, so to speak, time, instead of working the healing wheeze, went and pulled the most awful bone and put the lid on it. Opening the paper one morning, I read that Mrs. Alexander Worple had presented her husband with a son and heir.

I was so darned sorry for poor old Corky that I hadn't the heart to touch my breakfast. I told Jeeves to drink it himself. I was bowled over. Absolutely. It was the limit.

I hardly knew what to do. I wanted, of course, to rush down to Washington Square and grip the poor blighter silently by the hand; and then, thinking it over, I hadn't the nerve. Absent treatment seemed the touch. I gave it him in waves.

But after a month or so I began to hesitate again. It struck me that it was playing it a bit low-down on the poor chap, avoiding him like this just when he probably wanted his pals to surge round him most. I pictured him sitting in his lonely studio with no company but his bitter thoughts, and the pathos of it got me to such an extent that I bounded straight into a taxi and told the driver to go all out for the studio.

I rushed in, and there was Corky, hunched up at the easel, painting away, while on the model throne sat a severe-looking female of middle age, holding a baby.

A fellow has to be ready for that sort of thing.

"Oh, ah!" I said, and started to back out.

Corky looked over his shoulder.

"Halloa, Bertie. Don't go. We're just finishing for the day. That will be all this afternoon," he said to the nurse, who got up with the baby and decanted it into a perambulator which was standing in the fairway.

"At the same hour to-morrow, Mr. Corcoran?"

"Yes, please."

"Good afternoon."

"Good afternoon."

Corky stood there, looking at the door, and then he turned to me and began to get it off his chest. Fortunately, he seemed to take it for granted that I knew all about what had happened, so it wasn't as awkward as it might have been.

"It's my uncle's idea," he said. "Muriel doesn't know about it yet. The portrait's to be a surprise for her on her birthday. The nurse takes the kid out ostensibly to get a breather, and they beat it down here. If you want an instance of the irony of fate, Bertie, get acquainted with this. Here's the first commission I have ever had to paint a portrait, and the sitter is that human poached egg that has butted in and bounced me out of my inheritance. Can you beat it! I call it rubbing the thing in to expect me to spend my afternoons gazing into the ugly face of a little brat who to all intents and purposes has hit me behind the ear with a blackjack and swiped all I possess. I can't refuse to paint the portrait because if I did my uncle would stop my allowance; yet every time I look up and catch that kid's vacant eye, I suffer agonies. I tell you, Bertie, sometimes when he gives me a patronizing glance and then turns away and is sick, as if it revolted him to look at me, I come within an ace of occupying the entire front page of the evening papers as the latest murder sensation. There are moments when I can almost see the headlines: 'Promising Young Artist Beans Baby With Axe.'"

I patted his shoulder silently. My sympathy for the poor old scout was too deep for words.

I kept away from the studio for some time after that, because it didn't seem right to me to intrude on the poor chappie's sorrow. Besides, I'm bound to say that nurse intimidated me. She reminded me so infernally of Aunt Agatha. She was the same gimlet-eyed type.

But one afternoon Corky called me on the 'phone.

"Bertie."

"Halloa?"

"Are you doing anything this afternoon?"

"Nothing special."

"You couldn't come down here, could you?"

"What's the trouble? Anything up?"

"I've finished the portrait."

"Good boy! Stout work!"

"Yes." His voice sounded rather doubtful. "The fact is, Bertie, it doesn't look quite right to me. There's something about it—My uncle's coming in half an hour to inspect it, and—I don't know why it is, but I kind of feel I'd like your moral support!"

I began to see that I was letting myself in for something. The sympathetic co-operation of Jeeves seemed to me to be indicated.

"You think he'll cut up rough?"

"He may."

I threw my mind back to the red-faced chappie I had met at the restaurant, and tried to picture him cutting up rough. It was only too easy. I spoke to Corky firmly on the telephone.

"I'll come," I said.

"Good!"

"But only if I may bring Jeeves!"

"Why Jeeves? What's Jeeves got to do with it? Who wants Jeeves? Jeeves is the fool who suggested the scheme that has led——"

"Listen, Corky, old top! If you think I am going to face that uncle of yours without Jeeves's support, you're mistaken. I'd sooner go into a den of wild beasts and bite a lion on the back of the neck."

"Oh, all right," said Corky. Not cordially, but he said it; so I rang for Jeeves, and explained the situation.

"Very good, sir," said Jeeves.

That's the sort of chap he is. You can't rattle him.

We found Corky near the door, looking at the picture, with one hand up in a defensive sort of way, as if he thought it might swing on him.

"Stand right where you are, Bertie," he said, without moving. "Now, tell me honestly, how does it strike you?"

The light from the big window fell right on the picture. I took a good look at it. Then I shifted a bit nearer and took another look. Then I went back to where I had been at first, because it hadn't seemed quite so bad from there.

"Well?" said Corky, anxiously.

I hesitated a bit.

"Of course, old man, I only saw the kid once, and then only for a moment, but—but it *was* an ugly sort of kid, wasn't it, if I remember rightly?"

"As ugly as that?"

I looked again, and honesty compelled me to be frank.

"I don't see how it could have been, old chap."

Poor old Corky ran his fingers through his hair in a temperamental sort of way. He groaned.

"You're right quite, Bertie. Something's gone wrong with the darned thing. My private impression is that, without knowing it, I've worked that stunt that Sargent and those fellows pull—painting the soul of the sitter. I've got through the mere outward appearance, and have put the child's soul on canvas."

"But could a child of that age have a soul like that? I don't see how he could have managed it in the time. What do you think, Jeeves?"

"I doubt it, sir."

"It—it sorts of leers at you, doesn't it?"

"You've noticed that, too?" said Corky.

"I don't see how one could help noticing."

"All I tried to do was to give the little brute a cheerful expression.

But, as it worked out, he looks positively dissipated."

"Just what I was going to suggest, old man. He looks as if he were in the middle of a colossal spree, and enjoying every minute of it. Don't you think so, Jeeves?"

"He has a decidedly inebriated air, sir."

Corky was starting to say something when the door opened, and the uncle came in.

For about three seconds all was joy, jollity, and goodwill. The old boy shook hands with me, slapped Corky on the back, said that he didn't think he had ever seen such a fine day, and whacked his leg with his stick. Jeeves had projected himself into the background, and he didn't notice him.

"Well, Bruce, my boy; so the portrait is really finished, is it—really finished? Well, bring it out. Let's have a look at it. This will be a wonderful surprise for your aunt. Where is it? Let's——"

And then he got it—suddenly, when he wasn't set for the punch; and he rocked back on his heels.

"Oosh!" he exclaimed. And for perhaps a minute there was one of the scaliest silences I've ever run up against.

"Is this a practical joke?" he said at last, in a way that set about sixteen draughts cutting through the room at once.

I thought it was up to me to rally round old Corky.

"You want to stand a bit farther away from it," I said.

"You're perfectly right!" he snorted. "I do! I want to stand so far away from it that I can't see the thing with a telescope!" He turned on Corky like an untamed tiger of the jungle who has just located a chunk of meat. "And this—this—is what you have been wasting your time and my money for all these years! A painter! I wouldn't let you paint a house of mine! I gave you this commission, thinking that you were a competent worker, and this—this—this extract from a comic coloured supplement is the result!" He swung towards the door, lashing his tail and growling to himself. "This ends it! If you wish to continue this foolery of pretending to be an artist because you want an excuse for idleness, please yourself. But let me tell you this. Unless you report at my office on Monday morning, prepared to abandon all this idiocy and start in at the bottom of the business to work your way up, as you should have done half a dozen years ago, not another cent—not another cent—not another—Boosh!"

Then the door closed, and he was no longer with us. And I crawled out of the bombproof shelter.

"Corky, old top!" I whispered faintly.

Corky was standing staring at the picture. His face was set. There was a hunted look in his eye.

"Well, that finishes it!" he muttered brokenly.

"What are you going to do?"

"Do? What can I do? I can't stick on here if he cuts off supplies. You heard what he said. I shall have to go to the office on Monday."

I couldn't think of a thing to say. I knew exactly how he felt about the office. I don't know when I've been so infernally uncomfortable. It was like hanging round trying to make conversation to a pal who's just been sentenced to twenty years in quod.

And then a soothing voice broke the silence.

"If I might make a suggestion, sir!"

It was Jeeves. He had slid from the shadows and was gazing gravely at the picture. Upon my word, I can't give you a better idea of the shattering effect of Corky's uncle Alexander when in action than by saying that he had absolutely made me forget for the moment that Jeeves was there.

"I wonder if I have ever happened to mention to you, sir, a Mr. Digby Thistleton, with whom I was once in service? Perhaps you have met him? He was a financier. He is now Lord Bridgnorth. It was a favourite saying of his that there is always a way. The first time I heard him use the expression was after the failure of a patent depilatory which he promoted."

"Jeeves," I said, "what on earth are you talking about?"

"I mentioned Mr. Thistleton, sir, because his was in some respects a parallel case to the present one. His depilatory failed, but he did not despair. He put it on the market again under the name of Hair-o, guaranteed to produce a full crop of hair in a few months. It was advertised, if you remember, sir, by a humorous picture of a billiard-ball, before and after taking, and made such a substantial fortune that Mr. Thistleton was soon afterwards elevated to the peerage for services to his Party. It seems to me that, if Mr. Corcoran looks into the matter, he will find, like Mr. Thistleton, that there is always a way.

Mr. Worple himself suggested the solution of the difficulty. In the heat of the moment he compared the portrait to an extract from a coloured comic supplement. I consider the suggestion a very valuable one, sir. Mr. Corcoran's portrait may not have pleased Mr. Worple as a likeness of his only child, but I have no doubt that editors would gladly consider it as a foundation for a series of humorous drawings. If Mr. Corcoran will allow me to make the suggestion, his talent has always been for the humorous. There is something about this picture—something bold and vigorous, which arrests the attention. I feel sure it would be highly popular."

Corky was glaring at the picture, and making a sort of dry, sucking noise with his mouth. He seemed completely overwrought.

And then suddenly he began to laugh in a wild way.

"Corky, old man!" I said, massaging him tenderly. I feared the poor blighter was hysterical.

He began to stagger about all over the floor.

"He's right! The man's absolutely right! Jeeves, you're a life-saver! You've hit on the greatest idea of the age! Report at the office on Monday! Start at the bottom of the business! I'll buy the business if I feel like it. I know the man who runs the comic section of the *Sunday Star*. He'll eat this thing. He was telling me only the other day how hard it was to get a good new series. He'll give me anything I ask for a real winner like this. I've got a gold-mine. Where's my hat? I've got an income for life! Where's that confounded hat? Lend me a fiver, Bertie. I want to take a taxi down to Park Row!"

Jeeves smiled paternally. Or, rather, he had a kind of paternal muscular spasm about the mouth, which is the nearest he ever gets to smiling.

"If I might make the suggestion, Mr. Corcoran—for a title of the series which you have in mind—'The Adventures of Baby Blobbs.'"

Corky and I looked at the picture, then at each other in an awed way.

Jeeves was right. There could be no other title.

"Jeeves," I said. It was a few weeks later, and I had just finished looking at the comic section of the *Sunday Star.* "I'm an optimist. I always have been. The older I get, the more I agree with Shakespeare

261

and those poet Johnnies about it always being darkest before the dawn and there's a silver lining and what you lose on the swings you make up on the roundabouts. Look at Mr. Corcoran, for instance. There was a fellow, one would have said, clear up to the eyebrows in the soup. To all appearances he had got it right in the neck. Yet look at him now. Have you seen these pictures?"

"I took the liberty of glancing at them before bringing them to you, sir. Extremely diverting."

"They have made a big hit, you know."

"I anticipated it, sir."

I leaned back against the pillows.

"You know, Jeeves, you're a genius. You ought to be drawing a commission on these things."

"I have nothing to complain of in that respect, sir. Mr. Corcoran has been most generous. I am putting out the brown suit, sir."

"No, I think I'll wear the blue with the faint red stripe."

"Not the blue with the faint red stripe, sir."

"But I rather fancy myself in it."

"Not the blue with the faint red stripe, sir."

"Oh, all right, have it your own way."

"Very good, sir. Thank you, sir."

Of course, I know it's as bad as being henpecked; but then Jeeves is always right. You've got to consider that, you know. What?

JEEVES AND THE UNBIDDEN GUEST

I'm not absolutely certain of my facts, but I rather fancy it's Shakespeare—or, if not, it's some equally brainy lad—who says that it's always just when a chappie is feeling particularly top-hole, and more than usually braced with things in general that Fate sneaks up behind him with a bit of lead piping. There's no doubt the man's right. It's absolutely that way with me. Take, for instance, the fairly rummy matter of Lady Malvern and her son Wilmot. A moment before they turned up, I was just thinking how thoroughly all right everything was.

It was one of those topping mornings, and I had just climbed out from under the cold shower, feeling like a two-year-old. As a matter of fact, I was especially bucked just then because the day before I had asserted myself with Jeeves—absolutely asserted myself, don't you know. You see, the way things had been going on I was rapidly becoming a dashed serf. The man had jolly well oppressed me. I didn't so much mind when he made me give up one of my new suits, because, Jeeves's judgment about suits is sound. But I as near as a toucher rebelled when he wouldn't let me wear a pair of cloth-topped boots which I loved like a couple of brothers. And when he tried to tread on me like a worm in the matter of a hat, I jolly well put my foot down and showed him who was who. It's a long story, and I haven't time to tell you now, but the point is that he wanted me to wear the Longacre—as worn by John Drew—when I had set my heart on the Country Gentleman—as worn by another famous actor chappie—and the end of the matter was that, after a rather painful scene, I bought the Country Gentleman. So that's how things stood on this particular morning, and I was feeling kind of manly and independent.

Well, I was in the bathroom, wondering what there was going to be for breakfast while I massaged the good old spine with a rough towel and sang slightly, when there was a tap at the door. I stopped singing and opened the door an inch.

"What ho without there!"

"Lady Malvern wishes to see you, sir," said Jeeves.

"Eh?"

"Lady Malvern, sir. She is waiting in the sitting-room."

"Pull yourself together, Jeeves, my man," I said, rather severely, for I bar practical jokes before breakfast. "You know perfectly well there's no one waiting for me in the sitting-room. How could there be when it's barely ten o'clock yet?"

"I gathered from her ladyship, sir, that she had landed from an ocean liner at an early hour this morning."

This made the thing a bit more plausible. I remembered that when I had arrived in America about a year before, the proceedings had begun at some ghastly hour like six, and that I had been shot out on to a foreign shore considerably before eight.

"Who the deuce is Lady Malvern, Jeeves?"

"Her ladyship did not confide in me, sir."

"Is she alone?"

"Her ladyship is accompanied by a Lord Pershore, sir. I fancy that his lordship would be her ladyship's son."

"Oh, well, put out rich raiment of sorts, and I'll be dressing."

"Our heather-mixture lounge is in readiness, sir."

"Then lead me to it."

While I was dressing I kept trying to think who on earth Lady Malvern could be. It wasn't till I had climbed through the top of my shirt and was reaching out for the studs that I remembered.

"I've placed her, Jeeves. She's a pal of my Aunt Agatha."

"Indeed, sir?"

"Yes. I met her at lunch one Sunday before I left London. A very vicious specimen. Writes books. She wrote a book on social conditions in India when she came back from the Durbar."

"Yes, sir? Pardon me, sir, but not that tie!"

"Eh?"

"Not that tie with the heather-mixture lounge, sir!"

It was a shock to me. I thought I had quelled the fellow. It was rather a solemn moment. What I mean is, if I weakened now, all my good work the night before would be thrown away. I braced myself.

"What's wrong with this tie? I've seen you give it a nasty look before.
Speak out like a man! What's the matter with it?"

"Too ornate, sir."

"Nonsense! A cheerful pink. Nothing more."

"Unsuitable, sir."

"Jeeves, this is the tie I wear!"

"Very good, sir."

Dashed unpleasant. I could see that the man was wounded. But I was firm. I tied the tie, got into the coat and waistcoat, and went into the sitting-room.

"Halloa! Halloa! Halloa!" I said. "What?"

"Ah! How do you do, Mr. Wooster? You have never met my son, Wilmot, I think? Motty, darling, this is Mr. Wooster."

Lady Malvern was a hearty, happy, healthy, overpowering sort of dashed female, not so very tall but making up for it by measuring about six feet from the O.P. to the Prompt Side. She fitted into my biggest arm-chair as if it had been built round her by someone who knew they were wearing arm-chairs tight about the hips that season. She had bright, bulging eyes and a lot of yellow hair, and when she spoke she showed about fifty-seven front teeth. She was one of those women who kind of numb a fellow's faculties. She made me feel as if I were ten years old and had been brought into the drawing-room in my Sunday clothes to say how-d'you-do. Altogether by no means the sort of thing a chappie would wish to find in his sitting-room before breakfast.

Motty, the son, was about twenty-three, tall and thin and meek-looking. He had the same yellow hair as his mother, but he wore it plastered down and parted in the middle. His eyes bulged, too, but they weren't bright. They were a dull grey with pink rims. His chin gave up the struggle about half-way down, and he didn't appear to have any eyelashes. A mild, furtive, sheepish sort of blighter, in short.

"Awfully glad to see you," I said. "So you've popped over, eh? Making a long stay in America?"

"About a month. Your aunt gave me your address and told me to be sure and call on you."

I was glad to hear this, as it showed that Aunt Agatha was beginning to come round a bit. There had been some unpleasantness a year before, when she had sent me over to New York to disentangle my Cousin Gussie from the clutches of a girl on the music-hall stage. When I tell you that by the time I had finished my operations, Gussie had not only married the girl but had gone on the stage himself, and was doing well, you'll understand that Aunt Agatha was upset to no small extent. I simply hadn't dared go back and face her, and it was a relief to find that time had healed the wound and all that sort of thing enough to make her tell her pals to look me up. What I mean is, much as I liked America, I didn't want to have England barred to me for the rest of my natural; and, believe me, England is a jolly sight too small for anyone to live in with Aunt Agatha, if she's really on the warpath. So I braced on hearing these kind words and smiled genially on the assemblage.

"Your aunt said that you would do anything that was in your power to be of assistance to us."

"Rather? Oh, rather! Absolutely!"

"Thank you so much. I want you to put dear Motty up for a little while."

I didn't get this for a moment.

"Put him up? For my clubs?"

"No, no! Darling Motty is essentially a home bird. Aren't you, Motty darling?"

Motty, who was sucking the knob of his stick, uncorked himself.

"Yes, mother," he said, and corked himself up again.

"I should not like him to belong to clubs. I mean put him up here. Have him to live with you while I am away."

These frightful words trickled out of her like honey. The woman simply didn't seem to understand the ghastly nature of her proposal. I gave Motty the swift east-to-west. He was sitting with his mouth nuzzling the stick, blinking at the wall. The thought of having this planted on me for an indefinite period appalled me. Absolutely appalled me, don't you know. I was just starting to say that the shot wasn't on the board at any price, and that the first sign Motty gave of trying to nestle into my little home I would yell for the police, when she went on, rolling placidly over me, as it were.

There was something about this woman that sapped a chappie's will-power.

"I am leaving New York by the midday train, as I have to pay a visit to Sing-Sing prison. I am extremely interested in prison conditions in America. After that I work my way gradually across to the coast, visiting the points of interest on the journey. You see, Mr. Wooster, I am in America principally on business. No doubt you read my book, *India and the Indians*? My publishers are anxious for me to write a companion volume on the United States. I shall not be able to spend more than a month in the country, as I have to get back for the season, but a month should be ample. I was less than a month in India, and my dear friend Sir Roger Cremorne wrote his *America from Within* after a stay of only two weeks. I should love to take dear Motty with me, but the poor boy gets so sick when he travels by train. I shall have to pick him up on my return."

From where I sat I could see Jeeves in the dining-room, laying the breakfast-table. I wished I could have had a minute with him alone. I felt certain that he would have been able to think of some way of putting a stop to this woman.

"It will be such a relief to know that Motty is safe with you, Mr. Wooster. I know what the temptations of a great city are. Hitherto dear Motty has been sheltered from them. He has lived quietly with me in the country. I know that you will look after him carefully, Mr. Wooster. He will give very little trouble." She talked about the poor blighter as if he wasn't there. Not that Motty seemed to mind. He had stopped chewing his walking-stick and was sitting there with his mouth open. "He is a vegetarian and a teetotaller and is devoted to reading. Give him a nice book and he will be quite contented." She got up. "Thank you so much, Mr. Wooster! I don't know what I should have done without your help. Come, Motty! We have just time to see a few of the sights before my train goes. But I shall have to rely on you for most of my information about New York, darling. Be sure to keep your eyes open and take notes of your impressions! It will be such a help. Good-bye, Mr. Wooster. I will send Motty back early in the afternoon."

They went out, and I howled for Jeeves.

"Jeeves! What about it?"

"Sir?"

"What's to be done? You heard it all, didn't you? You were in the dining-room most of the time. That pill is coming to stay here."

"Pill, sir?"

"The excrescence."

"I beg your pardon, sir?"

I looked at Jeeves sharply. This sort of thing wasn't like him. It was as if he were deliberately trying to give me the pip. Then I understood. The man was really upset about that tie. He was trying to get his own back.

"Lord Pershore will be staying here from to-night, Jeeves," I said coldly.

"Very good, sir. Breakfast is ready, sir."

I could have sobbed into the bacon and eggs. That there wasn't any sympathy to be got out of Jeeves was what put the lid on it. For a moment I almost weakened and told him to destroy the hat and tie if he didn't like them, but I pulled myself together again. I was dashed if I was going to let Jeeves treat me like a bally one-man chain-gang!

But, what with brooding on Jeeves and brooding on Motty, I was in a pretty reduced sort of state. The more I examined the situation, the more blighted it became. There was nothing I could do. If I slung Motty out, he would report to his mother, and she would pass it on to Aunt Agatha, and I didn't like to think what would happen then. Sooner or later, I should be wanting to go back to England, and I didn't want to get there and find Aunt Agatha waiting on the quay for me with a stuffed eelskin. There was absolutely nothing for it but to put the fellow up and make the best of it.

About midday Motty's luggage arrived, and soon afterward a large parcel of what I took to be nice books. I brightened up a little when I saw it. It was one of those massive parcels and looked as if it had enough in it to keep the chappie busy for a year. I felt a trifle more cheerful, and I got my Country Gentleman hat and stuck it on my head, and gave the pink tie a twist, and reeled out to take a bite of lunch with one or two of the lads at a neighbouring hostelry; and what with excellent browsing and sluicing and cheery conversation and what-not, the afternoon passed quite happily. By dinner-time I had almost forgotten blighted Motty's existence.

I dined at the club and looked in at a show afterward, and it wasn't till fairly late that I got back to the flat. There were no signs of Motty, and I took it that he had gone to bed.

It seemed rummy to me, though, that the parcel of nice books was still there with the string and paper on it. It looked as if Motty, after seeing mother off at the station, had decided to call it a day.

Jeeves came in with the nightly whisky-and-soda. I could tell by the chappie's manner that he was still upset.

"Lord Pershore gone to bed, Jeeves?" I asked, with reserved hauteur and what-not.

"No, sir. His lordship has not yet returned."

"Not returned? What do you mean?"

"His lordship came in shortly after six-thirty, and, having dressed, went out again."

At this moment there was a noise outside the front door, a sort of scrabbling noise, as if somebody were trying to paw his way through the woodwork. Then a sort of thud.

"Better go and see what that is, Jeeves."

"Very good, sir."

He went out and came back again.

"If you would not mind stepping this way, sir, I think we might be able to carry him in."

"Carry him in?"

"His lordship is lying on the mat, sir."

I went to the front door. The man was right. There was Motty huddled up outside on the floor. He was moaning a bit.

"He's had some sort of dashed fit," I said. I took another look. "Jeeves! Someone's been feeding him meat!"

"Sir?"

"He's a vegetarian, you know. He must have been digging into a steak or something. Call up a doctor!"

"I hardly think it will be necessary, sir. If you would take his lordship's legs, while I——"

"Great Scot, Jeeves! You don't think—he can't be——"

"I am inclined to think so, sir."

And, by Jove, he was right! Once on the right track, you couldn't mistake it. Motty was under the surface.

It was the deuce of a shock.

"You never can tell, Jeeves!"

"Very seldom, sir."

"Remove the eye of authority and where are you?"

"Precisely, sir."

"Where is my wandering boy to-night and all that sort of thing, what?"

"It would seem so, sir."

"Well, we had better bring him in, eh?"

"Yes, sir."

So we lugged him in, and Jeeves put him to bed, and I lit a cigarette and sat down to think the thing over. I had a kind of foreboding. It seemed to me that I had let myself in for something pretty rocky.

Next morning, after I had sucked down a thoughtful cup of tea, I went into Motty's room to investigate. I expected to find the fellow a wreck, but there he was, sitting up in bed, quite chirpy, reading Gingery stories.

"What ho!" I said.

"What ho!" said Motty.

"What ho! What ho!"

"What ho! What ho! What ho!"

After that it seemed rather difficult to go on with the conversation.

"How are you feeling this morning?" I asked.

"Topping!" replied Motty, blithely and with abandon. "I say, you know, that fellow of yours—Jeeves, you know—is a corker. I had a most frightful headache when I woke up, and he brought me a sort of rummy dark drink, and it put me right again at once. Said it was his own invention. I must see more of that lad. He seems to me distinctly one of the ones!"

I couldn't believe that this was the same blighter who had sat and sucked his stick the day before.

"You ate something that disagreed with you last night, didn't you?" I said, by way of giving him a chance to slide out of it if he wanted to. But he wouldn't have it, at any price.

"No!" he replied firmly. "I didn't do anything of the kind. I drank too much! Much too much. Lots and lots too much! And, what's more, I'm going to do it again! I'm going to do it every night. If ever you see me sober, old top," he said, with a kind of holy exaltation, "tap me on the shoulder and say, 'Tut! Tut!' and I'll apologize and remedy the defect."

"But I say, you know, what about me?"

"What about you?"

"Well, I'm so to speak, as it were, kind of responsible for you. What I mean to say is, if you go doing this sort of thing I'm apt to get in the soup somewhat."

"I can't help your troubles," said Motty firmly. "Listen to me, old thing: this is the first time in my life that I've had a real chance to yield to the temptations of a great city. What's the use of a great city having temptations if fellows don't yield to them? Makes it so bally discouraging for a great city. Besides, mother told me to keep my eyes open and collect impressions."

I sat on the edge of the bed. I felt dizzy.

"I know just how you feel, old dear," said Motty consolingly. "And, if my principles would permit it, I would simmer down for your sake. But duty first! This is the first time I've been let out alone, and I mean to make the most of it. We're only young once. Why interfere with life's morning? Young man, rejoice in thy youth! Tra-la! What ho!"

Put like that, it did seem reasonable.

"All my bally life, dear boy," Motty went on, "I've been cooped up in the ancestral home at Much Middlefold, in Shropshire, and till you've been cooped up in Much Middlefold you don't know what cooping is! The only time we get any excitement is when one of the choir-boys is caught sucking chocolate during the sermon. When that happens, we talk about it for days. I've got about a month of New York, and I mean to store up a few happy memories for the long winter evenings. This is my only chance to collect a past, and I'm going to do it. Now tell me, old sport, as man to man, how does one get in touch with that very decent chappie Jeeves? Does one ring a bell or shout a bit? I should like to discuss the subject of a good stiff b.-and-s. with him!"

* * * * *

I had had a sort of vague idea, don't you know, that if I stuck close to Motty and went about the place with him, I might act as a bit of a damper on the gaiety. What I mean is, I thought that if, when he was being the life and soul of the party, he were to catch my reproving eye he might ease up a trifle on the revelry. So the next night I took him along to supper with me. It was the last time. I'm a quiet, peaceful sort of chappie who has lived all his life in London, and I can't stand the pace these swift sportsmen from the rural districts set. What I mean to say is this, I'm all for rational enjoyment and so forth, but I think a chappie makes himself conspicuous when he throws soft-boiled eggs at the electric fan. And decent mirth and all that sort of thing are all right, but I do bar dancing on tables and having to dash all over the place dodging waiters, managers, and chuckers-out, just when you want to sit still and digest.

Directly I managed to tear myself away that night and get home, I made up my mind that this was jolly well the last time that I went about with Motty. The only time I met him late at night after that was once when I passed the door of a fairly low-down sort of restaurant and had to step aside to dodge him as he sailed through the air *en route* for the opposite pavement, with a muscular sort of looking chappie peering out after him with a kind of gloomy satisfaction.

In a way, I couldn't help sympathizing with the fellow. He had about four weeks to have the good time that ought to have been spread over about ten years, and I didn't wonder at his wanting to be pretty busy. I should have been just the same in his place. Still, there was no denying that it was a bit thick. If it hadn't been for the thought of Lady Malvern and Aunt Agatha in the background, I should have regarded Motty's rapid work with an indulgent smile. But I couldn't get rid of the feeling that, sooner or later, I was the lad who was scheduled to get it behind the ear. And what with brooding on this prospect, and sitting up in the old flat waiting for the familiar footstep, and putting it to bed when it got there, and stealing into the sick-chamber next morning to contemplate the wreckage, I was beginning to lose weight. Absolutely becoming the good old shadow, I give you my honest word. Starting at sudden noises and what-not.

And no sympathy from Jeeves. That was what cut me to the quick. The man was still thoroughly pipped about the hat and tie, and simply wouldn't rally round. One morning I wanted comforting so much that I sank the pride of the Woosters and appealed to the fellow direct.

"Jeeves," I said, "this is getting a bit thick!"

"Sir?" Business and cold respectfulness.

"You know what I mean. This lad seems to have chucked all the principles of a well-spent boyhood. He has got it up his nose!"

"Yes, sir."

"Well, I shall get blamed, don't you know. You know what my Aunt Agatha is!"

"Yes, sir."

"Very well, then."

I waited a moment, but he wouldn't unbend.

"Jeeves," I said, "haven't you any scheme up your sleeve for coping with this blighter?"

"No, sir."

And he shimmered off to his lair. Obstinate devil! So dashed absurd, don't you know. It wasn't as if there was anything wrong with that Country Gentleman hat. It was a remarkably priceless effort, and much admired by the lads. But, just because he preferred the Longacre, he left me flat.

It was shortly after this that young Motty got the idea of bringing pals back in the small hours to continue the gay revels in the home. This was where I began to crack under the strain. You see, the part of town where I was living wasn't the right place for that sort of thing. I knew lots of chappies down Washington Square way who started the evening at about 2 a.m.—artists and writers and what-not, who frolicked considerably till checked by the arrival of the morning milk. That was all right. They like that sort of thing down there. The neighbours can't get to sleep unless there's someone dancing Hawaiian dances over their heads. But on Fifty-seventh Street the atmosphere wasn't right, and when Motty turned up at three in the morning with a collection of hearty lads, who only stopped singing their college song when they started singing "The Old Oaken Bucket," there was a marked peevishness among the old settlers in the flats. The management was extremely terse over the telephone at breakfast-time, and took a lot of soothing.

The next night I came home early, after a lonely dinner at a place which I'd chosen because there didn't seem any chance of meeting Motty there. The sitting-room was quite dark, and I was just moving to switch on the light, when there was a sort of explosion and something collared hold of my trouser-leg. Living with Motty had reduced me to such an extent that I was simply unable to cope with this thing. I jumped backward with a loud yell of anguish, and tumbled out into the hall just as Jeeves came out of his den to see what the matter was.

"Did you call, sir?"

"Jeeves! There's something in there that grabs you by the leg!"

"That would be Rollo, sir."

"Eh?"

"I would have warned you of his presence, but I did not hear you come in. His temper is a little uncertain at present, as he has not yet

273

settled down."

"Who the deuce is Rollo?"

"His lordship's bull-terrier, sir. His lordship won him in a raffle, and tied him to the leg of the table. If you will allow me, sir, I will go in and switch on the light."

There really is nobody like Jeeves. He walked straight into the sitting-room, the biggest feat since Daniel and the lions' den, without a quiver. What's more, his magnetism or whatever they call it was such that the dashed animal, instead of pinning him by the leg, calmed down as if he had had a bromide, and rolled over on his back with all his paws in the air. If Jeeves had been his rich uncle he couldn't have been more chummy. Yet directly he caught sight of me again, he got all worked up and seemed to have only one idea in life—to start chewing me where he had left off.

"Rollo is not used to you yet, sir," said Jeeves, regarding the bally quadruped in an admiring sort of way. "He is an excellent watchdog."

"I don't want a watchdog to keep me out of my rooms."

"No, sir."

"Well, what am I to do?"

"No doubt in time the animal will learn to discriminate, sir. He will learn to distinguish your peculiar scent."

"What do you mean—my peculiar scent? Correct the impression that I intend to hang about in the hall while life slips by, in the hope that one of these days that dashed animal will decide that I smell all right." I thought for a bit. "Jeeves!"

"Sir?"

"I'm going away—to-morrow morning by the first train. I shall go and stop with Mr. Todd in the country."

"Do you wish me to accompany you, sir?"

"No."

"Very good, sir."

"I don't know when I shall be back. Forward my letters."

"Yes, sir."

* * * * *

As a matter of fact, I was back within the week. Rocky Todd, the pal I went to stay with, is a rummy sort of a chap who lives all alone in the wilds of Long Island, and likes it; but a little of that sort of thing goes a long way with me. Dear old Rocky is one of the best, but after a few days in his cottage in the woods, miles away from anywhere, New York, even with Motty on the premises, began to look pretty good to me. The days down on Long Island have forty-eight hours in them; you can't get to sleep at night because of the bellowing of the crickets; and you have to walk two miles for a drink and six for an evening paper. I thanked Rocky for his kind hospitality, and caught the only train they have down in those parts. It landed me in New York about dinner-time. I went straight to the old flat. Jeeves came out of his lair. I looked round cautiously for Rollo.

"Where's that dog, Jeeves? Have you got him tied up?"

"The animal is no longer here, sir. His lordship gave him to the porter, who sold him. His lordship took a prejudice against the animal on account of being bitten by him in the calf of the leg."

I don't think I've ever been so bucked by a bit of news. I felt I had misjudged Rollo. Evidently, when you got to know him better, he had a lot of intelligence in him.

"Ripping!" I said. "Is Lord Pershore in, Jeeves?"

"No, sir."

"Do you expect him back to dinner?"

"No, sir."

"Where is he?"

"In prison, sir."

Have you ever trodden on a rake and had the handle jump up and hit   you? That's how I felt then.

"In prison!"

"Yes, sir."

"You don't mean—in prison?"

"Yes, sir."

I lowered myself into a chair.

"Why?" I said.

"He assaulted a constable, sir."

"Lord Pershore assaulted a constable!"

"Yes, sir."

I digested this.

"But, Jeeves, I say! This is frightful!"

"Sir?"

"What will Lady Malvern say when she finds out?"

"I do not fancy that her ladyship will find out, sir."

"But she'll come back and want to know where he is."

"I rather fancy, sir, that his lordship's bit of time will have run out by then."

"But supposing it hasn't?"

"In that event, sir, it may be judicious to prevaricate a little."

"How?"

"If I might make the suggestion, sir, I should inform her ladyship that his lordship has left for a short visit to Boston."

"Why Boston?"

"Very interesting and respectable centre, sir."

"Jeeves, I believe you've hit it."

"I fancy so, sir."

"Why, this is really the best thing that could have happened. If this hadn't turned up to prevent him, young Motty would have been in a sanatorium by the time Lady Malvern got back."

"Exactly, sir."

The more I looked at it in that way, the sounder this prison wheeze seemed to me. There was no doubt in the world that prison was just what the doctor ordered for Motty. It was the only thing that could have pulled him up. I was sorry for the poor blighter, but, after all, I reflected, a chappie who had lived all his life with Lady Malvern, in a small village in the interior of Shropshire, wouldn't have much to kick at in a prison. Altogether, I began to feel absolutely braced again. Life became like what the poet Johnnie says—one grand, sweet song. Things went on so comfortably and peacefully for a couple of weeks that I give you my word that I'd almost forgotten such a person as Motty existed. The only flaw in the scheme of things was that Jeeves was still pained and distant. It wasn't anything he said or did, mind you, but there was a rummy something about him all the time. Once when I was tying the pink tie I caught sight of him in the looking-glass. There was a kind of grieved look in his eye.

And then Lady Malvern came back, a good bit ahead of schedule. I hadn't been expecting her for days. I'd forgotten how time had been slipping along. She turned up one morning while I was still in bed sipping tea and thinking of this and that. Jeeves flowed in with the announcement that he had just loosed her into the sitting-room. I draped a few garments round me and went in.

There she was, sitting in the same arm-chair, looking as massive as ever. The only difference was that she didn't uncover the teeth, as she had done the first time.

"Good morning," I said. "So you've got back, what?"

"I have got back."

There was something sort of bleak about her tone, rather as if she had swallowed an east wind. This I took to be due to the fact that she probably hadn't breakfasted. It's only after a bit of breakfast that I'm able to regard the world with that sunny cheeriness which makes a fellow the universal favourite. I'm never much of a lad till I've engulfed an egg or two and a beaker of coffee.

"I suppose you haven't breakfasted?"

"I have not yet breakfasted."

"Won't you have an egg or something? Or a sausage or something? Or something?"

"No, thank you."

She spoke as if she belonged to an anti-sausage society or a league for the suppression of eggs. There was a bit of a silence.

"I called on you last night," she said, "but you were out."

"Awfully sorry! Had a pleasant trip?"

"Extremely, thank you."

"See everything? Niag'ra Falls, Yellowstone Park, and the jolly old Grand Canyon, and what-not?"

"I saw a great deal."

There was another slightly *frappé* silence. Jeeves floated silently into the dining-room and began to lay the breakfast-table.

"I hope Wilmot was not in your way, Mr. Wooster?"

I had been wondering when she was going to mention Motty.

"Rather not! Great pals! Hit it off splendidly."

"You were his constant companion, then?"

"Absolutely! We were always together. Saw all the sights, don't you know. We'd take in the Museum of Art in the morning, and have a bit of lunch at some good vegetarian place, and then toddle along to

277

a sacred concert in the afternoon, and home to an early dinner. We usually played dominoes after dinner. And then the early bed and the refreshing sleep. We had a great time. I was awfully sorry when he went away to Boston."

"Oh! Wilmot is in Boston?"

"Yes. I ought to have let you know, but of course we didn't know where you were. You were dodging all over the place like a snipe—I mean, don't you know, dodging all over the place, and we couldn't get at you. Yes, Motty went off to Boston."

"You're sure he went to Boston?"

"Oh, absolutely." I called out to Jeeves, who was now messing about in the next room with forks and so forth: "Jeeves, Lord Pershore didn't change his mind about going to Boston, did he?"

"No, sir."

"I thought I was right. Yes, Motty went to Boston."

"Then how do you account, Mr. Wooster, for the fact that when I went yesterday afternoon to Blackwell's Island prison, to secure material for my book, I saw poor, dear Wilmot there, dressed in a striped suit, seated beside a pile of stones with a hammer in his hands?"

I tried to think of something to say, but nothing came. A chappie has to be a lot broader about the forehead than I am to handle a jolt like this. I strained the old bean till it creaked, but between the collar and the hair parting nothing stirred. I was dumb. Which was lucky, because I wouldn't have had a chance to get any persiflage out of my system. Lady Malvern collared the conversation. She had been bottling it up, and now it came out with a rush:

"So this is how you have looked after my poor, dear boy, Mr. Wooster! So this is how you have abused my trust! I left him in your charge, thinking that I could rely on you to shield him from evil. He came to you innocent, unversed in the ways of the world, confiding, unused to the temptations of a large city, and you led him astray!"

I hadn't any remarks to make. All I could think of was the picture of Aunt Agatha drinking all this in and reaching out to sharpen the hatchet against my return.

"You deliberately——"

Far away in the misty distance a soft voice spoke:

"If I might explain, your ladyship."

Jeeves had projected himself in from the dining-room and materialized on the rug. Lady Malvern tried to freeze him with a look, but you can't do that sort of thing to Jeeves. He is look-proof.

"I fancy, your ladyship, that you have misunderstood Mr. Wooster, and that he may have given you the impression that he was in New York when his lordship—was removed. When Mr. Wooster informed your ladyship that his lordship had gone to Boston, he was relying on the version I had given him of his lordship's movements. Mr. Wooster was away, visiting a friend in the country, at the time, and knew nothing of the matter till your ladyship informed him."

Lady Malvern gave a kind of grunt. It didn't rattle Jeeves.

"I feared Mr. Wooster might be disturbed if he knew the truth, as he is so attached to his lordship and has taken such pains to look after him, so I took the liberty of telling him that his lordship had gone away for a visit. It might have been hard for Mr. Wooster to believe that his lordship had gone to prison voluntarily and from the best motives, but your ladyship, knowing him better, will readily understand."

"What!" Lady Malvern goggled at him. "Did you say that Lord Pershore went to prison voluntarily?"

"If I might explain, your ladyship. I think that your ladyship's parting words made a deep impression on his lordship. I have frequently heard him speak to Mr. Wooster of his desire to do something to follow your ladyship's instructions and collect material for your ladyship's book on America. Mr. Wooster will bear me out when I say that his lordship was frequently extremely depressed at the thought that he was doing so little to help."

"Absolutely, by Jove! Quite pipped about it!" I said.

"The idea of making a personal examination into the prison system of the country—from within—occurred to his lordship very suddenly one night. He embraced it eagerly. There was no restraining him."

Lady Malvern looked at Jeeves, then at me, then at Jeeves again. I could see her struggling with the thing.

"Surely, your ladyship," said Jeeves, "it is more reasonable to suppose that a gentleman of his lordship's character went to prison of his own volition than that he committed some breach of the law which necessitated his arrest?"

Lady Malvern blinked. Then she got up.

"Mr. Wooster," she said, "I apologize. I have done you an injustice. I should have known Wilmot better. I should have had more faith in his pure, fine spirit."

"Absolutely!" I said.

"Your breakfast is ready, sir," said Jeeves.

I sat down and dallied in a dazed sort of way with a poached egg.

"Jeeves," I said, "you are certainly a life-saver!"

"Thank you, sir."

"Nothing would have convinced my Aunt Agatha that I hadn't lured that blighter into riotous living."

"I fancy you are right, sir."

I champed my egg for a bit. I was most awfully moved, don't you know, by the way Jeeves had rallied round. Something seemed to tell me that this was an occasion that called for rich rewards. For a moment I hesitated. Then I made up my mind.

"Jeeves!"

"Sir?"

"That pink tie!"

"Yes, sir?"

"Burn it!"

"Thank you, sir."

"And, Jeeves!"

"Yes, sir?"

"Take a taxi and get me that Longacre hat, as worn by John Drew!"

"Thank you very much, sir."

I felt most awfully braced. I felt as if the clouds had rolled away and all was as it used to be. I felt like one of those chappies in the novels who calls off the fight with his wife in the last chapter and decides to forget and forgive. I felt I wanted to do all sorts of other things to show Jeeves that I appreciated him.

"Jeeves," I said, "it isn't enough. Is there anything else you would like?"

"Yes, sir. If I may make the suggestion—fifty dollars."

"Fifty dollars?"

"It will enable me to pay a debt of honour, sir. I owe it to his lordship."

"You owe Lord Pershore fifty dollars?"

"Yes, sir. I happened to meet him in the street the night his lordship was arrested. I had been thinking a good deal about the most suitable method of inducing him to abandon his mode of living, sir. His lordship was a little over-excited at the time and I fancy that he mistook me for a friend of his. At any rate when I took the liberty of wagering him fifty dollars that he would not punch a passing policeman in the eye, he accepted the bet very cordially and won it."

I produced my pocket-book and counted out a hundred.

"Take this, Jeeves," I said; "fifty isn't enough. Do you know, Jeeves, you're—well, you absolutely stand alone!"

"I endeavour to give satisfaction, sir," said Jeeves.

JEEVES AND THE HARD-BOILED EGG

Sometimes of a morning, as I've sat in bed sucking down the early cup of tea and watched my man Jeeves flitting about the room and putting out the raiment for the day, I've wondered what the deuce I should do if the fellow ever took it into his head to leave me. It's not so bad now I'm in New York, but in London the anxiety was frightful. There used to be all sorts of attempts on the part of low blighters to sneak him away from me. Young Reggie Foljambe to my certain knowledge offered him double what I was giving him, and Alistair Bingham-Reeves, who's got a valet who had been known to press his trousers sideways, used to look at him, when he came to see me, with a kind of glittering hungry eye which disturbed me deucedly. Bally pirates!

The thing, you see, is that Jeeves is so dashed competent. You can spot it even in the way he shoves studs into a shirt.

I rely on him absolutely in every crisis, and he never lets me down. And, what's more, he can always be counted on to extend himself on behalf of any pal of mine who happens to be to all appearances knee-deep in the bouillon. Take the rather rummy case, for instance, of dear old Bicky and his uncle, the hard-boiled egg.

It happened after I had been in America for a few months. I got back to the flat latish one night, and when Jeeves brought me the final drink he said:

"Mr. Bickersteth called to see you this evening, sir, while you were out."

"Oh?" I said.

"Twice, sir. He appeared a trifle agitated."

"What, pipped?"

"He gave that impression, sir."

I sipped the whisky. I was sorry if Bicky was in trouble, but, as a matter of fact, I was rather glad to have something I could discuss freely with Jeeves just then, because things had been a bit strained between us for some time, and it had been rather difficult to hit on anything to talk about that wasn't apt to take a personal turn. You see, I had decided—rightly or wrongly—to grow a moustache and this had cut Jeeves to the quick. He couldn't stick the thing at any price, and I had been living ever since in an atmosphere of bally disapproval till I was getting jolly well fed up with it. What I mean is, while there's no doubt that in certain matters of dress Jeeves's judgment is absolutely sound and should be followed, it seemed to me that it was getting a bit too thick if he was going to edit my face as well as my costume. No one can call me an unreasonable chappie, and many's the time I've given in like a lamb when Jeeves has voted against one of my pet suits or ties; but when it comes to a valet's staking out a claim on your upper lip you've simply got to have a bit of the good old bulldog pluck and defy the blighter.

"He said that he would call again later, sir."

"Something must be up, Jeeves."

"Yes, sir."

I gave the moustache a thoughtful twirl. It seemed to hurt Jeeves a good deal, so I chucked it.

"I see by the paper, sir, that Mr. Bickersteth's uncle is arriving on the *Carmantic*."

"Yes?"

"His Grace the Duke of Chiswick, sir."

This was news to me, that Bicky's uncle was a duke. Rum, how little one knows about one's pals! I had met Bicky for the first time at a species of beano or jamboree down in Washington Square, not long after my arrival in New York. I suppose I was a bit homesick at the time, and I rather took to Bicky when I found that he was an Englishman and had, in fact, been up at Oxford with me. Besides, he was a frightful chump, so we naturally drifted together; and while we were taking a quiet snort in a corner that wasn't all cluttered up with artists and sculptors and what-not, he furthermore endeared himself to me by a most extraordinarily gifted imitation of a bull-terrier chasing a cat up a tree. But, though we had subsequently become extremely pally, all I really knew about him was that he was generally hard up, and had an uncle who relieved the strain a bit from time to time by sending him monthly remittances.

"If the Duke of Chiswick is his uncle," I said, "why hasn't he a title?
Why isn't he Lord What-Not?"

"Mr. Bickersteth is the son of his grace's late sister, sir, who married Captain Rollo Bickersteth of the Coldstream Guards."

Jeeves knows everything.

"Is Mr. Bickersteth's father dead, too?"

"Yes, sir."

"Leave any money?"

"No, sir."

I began to understand why poor old Bicky was always more or less on the rocks. To the casual and irreflective observer, if you know what I mean, it may sound a pretty good wheeze having a duke for an uncle, but the trouble about old Chiswick was that, though an extremely wealthy old buster, owning half London and about five counties up north, he was notoriously the most prudent spender in England. He was what American chappies would call a hard-boiled egg. If Bicky's people hadn't left him anything and he depended on what he could prise out of the old duke, he was in a pretty bad way. Not that that explained why he was hunting me like this, because he was a chap who never borrowed money. He said he wanted to keep his pals, so never bit any one's ear on principle.

At this juncture the door bell rang. Jeeves floated out to answer it.

"Yes, sir. Mr. Wooster has just returned," I heard him say. And Bicky came trickling in, looking pretty sorry for himself.

"Halloa, Bicky!" I said. "Jeeves told me you had been trying to get me. Jeeves, bring another glass, and let the revels commence. What's the trouble, Bicky?"

"I'm in a hole, Bertie. I want your advice."

"Say on, old lad!"

"My uncle's turning up to-morrow, Bertie."

"So Jeeves told me."

"The Duke of Chiswick, you know."

"So Jeeves told me."

Bicky seemed a bit surprised.

"Jeeves seems to know everything."

"Rather rummily, that's exactly what I was thinking just now myself."

"Well, I wish," said Bicky gloomily, "that he knew a way to get me out of the hole I'm in."

Jeeves shimmered in with the glass, and stuck it competently on the table.

"Mr. Bickersteth is in a bit of a hole, Jeeves," I said, "and wants you to rally round."

"Very good, sir."

Bicky looked a bit doubtful.

"Well, of course, you know, Bertie, this thing is by way of being a bit private and all that."

"I shouldn't worry about that, old top. I bet Jeeves knows all about it already. Don't you, Jeeves?"

"Yes, sir."

"Eh!" said Bicky, rattled.

"I am open to correction, sir, but is not your dilemma due to the fact that you are at a loss to explain to his grace why you are in New York instead of in Colorado?"

Bicky rocked like a jelly in a high wind.

"How the deuce do you know anything about it?"

"I chanced to meet his grace's butler before we left England. He informed me that he happened to overhear his grace speaking to you on the matter, sir, as he passed the library door."

Bicky gave a hollow sort of laugh.

"Well, as everybody seems to know all about it, there's no need to try to keep it dark. The old boy turfed me out, Bertie, because he said I was a brainless nincompoop. The idea was that he would give me a remittance on condition that I dashed out to some blighted locality of the name of Colorado and learned farming or ranching, or whatever they call it, at some bally ranch or farm or whatever it's called. I didn't fancy the idea a bit. I should have had to ride horses and pursue cows, and so forth. I hate horses. They bite at you. I was all against the scheme. At the same time, don't you know, I had to have that remittance."

"I get you absolutely, dear boy."

"Well, when I got to New York it looked a decent sort of place to me, so I thought it would be a pretty sound notion to stop here. So I cabled to my uncle telling him that I had dropped into a good business wheeze in the city and wanted to chuck the ranch idea. He wrote back that it was all right, and here I've been ever since. He thinks I'm doing well at something or other over here. I never dreamed, don't you know, that he would ever come out here. What on earth am I to do?"

"Jeeves," I said, "what on earth is Mr. Bickersteth to do?"

"You see," said Bicky, "I had a wireless from him to say that he was coming to stay with me—to save hotel bills, I suppose. I've always given him the impression that I was living in pretty good style. I can't have him to stay at my boarding-house."

"Thought of anything, Jeeves?" I said.

"To what extent, sir, if the question is not a delicate one, are you prepared to assist Mr. Bickersteth?"

"I'll do anything I can for you, of course, Bicky, old man."

"Then, if I might make the suggestion, sir, you might lend Mr. Bickersteth——"

"No, by Jove!" said Bicky firmly. "I never have touched you, Bertie, and I'm not going to start now. I may be a chump, but it's my boast that I don't owe a penny to a single soul—not counting tradesmen, of course."

"I was about to suggest, sir, that you might lend Mr. Bickersteth

285

this flat. Mr. Bickersteth could give his grace the impression that he was the owner of it. With your permission I could convey the notion that I was in Mr. Bickersteth's employment, and not in yours. You would be residing here temporarily as Mr. Bickersteth's guest. His grace would occupy the second spare bedroom. I fancy that you would find this answer satisfactorily, sir."

Bicky had stopped rocking himself and was staring at Jeeves in an awed sort of way.

"I would advocate the dispatching of a wireless message to his grace on board the vessel, notifying him of the change of address. Mr. Bickersteth could meet his grace at the dock and proceed directly here.

Will that meet the situation, sir?"

"Absolutely."

"Thank you, sir."

Bicky followed him with his eye till the door closed.

"How does he do it, Bertie?" he said. "I'll tell you what I think it is. I believe it's something to do with the shape of his head. Have you ever noticed his head, Bertie, old man? It sort of sticks out at the back!"

* * * * *

I hopped out of bed early next morning, so as to be among those present when the old boy should arrive. I knew from experience that these ocean liners fetch up at the dock at a deucedly ungodly hour. It wasn't much after nine by the time I'd dressed and had my morning tea and was leaning out of the window, watching the street for Bicky and his uncle. It was one of those jolly, peaceful mornings that make a chappie wish he'd got a soul or something, and I was just brooding on life in general when I became aware of the dickens of a spate in progress down below. A taxi had driven up, and an old boy in a top hat had got out and was kicking up a frightful row about the fare. As far as I could make out, he was trying to get the cab chappie to switch from New York to London prices, and the cab chappie had apparently never heard of London before, and didn't seem to think a lot of it now. The old boy said that in London the trip would have set him back eightpence; and the cabby said he should worry. I called to Jeeves.

"The duke has arrived, Jeeves."

"Yes, sir?"

"That'll be him at the door now."

Jeeves made a long arm and opened the front door, and the old boy crawled in, looking licked to a splinter.

"How do you do, sir?" I said, bustling up and being the ray of sunshine. "Your nephew went down to the dock to meet you, but you must have missed him. My name's Wooster, don't you know. Great pal of Bicky's, and all that sort of thing. I'm staying with him, you know. Would you like a cup of tea? Jeeves, bring a cup of tea."

Old Chiswick had sunk into an arm-chair and was looking about the room.

"Does this luxurious flat belong to my nephew Francis?"

"Absolutely."

"It must be terribly expensive."

"Pretty well, of course. Everything costs a lot over here, you know."

He moaned. Jeeves filtered in with the tea. Old Chiswick took a stab at it to restore his tissues, and nodded.

"A terrible country, Mr. Wooster! A terrible country! Nearly eight shillings for a short cab-drive! Iniquitous!" He took another look round the room. It seemed to fascinate him. "Have you any idea how much my nephew pays for this flat, Mr. Wooster?"

"About two hundred dollars a month, I believe."

"What! Forty pounds a month!"

I began to see that, unless I made the thing a bit more plausible, the scheme might turn out a frost. I could guess what the old boy was thinking. He was trying to square all this prosperity with what he knew of poor old Bicky. And one had to admit that it took a lot of squaring, for dear old Bicky, though a stout fellow and absolutely unrivalled as an imitator of bull-terriers and cats, was in many ways one of the most pronounced fatheads that ever pulled on a suit of gent's underwear.

"I suppose it seems rummy to you," I said, "but the fact is New York often bucks chappies up and makes them show a flash of speed that you wouldn't have imagined them capable of. It sort of develops them. Something in the air, don't you know. I imagine that Bicky in the past, when you knew him, may have been something of a chump, but it's quite different now. Devilish efficient sort of chappie, and looked on in commercial circles as quite the nib!"

"I am amazed! What is the nature of my nephew's business, Mr. Wooster?"

"Oh, just business, don't you know. The same sort of thing Carnegie and Rockefeller and all these coves do, you know." I slid for the door. "Awfully sorry to leave you, but I've got to meet some of the lads elsewhere."

Coming out of the lift I met Bicky bustling in from the street.

"Halloa, Bertie! I missed him. Has he turned up?"

"He's upstairs now, having some tea."

"What does he think of it all?"

"He's absolutely rattled."

"Ripping! I'll be toddling up, then. Toodle-oo, Bertie, old man. See you later."

"Pip-pip, Bicky, dear boy."

He trotted off, full of merriment and good cheer, and I went off to the club to sit in the window and watch the traffic coming up one way and going down the other.

It was latish in the evening when I looked in at the flat to dress for dinner.

"Where's everybody, Jeeves?" I said, finding no little feet pattering about the place. "Gone out?"

"His grace desired to see some of the sights of the city, sir. Mr. Bickersteth is acting as his escort. I fancy their immediate objective was Grant's Tomb."

"I suppose Mr. Bickersteth is a bit braced at the way things are going—what?"

"Sir?"

"I say, I take it that Mr. Bickersteth is tolerably full of beans."

"Not altogether, sir."

"What's his trouble now?"

"The scheme which I took the liberty of suggesting to Mr. Bickersteth and yourself has, unfortunately, not answered entirely satisfactorily, sir."

"Surely the duke believes that Mr. Bickersteth is doing well in business, and all that sort of thing?"

"Exactly, sir. With the result that he has decided to cancel Mr. Bickersteth's monthly allowance, on the ground that, as Mr. Bickersteth is doing so well on his own account, he no longer requires pecuniary assistance."

"Great Scot, Jeeves! This is awful."

"Somewhat disturbing, sir."

"I never expected anything like this!"

"I confess I scarcely anticipated the contingency myself, sir."

"I suppose it bowled the poor blighter over absolutely?"

"Mr. Bickersteth appeared somewhat taken aback, sir."

My heart bled for Bicky.

"We must do something, Jeeves."

"Yes, sir."

"Can you think of anything?"

"Not at the moment, sir."

"There must be something we can do."

"It was a maxim of one of my former employers, sir—as I believe I mentioned to you once before—the present Lord Bridgnorth, that there is always a way. I remember his lordship using the expression on the occasion—he was then a business gentleman and had not yet received his title—when a patent hair-restorer which he chanced to be promoting failed to attract the public. He put it on the market under another name as a depilatory, and amassed a substantial fortune. I have generally found his lordship's aphorism based on sound foundations. No doubt we shall be able to discover some solution of Mr. Bickersteth's difficulty, sir."

"Well, have a stab at it, Jeeves!"

"I will spare no pains, sir."

I went and dressed sadly. It will show you pretty well how pipped I was when I tell you that I near as a toucher put on a white tie with a dinner-jacket. I sallied out for a bit of food more to pass the time than because I wanted it. It seemed brutal to be wading into the bill of fare with poor old Bicky headed for the breadline.

When I got back old Chiswick had gone to bed, but Bicky was

there, hunched up in an arm-chair, brooding pretty tensely, with a cigarette hanging out of the corner of his mouth and a more or less glassy stare in his eyes. He had the aspect of one who had been soaked with what the newspaper chappies call "some blunt instrument."

"This is a bit thick, old thing—what!" I said.

He picked up his glass and drained it feverishly, overlooking the fact that it hadn't anything in it.

"I'm done, Bertie!" he said.

He had another go at the glass. It didn't seem to do him any good.

"If only this had happened a week later, Bertie! My next month's money was due to roll in on Saturday. I could have worked a wheeze I've been reading about in the magazine advertisements. It seems that you can make a dashed amount of money if you can only collect a few dollars and start a chicken-farm. Jolly sound scheme, Bertie! Say you buy a hen—call it one hen for the sake of argument. It lays an egg every day of the week. You sell the eggs seven for twenty-five cents. Keep of hen costs nothing. Profit practically twenty-five cents on every seven eggs. Or look at it another way: Suppose you have a dozen eggs. Each of the hens has a dozen chickens. The chickens grow up and have more chickens. Why, in no time you'd have the place covered knee-deep in hens, all laying eggs, at twenty-five cents for every seven. You'd make a fortune. Jolly life, too, keeping hens!" He had begun to get quite worked up at the thought of it, but he slopped back in his chair at this juncture with a good deal of gloom. "But, of course, it's no good," he said, "because I haven't the cash."

"You've only to say the word, you know, Bicky, old top."

"Thanks awfully, Bertie, but I'm not going to sponge on you."

That's always the way in this world. The chappies you'd like to lend money to won't let you, whereas the chappies you don't want to lend it to will do everything except actually stand you on your head and lift the specie out of your pockets. As a lad who has always rolled tolerably free in the right stuff, I've had lots of experience of the second class. Many's the time, back in London, I've hurried along Piccadilly and felt the hot breath of the toucher on the back of my neck and heard his sharp, excited yapping as he closed in on me. I've simply spent my life scattering largesse to blighters I didn't care a hang for; yet here was I now, dripping doubloons and pieces of eight and longing to hand them over, and Bicky, poor fish, absolutely on his uppers, not taking any at any price.

"Well, there's only one hope, then."

"What's that?"

"Jeeves."

"Sir?"

There was Jeeves, standing behind me, full of zeal. In this matter of shimmering into rooms the chappie is rummy to a degree. You're sitting in the old armchair, thinking of this and that, and then suddenly you look up, and there he is. He moves from point to point with as little uproar as a jelly fish. The thing startled poor old Bicky considerably. He rose from his seat like a rocketing pheasant. I'm used to Jeeves now, but often in the days when he first came to me I've bitten my tongue freely on finding him unexpectedly in my midst.

"Did you call, sir?"

"Oh, there you are, Jeeves!"

"Precisely, sir."

"Jeeves, Mr. Bickersteth is still up the pole. Any ideas?"

"Why, yes, sir. Since we had our recent conversation I fancy I have found what may prove a solution. I do not wish to appear to be taking a liberty, sir, but I think that we have overlooked his grace's potentialities as a source of revenue."

Bicky laughed, what I have sometimes seen described as a hollow, mocking laugh, a sort of bitter cackle from the back of the throat, rather like a gargle.

"I do not allude, sir," explained Jeeves, "to the possibility of inducing his grace to part with money. I am taking the liberty of regarding his grace in the light of an at present—if I may say so—useless property, which is capable of being developed."

Bicky looked at me in a helpless kind of way. I'm bound to say I didn't get it myself.

"Couldn't you make it a bit easier, Jeeves!"

"In a nutshell, sir, what I mean is this: His grace is, in a sense, a prominent personage. The inhabitants of this country, as no doubt you are aware, sir, are peculiarly addicted to shaking hands with prominent personages. It occurred to me that Mr. Bickersteth or yourself might know of persons who would be willing to pay a small fee—let us say two dollars or three—for the privilege of an introduction, including handshake, to his grace."

Bicky didn't seem to think much of it.

"Do you mean to say that anyone would be mug enough to part with solid cash just to shake hands with my uncle?"

"I have an aunt, sir, who paid five shillings to a young fellow for bringing a moving-picture actor to tea at her house one Sunday. It gave her social standing among the neighbours."

Bicky wavered.

"If you think it could be done——"

"I feel convinced of it, sir."

"What do you think, Bertie?"

"I'm for it, old boy, absolutely. A very brainy wheeze."

"Thank you, sir. Will there be anything further? Good night, sir."

And he floated out, leaving us to discuss details.

Until we started this business of floating old Chiswick as a money-making proposition I had never realized what a perfectly foul time those Stock Exchange chappies must have when the public isn't biting freely. Nowadays I read that bit they put in the financial reports about "The market opened quietly" with a sympathetic eye, for, by Jove, it certainly opened quietly for us! You'd hardly believe how difficult it was to interest the public and make them take a flutter on the old boy. By the end of the week the only name we had on our list was a delicatessen-store keeper down in Bicky's part of the town, and as he wanted us to take it out in sliced ham instead of cash that didn't help much. There was a gleam of light when the brother of Bicky's pawnbroker offered ten dollars, money down, for an introduction to old Chiswick, but the deal fell through, owing to its turning out that the chap was an anarchist and intended to kick the old boy instead of shaking hands with him. At that, it took me the deuce of a time to persuade Bicky not to grab the cash and let things take their course. He seemed to regard the pawnbroker's brother rather as a sportsman and benefactor of his species than otherwise.

The whole thing, I'm inclined to think, would have been off if it hadn't been for Jeeves. There is no doubt that Jeeves is in a class of his own. In the matter of brain and resource I don't think I have ever met a chappie so supremely like mother made. He trickled into my room one morning with a good old cup of tea, and intimated that there was something doing.

"Might I speak to you with regard to that matter of his grace, sir?"

"It's all off. We've decided to chuck it."

"Sir?"

"It won't work. We can't get anybody to come."

"I fancy I can arrange that aspect of the matter, sir."

"Do you mean to say you've managed to get anybody?"

"Yes, sir. Eighty-seven gentlemen from Birdsburg, sir."

I sat up in bed and spilt the tea.

"Birdsburg?"

"Birdsburg, Missouri, sir."

"How did you get them?"

"I happened last night, sir, as you had intimated that you would be absent from home, to attend a theatrical performance, and entered into conversation between the acts with the occupant of the adjoining seat. I had observed that he was wearing a somewhat ornate decoration in his buttonhole, sir—a large blue button with the words 'Boost for Birdsburg' upon it in red letters, scarcely a judicious addition to a gentleman's evening costume. To my surprise I noticed that the auditorium was full of persons similarly decorated. I ventured to inquire the explanation, and was informed that these gentlemen, forming a party of eighty-seven, are a convention from a town of the name if Birdsburg, in the State of Missouri. Their visit, I gathered, was purely of a social and pleasurable nature, and my informant spoke at some length of the entertainments arranged for their stay in the city. It was when he related with a considerable amount of satisfaction and pride, that a deputation of their number had been introduced to and had shaken hands with a well-known prizefighter, that it occurred to me to broach the subject of his grace. To make a long story short, sir, I have arranged, subject to your approval, that the entire convention shall be presented to his grace to-morrow afternoon."

I was amazed. This chappie was a Napoleon.

"Eighty-seven, Jeeves. At how much a head?"

"I was obliged to agree to a reduction for quantity, sir. The terms finally arrived at were one hundred and fifty dollars for the party."

I thought a bit.

"Payable in advance?"

"No, sir. I endeavoured to obtain payment in advance, but was not successful."

"Well, any way, when we get it I'll make it up to five hundred. Bicky'll never know. Do you suspect Mr. Bickersteth would suspect anything, Jeeves, if I made it up to five hundred?"

"I fancy not, sir. Mr. Bickersteth is an agreeable gentleman, but not bright."

"All right, then. After breakfast run down to the bank and get me some money."

"Yes, sir."

"You know, you're a bit of a marvel, Jeeves."

"Thank you, sir."

"Right-o!"

"Very good, sir."

When I took dear old Bicky aside in the course of the morning and told him what had happened he nearly broke down. He tottered into the sitting-room and buttonholed old Chiswick, who was reading the comic section of the morning paper with a kind of grim resolution.

"Uncle," he said, "are you doing anything special to-morrow afternoon? I mean to say, I've asked a few of my pals in to meet you, don't you know."

The old boy cocked a speculative eye at him.

"There will be no reporters among them?"

"Reporters? Rather not! Why?"

"I refuse to be badgered by reporters. There were a number of adhesive young men who endeavoured to elicit from me my views on America while the boat was approaching the dock. I will not be subjected to this persecution again."

"That'll be absolutely all right, uncle. There won't be a newspaper-man in the place."

"In that case I shall be glad to make the acquaintance of your friends."

"You'll shake hands with them and so forth?"

"I shall naturally order my behaviour according to the accepted rules of civilized intercourse."

Bicky thanked him heartily and came off to lunch with me at the club, where he babbled freely of hens, incubators, and other rotten things.

After mature consideration we had decided to unleash the Birdsburg contingent on the old boy ten at a time. Jeeves brought his theatre pal round to see us, and we arranged the whole thing with him. A very decent chappie, but rather inclined to collar the conversation and turn it in the direction of his home-town's new water-supply system. We settled that, as an hour was about all he would be likely to stand, each gang should consider itself entitled to seven minutes of the duke's society by Jeeves's stop-watch, and that when their time was up Jeeves should slide into the room and cough meaningly. Then we parted with what I believe are called mutual expressions of goodwill, the Birdsburg chappie extending a cordial invitation to us all to pop out some day and take a look at the new water-supply system, for which we thanked him.

Next day the deputation rolled in. The first shift consisted of the cove we had met and nine others almost exactly like him in every respect. They all looked deuced keen and businesslike, as if from youth up they had been working in the office and catching the boss's eye and what-not. They shook hands with the old boy with a good deal of apparent satisfaction—all except one chappie, who seemed to be brooding about something—and then they stood off and became chatty.

"What message have you for Birdsburg, Duke?" asked our pal.

The old boy seemed a bit rattled.

"I have never been to Birdsburg."

The chappie seemed pained.

"You should pay it a visit," he said. "The most rapidly-growing city in the country. Boost for Birdsburg!"

"Boost for Birdsburg!" said the other chappies reverently.

The chappie who had been brooding suddenly gave tongue.

"Say!"

He was a stout sort of well-fed cove with one of those determined chins and a cold eye.

The assemblage looked at him.

"As a matter of business," said the chappie—"mind you, I'm not questioning anybody's good faith, but, as a matter of strict business— I think this gentleman here ought to put himself on record before witnesses as stating that he really is a duke."

"What do you mean, sir?" cried the old boy, getting purple.

"No offence, simply business. I'm not saying anything, mind you, but there's one thing that seems kind of funny to me. This gentleman here says his name's Mr. Bickersteth, as I understand it. Well, if you're the Duke of Chiswick, why isn't he Lord Percy Something? I've read English novels, and I know all about it."

"This is monstrous!"

"Now don't get hot under the collar. I'm only asking. I've a right to know. You're going to take our money, so it's only fair that we should see that we get our money's worth."

The water-supply cove chipped in:

"You're quite right, Simms. I overlooked that when making the agreement. You see, gentlemen, as business men we've a right to reasonable guarantees of good faith. We are paying Mr. Bickersteth here a hundred and fifty dollars for this reception, and we naturally want to know——"

Old Chiswick gave Bicky a searching look; then he turned to the water-supply chappie. He was frightfully calm.

"I can assure you that I know nothing of this," he said, quite politely. "I should be grateful if you would explain."

"Well, we arranged with Mr. Bickersteth that eighty-seven citizens of Birdsburg should have the privilege of meeting and shaking hands with you for a financial consideration mutually arranged, and what my friend Simms here means—and I'm with him—is that we have only Mr. Bickersteth's word for it—and he is a stranger to us—that you are the Duke of Chiswick at all."

Old Chiswick gulped.

"Allow me to assure you, sir," he said, in a rummy kind of voice, "that
I am the Duke of Chiswick."

"Then that's all right," said the chappie heartily. "That was all we wanted to know. Let the thing go on."

"I am sorry to say," said old Chiswick, "that it cannot go on. I am feeling a little tired. I fear I must ask to be excused."

"But there are seventy-seven of the boys waiting round the corner at this moment, Duke, to be introduced to you."

"I fear I must disappoint them."

"But in that case the deal would have to be off."

"That is a matter for you and my nephew to discuss."

The chappie seemed troubled.

"You really won't meet the rest of them?"

"No!"

"Well, then, I guess we'll be going."

They went out, and there was a pretty solid silence. Then old Chiswick turned to Bicky:

"Well?"

Bicky didn't seem to have anything to say.

"Was it true what that man said?"

"Yes, uncle."

"What do you mean by playing this trick?"

Bicky seemed pretty well knocked out, so I put in a word.

"I think you'd better explain the whole thing, Bicky, old top."

Bicky's Adam's-apple jumped about a bit; then he started:

"You see, you had cut off my allowance, uncle, and I wanted a bit of money to start a chicken farm. I mean to say it's an absolute cert if you once get a bit of capital. You buy a hen, and it lays an egg every day of the week, and you sell the eggs, say, seven for twenty-five cents.

"Keep of hens cost nothing. Profit practically——"

"What is all this nonsense about hens? You led me to suppose you were a substantial business man."

"Old Bicky rather exaggerated, sir," I said, helping the chappie out. "The fact is, the poor old lad is absolutely dependent on that remittance of yours, and when you cut it off, don't you know, he was pretty solidly in the soup, and had to think of some way of closing in on a bit of the ready pretty quick. That's why we thought of this handshaking scheme."

Old Chiswick foamed at the mouth.

"So you have lied to me! You have deliberately deceived me as to your financial status!"

"Poor old Bicky didn't want to go to that ranch," I explained. "He doesn't like cows and horses, but he rather thinks he would be hot stuff among the hens. All he wants is a bit of capital. Don't you think it would be rather a wheeze if you were to——"

"After what has happened? After this—this deceit and foolery? Not a penny!"

"But——"

"Not a penny!"

There was a respectful cough in the background.

"If I might make a suggestion, sir?"

Jeeves was standing on the horizon, looking devilish brainy.

"Go ahead, Jeeves!" I said.

"I would merely suggest, sir, that if Mr. Bickersteth is in need of a little ready money, and is at a loss to obtain it elsewhere, he might secure the sum he requires by describing the occurrences of this afternoon for the Sunday issue of one of the more spirited and enterprising newspapers."

"By Jove!" I said.

"By George!" said Bicky.

"Great heavens!" said old Chiswick.

"Very good, sir," said Jeeves.

Bicky turned to old Chiswick with a gleaming eye.

"Jeeves is right. I'll do it! The *Chronicle* would jump at it. They eat that sort of stuff."

Old Chiswick gave a kind of moaning howl.

"I absolutely forbid you, Francis, to do this thing!"

"That's all very well," said Bicky, wonderfully braced, "but if I can't get the money any other way——"

"Wait! Er—wait, my boy! You are so impetuous! We might arrange something."

"I won't go to that bally ranch."

"No, no! No, no, my boy! I would not suggest it. I would not for a moment suggest it. I—I think——"

He seemed to have a bit of a struggle with himself. "I—I think that, on the whole, it would be best if you returned with me to England. I—I might—in fact, I think I see my way to doing—to—I might be able to utilize your services in some secretarial position."

"I shouldn't mind that."

"I should not be able to offer you a salary, but, as you know, in English political life the unpaid secretary is a recognized figure——"

"The only figure I'll recognize," said Bicky firmly, "is five hundred quid a year, paid quarterly."

"My dear boy!"

"Absolutely!"

"But your recompense, my dear Francis, would consist in the unrivalled opportunities you would have, as my secretary, to gain experience, to accustom yourself to the intricacies of political life, to—in fact, you would be in an exceedingly advantageous position."

"Five hundred a year!" said Bicky, rolling it round his tongue. "Why, that would be nothing to what I could make if I started a chicken farm. It stands to reason. Suppose you have a dozen hens. Each of the hens has a dozen chickens. After a bit the chickens grow up and have a dozen chickens each themselves, and then they all start laying eggs! There's a fortune in it. You can get anything you like for eggs in America. Chappies keep them on ice for years and years, and don't sell them till they fetch about a dollar a whirl. You don't think I'm going to chuck a future like this for anything under five hundred o' goblins a year—what?"

A look of anguish passed over old Chiswick's face, then he seemed to be resigned to it. "Very well, my boy," he said.

"What-o!" said Bicky. "All right, then."

"Jeeves," I said. Bicky had taken the old boy off to dinner to celebrate, and we were alone. "Jeeves, this has been one of your best efforts."

"Thank you, sir."

"It beats me how you do it."

"Yes, sir."

"The only trouble is you haven't got much out of it—what!"

"I fancy Mr. Bickersteth intends—I judge from his remarks—to signify his appreciation of anything I have been fortunate enough to do to assist him, at some later date when he is in a more favourable position to do so."

299

"It isn't enough, Jeeves!"

"Sir?"

It was a wrench, but I felt it was the only possible thing to be done.

"Bring my shaving things."

A gleam of hope shone in the chappie's eye, mixed with doubt.

"You mean, sir?"

"And shave off my moustache."

There was a moment's silence. I could see the fellow was deeply moved.

"Thank you very much indeed, sir," he said, in a low voice, and popped off.

ABSENT TREATMENT

I want to tell you all about dear old Bobbie Cardew. It's a most interesting story. I can't put in any literary style and all that; but I don't have to, don't you know, because it goes on its Moral Lesson. If you're a man you mustn't miss it, because it'll be a warning to you; and if you're a woman you won't want to, because it's all about how a girl made a man feel pretty well fed up with things.

If you're a recent acquaintance of Bobbie's, you'll probably be surprised to hear that there was a time when he was more remarkable for the weakness of his memory than anything else. Dozens of fellows, who have only met Bobbie since the change took place, have been surprised when I told them that. Yet it's true. Believe *me*.

In the days when I first knew him Bobbie Cardew was about the most pronounced young rotter inside the four-mile radius. People have called me a silly ass, but I was never in the same class with Bobbie. When it came to being a silly ass, he was a plus-four man, while my handicap was about six. Why, if I wanted him to dine with me, I used to post him a letter at the beginning of the week, and then the day before send him a telegram and a phone-call on the day itself, and—half an hour before the time we'd fixed—a messenger in a taxi, whose business it was to see that he got in and that the chauffeur had the address all correct. By doing this I generally managed to get him, unless he had left town before my messenger arrived.

The funny thing was that he wasn't altogether a fool in other ways. Deep down in him there was a kind of stratum of sense. I had known him, once or twice, show an almost human intelligence. But to reach that stratum, mind you, you needed dynamite.

At least, that's what I thought. But there was another way which hadn't occurred to me. Marriage, I mean. Marriage, the dynamite of the soul; that was what hit Bobbie. He married. Have you ever seen a bull-pup chasing a bee? The pup sees the bee. It looks good to him. But he still doesn't know what's at the end of it till he gets there. It was like that with Bobbie. He fell in love, got married—with a sort of whoop, as if it were the greatest fun in the world—and then began to find out things.

She wasn't the sort of girl you would have expected Bobbie to rave about. And yet, I don't know. What I mean is, she worked for her living; and to a fellow who has never done a hand's turn in his life there's undoubtedly a sort of fascination, a kind of romance, about a girl who works for her living.

Her name was Anthony. Mary Anthony. She was about five feet six; she had a ton and a half of red-gold hair, grey eyes, and one of those determined chins. She was a hospital nurse. When Bobbie smashed himself up at polo, she was told off by the authorities to smooth his brow and rally round with cooling unguents and all that; and the old boy hadn't been up and about again for more than a week before they popped off to the registrar's and fixed it up. Quite the romance.

Bobbie broke the news to me at the club one evening, and next day he introduced me to her. I admired her. I've never worked myself—my name's Pepper, by the way. Almost forgot to mention it. Reggie Pepper. My uncle Edward was Pepper, Wells, and Co., the Colliery people. He left me a sizable chunk of bullion—I say I've never worked myself, but I admire any one who earns a living under difficulties, especially a girl. And this girl had had a rather unusually tough time of it, being an orphan and all that, and having had to do everything off her own bat for years.

Mary and I got along together splendidly. We don't now, but we'll come to that later. I'm speaking of the past. She seemed to think Bobbie the greatest thing on earth, judging by the way she looked at him when she thought I wasn't noticing. And Bobbie seemed to think the same about her. So that I came to the conclusion that, if only dear old Bobbie didn't forget to go to the wedding, they had a sporting chance of being quite happy.

Well, let's brisk up a bit here, and jump a year. The story doesn't really start till then.

They took a flat and settled down. I was in and out of the place quite a good deal. I kept my eyes open, and everything seemed to me to be running along as smoothly as you could want. If this was marriage, I thought, I couldn't see why fellows were so frightened of it. There were a lot of worse things that could happen to a man.

But we now come to the incident of the quiet Dinner, and it's just here that love's young dream hits a snag, and things begin to occur.

I happened to meet Bobbie in Piccadilly, and he asked me to come back to dinner at the flat. And, like a fool, instead of bolting and putting myself under police protection, I went.

When we got to the flat, there was Mrs. Bobbie looking—well, I tell you, it staggered me. Her gold hair was all piled up in waves and crinkles and things, with a what-d'-you-call-it of diamonds in it. And she was wearing the most perfectly ripping dress. I couldn't begin to describe it. I can only say it was the limit. It struck me that if this was how she was in the habit of looking every night when they were dining quietly at home together, it was no wonder that Bobbie liked domesticity.

"Here's old Reggie, dear," said Bobbie. "I've brought him home to have a bit of dinner. I'll phone down to the kitchen and ask them to send it up now—what?"

She stared at him as if she had never seen him before. Then she turned scarlet. Then she turned as white as a sheet. Then she gave a little laugh. It was most interesting to watch. Made me wish I was up a tree about eight hundred miles away. Then she recovered herself.

"I am so glad you were able to come, Mr. Pepper," she said, smiling at me.

And after that she was all right. At least, you would have said so. She talked a lot at dinner, and chaffed Bobbie, and played us ragtime on the piano afterwards, as if she hadn't a care in the world. Quite a jolly little party it was—not. I'm no lynx-eyed sleuth, and all that sort of thing, but I had seen her face at the beginning, and I knew that she was working the whole time and working hard, to keep herself in hand, and that she would have given that diamond what's-its-name in her hair and everything else she possessed to have one good scream—just one. I've sat through some pretty thick evenings in my time, but that one had the rest beaten in a canter. At the very earliest moment I grabbed my hat and got away.

Having seen what I did, I wasn't particularly surprised to meet Bobbie at the club next day looking about as merry and bright as a lonely gum-drop at an Eskimo tea-party.

He started in straightway. He seemed glad to have someone to talk to about it.

"Do you know how long I've been married?" he said.

I didn't exactly.

"About a year, isn't it?"

"Not *about* a year," he said sadly. "Exactly a year—yesterday!"

Then I understood. I saw light—a regular flash of light.

"Yesterday was———?"

"The anniversary of the wedding. I'd arranged to take Mary to the Savoy, and on to Covent Garden. She particularly wanted to hear Caruso. I had the ticket for the box in my pocket. Do you know, all through dinner I had a kind of rummy idea that there was something I'd forgotten, but I couldn't think what?"

"Till your wife mentioned it?"

He nodded———

"She—mentioned it," he said thoughtfully.

I didn't ask for details. Women with hair and chins like Mary's may be angels most of the time, but, when they take off their wings for a bit, they aren't half-hearted about it.

"To be absolutely frank, old top," said poor old Bobbie, in a broken sort of way, "my stock's pretty low at home."

There didn't seem much to be done. I just lit a cigarette and sat there. He didn't want to talk. Presently he went out. I stood at the window of our upper smoking-room, which looks out on to

303

Piccadilly, and watched him. He walked slowly along for a few yards, stopped, then walked on again, and finally turned into a jeweller's. Which was an instance of what I meant when I said that deep down in him there was a certain stratum of sense.

* * * * *

It was from now on that I began to be really interested in this problem of Bobbie's married life. Of course, one's always mildly interested in one's friends' marriages, hoping they'll turn out well and all that; but this was different. The average man isn't like Bobbie, and the average girl isn't like Mary. It was that old business of the immovable mass and the irresistible force. There was Bobbie, ambling gently through life, a dear old chap in a hundred ways, but undoubtedly a chump of the first water.

And there was Mary, determined that he shouldn't be a chump. And Nature, mind you, on Bobbie's side. When Nature makes a chump like dear old Bobbie, she's proud of him, and doesn't want her handiwork disturbed. She gives him a sort of natural armour to protect him against outside interference. And that armour is shortness of memory. Shortness of memory keeps a man a chump, when, but for it, he might cease to be one. Take my case, for instance. I'm a chump. Well, if I had remembered half the things people have tried to teach me during my life, my size in hats would be about number nine. But I didn't. I forgot them. And it was just the same with Bobbie.

For about a week, perhaps a bit more, the recollection of that quiet little domestic evening bucked him up like a tonic. Elephants, I read somewhere, are champions at the memory business, but they were fools to Bobbie during that week. But, bless you, the shock wasn't nearly big enough. It had dinted the armour, but it hadn't made a hole in it. Pretty soon he was back at the old game.

It was pathetic, don't you know. The poor girl loved him, and she was frightened. It was the thin edge of the wedge, you see, and she knew it. A man who forgets what day he was married, when he's been married one year, will forget, at about the end of the fourth, that he's married at all. If she meant to get him in hand at all, she had got to do it now, before he began to drift away.

I saw that clearly enough, and I tried to make Bobbie see it, when he was by way of pouring out his troubles to me one afternoon. I can't remember what it was that he had forgotten the day before, but it was something she had asked him to bring home for her—it may have been a book.

"It's such a little thing to make a fuss about," said Bobbie. "And she knows that it's simply because I've got such an infernal memory about everything. I can't remember anything. Never could."

He talked on for a while, and, just as he was going, he pulled out a couple of sovereigns.

"Oh, by the way," he said.

"What's this for?" I asked, though I knew.

"I owe it you."

"How's that?" I said.

"Why, that bet on Tuesday. In the billiard-room. Murray and Brown were playing a hundred up, and I gave you two to one that Brown would win, and Murray beat him by twenty odd."

"So you do remember some things?" I said.

He got quite excited. Said that if I thought he was the sort of rotter who forgot to pay when he lost a bet, it was pretty rotten of me after knowing him all these years, and a lot more like that.

"Subside, laddie," I said.

Then I spoke to him like a father.

"What you've got to do, my old college chum," I said, "is to pull yourself together, and jolly quick, too. As things are shaping, you're due for a nasty knock before you know what's hit you. You've got to make an effort. Don't say you can't. This two quid business shows that, even if your memory is rocky, you can remember some things. What you've got to do is to see that wedding anniversaries and so on are included in the list. It may be a brainstrain, but you can't get out of it."

"I suppose you're right," said Bobbie. "But it beats me why she thinks such a lot of these rotten little dates. What's it matter if I forgot what day we were married on or what day she was born on or what day the cat had the measles? She knows I love her just as much as if I were a memorizing freak at the halls."

"That's not enough for a woman," I said. "They want to be shown. Bear that in mind, and you're all right. Forget it, and there'll be trouble."

He chewed the knob of his stick.

"Women are frightfully rummy," he said gloomily.

"You should have thought of that before you married one," I said.

* * * * *

I don't see that I could have done any more. I had put the whole thing in a nutshell for him. You would have thought he'd have seen the point, and that it would have made him brace up and get a hold on himself. But no. Off he went again in the same old way. I gave up arguing with him. I had a good deal of time on my hands, but not enough to amount to anything when it was a question of reforming dear old Bobbie by argument. If you see a man asking for trouble, and insisting on getting it, the only thing to do is to stand by and wait till it comes to him. After that you may get a chance. But till then there's nothing to be done. But I thought a lot about him.

Bobbie didn't get into the soup all at once. Weeks went by, and months, and still nothing happened. Now and then he'd come into the club with a kind of cloud on his shining morning face, and I'd know that there had been doings in the home; but it wasn't till well on in the spring that he got the thunderbolt just where he had been asking for it—in the thorax.

I was smoking a quiet cigarette one morning in the window looking out over Piccadilly, and watching the buses and motors going up one way and down the other—most interesting it is; I often do it—when in rushed Bobbie, with his eyes bulging and his face the colour of an oyster, waving a piece of paper in his hand.

"Reggie," he said. "Reggie, old top, she's gone!"

"Gone!" I said. "Who?"

"Mary, of course! Gone! Left me! Gone!"

"Where?" I said.

Silly question? Perhaps you're right. Anyhow, dear old Bobbie nearly foamed at the mouth.

"Where? How should I know where? Here, read this."

He pushed the paper into my hand. It was a letter.

"Go on," said Bobbie. "Read it."

So I did. It certainly was quite a letter. There was not much of it, but it was all to the point. This is what it said:

"MY DEAR BOBBIE,—I am going away. When you care enough

about me to remember to wish me many happy returns on my birthday, I will come back. My address will be Box 341, *London Morning News*."

I read it twice, then I said, "Well, why don't you?"

"Why don't I what?"

"Why don't you wish her many happy returns? It doesn't seem much to ask."

"But she says on her birthday."

"Well, when is her birthday?"

"Can't you understand?" said Bobbie. "I've forgotten."

"Forgotten!" I said.

"Yes," said Bobbie. "Forgotten."

"How do you mean, forgotten?" I said. "Forgotten whether it's the twentieth or the twenty-first, or what? How near do you get to it?"

"I know it came somewhere between the first of January and the thirty-first of December. That's how near I get to it."

"Think."

"Think? What's the use of saying 'Think'? Think I haven't thought? I've been knocking sparks out of my brain ever since I opened that letter."

"And you can't remember?"

"No."

I rang the bell and ordered restoratives.

"Well, Bobbie," I said, "it's a pretty hard case to spring on an untrained amateur like me. Suppose someone had come to Sherlock Holmes and said, 'Mr. Holmes, here's a case for you. When is my wife's birthday?' Wouldn't that have given Sherlock a jolt? However, I know enough about the game to understand that a fellow can't shoot off his deductive theories unless you start him with a clue, so rouse yourself out of that pop-eyed trance and come across with two or three. For instance, can't you remember the last time she had a birthday? What sort of weather was it? That might fix the month."

Bobbie shook his head.

"It was just ordinary weather, as near as I can recollect."

"Warm?"

"Warmish."

"Or cold?"

"Well, fairly cold, perhaps. I can't remember."

I ordered two more of the same. They seemed indicated in the Young Detective's Manual. "You're a great help, Bobbie," I said. "An invaluable assistant. One of those indispensable adjuncts without which no home is complete."

Bobbie seemed to be thinking.

"I've got it," he said suddenly. "Look here. I gave her a present on her last birthday. All we have to do is to go to the shop, hunt up the date when it was bought, and the thing's done."

"Absolutely. What did you give her?"

He sagged.

"I can't remember," he said.

Getting ideas is like golf. Some days you're right off, others it's as easy as falling off a log. I don't suppose dear old Bobbie had ever had two ideas in the same morning before in his life; but now he did it without an effort. He just loosed another dry Martini into the undergrowth, and before you could turn round it had flushed quite a brain-wave.

Do you know those little books called *When were you Born?* There's one for each month. They tell you your character, your talents, your strong points, and your weak points at fourpence halfpenny a go. Bobbie's idea was to buy the whole twelve, and go through them till we found out which month hit off Mary's character. That would give us the month, and narrow it down a whole lot.

A pretty hot idea for a non-thinker like dear old Bobbie. We sallied out at once. He took half and I took half, and we settled down to work. As I say, it sounded good. But when we came to go into the thing, we saw that there was a flaw. There was plenty of information all right, but there wasn't a single month that didn't have something that exactly hit off Mary. For instance, in the December book it said, "December people are apt to keep their own secrets. They are extensive travellers." Well, Mary had certainly kept her secret, and she had travelled quite extensively enough for Bobbie's needs. Then, October people were "born with original ideas" and "loved moving." You couldn't have summed up Mary's little jaunt more neatly. February people had "wonderful memories"—Mary's speciality.

We took a bit of a rest, then had another go at the thing.

Bobbie was all for May, because the book said that women born in that month were "inclined to be capricious, which is always a barrier to a happy married life"; but I plumped for February, because February women "are unusually determined to have their own way, are very earnest, and expect a full return in their companion or mates." Which he owned was about as like Mary as anything could be.

In the end he tore the books up, stamped on them, burnt them, and went home.

It was wonderful what a change the next few days made in dear old Bobbie. Have you ever seen that picture, "The Soul's Awakening"? It represents a flapper of sorts gazing in a startled sort of way into the middle distance with a look in her eyes that seems to say, "Surely that is George's step I hear on the mat! Can this be love?" Well, Bobbie had a soul's awakening too. I don't suppose he had ever troubled to think in his life before—not really *think*. But now he was wearing his brain to the bone. It was painful in a way, of course, to see a fellow human being so thoroughly in the soup, but I felt strongly that it was all for the best. I could see as plainly as possible that all these brainstorms were improving Bobbie out of knowledge. When it was all over he might possibly become a rotter again of a sort, but it would only be a pale reflection of the rotter he had been. It bore out the idea I had always had that what he needed was a real good jolt.

I saw a great deal of him these days. I was his best friend, and he came to me for sympathy. I gave it him, too, with both hands, but I never failed to hand him the Moral Lesson when I had him weak.

One day he came to me as I was sitting in the club, and I could see that he had had an idea. He looked happier than he had done in weeks.

"Reggie," he said, "I'm on the trail. This time I'm convinced that I shall pull it off. I've remembered something of vital importance."

"Yes?" I said.

"I remember distinctly," he said, "that on Mary's last birthday we went together to the Coliseum. How does that hit you?"

"It's a fine bit of memorizing," I said; "but how does it help?"

"Why, they change the programme every week there."

"Ah!" I said. "Now you are talking."

"And the week we went one of the turns was Professor Some One's Terpsichorean Cats. I recollect them distinctly. Now, are we narrowing it down, or aren't we? Reggie, I'm going round to the Coliseum this minute, and I'm going to dig the date of those Terpsichorean Cats out of them, if I have to use a crowbar."

So that got him within six days; for the management treated us like brothers; brought out the archives, and ran agile fingers over the pages till they treed the cats in the middle of May.

"I told you it was May," said Bobbie. "Maybe you'll listen to me another time."

"If you've any sense," I said, "there won't be another time."

And Bobbie said that there wouldn't.

Once you get your money on the run, it parts as if it enjoyed doing it. I had just got off to sleep that night when my telephone-bell rang. It was Bobbie, of course. He didn't apologize.

"Reggie," he said, "I've got it now for certain. It's just come to me. We saw those Terpsichorean Cats at a matinee, old man."

"Yes?" I said.

"Well, don't you see that that brings it down to two days? It must have been either Wednesday the seventh or Saturday the tenth."

"Yes," I said, "if they didn't have daily matinees at the Coliseum."

I heard him give a sort of howl.

"Bobbie," I said. My feet were freezing, but I was fond of him.

"Well?"

"I've remembered something too. It's this. The day you went to the Coliseum I lunched with you both at the Ritz. You had forgotten to bring any money with you, so you wrote a cheque."

"But I'm always writing cheques."

"You are. But this was for a tenner, and made out to the hotel. Hunt up your cheque-book and see how many cheques for ten pounds payable to the Ritz Hotel you wrote out between May the fifth and May the tenth."

He gave a kind of gulp.

"Reggie," he said, "you're a genius. I've always said so. I believe you've got it. Hold the line."

Presently he came back again.

"Halloa!" he said.

"I'm here," I said.

"It was the eighth. Reggie, old man, I——"

"Topping," I said. "Good night."

It was working along into the small hours now, but I thought I might as well make a night of it and finish the thing up, so I rang up an hotel near the Strand.

"Put me through to Mrs. Cardew," I said.

"It's late," said the man at the other end.

"And getting later every minute," I said. "Buck along, laddie."

I waited patiently. I had missed my beauty-sleep, and my feet had frozen hard, but I was past regrets.

"What is the matter?" said Mary's voice.

"My feet are cold," I said. "But I didn't call you up to tell you that particularly. I've just been chatting with Bobbie, Mrs. Cardew."

"Oh! is that Mr. Pepper?"

"Yes. He's remembered it, Mrs. Cardew."

She gave a sort of scream. I've often thought how interesting it must be to be one of those Exchange girls. The things they must hear, don't you know. Bobbie's howl and gulp and Mrs. Bobbie's scream and all about my feet and all that. Most interesting it must be.

"He's remembered it!" she gasped. "Did you tell him?"

"No."

Well, I hadn't.

"Mr. Pepper."

"Yes?"

"Was he—has he been—was he very worried?"

I chuckled. This was where I was billed to be the life and soul of the party.

"Worried! He was about the most worried man between here and Edinburgh. He has been worrying as if he was paid to do it by the nation. He has started out to worry after breakfast, and——"

Oh, well, you can never tell with women. My idea was that we should pass the rest of the night slapping each other on the back across the wire, and telling each other what bally brainy conspirators we were, don't you know, and all that. But I'd got just as far as this, when she bit at me. Absolutely! I heard the snap. And then she said "Oh!" in that choked kind of way. And when a woman says "Oh!" like that, it means all the bad words she'd love to say if she only knew them.

And then she began.

"What brutes men are! What horrid brutes! How you could stand by and see poor dear Bobbie worrying himself into a fever, when a word from you would have put everything right, I can't——"

"But——"

"And you call yourself his friend! His friend!" (Metallic laugh, most unpleasant.) "It shows how one can be deceived. I used to think you a kind-hearted man."

"But, I say, when I suggested the thing, you thought it perfectly——"

"I thought it hateful, abominable."

"But you said it was absolutely top——"

"I said nothing of the kind. And if I did, I didn't mean it. I don't wish to be unjust, Mr. Pepper, but I must say that to me there seems to be something positively fiendish in a man who can go out of his way to separate a husband from his wife, simply in order to amuse himself by gloating over his agony——"

"But——!"

"When one single word would have——"

"But you made me promise not to——" I bleated.

"And if I did, do you suppose I didn't expect you to have the sense to break your promise?"

I had finished. I had no further observations to make. I hung up the receiver, and crawled into bed.

* * * * *

I still see Bobbie when he comes to the club, but I do not visit the old homestead. He is friendly, but he stops short of issuing invitations. I ran across Mary at the Academy last week, and her eyes went through me like a couple of bullets through a pat of butter. And as they came out the other side, and I limped off to piece myself together again, there occurred to me the simple epitaph which, when I am no more, I intend to have inscribed on my tombstone. It was this: "He was a man who acted from the best motives. There is one born every minute."

HELPING FREDDIE

I don't want to bore you, don't you know, and all that sort of rot, but I must tell you about dear old Freddie Meadowes. I'm not a flier at literary style, and all that, but I'll get some writer chappie to give the thing a wash and brush up when I've finished, so that'll be all right.

Dear old Freddie, don't you know, has been a dear old pal of mine for years and years; so when I went into the club one morning and found him sitting alone in a dark corner, staring glassily at nothing, and generally looking like the last rose of summer, you can understand I was quite disturbed about it. As a rule, the old rotter is the life and soul of our set. Quite the little lump of fun, and all that sort of thing.

Jimmy Pinkerton was with me at the time. Jimmy's a fellow who writes plays—a deuced brainy sort of fellow—and between us we set to work to question the poor pop-eyed chappie, until finally we got at what the matter was.

As we might have guessed, it was a girl. He had had a quarrel with Angela West, the girl he was engaged to, and she had broken off the engagement. What the row had been about he didn't say, but apparently she was pretty well fed up. She wouldn't let him come near her, refused to talk on the phone, and sent back his letters unopened.

I was sorry for poor old Freddie. I knew what it felt like. I was once in love myself with a girl called Elizabeth Shoolbred, and the fact that she couldn't stand me at any price will be recorded in my autobiography. I knew the thing for Freddie.

"Change of scene is what you want, old scout," I said. "Come with me to Marvis Bay. I've taken a cottage there. Jimmy's coming down on the twenty-fourth. We'll be a cosy party."

"He's absolutely right," said Jimmy. "Change of scene's the thing. I knew a man. Girl refused him. Man went abroad. Two months later girl wired him, 'Come back. Muriel.' Man started to write out a reply; suddenly found that he couldn't remember girl's surname; so never answered at all."

But Freddie wouldn't be comforted. He just went on looking as if he had swallowed his last sixpence. However, I got him to promise to come to Marvis Bay with me. He said he might as well be there as anywhere.

Do you know Marvis Bay? It's in Dorsetshire. It isn't what you'd call a fiercely exciting spot, but it has its good points. You spend the day there bathing and sitting on the sands, and in the evening you stroll out on the shore with the gnats. At nine o'clock you rub ointment on the wounds and go to bed.

It seemed to suit poor old Freddie. Once the moon was up and the breeze sighing in the trees, you couldn't drag him from that beach with a rope. He became quite a popular pet with the gnats. They'd hang round waiting for him to come out, and would give perfectly good strollers the miss-in-baulk just so as to be in good condition for him.

Yes, it was a peaceful sort of life, but by the end of the first week I began to wish that Jimmy Pinkerton had arranged to come down earlier: for as a companion Freddie, poor old chap, wasn't anything to write home to mother about. When he wasn't chewing a pipe and scowling at the carpet, he was sitting at the piano, playing "The Rosary" with one finger. He couldn't play anything except "The Rosary," and he couldn't play much of that. Somewhere round about the third bar a fuse would blow out, and he'd have to start all over again.

He was playing it as usual one morning when I came in from bathing.

"Reggie," he said, in a hollow voice, looking up, "I've seen her."

"Seen her?" I said. "What, Miss West?"

"I was down at the post office, getting the letters, and we met in the doorway. She cut me!"

He started "The Rosary" again, and side-slipped in the second bar.

"Reggie," he said, "you ought never to have brought me here. I must go away."

"Go away?" I said. "Don't talk such rot. This is the best thing that could have happened. This is where you come out strong."

"She cut me."

"Never mind. Be a sportsman. Have another dash at her."

"She looked clean through me!"

"Of course she did. But don't mind that. Put this thing in my hands. I'll see you through. Now, what you want," I said, "is to place her under some obligation to you. What you want is to get her timidly thanking you. What you want——"

"But what's she going to thank me timidly for?"

I thought for a moment.

"Look out for a chance and save her from drowning," I said.

"I can't swim," said Freddie.

That was Freddie all over, don't you know. A dear old chap in a thousand ways, but no help to a fellow, if you know what I mean.

He cranked up the piano once more and I sprinted for the open.

I strolled out on to the sands and began to think this thing over. There was no doubt that the brain-work had got to be done by me. Dear old Freddie had his strong qualities. He was top-hole at polo, and in happier days I've heard him give an imitation of cats fighting in a backyard that would have surprised you. But apart from that he wasn't a man of enterprise.

Well, don't you know, I was rounding some rocks, with my brain whirring like a dynamo, when I caught sight of a blue dress, and, by Jove, it was the girl. I had never met her, but Freddie had sixteen photographs of her sprinkled round his bedroom, and I knew I couldn't be mistaken. She was sitting on the sand, helping a small, fat child build a castle. On a chair close by was an elderly lady reading a novel. I heard the girl call her "aunt." So, doing the Sherlock Holmes business, I deduced that the fat child was her cousin. It struck me that if Freddie had been there he would probably have tried to work up some sentiment about the kid on the strength of it. Personally I couldn't manage it. I don't think I ever saw a child who made me feel less sentimental. He was one of those round, bulging kids.

After he had finished the castle he seemed to get bored with life, and began to whimper. The girl took him off to where a fellow was selling sweets at a stall. And I walked on.

Now, fellows, if you ask them, will tell you that I'm a chump. Well, I don't mind. I admit it. I *am* a chump. All the Peppers have been chumps. But what I do say is that every now and then, when you'd least expect it, I get a pretty hot brain-wave; and that's what happened now. I doubt if the idea that came to me then would have occurred to a single one of any dozen of the brainiest chappies you care to name.

It came to me on my return journey. I was walking back along the shore, when I saw the fat kid meditatively smacking a jelly-fish with a spade. The girl wasn't with him. In fact, there didn't seem to be any one in sight. I was just going to pass on when I got the brain-wave. I thought the whole thing out in a flash, don't you know. From what I had seen of the two, the girl was evidently fond of this kid, and, anyhow, he was her cousin, so what I said to myself was this: If I kidnap this young heavy-weight for the moment, and if, when the girl has got frightfully anxious about where he can have got to, dear old Freddie suddenly appears leading the infant by the hand and telling a story to the effect that he has found him wandering at large about the country and practically saved his life, why, the girl's gratitude is bound to make her chuck hostilities and be friends again. So I gathered in the kid and made off with him. All the way home I pictured that scene of reconciliation. I could see it so vividly, don't you know, that, by George, it gave me quite a choky feeling in my throat.

Freddie, dear old chap, was rather slow at getting on to the fine points of the idea. When I appeared, carrying the kid, and dumped him down in our sitting-room, he didn't absolutely effervesce with joy, if you know what I mean. The kid had started to bellow by this time, and poor old Freddie seemed to find it rather trying.

"Stop it!" he said. "Do you think nobody's got any troubles except you?
What the deuce is all this, Reggie?"

The kid came back at him with a yell that made the window rattle. I raced to the kitchen and fetched a jar of honey. It was the right stuff. The kid stopped bellowing and began to smear his face with the stuff.

"Well?" said Freddie, when silence had set in. I explained the idea. After a while it began to strike him.

"You're not such a fool as you look, sometimes, Reggie," he said handsomely. "I'm bound to say this seems pretty good."

And he disentangled the kid from the honey-jar and took him out, to scour the beach for Angela.

I don't know when I've felt so happy. I was so fond of dear old Freddie that to know that he was soon going to be his old bright self again made me feel as if somebody had left me about a million pounds. I was leaning back in a chair on the veranda, smoking peacefully, when down the road I saw the old boy returning, and, by George, the kid was still with him. And Freddie looked as if he hadn't a friend in the world.

"Hello!" I said. "Couldn't you find her?"

"Yes, I found her," he replied, with one of those bitter, hollow laughs.

"Well, then——?"

Freddie sank into a chair and groaned.

"This isn't her cousin, you idiot!" he said.

"He's no relation at all. He's just a kid she happened to meet on the beach. She had never seen him before in her life."

"What! Who is he, then?"

"I don't know. Oh, Lord, I've had a time! Thank goodness you'll probably spend the next few years of your life in Dartmoor for kidnapping. That's my only consolation. I'll come and jeer at you through the bars."

"Tell me all, old boy," I said.

It took him a good long time to tell the story, for he broke off in the middle of nearly every sentence to call me names, but I gathered gradually what had happened. She had listened like an iceberg while he told the story he had prepared, and then—well, she didn't actually call him a liar, but she gave him to understand in a general sort of way that if he and Dr. Cook ever happened to meet, and started swapping stories, it would be about the biggest duel on record. And then he had crawled away with the kid, licked to a splinter.

"And mind, this is your affair," he concluded. "I'm not mixed up in it at all. If you want to escape your sentence, you'd better go and find the kid's parents and return him before the police come for you."

* * * * *

By Jove, you know, till I started to tramp the place with this infernal kid, I never had a notion it would have been so deuced

317

difficult to restore a child to its anxious parents. It's a mystery to me how kidnappers ever get caught. I searched Marvis Bay like a bloodhound, but nobody came forward to claim the infant. You'd have thought, from the lack of interest in him, that he was stopping there all by himself in a cottage of his own. It wasn't till, by an inspiration, I thought to ask the sweet-stall man that I found out that his name was Medwin, and that his parents lived at a place called Ocean Rest, in Beach Road.

I shot off there like an arrow and knocked at the door. Nobody answered. I knocked again. I could hear movements inside, but nobody came. I was just going to get to work on that knocker in such a way that the idea would filter through into these people's heads that I wasn't standing there just for the fun of the thing, when a voice from somewhere above shouted, "Hi!"

I looked up and saw a round, pink face, with grey whiskers east and west of it, staring down from an upper window.

"Hi!" it shouted again.

"What the deuce do you mean by 'Hi'?" I said.

"You can't come in," said the face. "Hello, is that Tootles?"

"My name is not Tootles, and I don't want to come in," I said. "Are   you Mr. Medwin? I've brought back your son."

"I see him. Peep-bo, Tootles! Dadda can see 'oo!"

The face disappeared with a jerk. I could hear voices. The face reappeared.

"Hi!"

I churned the gravel madly.

"Do you live here?" said the face.

"I'm staying here for a few weeks."

"What's your name?"

"Pepper. But——"

"Pepper? Any relation to Edward Pepper, the colliery owner?"

"My uncle. But——"

"I used to know him well. Dear old Edward Pepper! I wish I was with him now."

"I wish you were," I said.

He beamed down at me.

"This is most fortunate," he said. "We were wondering what we

318

were to do with Tootles. You see, we have the mumps here. My daughter Bootles has just developed mumps. Tootles must not be exposed to the risk of infection. We could not think what we were to do with him. It was most fortunate your finding him. He strayed from his nurse. I would hesitate to trust him to the care of a stranger, but you are different. Any nephew of Edward Pepper's has my implicit confidence. You must take Tootles to your house. It will be an ideal arrangement. I have written to my brother in London to come and fetch him. He may be here in a few days."

"May!"

"He is a busy man, of course; but he should certainly be here within a week. Till then Tootles can stop with you. It is an excellent plan. Very much obliged to you. Your wife will like Tootles."

"I haven't got a wife," I yelled; but the window had closed with a bang, as if the man with the whiskers had found a germ trying to escape, don't you know, and had headed it off just in time.

I breathed a deep breath and wiped my forehead.

The window flew up again.

"Hi!"

A package weighing about a ton hit me on the head and burst like a bomb.

"Did you catch it?" said the face, reappearing. "Dear me, you missed it! Never mind. You can get it at the grocer's. Ask for Bailey's Granulated Breakfast Chips. Tootles takes them for breakfast with a little milk. Be certain to get Bailey's."

My spirit was broken, if you know what I mean. I accepted the situation. Taking Tootles by the hand, I walked slowly away. Napoleon's retreat from Moscow was a picnic by the side of it.

As we turned up the road we met Freddie's Angela.

The sight of her had a marked effect on the kid Tootles. He pointed at her and said, "Wah!"

The girl stopped and smiled. I loosed the kid, and he ran to her.

"Well, baby?" she said, bending down to him. "So father found you again, did he? Your little son and I made friends on the beach this morning," she said to me.

This was the limit. Coming on top of that interview with the whiskered lunatic it so utterly unnerved me, don't you know, that she had nodded good-bye and was half-way down the road before I caught up with my breath enough to deny the charge of being the infant's father.

I hadn't expected dear old Freddie to sing with joy when he found out what had happened, but I did think he might have shown a little more manly fortitude. He leaped up, glared at the kid, and clutched his head. He didn't speak for a long time, but, on the other hand, when he began he did not leave off for a long time. He was quite emotional, dear old boy. It beat me where he could have picked up such expressions.

"Well," he said, when he had finished, "say something! Heavens! man, why don't you say something?"

"You don't give me a chance, old top," I said soothingly.

"What are you going to do about it?"

"What can we do about it?"

"We can't spend our time acting as nurses to this—this exhibit."

He got up.

"I'm going back to London," he said.

"Freddie!" I cried. "Freddie, old man!" My voice shook. "Would you desert a pal at a time like this?"

"I would. This is your business, and you've got to manage it."

"Freddie," I said, "you've got to stand by me. You must. Do you realize that this child has to be undressed, and bathed, and dressed again? You wouldn't leave me to do all that single-handed? Freddie, old scout, we were at school together. Your mother likes me. You owe me a tenner."

He sat down again.

"Oh, well," he said resignedly.

"Besides, old top," I said, "I did it all for your sake, don't you know?"

He looked at me in a curious way.

"Reggie," he said, in a strained voice, "one moment. I'll stand a good deal, but I won't stand for being expected to be grateful."

Looking back at it, I see that what saved me from Colney Hatch in that crisis was my bright idea of buying up most of the contents of the local sweet-shop. By serving out sweets to the kid practically incessantly we managed to get through the rest of that day pretty satisfactorily. At eight o'clock he fell asleep in a chair, and, having undressed him by unbuttoning every button in sight and, where there were no buttons, pulling till something gave, we carried him up to bed.

Freddie stood looking at the pile of clothes on the floor and I knew what he was thinking. To get the kid undressed had been simple—a mere matter of muscle. But how were we to get him into his clothes again? I stirred the pile with my foot. There was a long linen arrangement which might have been anything. Also a strip of pink flannel which was like nothing on earth. We looked at each other and smiled wanly.

But in the morning I remembered that there were children at the next bungalow but one. We went there before breakfast and borrowed their nurse. Women are wonderful, by George they are! She had that kid dressed and looking fit for anything in about eight minutes. I showered wealth on her, and she promised to come in morning and evening. I sat down to breakfast almost cheerful again. It was the first bit of silver lining there had been to the cloud up to date.

"And after all," I said, "there's lots to be said for having a child about the house, if you know what I mean. Kind of cosy and domestic—what!"

Just then the kid upset the milk over Freddie's trousers, and when he had come back after changing his clothes he began to talk about what a much-maligned man King Herod was. The more he saw of Tootles, he said, the less he wondered at those impulsive views of his on infanticide.

Two days later Jimmy Pinkerton came down. Jimmy took one look at the kid, who happened to be howling at the moment, and picked up his portmanteau.

"For me," he said, "the hotel. I can't write dialogue with that sort of thing going on. Whose work is this? Which of you adopted this little treasure?"

I told him about Mr. Medwin and the mumps. Jimmy seemed interested.

"I might work this up for the stage," he said. "It wouldn't make a bad situation for act two of a farce."

"Farce!" snarled poor old Freddie.

"Rather. Curtain of act one on hero, a well-meaning, half-baked sort of idiot just like—that is to say, a well-meaning, half-baked sort of idiot, kidnapping the child. Second act, his adventures with it. I'll rough it out to-night. Come along and show me the hotel, Reggie."

As we went I told him the rest of the story—the Angela part. He laid down his portmanteau and looked at me like an owl through his glasses.

"What!" he said. "Why, hang it, this is a play, ready-made. It's the old 'Tiny Hand' business. Always safe stuff. Parted lovers. Lisping child. Reconciliation over the little cradle. It's big. Child, centre. Girl L.C.; Freddie, up stage, by the piano. Can Freddie play the piano?"

"He can play a little of 'The Rosary' with one finger."

Jimmy shook his head.

"No; we shall have to cut out the soft music. But the rest's all right. Look here." He squatted in the sand. "This stone is the girl. This bit of seaweed's the child. This nutshell is Freddie. Dialogue leading up to child's line. Child speaks like, 'Boofer lady, does 'oo love dadda?' Business of outstretched hands. Hold picture for a moment. Freddie crosses L., takes girl's hand. Business of swallowing lump in throat. Then big speech. 'Ah, Marie,' or whatever her name is—Jane—Agnes—Angela? Very well. 'Ah, Angela, has not this gone on too long? A little child rebukes us! Angela!' And so on. Freddie must work up his own part. I'm just giving you the general outline. And we must get a good line for the child. 'Boofer lady, does 'oo love dadda?' isn't definite enough. We want something more—ah! 'Kiss Freddie,' that's it. Short, crisp, and has the punch."

"But, Jimmy, old top," I said, "the only objection is, don't you know, that there's no way of getting the girl to the cottage. She cuts Freddie. She wouldn't come within a mile of him."

Jimmy frowned.

"That's awkward," he said. "Well, we shall have to make it an exterior set instead of an interior. We can easily corner her on the beach somewhere, when we're ready. Meanwhile, we must get the kid letter-perfect. First rehearsal for lines and business eleven sharp to-morrow."

Poor old Freddie was in such a gloomy state of mind that we

decided not to tell him the idea till we had finished coaching the kid. He wasn't in the mood to have a thing like that hanging over him. So we concentrated on Tootles. And pretty early in the proceedings we saw that the only way to get Tootles worked up to the spirit of the thing was to introduce sweets of some sort as a sub-motive, so to speak.

"The chief difficulty," said Jimmy Pinkerton at the end of the first rehearsal, "is to establish a connection in the kid's mind between his line and the sweets. Once he has grasped the basic fact that those two words, clearly spoken, result automatically in acid-drops, we have got a success."

I've often thought, don't you know, how interesting it must be to be one of those animal-trainer Johnnies: to stimulate the dawning intelligence, and that sort of thing. Well, this was every bit as exciting. Some days success seemed to be staring us in the eye, and the kid got the line out as if he'd been an old professional. And then he'd go all to pieces again. And time was flying.

"We must hurry up, Jimmy," I said. "The kid's uncle may arrive any day now and take him away."

"And we haven't an understudy," said Jimmy. "There's something in that. We must work! My goodness, that kid's a bad study. I've known deaf-mutes who would have learned the part quicker."

I will say this for the kid, though: he was a trier. Failure didn't discourage him. Whenever there was any kind of sweet near he had a dash at his line, and kept on saying something till he got what he was after. His only fault was his uncertainty. Personally, I would have been prepared to risk it, and start the performance at the first opportunity, but Jimmy said no.

"We're not nearly ready," said Jimmy. "To-day, for instance, he said 'Kick Freddie.' That's not going to win any girl's heart. And she might do it, too. No; we must postpone production awhile yet."

But, by George, we didn't. The curtain went up the very next afternoon.

It was nobody's fault—certainly not mine. It was just Fate. Freddie had settled down at the piano, and I was leading the kid out of the house to exercise it, when, just as we'd got out to the veranda, along came the girl Angela on her way to the beach. The kid set up his usual yell at the sight of her, and she stopped at the foot of the steps.

"Hello, baby!" she said. "Good morning," she said to me. "May I come up?"

She didn't wait for an answer. She just came. She seemed to be that sort of girl. She came up on the veranda and started fussing over the kid. And six feet away, mind you, Freddie smiting the piano in the sitting-room. It was a dash disturbing situation, don't you know. At any minute Freddie might take it into his head to come out on to the veranda, and we hadn't even begun to rehearse him in his part.

I tried to break up the scene.

"We were just going down to the beach," I said.

"Yes?" said the girl. She listened for a moment. "So you're having your piano tuned?" she said. "My aunt has been trying to find a tuner for ours. Do you mind if I go in and tell this man to come on to us when he's finished here?"

"Er—not yet!" I said. "Not yet, if you don't mind. He can't bear to be disturbed when he's working. It's the artistic temperament. I'll tell him later."

"Very well," she said, getting up to go. "Ask him to call at Pine Bungalow. West is the name. Oh, he seems to have stopped. I suppose he will be out in a minute now. I'll wait."

"Don't you think—shouldn't we be going on to the beach?" I said.

She had started talking to the kid and didn't hear. She was feeling in her pocket for something.

"The beach," I babbled.

"See what I've brought for you, baby," she said. And, by George, don't you know, she held up in front of the kid's bulging eyes a chunk of toffee about the size of the Automobile Club.

That finished it. We had just been having a long rehearsal, and the kid was all worked up in his part. He got it right first time.

"Kiss Fweddie!" he shouted.

And the front door opened, and Freddie came out on to the veranda, for all the world as if he had been taking a cue.

He looked at the girl, and the girl looked at him. I looked at the ground, and the kid looked at the toffee.

"Kiss Fweddie!" he yelled. "Kiss Fweddie!"

The girl was still holding up the toffee, and the kid did what Jimmy Pinkerton would have called "business of outstretched hands" towards it.

"Kiss Fweddie!" he shrieked.

"What does this mean?" said the girl, turning to me.

"You'd better give it to him, don't you know," I said. "He'll go on till you do."

She gave the kid his toffee, and he subsided. Poor old Freddie still stood there gaping, without a word.

"What does it mean?" said the girl again. Her face was pink, and her eyes were sparkling in the sort of way, don't you know, that makes a fellow feel as if he hadn't any bones in him, if you know what I mean. Did you ever tread on your partner's dress at a dance and tear it, and see her smile at you like an angel and say: "*Please* don't apologize. It's nothing," and then suddenly meet her clear blue eyes and feel as if you had stepped on the teeth of a rake and had the handle jump up and hit you in the face? Well, that's how Freddie's Angela looked.

"*Well?*" she said, and her teeth gave a little click.

I gulped. Then I said it was nothing. Then I said it was nothing much. Then I said, "Oh, well, it was this way." And, after a few brief remarks about Jimmy Pinkerton, I told her all about it. And all the while Idiot Freddie stood there gaping, without a word.

And the girl didn't speak, either. She just stood listening.

And then she began to laugh. I never heard a girl laugh so much. She leaned against the side of the veranda and shrieked. And all the while Freddie, the World's Champion Chump, stood there, saying nothing.

Well I sidled towards the steps. I had said all I had to say, and it seemed to me that about here the stage-direction "exit" was written in my part. I gave poor old Freddie up in despair. If only he had said a word, it might have been all right. But there he stood, speechless. What can a fellow do with a fellow like that?

Just out of sight of the house I met Jimmy Pinkerton.

"Hello, Reggie!" he said. "I was just coming to you. Where's the kid?

325

We must have a big rehearsal to-day."

"No good," I said sadly. "It's all over. The thing's finished. Poor dear old Freddie has made an ass of himself and killed the whole show."

"Tell me," said Jimmy.

I told him.

"Fluffed in his lines, did he?" said Jimmy, nodding thoughtfully. "It's always the way with these amateurs. We must go back at once. Things look bad, but it may not be too late," he said as we started. "Even now a few well-chosen words from a man of the world, and——"

"Great Scot!" I cried. "Look!"

In front of the cottage stood six children, a nurse, and the fellow from the grocer's staring. From the windows of the houses opposite projected about four hundred heads of both sexes, staring. Down the road came galloping five more children, a dog, three men, and a boy, about to stare. And on our porch, as unconscious of the spectators as if they had been alone in the Sahara, stood Freddie and Angela, clasped in each other's arms.

* * * * *

Dear old Freddie may have been fluffy in his lines, but, by George, his business had certainly gone with a bang!

RALLYING ROUND OLD GEORGE

I think one of the rummiest affairs I was ever mixed up with, in the course of a lifetime devoted to butting into other people's business, was that affair of George Lattaker at Monte Carlo. I wouldn't bore you, don't you know, for the world, but I think you ought to hear about it.

We had come to Monte Carlo on the yacht *Circe*, belonging to an old sportsman of the name of Marshall. Among those present were myself, my man Voules, a Mrs. Vanderley, her daughter Stella, Mrs. Vanderley's maid Pilbeam and George.

George was a dear old pal of mine. In fact, it was I who had worked him into the party. You see, George was due to meet his Uncle Augustus, who was scheduled, George having just reached his twenty-fifth birthday, to hand over to him a legacy left by one of George's aunts, for which he had been trustee. The aunt had died when George was quite a kid. It was a date that George had been looking forward to; for, though he had a sort of income—an income, after-all, is only an income, whereas a chunk of o' goblins is a pile. George's uncle was in Monte Carlo, and had written George that he would come to London and unbelt; but it struck me that a far better plan was for George to go to his uncle at Monte Carlo instead. Kill two birds with one stone, don't you know. Fix up his affairs and have a pleasant holiday simultaneously. So George had tagged along, and at the time when the trouble started we were anchored in Monaco Harbour, and Uncle Augustus was due next day.

     * * * * *

Looking back, I may say that, so far as I was mixed up in it, the thing began at seven o'clock in the morning, when I was aroused from a dreamless sleep by the dickens of a scrap in progress outside my state-room door. The chief ingredients were a female voice that sobbed and said: "Oh, Harold!" and a male voice "raised in anger," as they say, which after considerable difficulty, I identified as Voules's. I hardly recognized it. In his official capacity Voules talks exactly like you'd expect a statue to talk, if it could. In private, however, he evidently relaxed to some extent, and to have that sort of thing going on in my midst at that hour was too much for me.

"Voules!" I yelled.

Spion Kop ceased with a jerk. There was silence, then sobs diminishing in the distance, and finally a tap at the door. Voules entered with that impressive, my-lord-the-carriage-waits look which is what I pay him for. You wouldn't have believed he had a drop of any sort of emotion in him.

"Voules," I said, "are you under the delusion that I'm going to be Queen of the May? You've called me early all right. It's only just seven."

"I understood you to summon me, sir."

"I summoned you to find out why you were making that infernal noise outside."

"I owe you an apology, sir. I am afraid that in the heat of the moment
I raised my voice."

"It's a wonder you didn't raise the roof. Who was that with you?"

"Miss Pilbeam, sir; Mrs. Vanderley's maid."

"What was all the trouble about?"

"I was breaking our engagement, sir."

I couldn't help gaping. Somehow one didn't associate Voules with engagements. Then it struck me that I'd no right to butt in on his secret sorrows, so I switched the conversation.

"I think I'll get up," I said.

"Yes, sir."

"I can't wait to breakfast with the rest. Can you get me some right away?"

"Yes, sir."

So I had a solitary breakfast and went up on deck to smoke. It was a lovely morning. Blue sea, gleaming Casino, cloudless sky, and all the rest of the hippodrome. Presently the others began to trickle up. Stella Vanderley was one of the first. I thought she looked a bit pale and tired. She said she hadn't slept well. That accounted for it. Unless you get your eight hours, where are you?

"Seen George?" I asked.

I couldn't help thinking the name seemed to freeze her a bit. Which was queer, because all the voyage she and George had been particularly close pals. In fact, at any moment I expected George to come to me and slip his little hand in mine, and whisper: "I've done it, old scout; she loves muh!"

"I have not seen Mr. Lattaker," she said.

I didn't pursue the subject. George's stock was apparently low that a.m.

The next item in the day's programme occurred a few minutes later when the morning papers arrived.

Mrs. Vanderley opened hers and gave a scream.

"The poor, dear Prince!" she said.

"What a shocking thing!" said old Marshall.

"I knew him in Vienna," said Mrs. Vanderley. "He waltzed divinely."

Then I got at mine and saw what they were talking about. The paper was full of it. It seemed that late the night before His Serene Highness the Prince of Saxburg-Leignitz (I always wonder why they call these chaps "Serene") had been murderously assaulted in a dark street on his way back from the Casino to his yacht. Apparently he had developed the habit of going about without an escort, and some rough-neck, taking advantage of this, had laid for him and slugged him with considerable vim. The Prince had been found lying pretty well beaten up and insensible in the street by a passing pedestrian, and had been taken back to his yacht, where he still lay unconscious.

"This is going to do somebody no good," I said. "What do you get for slugging a Serene Highness? I wonder if they'll catch the fellow?"

"'Later,'" read old Marshall, "'the pedestrian who discovered His Serene Highness proves to have been Mr. Denman Sturgis, the eminent private investigator. Mr. Sturgis has offered his services to the police, and is understood to be in possession of a most important clue.' That's the fellow who had charge of that kidnapping case in Chicago. If anyone can catch the man, he can."

About five minutes later, just as the rest of them were going to move off to breakfast, a boat hailed us and came alongside. A tall, thin man came up the gangway. He looked round the group, and fixed on old Marshall as the probable owner of the yacht.

"Good morning," he said. "I believe you have a Mr. Lattaker on board—Mr. George Lattaker?"

"Yes," said Marshall. "He's down below. Want to see him? Whom shall I say?"

"He would not know my name. I should like to see him for a moment on somewhat urgent business."

"Take a seat. He'll be up in a moment. Reggie, my boy, go and hurry him up."

I went down to George's state-room.

"George, old man!" I shouted.

No answer. I opened the door and went in. The room was empty. What's more, the bunk hadn't been slept in. I don't know when I've been more surprised. I went on deck.

"He isn't there," I said.

"Not there!" said old Marshall. "Where is he, then? Perhaps he's gone for a stroll ashore. But he'll be back soon for breakfast. You'd better wait for him. Have you breakfasted? No? Then will you join us?"

The man said he would, and just then the gong went and they trooped down, leaving me alone on deck.

I sat smoking and thinking, and then smoking a bit more, when I thought I heard somebody call my name in a sort of hoarse whisper. I looked over my shoulder, and, by Jove, there at the top of the gangway in evening dress, dusty to the eyebrows and without a hat, was dear old George.

"Great Scot!" I cried.

"'Sh!" he whispered. "Anyone about?"

"They're all down at breakfast."

He gave a sigh of relief, sank into my chair, and closed his eyes. I regarded him with pity. The poor old boy looked a wreck.

"I say!" I said, touching him on the shoulder.

He leaped out of the chair with a smothered yell.

"Did you do that? What did you do it for? What's the sense of it? How do you suppose you can ever make yourself popular if you go about touching people on the shoulder? My nerves are sticking a yard out of my body this morning, Reggie!"

"Yes, old boy?"

"I did a murder last night."

"What?"

"It's the sort of thing that might happen to anybody. Directly Stella Vanderley broke off our engagement I——"

"Broke off your engagement? How long were you engaged?"

"About two minutes. It may have been less. I hadn't a stop-watch. I proposed to her at ten last night in the saloon. She accepted me. I was just going to kiss her when we heard someone coming. I went out. Coming along the corridor was that infernal what's-her-name— Mrs. Vanderley's maid—Pilbeam. Have you ever been accepted by the girl you love, Reggie?"

"Never. I've been refused dozens——"

"Then you won't understand how I felt. I was off my head with joy. I hardly knew what I was doing. I just felt I had to kiss the nearest thing handy. I couldn't wait. It might have been the ship's cat. It wasn't. It was Pilbeam."

"You kissed her?"

"I kissed her. And just at that moment the door of the saloon opened and out came Stella."

"Great Scott!"

"Exactly what I said. It flashed across me that to Stella, dear girl, not knowing the circumstances, the thing might seem a little odd. It did. She broke off the engagement, and I got out the dinghy and rowed off. I was mad. I didn't care what became of me. I simply wanted to forget. I went ashore. I—It's just on the cards that I may have drowned my sorrows a bit. Anyhow, I don't remember a thing, except that I can recollect having the deuce of a scrap with somebody in a dark street and somebody falling, and myself falling, and myself legging it for all I was worth. I woke up this morning in the Casino gardens. I've lost my hat."

I dived for the paper.

"Read," I said. "It's all there."

He read.

"Good heavens!" he said.

"You didn't do a thing to His Serene Nibs, did you?"

"Reggie, this is awful."

"Cheer up. They say he'll recover."

"That doesn't matter."

"It does to him."

He read the paper again.

"It says they've a clue."

"They always say that."

"But—My hat!"

"Eh?"

"My hat. I must have dropped it during the scrap. This man, Denman
Sturgis, must have found it. It had my name in it!"

"George," I said, "you mustn't waste time. Oh!"

He jumped a foot in the air.

"Don't do it!" he said, irritably. "Don't bark like that. What's the matter?"

"The man!"

"What man?"

"A tall, thin man with an eye like a gimlet. He arrived just before you did. He's down in the saloon now, having breakfast. He said he wanted to see you on business, and wouldn't give his name. I didn't like the look of him from the first. It's this fellow Sturgis. It must be."

"No!"

"I feel it. I'm sure of it."

"Had he a hat?"

"Of course he had a hat."

"Fool! I mean mine. Was he carrying a hat?"

"By Jove, he *was* carrying a parcel. George, old scout, you must get a move on. You must light out if you want to spend the rest of your life out of prison. Slugging a Serene Highness is *lèse-majesté*. It's worse than hitting a policeman. You haven't got a moment to waste."

"But I haven't any money. Reggie, old man, lend me a tenner or something. I must get over the frontier into Italy at once. I'll wire my uncle to meet me in———"

"Look out," I cried; "there's someone coming!"

He dived out of sight just as Voules came up the companion-way, carrying a letter on a tray.

"What's the matter!" I said. "What do you want?"

"I beg your pardon, sir. I thought I heard Mr. Lattaker's voice. A letter has arrived for him."

"He isn't here."

"No, sir. Shall I remove the letter?"

"No; give it to me. I'll give it to him when he comes."

"Very good, sir."

"Oh, Voules! Are they all still at breakfast? The gentleman who came to see Mr. Lattaker? Still hard at it?"

"He is at present occupied with a kippered herring, sir."

"Ah! That's all, Voules."

"Thank you, sir."

He retired. I called to George, and he came out.

"Who was it?"

"Only Voules. He brought a letter for you. They're all at breakfast still. The sleuth's eating kippers."

"That'll hold him for a bit. Full of bones." He began to read his letter. He gave a kind of grunt of surprise at the first paragraph.

"Well, I'm hanged!" he said, as he finished.

"Reggie, this is a queer thing."

"What's that?"

He handed me the letter, and directly I started in on it I saw why he had grunted. This is how it ran:

"My dear George—I shall be seeing you to-morrow, I hope; but I think it is better, before we meet, to prepare you for a curious situation that has arisen in connection with the legacy which your father inherited from your Aunt Emily, and which you are expecting me, as trustee, to hand over to you, now that you have reached your twenty-fifth birthday. You have doubtless heard your father speak of your twin-brother Alfred, who was lost or kidnapped—which, was never ascertained—when you were both babies. When no news was received of him for so many years, it was supposed that he was dead. Yesterday, however, I received a letter purporting that he had been living all this time in Buenos Ayres as the adopted son of a wealthy South American, and has only recently discovered his identity. He states that he is on his way to meet me, and will arrive any day now. Of course, like other claimants, he may prove to be an impostor, but meanwhile his intervention will, I fear, cause a certain delay before I can hand over your money to you. It will be necessary to go into a thorough examination of credentials, etc., and this will take some time. But I will go fully into the matter with you when we meet.— Your affectionate uncle,

"AUGUSTUS ARBUTT."

I read it through twice, and the second time I had one of those ideas I do sometimes get, though admittedly a chump of the premier class. I have seldom had such a thoroughly corking brain-wave.

"Why, old top," I said, "this lets you out."

"Lets me out of half the darned money, if that's what you mean. If this chap's not an imposter—and there's no earthly reason to suppose he is, though I've never heard my father say a word about him—we shall have to split the money. Aunt Emily's will left the money to my father, or, failing him, his 'offspring.' I thought that meant me, but apparently there are a crowd of us. I call it rotten work, springing unexpected offspring on a fellow at the eleventh hour like this."

"Why, you chump," I said, "it's going to save you. This lets you out of your spectacular dash across the frontier. All you've got to do is to stay here and be your brother Alfred. It came to me in a flash."

He looked at me in a kind of dazed way.

"You ought to be in some sort of a home, Reggie."

"Ass!" I cried. "Don't you understand? Have you ever heard of twin-brothers who weren't exactly alike? Who's to say you aren't Alfred if you swear you are? Your uncle will be there to back you up that you have a brother Alfred."

"And Alfred will be there to call me a liar."

"He won't. It's not as if you had to keep it up for the rest of your life. It's only for an hour or two, till we can get this detective off the yacht. We sail for England to-morrow morning."

At last the thing seemed to sink into him. His face brightened.

"Why, I really do believe it would work," he said.

"Of course it would work. If they want proof, show them your mole. I'll swear George hadn't one."

"And as Alfred I should get a chance of talking to Stella and making things all right for George. Reggie, old top, you're a genius."

"No, no."

"You *are*."

"Well, it's only sometimes. I can't keep it up."

And just then there was a gentle cough behind us. We spun round.

"What the devil are you doing here, Voules," I said.

"I beg your pardon, sir. I have heard all."

I looked at George. George looked at me.

"Voules is all right," I said. "Decent Voules! Voules wouldn't give us away, would you, Voules?"

"Yes, sir."

"You would?"

"Yes, sir."

"But, Voules, old man," I said, "be sensible. What would you gain by it?"

"Financially, sir, nothing."

"Whereas, by keeping quiet"—I tapped him on the chest—"by

holding your tongue, Voules, by saying nothing about it to anybody, Voules, old fellow, you might gain a considerable sum."

"Am I to understand, sir, that, because you are rich and I am poor, you think that you can buy my self-respect?"

"Oh, come!" I said.

"How much?" said Voules.

So we switched to terms. You wouldn't believe the way the man haggled. You'd have thought a decent, faithful servant would have been delighted to oblige one in a little matter like that for a fiver. But not Voules. By no means. It was a hundred down, and the promise of another hundred when we had got safely away, before he was satisfied. But we fixed it up at last, and poor old George got down to his state-room and changed his clothes.

He'd hardly gone when the breakfast-party came on deck.

"Did you meet him?" I asked.

"Meet whom?" said old Marshall.

"George's twin-brother Alfred."

"I didn't know George had a brother."

"Nor did he till yesterday. It's a long story. He was kidnapped in infancy, and everyone thought he was dead. George had a letter from his uncle about him yesterday. I shouldn't wonder if that's where George has gone, to see his uncle and find out about it. In the meantime, Alfred has arrived. He's down in George's state-room now, having a brush-up. It'll amaze you, the likeness between them. You'll think it *is* George at first. Look! Here he comes."

And up came George, brushed and clean, in an ordinary yachting suit.

They were rattled. There was no doubt about that. They stood looking at him, as if they thought there was a catch somewhere, but weren't quite certain where it was. I introduced him, and still they looked doubtful.

"Mr. Pepper tells me my brother is not on board," said George.

"It's an amazing likeness," said old Marshall.

"Is my brother like me?" asked George amiably.

"No one could tell you apart," I said.

"I suppose twins always are alike," said George. "But if it ever came to a question of identification, there would be one way of distinguishing us. Do you know George well, Mr. Pepper?"

"He's a dear old pal of mine."

"You've been swimming with him perhaps?"

"Every day last August."

"Well, then, you would have noticed it if he had had a mole like this on the back of his neck, wouldn't you?" He turned his back and stooped and showed the mole. His collar hid it at ordinary times. I had seen it often when we were bathing together.

"Has George a mole like that?" he asked.

"No," I said. "Oh, no."

"You would have noticed it if he had?"

"Yes," I said. "Oh, yes."

"I'm glad of that," said George. "It would be a nuisance not to be able to prove one's own identity."

That seemed to satisfy them all. They couldn't get away from it. It seemed to me that from now on the thing was a walk-over. And I think George felt the same, for, when old Marshall asked him if he had had breakfast, he said he had not, went below, and pitched in as if he hadn't a care in the world.

Everything went right till lunch-time. George sat in the shade on the foredeck talking to Stella most of the time. When the gong went and the rest had started to go below, he drew me back. He was beaming.

"It's all right," he said. "What did I tell you?"

"What did you tell me?"

"Why, about Stella. Didn't I say that Alfred would fix things for George? I told her she looked worried, and got her to tell me what the trouble was. And then——"

"You must have shown a flash of speed if you got her to confide in you after knowing you for about two hours."

"Perhaps I did," said George modestly, "I had no notion, till I became him, what a persuasive sort of chap my brother Alfred was. Anyway, she told me all about it, and I started in to show her that George was a pretty good sort of fellow on the whole, who oughtn't to be turned down for what was evidently merely temporary insanity. She saw my point."

"And it's all right?"

"Absolutely, if only we can produce George. How much longer does that infernal sleuth intend to stay here? He seems to have taken root."

"I fancy he thinks that you're bound to come back sooner or later, and is waiting for you."

"He's an absolute nuisance," said George.

We were moving towards the companion way, to go below for lunch, when a boat hailed us. We went to the side and looked over.

"It's my uncle," said George.

A stout man came up the gangway.

"Halloa, George!" he said. "Get my letter?"

"I think you are mistaking me for my brother," said George. "My name is Alfred Lattaker."

"What's that?"

"I am George's brother Alfred. Are you my Uncle Augustus?"

The stout man stared at him.

"You're very like George," he said.

"So everyone tells me."

"And you're really Alfred?"

"I am."

"I'd like to talk business with you for a moment."

He cocked his eye at me. I sidled off and went below.

At the foot of the companion-steps I met Voules,

"I beg your pardon, sir," said Voules. "If it would be convenient I should be glad to have the afternoon off."

I'm bound to say I rather liked his manner. Absolutely normal. Not a trace of the fellow-conspirator about it. I gave him the afternoon off.

I had lunch—George didn't show up—and as I was going out I was waylaid by the girl Pilbeam. She had been crying.

"I beg your pardon, sir, but did Mr. Voules ask you for the afternoon?"

I didn't see what business if was of hers, but she seemed all worked up about it, so I told her.

"Yes, I have given him the afternoon off."

337

She broke down—absolutely collapsed. Devilish unpleasant it was. I'm hopeless in a situation like this. After I'd said, "There, there!" which didn't seem to help much, I hadn't any remarks to make.

"He s-said he was going to the tables to gamble away all his savings and then shoot himself, because he had nothing left to live for."

I suddenly remembered the scrap in the small hours outside my state-room door. I hate mysteries. I meant to get to the bottom of this. I couldn't have a really first-class valet like Voules going about the place shooting himself up. Evidently the girl Pilbeam was at the bottom of the thing. I questioned her. She sobbed.

I questioned her more. I was firm. And eventually she yielded up the facts. Voules had seen George kiss her the night before; that was the trouble.

Things began to piece themselves together. I went up to interview George. There was going to be another job for persuasive Alfred. Voules's mind had got to be eased as Stella's had been. I couldn't afford to lose a fellow with his genius for preserving a trouser-crease.

I found George on the foredeck. What is it Shakespeare or somebody says about some fellow's face being sicklied o'er with the pale cast of care? George's was like that. He looked green.

"Finished with your uncle?" I said.

He grinned a ghostly grin.

"There isn't any uncle," he said. "There isn't any Alfred. And there isn't any money."

"Explain yourself, old top," I said.

"It won't take long. The old crook has spent every penny of the trust money. He's been at it for years, ever since I was a kid. When the time came to cough up, and I was due to see that he did it, he went to the tables in the hope of a run of luck, and lost the last remnant of the stuff. He had to find a way of holding me for a while and postponing the squaring of accounts while he got away, and he invented this twin-brother business. He knew I should find out sooner or later, but meanwhile he would be able to get off to South America, which he has done. He's on his way now."

"You let him go?"

"What could I do? I can't afford to make a fuss with that man Sturgis around. I can't prove there's no Alfred when my only chance of avoiding prison is to be Alfred."

"Well, you've made things right for yourself with Stella Vanderley, anyway," I said, to cheer him up.

"What's the good of that now? I've hardly any money and no prospects.
How can I marry her?"

I pondered.

"It looks to me, old top," I said at last, "as if things were in a bit of a mess."

"You've guessed it," said poor old George.

I spent the afternoon musing on Life. If you come to think of it, what a queer thing Life is! So unlike anything else, don't you know, if you see what I mean. At any moment you may be strolling peacefully along, and all the time Life's waiting around the corner to fetch you one. You can't tell when you may be going to get it. It's all dashed puzzling. Here was poor old George, as well-meaning a fellow as ever stepped, getting swatted all over the ring by the hand of Fate. Why? That's what I asked myself. Just Life, don't you know. That's all there was about it.

It was close on six o'clock when our third visitor of the day arrived. We were sitting on the afterdeck in the cool of the evening—old Marshall, Denman Sturgis, Mrs. Vanderley, Stella, George, and I—when he came up. We had been talking of George, and old Marshall was suggesting the advisability of sending out search-parties. He was worried. So was Stella Vanderley. So, for that matter, were George and I, only not for the same reason.

We were just arguing the thing out when the visitor appeared. He was a well-built, stiff sort of fellow. He spoke with a German accent.

"Mr. Marshall?" he said. "I am Count Fritz von Cöslin, equerry to His
Serene Highness"—he clicked his heels together and saluted—"the Prince of Saxburg-Leignitz."

Mrs. Vanderley jumped up.

"Why, Count," she said, "what ages since we met in Vienna! You remember?"

"Could I ever forget? And the charming Miss Stella, she is well, I suppose not?"

"Stella, you remember Count Fritz?"

Stella shook hands with him.

"And how is the poor, dear Prince?" asked Mrs. Vanderley. "What a terrible thing to have happened!"

"I rejoice to say that my high-born master is better. He has regained consciousness and is sitting up and taking nourishment."

"That's good," said old Marshall.

"In a spoon only," sighed the Count. "Mr. Marshall, with your permission I should like a word with Mr. Sturgis."

"Mr. Who?"

The gimlet-eyed sportsman came forward.

"I am Denman Sturgis, at your service."

"The deuce you are! What are you doing here?"

"Mr. Sturgis," explained the Count, "graciously volunteered his services——"

"I know. But what's he doing here?"

"I am waiting for Mr. George Lattaker, Mr. Marshall."

"Eh?"

"You have not found him?" asked the Count anxiously.

"Not yet, Count; but I hope to do so shortly. I know what he looks like now. This gentleman is his twin-brother. They are doubles."

"You are sure this gentleman is not Mr. George Lattaker?"

George put his foot down firmly on the suggestion.

"Don't go mixing me up with my brother," he said. "I am Alfred. You can tell me by my mole."

He exhibited the mole. He was taking no risks.

The Count clicked his tongue regretfully.

"I am sorry," he said.

George didn't offer to console him,

"Don't worry," said Sturgis. "He won't escape me. I shall find him."

"Do, Mr. Sturgis, do. And quickly. Find swiftly that noble young man."

"What?" shouted George.

"That noble young man, George Lattaker, who, at the risk of his life, saved my high-born master from the assassin."

George sat down suddenly.

"I don't understand," he said feebly.

"We were wrong, Mr. Sturgis," went on the Count. "We leaped to the conclusion—was it not so?—that the owner of the hat you found was also the assailant of my high-born master. We were wrong. I have heard the story from His Serene Highness's own lips. He was passing down a dark street when a ruffian in a mask sprang out upon him. Doubtless he had been followed from the Casino, where he had been winning heavily. My high-born master was taken by surprise. He was felled. But before he lost consciousness he perceived a young man in evening dress, wearing the hat you found, running swiftly towards him. The hero engaged the assassin in combat, and my high-born master remembers no more. His Serene Highness asks repeatedly, 'Where is my brave preserver?' His gratitude is princely. He seeks for this young man to reward him. Ah, you should be proud of your brother, sir!"

"Thanks," said George limply.

"And you, Mr. Sturgis, you must redouble your efforts. You must search the land; you must scour the sea to find George Lattaker."

"He needn't take all that trouble," said a voice from the gangway.

It was Voules. His face was flushed, his hat was on the back of his head, and he was smoking a fat cigar.

"I'll tell you where to find George Lattaker!" he shouted.

He glared at George, who was staring at him.

"Yes, look at me," he yelled. "Look at me. You won't be the first this afternoon who's stared at the mysterious stranger who won for two hours without a break. I'll be even with you now, Mr. Blooming Lattaker. I'll learn you to break a poor man's heart. Mr. Marshall and gents, this morning I was on deck, and I over'eard 'im plotting to put up a game on you. They'd spotted that gent there as a detective, and they arranged that blooming Lattaker was to pass himself off as his own twin-brother. And if you wanted proof, blooming Pepper tells him to show them his mole and he'd swear George hadn't one. Those were his very words. That man there is George Lattaker, Hesquire, and let him deny it if he can."

George got up.

"I haven't the least desire to deny it, Voules."

"Mr. Voules, if *you* please."

"It's true," said George, turning to the Count. "The fact is, I had rather a foggy recollection of what happened last night. I only remembered knocking some one down, and, like you, I jumped to the conclusion that I must have assaulted His Serene Highness."

"Then you are really George Lattaker?" asked the Count.

"I am."

"'Ere, what does all this mean?" demanded Voules.

"Merely that I saved the life of His Serene Highness the Prince of Saxburg-Leignitz, Mr. Voules."

"It's a swindle!" began Voules, when there was a sudden rush and the girl Pilbeam cannoned into the crowd, sending me into old Marshall's chair, and flung herself into the arms of Voules.

"Oh, Harold!" she cried. "I thought you were dead. I thought you'd shot yourself."

He sort of braced himself together to fling her off, and then he seemed to think better of it and fell into the clinch.

It was all dashed romantic, don't you know, but there *are* limits.

"Voules, you're sacked," I said.

"Who cares?" he said. "Think I was going to stop on now I'm a gentleman of property? Come along, Emma, my dear. Give a month's notice and get your 'at, and I'll take you to dinner at Ciro's."

"And you, Mr. Lattaker," said the Count, "may I conduct you to the presence of my high-born master? He wishes to show his gratitude to his preserver."

"You may," said George. "May I have my hat, Mr. Sturgis?"

There's just one bit more. After dinner that night I came up for a smoke, and, strolling on to the foredeck, almost bumped into George and Stella. They seemed to be having an argument.

"I'm not sure," she was saying, "that I believe that a man can be so happy that he wants to kiss the nearest thing in sight, as you put it."

"Don't you?" said George. "Well, as it happens, I'm feeling just that way now."

I coughed and he turned round.

"Halloa, Reggie!" he said.

"Halloa, George!" I said. "Lovely night."

"Beautiful," said Stella.

"The moon," I said.
"Ripping," said George.
"Lovely," said Stella.
"And look at the reflection of the stars on the——"
George caught my eye. "Pop off," he said.
I popped.

DOING CLARENCE A BIT OF GOOD

Have you ever thought about—and, when I say thought about, I mean really carefully considered the question of—the coolness, the cheek, or, if you prefer it, the gall with which Woman, as a sex, fairly bursts? *I* have, by Jove! But then I've had it thrust on my notice, by George, in a way I should imagine has happened to pretty few fellows. And the limit was reached by that business of the Yeardsley "Venus."

To make you understand the full what-d'you-call-it of the situation, I shall have to explain just how matters stood between Mrs. Yeardsley and myself.

When I first knew her she was Elizabeth Shoolbred. Old Worcestershire family; pots of money; pretty as a picture. Her brother Bill was at Oxford with me.

I loved Elizabeth Shoolbred. I loved her, don't you know. And there was a time, for about a week, when we were engaged to be married. But just as I was beginning to take a serious view of life and study furniture catalogues and feel pretty solemn when the restaurant orchestra played "The Wedding Glide," I'm hanged if she didn't break it off, and a month later she was married to a fellow of the name of Yeardsley—Clarence Yeardsley, an artist.

What with golf, and billiards, and a bit of racing, and fellows at the club rallying round and kind of taking me out of myself, as it were, I got over it, and came to look on the affair as a closed page in the book of my life, if you know what I mean. It didn't seem likely to me that we should meet again, as she and Clarence had settled down in the country somewhere and never came to London, and I'm bound to own that, by the time I got her letter, the wound had pretty well healed, and I was to a certain extent sitting up and taking nourishment. In fact, to be absolutely honest, I was jolly thankful the thing had ended as it had done.

This letter I'm telling you about arrived one morning out of a blue sky, as it were. It ran like this:

"MY DEAR OLD REGGIE,—What ages it seems since I saw anything of you. How are you? We have settled down here in the most perfect old house, with a lovely garden, in the middle of delightful country. Couldn't you run down here for a few days? Clarence and I would be so glad to see you. Bill is here, and is most anxious to meet you again. He was speaking of you only this morning. *Do* come. Wire your train, and I will send the car to meet you. —Yours most sincerely,

ELIZABETH YEARDSLEY.

"P.S.—We can give you new milk and fresh eggs. Think of that!

"P.P.S.—Bill says our billiard-table is one of the best he has ever played on.

"P.P.S.S.—We are only half a mile from a golf course. Bill says it is better than St. Andrews.

"P.P.S.S.S.—You *must* come!"

Well, a fellow comes down to breakfast one morning, with a bit of a head on, and finds a letter like that from a girl who might quite easily have blighted his life! It rattled me rather, I must confess.

However, that bit about the golf settled me. I knew Bill knew what he was talking about, and, if he said the course was so topping, it must be something special. So I went.

Old Bill met me at the station with the car. I hadn't come across him for some months, and I was glad to see him again. And he apparently was glad to see me.

"Thank goodness you've come," he said, as we drove off. "I was just about at my last grip."

"What's the trouble, old scout?" I asked.

"If I had the artistic what's-its-name," he went on, "if the mere mention of pictures didn't give me the pip, I dare say it wouldn't be so bad. As it is, it's rotten!"

344

"Pictures?"

"Pictures. Nothing else is mentioned in this household. Clarence is an artist. So is his father. And you know yourself what Elizabeth is like when one gives her her head?"

I remembered then—it hadn't come back to me before—that most of my time with Elizabeth had been spent in picture-galleries. During the period when I had let her do just what she wanted to do with me, I had had to follow her like a dog through gallery after gallery, though pictures are poison to me, just as they are to old Bill. Somehow it had never struck me that she would still be going on in this way after marrying an artist. I should have thought that by this time the mere sight of a picture would have fed her up. Not so, however, according to old Bill.

"They talk pictures at every meal," he said. "I tell you, it makes a chap feel out of it. How long are you down for?"

"A few days."

"Take my tip, and let me send you a wire from London. I go there to-morrow. I promised to play against the Scottish. The idea was that I was to come back after the match. But you couldn't get me back with a lasso."

I tried to point out the silver lining.

"But, Bill, old scout, your sister says there's a most corking links near here."

He turned and stared at me, and nearly ran us into the bank.

"You don't mean honestly she said that?"

"She said you said it was better than St. Andrews."

"So I did. Was that all she said I said?"

"Well, wasn't it enough?"

"She didn't happen to mention that I added the words, 'I don't think'?"

"No, she forgot to tell me that."

"It's the worst course in Great Britain."

I felt rather stunned, don't you know. Whether it's a bad habit to have got into or not, I can't say, but I simply can't do without my daily allowance of golf when I'm not in London.

I took another whirl at the silver lining.

"We'll have to take it out in billiards," I said. "I'm glad the table's good."

"It depends what you call good. It's half-size, and there's a seven-inch cut just out of baulk where Clarence's cue slipped. Elizabeth has mended it with pink silk. Very smart and dressy it looks, but it doesn't improve the thing as a billiard-table."

"But she said you said——"

"Must have been pulling your leg."

We turned in at the drive gates of a good-sized house standing well back from the road. It looked black and sinister in the dusk, and I couldn't help feeling, you know, like one of those Johnnies you read about in stories who are lured to lonely houses for rummy purposes and hear a shriek just as they get there. Elizabeth knew me well enough to know that a specially good golf course was a safe draw to me. And she had deliberately played on her knowledge. What was the game? That was what I wanted to know. And then a sudden thought struck me which brought me out in a cold perspiration. She had some girl down here and was going to have a stab at marrying me off. I've often heard that young married women are all over that sort of thing. Certainly she had said there was nobody at the house but Clarence and herself and Bill and Clarence's father, but a woman who could take the name of St. Andrews in vain as she had done wouldn't be likely to stick at a trifle.

"Bill, old scout," I said, "there aren't any frightful girls or any rot of that sort stopping here, are there?"

"Wish there were," he said. "No such luck."

As we pulled up at the front door, it opened, and a woman's figure appeared.

"Have you got him, Bill?" she said, which in my present frame of mind struck me as a jolly creepy way of putting it. The sort of thing Lady Macbeth might have said to Macbeth, don't you know.

"Do you mean me?" I said.

She came down into the light. It was Elizabeth, looking just the same as in the old days.

"Is that you, Reggie? I'm so glad you were able to come. I was afraid you might have forgotten all about it. You know what you are. Come along in and have some tea."

* * * * *

346

Have you ever been turned down by a girl who afterwards married and then been introduced to her husband? If so you'll understand how I felt when Clarence burst on me. You know the feeling. First of all, when you hear about the marriage, you say to yourself, "I wonder what he's like." Then you meet him, and think, "There must be some mistake. She can't have preferred *this* to me!" That's what I thought, when I set eyes on Clarence.

He was a little thin, nervous-looking chappie of about thirty-five. His hair was getting grey at the temples and straggly on top. He wore pince-nez, and he had a drooping moustache. I'm no Bombardier Wells myself, but in front of Clarence I felt quite a nut. And Elizabeth, mind you, is one of those tall, splendid girls who look like princesses. Honestly, I believe women do it out of pure cussedness.

"How do you do, Mr. Pepper? Hark! Can you hear a mewing cat?" said
Clarence. All in one breath, don't you know.

"Eh?" I said.

"A mewing cat. I feel sure I hear a mewing cat. Listen!"

While we were listening the door opened, and a white-haired old gentleman came in. He was built on the same lines as Clarence, but was an earlier model. I took him correctly, to be Mr. Yeardsley, senior. Elizabeth introduced us.

"Father," said Clarence, "did you meet a mewing cat outside? I feel positive I heard a cat mewing."

"No," said the father, shaking his head; "no mewing cat."

"I can't bear mewing cats," said Clarence. "A mewing cat gets on my nerves!"

"A mewing cat is so trying," said Elizabeth.

"*I* dislike mewing cats," said old Mr. Yeardsley.

That was all about mewing cats for the moment. They seemed to think they had covered the ground satisfactorily, and they went back to pictures.

We talked pictures steadily till it was time to dress for dinner. At least, they did. I just sort of sat around. Presently the subject of picture-robberies came up. Somebody mentioned the "Monna Lisa," and then I happened to remember seeing something in the evening paper, as I was coming down in the train, about some fellow somewhere having had a valuable painting pinched by burglars the night before. It was the first time I had had a chance of breaking into the conversation with any effect, and I meant to make the most of it. The paper was in the pocket of my overcoat in the hall. I went and fetched it.

"Here it is," I said. "A Romney belonging to Sir Bellamy Palmer——"

They all shouted "What!" exactly at the same time, like a chorus. Elizabeth grabbed the paper.

"Let me look! Yes. 'Late last night burglars entered the residence of
Sir Bellamy Palmer, Dryden Park, Midford, Hants——'"

"Why, that's near here," I said. "I passed through Midford——"

"Dryden Park is only two miles from this house," said Elizabeth. I noticed her eyes were sparkling.

"Only two miles!" she said. "It might have been us! It might have been the 'Venus'!"

Old Mr. Yeardsley bounded in his chair.

"The 'Venus'!" he cried.

They all seemed wonderfully excited. My little contribution to the evening's chat had made quite a hit.

Why I didn't notice it before I don't know, but it was not till Elizabeth showed it to me after dinner that I had my first look at the Yeardsley "Venus." When she led me up to it, and switched on the light, it seemed impossible that I could have sat right through dinner without noticing it. But then, at meals, my attention is pretty well riveted on the foodstuffs. Anyway, it was not till Elizabeth showed it to me that I was aware of its existence.

She and I were alone in the drawing-room after dinner. Old Yeardsley was writing letters in the morning-room, while Bill and Clarence were rollicking on the half-size billiard table with the pink silk tapestry effects. All, in fact, was joy, jollity, and song, so to speak, when Elizabeth, who had been sitting wrapped in thought for a bit, bent towards me and said, "Reggie."

And the moment she said it I knew something was going to happen. You know that pre-what-d'you-call-it you get sometimes? Well, I got it then.

"What-o?" I said nervously.

"Reggie," she said, "I want to ask a great favour of you."

"Yes?"

She stooped down and put a log on the fire, and went on, with her back to me:

"Do you remember, Reggie, once saying you would do anything in the world for me?"

There! That's what I meant when I said that about the cheek of Woman as a sex. What I mean is, after what had happened, you'd have thought she would have preferred to let the dead past bury its dead, and all that sort of thing, what?

Mind you, I *had* said I would do anything in the world for her. I admit that. But it was a distinctly pre-Clarence remark. He hadn't appeared on the scene then, and it stands to reason that a fellow who may have been a perfect knight-errant to a girl when he was engaged to her, doesn't feel nearly so keen on spreading himself in that direction when she has given him the miss-in-baulk, and gone and married a man who reason and instinct both tell him is a decided blighter.

I couldn't think of anything to say but "Oh, yes."

"There's something you can do for me now, which will make me everlastingly grateful."

"Yes," I said.

"Do you know, Reggie," she said suddenly, "that only a few months ago Clarence was very fond of cats?"

"Eh! Well, he still seems—er—*interested* in them, what?"

"Now they get on his nerves. Everything gets on his nerves."

"Some fellows swear by that stuff you see advertised all over the———"

"No, that wouldn't help him. He doesn't need to take anything. He wants to get rid of something."

"I don't quite fellow. Get rid of something?"

"The 'Venus,'" said Elizabeth.

She looked up and caught my bulging eye.

"You saw the 'Venus,'" she said.

"Not that I remember."

"Well, come into the dining-room."

We went into the dining-room, and she switched on the lights.

"There," she said.

On the wall close to the door—that may have been why I hadn't noticed it before; I had sat with my back to it—was a large oil-painting. It was what you'd call a classical picture, I suppose. What I mean is—well, you know what I mean. All I can say is that it's funny I *hadn't* noticed it.

"Is that the 'Venus'?" I said.

She nodded.

"How would you like to have to look at that every time you sat down to a meal?"

"Well, I don't know. I don't think it would affect me much. I'd worry through all right."

She jerked her head impatiently.

"But you're not an artist," she said. "Clarence is."

And then I began to see daylight. What exactly was the trouble I didn't understand, but it was evidently something to do with the good old Artistic Temperament, and I could believe anything about that. It explains everything. It's like the Unwritten Law, don't you know, which you plead in America if you've done anything they want to send you to chokey for and you don't want to go. What I mean is, if you're absolutely off your rocker, but don't find it convenient to be scooped into the luny-bin, you simply explain that, when you said you were a teapot, it was just your Artistic Temperament, and they apologize and go away. So I stood by to hear just how the A.T. had affected Clarence, the Cat's Friend, ready for anything.

And, believe me, it had hit Clarence badly.

It was this way. It seemed that old Yeardsley was an amateur artist and that this "Venus" was his masterpiece. He said so, and he ought to have known. Well, when Clarence married, he had given it to him, as a wedding present, and had hung it where it stood with his own hands. All right so far, what? But mark the sequel. Temperamental Clarence, being a professional artist and consequently some streets ahead of the dad at the game, saw flaws in the "Venus." He couldn't stand it at any price. He didn't like the drawing. He didn't like the expression of the face. He didn't like the colouring. In fact, it made him feel quite ill to look at it. Yet, being devoted to his father and wanting to do anything rather than give him pain, he had not been able to bring himself to store the thing in the cellar, and the strain of confronting the picture three times a day had begun to tell on him to such an extent that Elizabeth felt something had to be done.

"Now you see," she said.

"In a way," I said. "But don't you think it's making rather heavy weather over a trifle?"

"Oh, can't you understand? Look!" Her voice dropped as if she was in church, and she switched on another light. It shone on the picture next to old Yeardsley's. "There!" she said. "Clarence painted that!"

She looked at me expectantly, as if she were waiting for me to swoon, or yell, or something. I took a steady look at Clarence's effort. It was another Classical picture. It seemed to me very much like the other one.

Some sort of art criticism was evidently expected of me, so I made a dash at it.

"Er—'Venus'?" I said.

Mark you, Sherlock Holmes would have made the same mistake. On the evidence, I mean.

"No. 'Jocund Spring,'" she snapped. She switched off the light. "I see you don't understand even now. You never had any taste about pictures. When we used to go to the galleries together, you would far rather have been at your club."

This was so absolutely true, that I had no remark to make. She came up to me, and put her hand on my arm.

"I'm sorry, Reggie. I didn't mean to be cross. Only I do want to make you understand that Clarence is *suffering*. Suppose—suppose—well, let us take the case of a great musician. Suppose a great musician had to sit and listen to a cheap vulgar tune—the same tune—day after day, day after day, wouldn't you expect his nerves to break! Well, it's just like that with Clarence. Now you see?"

"Yes, but——"

"But what? Surely I've put it plainly enough?"

"Yes. But what I mean is, where do I come in? What do you want

351

me to do?"

"I want you to steal the 'Venus.'"

I looked at her.

"You want me to——?"

"Steal it. Reggie!" Her eyes were shining with excitement. "Don't you see? It's Providence. When I asked you to come here, I had just got the idea. I knew I could rely on you. And then by a miracle this robbery of the Romney takes place at a house not two miles away. It removes the last chance of the poor old man suspecting anything and having his feelings hurt. Why, it's the most wonderful compliment to him. Think! One night thieves steal a splendid Romney; the next the same gang take his 'Venus.' It will be the proudest moment of his life. Do it to-night, Reggie. I'll give you a sharp knife. You simply cut the canvas out of the frame, and it's done."

"But one moment," I said. "I'd be delighted to be of any use to you, but in a purely family affair like this, wouldn't it be better—in fact, how about tackling old Bill on the subject?"

"I have asked Bill already. Yesterday. He refused."

"But if I'm caught?"

"You can't be. All you have to do is to take the picture, open one of the windows, leave it open, and go back to your room."

It sounded simple enough.

"And as to the picture itself—when I've got it?"

"Burn it. I'll see that you have a good fire in your room."

"But——"

She looked at me. She always did have the most wonderful eyes.

"Reggie," she said; nothing more. Just "Reggie."

She looked at me.

"Well, after all, if you see what I mean—The days that are no more, don't you know. Auld Lang Syne, and all that sort of thing. You follow me?"

"All right," I said. "I'll do it."

I don't know if you happen to be one of those Johnnies who are steeped in crime, and so forth, and think nothing of pinching diamond necklaces. If you're not, you'll understand that I felt a lot less keen on the job I'd taken on when I sat in my room, waiting to get busy, than I had done when I promised to tackle it in the dining-room. On paper it all seemed easy enough, but I couldn't help feeling there was a catch somewhere, and I've never known time pass slower. The kick-off was scheduled for one o'clock in the morning, when the household might be expected to be pretty sound asleep, but at a quarter to I couldn't stand it any longer. I lit the lantern I had taken from Bill's bicycle, took a grip of my knife, and slunk downstairs.

The first thing I did on getting to the dining-room was to open the window. I had half a mind to smash it, so as to give an extra bit of local colour to the affair, but decided not to on account of the noise. I had put my lantern on the table, and was just reaching out for it, when something happened. What it was for the moment I couldn't have said. It might have been an explosion of some sort or an earthquake. Some solid object caught me a frightful whack on the chin. Sparks and things occurred inside my head and the next thing I remember is feeling something wet and cold splash into my face, and hearing a voice that sounded like old Bill's say, "Feeling better now?"

I sat up. The lights were on, and I was on the floor, with old Bill kneeling beside me with a soda siphon.

"What happened?" I said.

"I'm awfully sorry, old man," he said. "I hadn't a notion it was you. I came in here, and saw a lantern on the table, and the window open and a chap with a knife in his hand, so I didn't stop to make inquiries. I just let go at his jaw for all I was worth. What on earth do you think you're doing? Were you walking in your sleep?"

"It was Elizabeth," I said. "Why, you know all about it. She said she had told you."

"You don't mean——"

"The picture. You refused to take it on, so she asked me."

"Reggie, old man," he said. "I'll never believe what they say about repentance again. It's a fool's trick and upsets everything. If I hadn't repented, and thought it was rather rough on Elizabeth not to do a little thing like that for her, and come down here to do it after all, you wouldn't have stopped that sleep-producer with your chin. I'm sorry."

"Me, too," I said, giving my head another shake to make certain it was still on.

"Are you feeling better now?"

"Better than I was. But that's not saying much."

"Would you like some more soda-water? No? Well, how about getting this job finished and going to bed? And let's be quick about it too. You made a noise like a ton of bricks when you went down just now, and it's on the cards some of the servants may have heard. Toss you who carves."

"Heads."

"Tails it is," he said, uncovering the coin. "Up you get. I'll hold the light. Don't spike yourself on that sword of yours."

It was as easy a job as Elizabeth had said. Just four quick cuts, and the thing came out of its frame like an oyster. I rolled it up. Old Bill had put the lantern on the floor and was at the sideboard, collecting whisky, soda, and glasses.

"We've got a long evening before us," he said. "You can't burn a picture of that size in one chunk. You'd set the chimney on fire. Let's do the thing comfortably. Clarence can't grudge us the stuff. We've done him a bit of good this trip. To-morrow'll be the maddest, merriest day of Clarence's glad New Year. On we go."

We went up to my room, and sat smoking and yarning away and sipping our drinks, and every now and then cutting a slice off the picture and shoving it in the fire till it was all gone. And what with the cosiness of it and the cheerful blaze, and the comfortable feeling of doing good by stealth, I don't know when I've had a jollier time since the days when we used to brew in my study at school.

We had just put the last slice on when Bill sat up suddenly, and gripped my arm.

"I heard something," he said.

I listened, and, by Jove, I heard something, too. My room was just over the dining-room, and the sound came up to us quite distinctly. Stealthy footsteps, by George! And then a chair falling over.

"There's somebody in the dining-room," I whispered.

There's a certain type of chap who takes a pleasure in positively chivvying trouble. Old Bill's like that. If I had been alone, it would have taken me about three seconds to persuade myself that I hadn't really heard anything after all. I'm a peaceful sort of cove, and believe in living and letting live, and so forth. To old Bill, however, a visit from burglars was pure jam. He was out of his chair in one jump.

"Come on," he said. "Bring the poker."

I brought the tongs as well. I felt like it. Old Bill collared the knife. We crept downstairs.

"We'll fling the door open and make a rush," said Bill.

"Supposing they shoot, old scout?"

"Burglars never shoot," said Bill.

Which was comforting provided the burglars knew it.

Old Bill took a grip of the handle, turned it quickly, and in he went.

And then we pulled up sharp, staring.

The room was in darkness except for a feeble splash of light at the near end. Standing on a chair in front of Clarence's "Jocund Spring," holding a candle in one hand and reaching up with a knife in the other, was old Mr. Yeardsley, in bedroom slippers and a grey dressing-gown. He had made a final cut just as we rushed in. Turning at the sound, he stopped, and he and the chair and the candle and the picture came down in a heap together. The candle went out.

"What on earth?" said Bill.

I felt the same. I picked up the candle and lit it, and then a most fearful thing happened. The old man picked himself up, and suddenly collapsed into a chair and began to cry like a child. Of course, I could see it was only the Artistic Temperament, but still, believe me, it was devilish unpleasant. I looked at old Bill. Old Bill looked at me. We shut the door quick, and after that we didn't know what to do. I saw Bill look at the sideboard, and I knew what he was looking for. But we had taken the siphon upstairs, and his ideas of first-aid stopped short at squirting soda-water. We just waited, and presently old Yeardsley switched off, sat up, and began talking with a rush.

"Clarence, my boy, I was tempted. It was that burglary at Dryden Park. It tempted me. It made it all so simple. I knew you would put it down to the same gang, Clarence, my boy. I——"

It seemed to dawn upon him at this point that Clarence was not among those present.

"Clarence?" he said hesitatingly.

"He's in bed," I said.

"In bed! Then he doesn't know? Even now—Young men, I throw myself on your mercy. Don't be hard on me. Listen." He grabbed at

Bill, who sidestepped. "I can explain everything—everything."

He gave a gulp.

"You are not artists, you two young men, but I will try to make you understand, make you realise what this picture means to me. I was two years painting it. It is my child. I watched it grow. I loved it. It was part of my life. Nothing would have induced me to sell it. And then Clarence married, and in a mad moment I gave my treasure to him. You cannot understand, you two young men, what agonies I suffered. The thing was done. It was irrevocable. I saw how Clarence valued the picture. I knew that I could never bring myself to ask him for it back. And yet I was lost without it. What could I do? Till this evening I could see no hope. Then came this story of the theft of the Romney from a house quite close to this, and I saw my way. Clarence would never suspect. He would put the robbery down to the same band of criminals who stole the Romney. Once the idea had come, I could not drive it out. I fought against it, but to no avail. At last I yielded, and crept down here to carry out my plan. You found me." He grabbed again, at me this time, and got me by the arm. He had a grip like a lobster. "Young man," he said, "you would not betray me? You would not tell Clarence?"

I was feeling most frightfully sorry for the poor old chap by this time, don't you know, but I thought it would be kindest to give it him straight instead of breaking it by degrees.

"I won't say a word to Clarence, Mr. Yeardsley," I said. "I quite understand your feelings. The Artistic Temperament, and all that sort of thing. I mean—what? *I* know. But I'm afraid—Well, look!"

I went to the door and switched on the electric light, and there, staring him in the face, were the two empty frames. He stood goggling at them in silence. Then he gave a sort of wheezy grunt.

"The gang! The burglars! They *have* been here, and they have taken Clarence's picture!" He paused. "It might have been mine! My Venus!" he whispered It was getting most fearfully painful, you know, but he had to know the truth.

"I'm awfully sorry, you know," I said. "But it *was*."

He started, poor old chap.

"Eh? What do you mean?"

"They *did* take your Venus."

"But I have it here."

I shook my head.

"That's Clarence's 'Jocund Spring,'" I said.

He jumped at it and straightened it out.

"What! What are you talking about? Do you think I don't know my own picture—my child—my Venus. See! My own signature in the corner. Can you read, boy? Look: 'Matthew Yeardsley.' This is *my* picture!"

And—well, by Jove, it *was*, don't you know!

* * * * *

Well, we got him off to bed, him and his infernal Venus, and we settled down to take a steady look at the position of affairs. Bill said it was my fault for getting hold of the wrong picture, and I said it was Bill's fault for fetching me such a crack on the jaw that I couldn't be expected to see what I was getting hold of, and then there was a pretty massive silence for a bit.

"Reggie," said Bill at last, "how exactly do you feel about facing Clarence and Elizabeth at breakfast?"

"Old scout," I said. "I was thinking much the same myself."

"Reggie," said Bill, "I happen to know there's a milk-train leaving Midford at three-fifteen. It isn't what you'd call a flier. It gets to London at about half-past nine. Well—er—in the circumstances, how

about it?"

THE AUNT AND THE SLUGGARD

Now that it's all over, I may as well admit that there was a time during the rather funny affair of Rockmetteller Todd when I thought that Jeeves was going to let me down. The man had the appearance of being baffled.

Jeeves is my man, you know. Officially he pulls in his weekly wages for pressing my clothes and all that sort of thing; but actually he's more like what the poet Johnnie called some bird of his acquaintance who was apt to rally round him in times of need—a guide, don't you know; philosopher, if I remember rightly, and—I rather fancy—friend. I rely on him at every turn.

So naturally, when Rocky Todd told me about his aunt, I didn't hesitate. Jeeves was in on the thing from the start.

The affair of Rocky Todd broke loose early one morning of spring. I was in bed, restoring the good old tissues with about nine hours of the dreamless, when the door flew open and somebody prodded me in the lower ribs and began to shake the bedclothes. After blinking a bit and generally pulling myself together, I located Rocky, and my first impression was that it was some horrid dream.

Rocky, you see, lived down on Long Island somewhere, miles away from New York; and not only that, but he had told me himself more than once that he never got up before twelve, and seldom earlier than one. Constitutionally the laziest young devil in America, he had hit on a walk in life which enabled him to go the limit in that direction. He was a poet. At least, he wrote poems when he did anything; but most of his time, as far as I could make out, he spent in a sort of trance. He told me once that he could sit on a fence, watching a worm and wondering what on earth it was up to, for hours at a stretch.

He had his scheme of life worked out to a fine point. About once a month he would take three days writing a few poems; the other three hundred and twenty-nine days of the year he rested. I didn't know there was enough money in poetry to support a chappie, even in the way in which Rocky lived; but it seems that, if you stick to exhortations to young men to lead the strenuous life and don't shove in any rhymes, American editors fight for the stuff. Rocky showed me one of his things once. It began:

Be!
Be!
The   past   is   dead.
To-morrow   is   not   born.
Be   to-day!
To-day!
Be   with   every   nerve,
With   every   muscle,
With   every   drop   of   your   red   blood!

Be!

It was printed opposite the frontispiece of a magazine with a sort of scroll round it, and a picture in the middle of a fairly-nude chappie, with bulging muscles, giving the rising sun the glad eye. Rocky said they gave him a hundred dollars for it, and he stayed in bed till four in the afternoon for over a month.

As regarded the future he was pretty solid, owing to the fact that he had a moneyed aunt tucked away somewhere in Illinois; and, as he had been named Rockmetteller after her, and was her only nephew, his position was pretty sound. He told me that when he did come into the money he meant to do no work at all, except perhaps an occasional poem recommending the young man with life opening out before him, with all its splendid possibilities, to light a pipe and shove his feet upon the mantelpiece.

And this was the man who was prodding me in the ribs in the grey dawn!

"Read this, Bertie!" I could just see that he was waving a letter or something equally foul in my face. "Wake up and read this!"

I can't read before I've had my morning tea and a cigarette. I groped for the bell.

Jeeves came in looking as fresh as a dewy violet. It's a mystery to me how he does it.

"Tea, Jeeves."

"Very good, sir."

He flowed silently out of the room—he always gives you the impression of being some liquid substance when he moves; and I found that Rocky was surging round with his beastly letter again.

"What is it?" I said. "What on earth's the matter?"

"Read it!"

"I can't. I haven't had my tea."

"Well, listen then."

"Who's it from?"

"My aunt."

At this point I fell asleep again. I woke to hear him saying:

"So what on earth am I to do?"

Jeeves trickled in with the tray, like some silent stream meandering over its mossy bed; and I saw daylight.

"Read it again, Rocky, old top," I said. "I want Jeeves to hear it. Mr. Todd's aunt has written him a rather rummy letter, Jeeves, and we want your advice."

"Very good, sir."

He stood in the middle of the room, registering devotion to the cause, and Rocky started again:

"MY DEAR ROCKMETTELLER.—I have been thinking things over for a long while, and I have come to the conclusion that I have been very thoughtless to wait so long before doing what I have made up my mind to do now."

"What do you make of that, Jeeves?"

"It seems a little obscure at present, sir, but no doubt it becomes cleared at a later point in the communication."

"It becomes as clear as mud!" said Rocky.

"Proceed, old scout," I said, champing my bread and butter.

"You know how all my life I have longed to visit New York and see

for myself the wonderful gay life of which I have read so much. I fear that now it will be impossible for me to fulfil my dream. I am old and worn out. I seem to have no strength left in me."

"Sad, Jeeves, what?"

"Extremely, sir."

"Sad nothing!" said Rocky. "It's sheer laziness. I went to see her last Christmas and she was bursting with health. Her doctor told me himself that there was nothing wrong with her whatever. But she will insist that she's a hopeless invalid, so he has to agree with her. She's got a fixed idea that the trip to New York would kill her; so, though it's been her ambition all her life to come here, she stays where she is."

"Rather like the chappie whose heart was 'in the Highlands a-chasing of the deer,' Jeeves?"

"The cases are in some respects parallel, sir."

"Carry on, Rocky, dear boy."

"So I have decided that, if I cannot enjoy all the marvels of the city myself, I can at least enjoy them through you. I suddenly thought of this yesterday after reading a beautiful poem in the Sunday paper about a young man who had longed all his life for a certain thing and won it in the end only when he was too old to enjoy it. It was very sad, and it touched me."

"A thing," interpolated Rocky bitterly, "that I've not been able to do in ten years."

"As you know, you will have my money when I am gone; but until now I have never been able to see my way to giving you an allowance. I have now decided to do so—on one condition. I have written to a firm of lawyers in New York, giving them instructions to pay you quite a substantial sum each month. My one condition is that you live in New York and enjoy yourself as I have always wished to do. I want you to be my representative, to spend this money for me as I should do myself. I want you to plunge into the gay, prismatic life of New York. I want you to be the life and soul of brilliant supper parties.

"Above all, I want you—indeed, I insist on this—to write me letters at least once a week giving me a full description of all you are doing and all that is going on in the city, so that I may enjoy at second-hand what my wretched health prevents my enjoying for myself. Remember that I shall expect full details, and that no detail is too trivial to interest.—Your affectionate Aunt,

"ISABEL ROCKMETTELLER."

"What about it?" said Rocky.

"What about it?" I said.

"Yes. What on earth am I going to do?"

It was only then that I really got on to the extremely rummy attitude of the chappie, in view of the fact that a quite unexpected mess of the right stuff had suddenly descended on him from a blue sky. To my mind it was an occasion for the beaming smile and the joyous whoop; yet here the man was, looking and talking as if Fate had swung on his solar plexus. It amazed me.

"Aren't you bucked?" I said.

"Bucked!"

"If I were in your place I should be frightfully braced. I consider this pretty soft for you."

He gave a kind of yelp, stared at me for a moment, and then began to talk of New York in a way that reminded me of Jimmy

Mundy, the reformer chappie. Jimmy had just come to New York on a hit-the-trail campaign, and I had popped in at the Garden a couple of days before, for half an hour or so, to hear him. He had certainly told New York some pretty straight things about itself, having apparently taken a dislike to the place, but, by Jove, you know, dear old Rocky made him look like a publicity agent for the old metrop.!

"Pretty soft!" he cried. "To have to come and live in New York! To have to leave my little cottage and take a stuffy, smelly, over-heated hole of an apartment in this Heaven-forsaken, festering Gehenna. To have to mix night after night with a mob who think that life is a sort of St. Vitus's dance, and imagine that they're having a good time because they're making enough noise for six and drinking too much for ten. I loathe New York, Bertie. I wouldn't come near the place if I hadn't got to see editors occasionally. There's a blight on it. It's got moral delirium tremens. It's the limit. The very thought of staying more than a day in it makes me sick. And you call this thing pretty soft for me!"

I felt rather like Lot's friends must have done when they dropped in for a quiet chat and their genial host began to criticise the Cities of the Plain. I had no idea old Rocky could be so eloquent.

"It would kill me to have to live in New York," he went on. "To have to share the air with six million people! To have to wear stiff collars and decent clothes all the time! To——" He started. "Good Lord! I suppose I should have to dress for dinner in the evenings. What a ghastly notion!"

I was shocked, absolutely shocked.

"My dear chap!" I said reproachfully.

"Do you dress for dinner every night, Bertie?"

"Jeeves," I said coldly. The man was still standing like a statue by the door. "How many suits of evening clothes have I?"

"We have three suits full of evening dress, sir; two dinner jackets——"

"Three."

"For practical purposes two only, sir. If you remember we cannot wear the third. We have also seven white waistcoats."

"And shirts?"

"Four dozen, sir."

"And white ties?"

"The first two shallow shelves in the chest of drawers are completely filled with our white ties, sir."

I turned to Rocky.

"You see?"

The chappie writhed like an electric fan.

"I won't do it! I can't do it! I'll be hanged if I'll do it! How on earth can I dress up like that? Do you realize that most days I don't get out of my pyjamas till five in the afternoon, and then I just put on an old sweater?"

I saw Jeeves wince, poor chap! This sort of revelation shocked his finest feelings.

"Then, what are you going to do about it?" I said.

"That's what I want to know."

"You might write and explain to your aunt."

"I might—if I wanted her to get round to her lawyer's in two rapid leaps and cut me out of her will."

I saw his point.

"What do you suggest, Jeeves?" I said.

Jeeves cleared his throat respectfully.

"The crux of the matter would appear to be, sir, that Mr. Todd is obliged by the conditions under which the money is delivered into his possession to write Miss Rockmetteller long and detailed letters relating to his movements, and the only method by which this can be accomplished, if Mr. Todd adheres to his expressed intention of remaining in the country, is for Mr. Todd to induce some second party to gather the actual experiences which Miss Rockmetteller wishes reported to her, and to convey these to him in the shape of a careful report, on which it would be possible for him, with the aid of his imagination, to base the suggested correspondence."

Having got which off the old diaphragm, Jeeves was silent. Rocky looked at me in a helpless sort of way. He hasn't been brought up on Jeeves as I have, and he isn't on to his curves.

"Could he put it a little clearer, Bertie?" he said. "I thought at the start it was going to make sense, but it kind of flickered. What's the idea?"

"My dear old man, perfectly simple. I knew we could stand on

363

Jeeves.
All you've got to do is to get somebody to go round the town for you and take a few notes, and then you work the notes up into letters. That's it, isn't it, Jeeves?"

"Precisely, sir."

The light of hope gleamed in Rocky's eyes. He looked at Jeeves in a startled way, dazed by the man's vast intellect.

"But who would do it?" he said. "It would have to be a pretty smart sort of man, a man who would notice things."

"Jeeves!" I said. "Let Jeeves do it."

"But would he?"

"You would do it, wouldn't you, Jeeves?"

For the first time in our long connection I observed Jeeves almost smile. The corner of his mouth curved quite a quarter of an inch, and for a moment his eye ceased to look like a meditative fish's.

"I should be delighted to oblige, sir. As a matter of fact, I have already visited some of New York's places of interest on my evening out, and it would be most enjoyable to make a practice of the pursuit."

"Fine! I know exactly what your aunt wants to hear about, Rocky. She wants an earful of cabaret stuff. The place you ought to go to first, Jeeves, is Reigelheimer's. It's on Forty-second Street. Anybody will show you the way."

Jeeves shook his head.

"Pardon me, sir. People are no longer going to Reigelheimer's. The place at the moment is Frolics on the Roof."

"You see?" I said to Rocky. "Leave it to Jeeves. He knows."

It isn't often that you find an entire group of your fellow-humans happy in this world; but our little circle was certainly an example of the fact that it can be done. We were all full of beans. Everything went absolutely right from the start.

Jeeves was happy, partly because he loves to exercise his giant brain, and partly because he was having a corking time among the bright lights. I saw him one night at the Midnight Revels. He was sitting at a table on the edge of the dancing floor, doing himself remarkably well with a fat cigar and a bottle of the best. I'd never imagined he could look so nearly human. His face wore an expression of austere benevolence, and he was making notes in a small book.

As for the rest of us, I was feeling pretty good, because I was fond of old Rocky and glad to be able to do him a good turn. Rocky was perfectly contented, because he was still able to sit on fences in his pyjamas and watch worms. And, as for the aunt, she seemed tickled to death. She was getting Broadway at pretty long range, but it seemed to be hitting her just right. I read one of her letters to Rocky, and it was full of life.

But then Rocky's letters, based on Jeeves's notes, were enough to buck anybody up. It was rummy when you came to think of it. There was I, loving the life, while the mere mention of it gave Rocky a tired feeling; yet here is a letter I wrote to a pal of mine in London:

"DEAR FREDDIE,—Well, here I am in New York. It's not a bad place. I'm not having a bad time. Everything's pretty all right. The cabarets aren't bad. Don't know when I shall be back. How's everybody? Cheer-o!—Yours,

"BERTIE.

"PS.—Seen old Ted lately?"

Not that I cared about Ted; but if I hadn't dragged him in I couldn't have got the confounded thing on to the second page.

Now here's old Rocky on exactly the same subject:

"DEAREST AUNT ISABEL,—How can I ever thank you enough for giving me the opportunity to live in this astounding city! New York seems more wonderful every day.

"Fifth Avenue is at its best, of course, just now. The dresses are magnificent!"

Wads of stuff about the dresses. I didn't know Jeeves was such an authority.

"I was out with some of the crowd at the Midnight Revels the other night. We took in a show first, after a little dinner at a new place on Forty-third Street. We were quite a gay party. Georgie Cohan looked in about midnight and got off a good one about Willie Collier. Fred Stone could only stay a minute, but Doug. Fairbanks did all sorts of stunts and made us roar. Diamond Jim Brady was there, as usual, and Laurette Taylor showed up with a party. The show at the Revels is quite good. I am enclosing a programme.

"Last night a few of us went round to Frolics on the Roof——"

And so on and so forth, yards of it. I suppose it's the artistic temperament or something. What I mean is, it's easier for a chappie who's used to writing poems and that sort of tosh to put a bit of a punch into a letter than it is for a chappie like me. Anyway, there's no doubt that Rocky's correspondence was hot stuff. I called Jeeves in and congratulated him.

"Jeeves, you're a wonder!"

"Thank you, sir."

"How you notice everything at these places beats me. I couldn't tell you a thing about them, except that I've had a good time."

"It's just a knack, sir."

"Well, Mr. Todd's letters ought to brace Miss Rockmetteller all right, what?"

"Undoubtedly, sir," agreed Jeeves.

And, by Jove, they did! They certainly did, by George! What I mean to say is, I was sitting in the apartment one afternoon, about a month after the thing had started, smoking a cigarette and resting the old bean, when the door opened and the voice of Jeeves burst the silence like a bomb.

It wasn't that he spoke loud. He has one of those soft, soothing voices that slide through the atmosphere like the note of a far-off sheep. It was what he said made me leap like a young gazelle.

"Miss Rockmetteller!"

And in came a large, solid female.

The situation floored me. I'm not denying it. Hamlet must have felt much as I did when his father's ghost bobbed up in the fairway. I'd come to look on Rocky's aunt as such a permanency at her own home that it didn't seem possible that she could really be here in New York. I stared at her. Then I looked at Jeeves. He was standing there in an attitude of dignified detachment, the chump, when, if ever he should have been rallying round the young master, it was now.

Rocky's aunt looked less like an invalid than any one I've ever seen, except my Aunt Agatha. She had a good deal of Aunt Agatha about her, as a matter of fact. She looked as if she might be deucedly dangerous if put upon; and something seemed to tell me that she would certainly regard herself as put upon if she ever found out the game which poor old Rocky had been pulling on her.

"Good afternoon," I managed to say.

"How do you do?" she said. "Mr. Cohan?"

"Er—no."

"Mr. Fred Stone?"

"Not absolutely. As a matter of fact, my name's Wooster—Bertie Wooster."

She seemed disappointed. The fine old name of Wooster appeared to mean nothing in her life.

"Isn't Rockmetteller home?" she said. "Where is he?"

She had me with the first shot. I couldn't think of anything to say. I couldn't tell her that Rocky was down in the country, watching worms.

There was the faintest flutter of sound in the background. It was the respectful cough with which Jeeves announces that he is about to speak without having been spoken to.

"If you remember, sir, Mr. Todd went out in the automobile with a party in the afternoon."

"So he did, Jeeves; so he did," I said, looking at my watch. "Did he say when he would be back?"

"He gave me to understand, sir, that he would be somewhat late in returning."

He vanished; and the aunt took the chair which I'd forgotten to offer her. She looked at me in rather a rummy way. It was a nasty look. It made me feel as if I were something the dog had brought in and intended to bury later on, when he had time. My own Aunt Agatha, back in England, has looked at me in exactly the same way many a time, and it never fails to make my spine curl.

"You seem very much at home here, young man. Are you a great friend of Rockmetteller's?"

"Oh, yes, rather!"

She frowned as if she had expected better things of old Rocky.

"Well, you need to be," she said, "the way you treat his flat as your own!"

I give you my word, this quite unforeseen slam simply robbed me of the power of speech. I'd been looking on myself in the light of the dashing host, and suddenly to be treated as an intruder jarred me. It wasn't, mark you, as if she had spoken in a way to suggest that she considered my presence in the place as an ordinary social call. She obviously looked on me as a cross between a burglar and the plumber's man come to fix the leak in the bathroom. It hurt her—my being there.

At this juncture, with the conversation showing every sign of being about to die in awful agonies, an idea came to me. Tea—the good old stand-by.

"Would you care for a cup of tea?" I said.

"Tea?"

She spoke as if she had never heard of the stuff.

"Nothing like a cup after a journey," I said. "Bucks you up! Puts a bit of zip into you. What I mean is, restores you, and so on, don't you know. I'll go and tell Jeeves."

I tottered down the passage to Jeeves's lair. The man was reading the evening paper as if he hadn't a care in the world.

"Jeeves," I said, "we want some tea."

"Very good, sir."

"I say, Jeeves, this is a bit thick, what?"

I wanted sympathy, don't you know—sympathy and kindness. The old nerve centres had had the deuce of a shock.

"She's got the idea this place belongs to Mr. Todd. What on earth put that into her head?"

Jeeves filled the kettle with a restrained dignity.

"No doubt because of Mr. Todd's letters, sir," he said. "It was my suggestion, sir, if you remember, that they should be addressed from this apartment in order that Mr. Todd should appear to possess a good central residence in the city."

I remembered. We had thought it a brainy scheme at the time.

"Well, it's bally awkward, you know, Jeeves. She looks on me as an intruder. By Jove! I suppose she thinks I'm someone who hangs about here, touching Mr. Todd for free meals and borrowing his shirts."

"Yes, sir."

"It's pretty rotten, you know."

"Most disturbing, sir."

"And there's another thing: What are we to do about Mr. Todd?

We've got to get him up here as soon as ever we can. When you have brought the tea you had better go out and send him a telegram, telling him to come up by the next train."

"I have already done so, sir. I took the liberty of writing the message and dispatching it by the lift attendant."

"By Jove, you think of everything, Jeeves!"

"Thank you, sir. A little buttered toast with the tea? Just so, sir. Thank you."

I went back to the sitting-room. She hadn't moved an inch. She was still bolt upright on the edge of her chair, gripping her umbrella like a hammer-thrower. She gave me another of those looks as I came in. There was no doubt about it; for some reason she had taken a dislike to me. I suppose because I wasn't George M. Cohan. It was a bit hard on a chap.

"This is a surprise, what?" I said, after about five minutes' restful silence, trying to crank the conversation up again.

"What is a surprise?"

"Your coming here, don't you know, and so on."

She raised her eyebrows and drank me in a bit more through her glasses.

"Why is it surprising that I should visit my only nephew?" she said.

Put like that, of course, it did seem reasonable.

"Oh, rather," I said. "Of course! Certainly. What I mean is——"

Jeeves projected himself into the room with the tea. I was jolly glad to see him. There's nothing like having a bit of business arranged for one when one isn't certain of one's lines. With the teapot to fool about with I felt happier.

"Tea, tea, tea—what? What?" I said.

It wasn't what I had meant to say. My idea had been to be a good deal more formal, and so on. Still, it covered the situation. I poured her out a cup. She sipped it and put the cup down with a shudder.

"Do you mean to say, young man," she said frostily, "that you expect me to drink this stuff?"

"Rather! Bucks you up, you know."

"What do you mean by the expression 'Bucks you up'?"

369

"Well, makes you full of beans, you know. Makes you fizz."

"I don't understand a word you say. You're English, aren't you?"

I admitted it. She didn't say a word. And somehow she did it in a way that made it worse than if she had spoken for hours. Somehow it was brought home to me that she didn't like Englishmen, and that if she had had to meet an Englishman, I was the one she'd have chosen last.

Conversation languished again after that.

Then I tried again. I was becoming more convinced every moment that you can't make a real lively *salon* with a couple of people, especially if one of them lets it go a word at a time.

"Are you comfortable at your hotel?" I said.

"At which hotel?"

"The hotel you're staying at."

"I am not staying at an hotel."

"Stopping with friends—what?"

"I am naturally stopping with my nephew."

I didn't get it for the moment; then it hit me.

"What! Here?" I gurgled.

"Certainly! Where else should I go?"

The full horror of the situation rolled over me like a wave. I couldn't see what on earth I was to do. I couldn't explain that this wasn't Rocky's flat without giving the poor old chap away hopelessly, because she would then ask me where he did live, and then he would be right in the soup. I was trying to induce the old bean to recover from the shock and produce some results when she spoke again.

"Will you kindly tell my nephew's man-servant to prepare my room? I wish to lie down."

"Your nephew's man-servant?"

"The man you call Jeeves. If Rockmetteller has gone for an automobile ride, there is no need for you to wait for him. He will naturally wish to be alone with me when he returns."

I found myself tottering out of the room. The thing was too much for me. I crept into Jeeves's den.

"Jeeves!" I whispered.

"Sir?"

"Mix me a b.-and-s., Jeeves. I feel weak."

"Very good, sir."

"This is getting thicker every minute, Jeeves."

"Sir?"

"She thinks you're Mr. Todd's man. She thinks the whole place is his, and everything in it. I don't see what you're to do, except stay on and keep it up. We can't say anything or she'll get on to the whole thing, and I don't want to let Mr. Todd down. By the way, Jeeves, she wants you to prepare her bed."

He looked wounded.

"It is hardly my place, sir——"

"I know—I know. But do it as a personal favour to me. If you come to that, it's hardly my place to be flung out of the flat like this and have to go to an hotel, what?"

"Is it your intention to go to an hotel, sir? What will you do for clothes?"

"Good Lord! I hadn't thought of that. Can you put a few things in a bag when she isn't looking, and sneak them down to me at the St. Aurea?"

"I will endeavour to do so, sir."

"Well, I don't think there's anything more, is there? Tell Mr. Todd where I am when he gets here."

"Very good, sir."

I looked round the place. The moment of parting had come. I felt sad. The whole thing reminded me of one of those melodramas where they drive chappies out of the old homestead into the snow.

"Good-bye, Jeeves," I said.

"Good-bye, sir."

And I staggered out.

* * * * *

You know, I rather think I agree with those poet-and-philosopher Johnnies who insist that a fellow ought to be devilish pleased if he has a bit of trouble. All that stuff about being refined by suffering, you know. Suffering does give a chap a sort of broader and more sympathetic outlook. It helps you to understand other people's misfortunes if you've been through the same thing yourself.

As I stood in my lonely bedroom at the hotel, trying to tie my white tie myself, it struck me for the first time that there must be whole squads of chappies in the world who had to get along without a man to look after them. I'd always thought of Jeeves as a kind of natural phenomenon; but, by Jove! of course, when you come to think of it, there must be quite a lot of fellows who have to press their own clothes themselves and haven't got anybody to bring them tea in the morning, and so on. It was rather a solemn thought, don't you know. I mean to say, ever since then I've been able to appreciate the frightful privations the poor have to stick.

I got dressed somehow. Jeeves hadn't forgotten a thing in his packing. Everything was there, down to the final stud. I'm not sure this didn't make me feel worse. It kind of deepened the pathos. It was like what somebody or other wrote about the touch of a vanished hand.

I had a bit of dinner somewhere and went to a show of some kind; but nothing seemed to make any difference. I simply hadn't the heart to go on to supper anywhere. I just sucked down a whisky-and-soda in the hotel smoking-room and went straight up to bed. I don't know when I've felt so rotten. Somehow I found myself moving about the room softly, as if there had been a death in the family. If I had anybody to talk to I should have talked in a whisper; in fact, when the telephone-bell rang I answered in such a sad, hushed voice that the fellow at the other end of the wire said "Halloa!" five times, thinking he hadn't got me.

It was Rocky. The poor old scout was deeply agitated.

"Bertie! Is that you, Bertie! Oh, gosh? I'm having a time!"

"Where are you speaking from?"

"The Midnight Revels. We've been here an hour, and I think we're a fixture for the night. I've told Aunt Isabel I've gone out to call up a friend to join us. She's glued to a chair, with this-is-the-life written all over her, taking it in through the pores. She loves it, and I'm nearly crazy."

"Tell me all, old top," I said.

"A little more of this," he said, "and I shall sneak quietly off to the river and end it all. Do you mean to say you go through this sort of thing every night, Bertie, and enjoy it? It's simply infernal! I was just snatching a wink of sleep behind the bill of fare just now when about a million yelling girls swooped down, with toy balloons. There are two orchestras here, each trying to see if it can't play louder than the other. I'm a mental and physical wreck. When your telegram arrived I was just lying down for a quiet pipe, with a sense of absolute peace stealing over me. I had to get dressed and sprint two miles to catch the train. It nearly gave me heart-failure; and on top of that I almost got brain fever inventing lies to tell Aunt Isabel. And then I had to cram myself into these confounded evening clothes of yours."

I gave a sharp wail of agony. It hadn't struck me till then that Rocky was depending on my wardrobe to see him through.

"You'll ruin them!"

"I hope so," said Rocky, in the most unpleasant way. His troubles seemed to have had the worst effect on his character. "I should like to get back at them somehow; they've given me a bad enough time. They're about three sizes too small, and something's apt to give at any moment. I wish to goodness it would, and give me a chance to breathe. I haven't breathed since half-past seven. Thank Heaven, Jeeves managed to get out and buy me a collar that fitted, or I should be a strangled corpse by now! It was touch and go till the stud broke. Bertie, this is pure Hades! Aunt Isabel keeps on urging me to dance. How on earth can I dance when I don't know a soul to dance with? And how the deuce could I, even if I knew every girl in the place? It's taking big chances even to move in these trousers. I had to tell her I've hurt my ankle. She keeps asking me when Cohan and Stone are going to turn up; and it's simply a question of time before she discovers that Stone is sitting two tables away. Something's got to be done, Bertie! You've got to think up some way of getting me out of this mess. It was you who got me into it."

"Me! What do you mean?"

"Well, Jeeves, then. It's all the same. It was you who suggested leaving it to Jeeves. It was those letters I wrote from his notes that did the mischief. I made them too good! My aunt's just been telling me about it. She says she had resigned herself to ending her life where she was, and then my letters began to arrive, describing the joys of New York; and they stimulated her to such an extent that she pulled herself together and made the trip. She seems to think she's had some miraculous kind of faith cure. I tell you I can't stand it, Bertie! It's got to end!"

"Can't Jeeves think of anything?"

"No. He just hangs round saying: 'Most disturbing, sir!' A fat lot of help that is!"

"Well, old lad," I said, "after all, it's far worse for me than it is for you. You've got a comfortable home and Jeeves. And you're saving a lot of money."

"Saving money? What do you mean—saving money?"

"Why, the allowance your aunt was giving you. I suppose she's paying all the expenses now, isn't she?"

"Certainly she is; but she's stopped the allowance. She wrote the lawyers to-night. She says that, now she's in New York, there is no necessity for it to go on, as we shall always be together, and it's simpler for her to look after that end of it. I tell you, Bertie, I've examined the darned cloud with a microscope, and if it's got a silver lining it's some little dissembler!"

"But, Rocky, old top, it's too bally awful! You've no notion of what I'm going through in this beastly hotel, without Jeeves. I must get back to the flat."

"Don't come near the flat."

"But it's my own flat."

"I can't help that. Aunt Isabel doesn't like you. She asked me what you did for a living. And when I told her you didn't do anything she said she thought as much, and that you were a typical specimen of a useless and decaying aristocracy. So if you think you have made a hit, forget it. Now I must be going back, or she'll be coming out here after me. Good-bye."

* * * * *

Next morning Jeeves came round. It was all so home-like when he floated noiselessly into the room that I nearly broke down.

"Good morning, sir," he said. "I have brought a few more of your personal belongings."

He began to unstrap the suit-case he was carrying.

"Did you have any trouble sneaking them away?"

"It was not easy, sir. I had to watch my chance. Miss Rockmetteller is a remarkably alert lady."

"You know, Jeeves, say what you like—this is a bit thick, isn't it?"

"The situation is certainly one that has never before come under my notice, sir. I have brought the heather-mixture suit, as the climatic conditions are congenial. To-morrow, if not prevented, I will endeavour to add the brown lounge with the faint green twill."

"It can't go on—this sort of thing—Jeeves."

"We must hope for the best, sir."

"Can't you think of anything to do?"

"I have been giving the matter considerable thought, sir, but so far without success. I am placing three silk shirts—the dove-coloured, the light blue, and the mauve—in the first long drawer, sir."

"You don't mean to say you can't think of anything, Jeeves?"

"For the moment, sir, no. You will find a dozen handkerchiefs and the tan socks in the upper drawer on the left." He strapped the suit-case and put it on a chair. "A curious lady, Miss Rockmetteller, sir."

"You understate it, Jeeves."

He gazed meditatively out of the window.

"In many ways, sir, Miss Rockmetteller reminds me of an aunt of mine who resides in the south-east portion of London. Their temperaments are much alike. My aunt has the same taste for the pleasures of the great city. It is a passion with her to ride in hansom cabs, sir. Whenever the family take their eyes off her she escapes from the house and spends the day riding about in cabs. On several occasions she has broken into the children's savings bank to secure the means to enable her to gratify this desire."

"I love to have these little chats with you about your female relatives, Jeeves," I said coldly, for I felt that the man had let me down, and I was fed up with him. "But I don't see what all this has got to do with my trouble."

"I beg your pardon, sir. I am leaving a small assortment of neckties on the mantelpiece, sir, for you to select according to your preference. I should recommend the blue with the red domino pattern, sir."

Then he streamed imperceptibly toward the door and flowed silently out.

* * * * *

I've often heard that chappies, after some great shock or loss, have a habit, after they've been on the floor for a while wondering what hit them, of picking themselves up and piecing themselves together, and sort of taking a whirl at beginning a new life. Time, the great healer, and Nature, adjusting itself, and so on and so forth. There's a lot in it. I know, because in my own case, after a day or two of what you might call prostration, I began to recover. The frightful loss of Jeeves made any thought of pleasure more or less a mockery, but at least I found that I was able to have a dash at enjoying life again. What I mean is, I braced up to the extent of going round the cabarets once more, so as to try to forget, if only for the moment.

New York's a small place when it comes to the part of it that wakes up just as the rest is going to bed, and it wasn't long before my tracks began to cross old Rocky's. I saw him once at Peale's, and again at Frolics on the roof. There wasn't anybody with him either time except the aunt, and, though he was trying to look as if he had struck the ideal life, it wasn't difficult for me, knowing the circumstances, to see that beneath the mask the poor chap was suffering. My heart bled for the fellow. At least, what there was of it that wasn't bleeding for myself bled for him. He had the air of one who was about to crack under the strain.

It seemed to me that the aunt was looking slightly upset also. I took it that she was beginning to wonder when the celebrities were going to surge round, and what had suddenly become of all those wild, careless spirits Rocky used to mix with in his letters. I didn't blame her. I had only read a couple of his letters, but they certainly gave the impression that poor old Rocky was by way of being the hub of New York night life, and that, if by any chance he failed to show up at a cabaret, the management said: "What's the use?" and put up the shutters.

The next two nights I didn't come across them, but the night after that I was sitting by myself at the Maison Pierre when somebody tapped me on the shoulder-blade, and I found Rocky standing beside me, with a sort of mixed expression of wistfulness and apoplexy on his face. How the chappie had contrived to wear my evening clothes so many times without disaster was a mystery to me. He confided later that early in the proceedings he had slit the waistcoat up the back and that that had helped a bit.

For a moment I had the idea that he had managed to get away from his aunt for the evening; but, looking past him, I saw that she was in again. She was at a table over by the wall, looking at me as if I were something the management ought to be complained to about.

"Bertie, old scout," said Rocky, in a quiet, sort of crushed voice, "we've always been pals, haven't we? I mean, you know I'd do you a good turn if you asked me?"

"My dear old lad," I said. The man had moved me.

"Then, for Heaven's sake, come over and sit at our table for the rest of the evening."

Well, you know, there are limits to the sacred claims of friendship.

"My dear chap," I said, "you know I'd do anything in reason; but——"

"You must come, Bertie. You've got to. Something's got to be done to divert her mind. She's brooding about something. She's been like that for the last two days. I think she's beginning to suspect. She can't understand why we never seem to meet anyone I know at these joints. A few nights ago I happened to run into two newspaper men I used to know fairly well. That kept me going for a while. I introduced them to Aunt Isabel as David Belasco and Jim Corbett, and it went well. But the effect has worn off now, and she's beginning to wonder again. Something's got to be done, or she will find out everything, and if she does I'd take a nickel for my chance of getting a cent from her later on. So, for the love of Mike, come across to our table and help things along."

I went along. One has to rally round a pal in distress. Aunt Isabel was sitting bolt upright, as usual. It certainly did seem as if she had lost a bit of the zest with which she had started out to explore Broadway. She looked as if she had been thinking a good deal about rather unpleasant things.

"You've met Bertie Wooster, Aunt Isabel?" said Rocky.

"I have."

There was something in her eye that seemed to say:

"Out of a city of six million people, why did you pick on me?"

"Take a seat, Bertie. What'll you have?" said Rocky.

And so the merry party began. It was one of those jolly, happy, bread-crumbling parties where you cough twice before you speak, and then decide not to say it after all. After we had had an hour of this wild dissipation, Aunt Isabel said she wanted to go home. In the light of what Rocky had been telling me, this struck me as sinister. I had gathered that at the beginning of her visit she had had to be dragged home with ropes.

It must have hit Rocky the same way, for he gave me a pleading look.

"You'll come along, won't you, Bertie, and have a drink at the flat?"

I had a feeling that this wasn't in the contract, but there wasn't anything to be done. It seemed brutal to leave the poor chap alone with the woman, so I went along.

Right from the start, from the moment we stepped into the taxi, the feeling began to grow that something was about to break loose. A massive silence prevailed in the corner where the aunt sat, and, though Rocky, balancing himself on the little seat in front, did his best to supply dialogue, we weren't a chatty party.

I had a glimpse of Jeeves as we went into the flat, sitting in his lair, and I wished I could have called to him to rally round. Something told me that I was about to need him.

The stuff was on the table in the sitting-room. Rocky took up the decanter.

"Say when, Bertie."

"Stop!" barked the aunt, and he dropped it.

I caught Rocky's eye as he stooped to pick up the ruins. It was the eye of one who sees it coming.

"Leave it there, Rockmetteller!" said Aunt Isabel; and Rocky left it there.

"The time has come to speak," she said. "I cannot stand idly by and see a young man going to perdition!"

Poor old Rocky gave a sort of gurgle, a kind of sound rather like the whisky had made running out of the decanter on to my carpet.

"Eh?" he said, blinking.

The aunt proceeded.

"The fault," she said, "was mine. I had not then seen the light. But now my eyes are open. I see the hideous mistake I have made. I shudder at the thought of the wrong I did you, Rockmetteller, by urging you into contact with this wicked city."

I saw Rocky grope feebly for the table. His fingers touched it, and a look of relief came into the poor chappie's face. I understood his feelings.

"But when I wrote you that letter, Rockmetteller, instructing you to go to the city and live its life, I had not had the privilege of hearing Mr. Mundy speak on the subject of New York."

"Jimmy Mundy!" I cried.

You know how it is sometimes when everything seems all mixed up and you suddenly get a clue. When she mentioned Jimmy Mundy I began to understand more or less what had happened. I'd seen it happen before. I remember, back in England, the man I had before Jeeves sneaked off to a meeting on his evening out and came back and denounced me in front of a crowd of chappies I was giving a bit of supper to as a moral leper.

The aunt gave me a withering up and down.

"Yes; Jimmy Mundy!" she said. "I am surprised at a man of your stamp having heard of him. There is no music, there are no drunken, dancing men, no shameless, flaunting women at his meetings; so for you they would have no attraction. But for others, less dead in sin, he has his message. He has come to save New York from itself; to force it—in his picturesque phrase—to hit the trail. It was three days ago, Rockmetteller, that I first heard him. It was an accident that took me to his meeting. How often in this life a mere accident may shape our whole future!

"You had been called away by that telephone message from Mr. Belasco; so you could not take me to the Hippodrome, as we had arranged. I asked your manservant, Jeeves, to take me there. The man has very little intelligence. He seems to have misunderstood me. I am thankful that he did. He took me to what I subsequently learned was Madison Square Garden, where Mr. Mundy is holding his meetings. He escorted me to a seat and then left me. And it was not till the meeting had begun that I discovered the mistake which had been made. My seat was in the middle of a row. I could not leave without inconveniencing a great many people, so I remained."

She gulped.

"Rockmetteller, I have never been so thankful for anything else. Mr. Mundy was wonderful! He was like some prophet of old, scourging the sins of the people. He leaped about in a frenzy of inspiration till I feared he would do himself an injury. Sometimes he expressed himself in a somewhat odd manner, but every word carried conviction. He showed me New York in its true colours. He showed me the vanity and wickedness of sitting in gilded haunts of vice, eating lobster when decent people should be in bed.

"He said that the tango and the fox-trot were devices of the devil to drag people down into the Bottomless Pit. He said that there was more sin in ten minutes with a negro banjo orchestra than in all the ancient revels of Nineveh and Babylon. And when he stood on one leg and pointed right at where I was sitting and shouted, 'This means you!' I could have sunk through the floor. I came away a changed woman. Surely you must have noticed the change in me, Rockmetteller? You must have seen that I was no longer the careless, thoughtless person who had urged you to dance in those places of wickedness?"

Rocky was holding on to the table as if it was his only friend.

"Y-yes," he stammered; "I—I thought something was wrong."

"Wrong? Something was right! Everything was right! Rockmetteller, it is not too late for you to be saved. You have only sipped of the evil cup. You have not drained it. It will be hard at first, but you will find that you can do it if you fight with a stout heart against the glamour and fascination of this dreadful city. Won't you, for my sake, try, Rockmetteller? Won't you go back to the country to-morrow and begin the struggle? Little by little, if you use your will——"

I can't help thinking it must have been that word "will" that roused dear old Rocky like a trumpet call. It must have brought home to him the realisation that a miracle had come off and saved him from being cut out of Aunt Isabel's. At any rate, as she said it he perked up, let go of the table, and faced her with gleaming eyes.

"Do you want me to go back to the country, Aunt Isabel?"

"Yes."

"Not to live in the country?"

"Yes, Rockmetteller."

"Stay in the country all the time, do you mean? Never come to New
York?"

"Yes, Rockmetteller; I mean just that. It is the only way. Only there can you be safe from temptation. Will you do it, Rockmetteller? Will you—for my sake?"

Rocky grabbed the table again. He seemed to draw a lot of encouragement from that table.

"I will!" he said.

* * * * *

"Jeeves," I said. It was next day, and I was back in the old flat, lying in the old arm-chair, with my feet upon the good old table. I had just come from seeing dear old Rocky off to his country cottage, and an hour before he had seen his aunt off to whatever hamlet it was that she was the curse of; so we were alone at last. "Jeeves, there's no place like home—what?"

"Very true, sir."

"The jolly old roof-tree, and all that sort of thing—what?"

"Precisely, sir."

I lit another cigarette.

"Jeeves."

"Sir?"

"Do you know, at one point in the business I really thought you were baffled."

"Indeed, sir?"

"When did you get the idea of taking Miss Rockmetteller to the meeting?
It was pure genius!"

"Thank you, sir. It came to me a little suddenly, one morning when I was thinking of my aunt, sir."

"Your aunt? The hansom cab one?"

"Yes, sir. I recollected that, whenever we observed one of her attacks coming on, we used to send for the clergyman of the parish. We always found that if he talked to her a while of higher things it diverted her mind from hansom cabs. It occurred to me that the same treatment might prove efficacious in the case of Miss Rockmetteller."

I was stunned by the man's resource.

"It's brain," I said; "pure brain! What do you do to get like that,

Jeeves? I believe you must eat a lot of fish, or something. Do you eat a lot of fish, Jeeves?"

"No, sir."

"Oh, well, then, it's just a gift, I take it; and if you aren't born that way there's no use worrying."

"Precisely, sir," said Jeeves. "If I might make the suggestion, sir, I should not continue to wear your present tie. The green shade gives you a slightly bilious air. I should strongly advocate the blue with the red domino pattern instead, sir."

"All right, Jeeves." I said humbly. "You know!"

BONUS STORY – "EXTRICATING YOUNG GUSSIE"

She sprang it on me before breakfast. There in seven words you have a complete character sketch of my Aunt Agatha. I could go on indefinitely about brutality and lack of consideration. I merely say that she routed me out of bed to listen to her painful story somewhere in the small hours. It can't have been half past eleven when Jeeves, my man, woke me out of the dreamless and broke the news:

'Mrs Gregson to see you, sir.'

I thought she must be walking in her sleep, but I crawled out of bed and got into a dressing-gown. I knew Aunt Agatha well enough to know that, if she had come to see me, she was going to see me. That's the sort of woman she is.

She was sitting bolt upright in a chair, staring into space. When I came in she looked at me in that darn critical way that always makes me feel as if I had gelatine where my spine ought to be. Aunt Agatha is one of those strong-minded women. I should think Queen Elizabeth must have been something like her. She bosses her husband, Spencer Gregson, a battered little chappie on the Stock Exchange. She bosses my cousin, Gussie Mannering-Phipps. She bosses her sister-in-law, Gussie's mother.

And, worst of all, she bosses me. She has an eye like a man-eating fish, and she has got moral suasion down to a fine point.

I dare say there are fellows in the world--men of blood and iron, don't you know, and all that sort of thing--whom she couldn't intimidate; but if you're a chappie like me, fond of a quiet life, you simply curl into a ball when you see her coming, and hope for the best. My experience is that when Aunt Agatha wants you to do a thing you do it, or else you find yourself wondering why those fellows in the olden days made such a fuss when they had trouble with the Spanish Inquisition.

'Halloa, Aunt Agatha!' I said

'Bertie,' she said, 'you look a sight. You look perfectly dissipated.'

I was feeling like a badly wrapped brown-paper parcel. I'm never at my best in the early morning. I said so.

'Early morning! I had breakfast three hours ago, and have been walking in the park ever since, trying to compose my thoughts.'

If I ever breakfasted at half past eight I should walk on the Embankment, trying to end it all in a watery grave.

'I am extremely worried, Bertie. That is why I have come to you.'

And then I saw she was going to start something, and I bleated weakly to Jeeves to bring me tea. But she had begun before I could get it.

'What are your immediate plans, Bertie?'

'Well, I rather thought of tottering out for a bite of lunch later on, and then possibly staggering round to the club, and after that, if I felt strong enough, I might trickle off to Walton Heath for a round of golf.'

I am not interested in your totterings and tricklings. I mean, have you any important engagements in the next week or so?'

I scented danger. 'Rather,' I said. 'Heaps! Millions! Booked solid!'

'What are they?'

'I--er--well, I don't quite know.'

'I thought as much. You have no engagements. Very well, then, I want you to start immediately for America.'

'America!'

Do not lose sight of the fact that all this was taking place on an empty stomach, shortly after the rising of the lark.

'Yes, America. I suppose even you have heard of America?'

'But why America?'

'Because that is where your Cousin Gussie is. He is in New York, and I can't get at him.'

'What's Gussie been doing?'

'Gussie is making a perfect idiot of himself.'

To one who knew young Gussie as well as I did, the words opened up a wide field for speculation.

'In what way?'

'He has lost his head over a creature.'

On past performances this rang true. Ever since he arrived at man's estate Gussie had been losing his head over creatures. He's that sort of chap. But, as the creatures never seemed to lose their heads over him, it had never amounted to much.

'I imagine you know perfectly well why Gussie went to America, Bertie. You know how wickedly extravagant your Uncle Cuthbert was.'

She alluded to Gussie's governor, the late head of the family, and I am bound to say she spoke the truth. Nobody was fonder of old Uncle Cuthbert than I was, but everybody knows that, where money was concerned, he was the most complete chump in the annals of the nation. He had an expensive thirst. He never backed a horse that didn't get housemaid's knee in the middle of the race. He had a system of beating the bank at Monte Carlo which used to make the administration hang out the bunting and ring the joy-bells when he was sighted in the offing.

Take him for all in all, dear old Uncle Cuthbert was as willing a spender as ever called the family lawyer a bloodsucking vampire because he wouldn't let Uncle Cuthbert cut down the timber to raise another thousand.

'He left your Aunt Julia very little money for a woman in her position. Beechwood requires a great deal of keeping up, and poor dear Spencer, though he does his best to help, has not unlimited resources. It was clearly understood why Gussie went to America. He is not clever, but he is very good-looking, and, though he has no title, the Mannering-Phippses are one of the best and oldest families in England. He had some excellent letters of introduction, and when he wrote home to say that he had met the most charming and beautiful girl in the world I felt quite happy. He continued to rave about her for several mails, and then this morning a letter has come from him in which he says, quite casually as a sort of afterthought, that he knows we are broadminded enough not to think any the worse of her because she is on the vaudeville stage.'

'Oh, I say!'

'It was like a thunderbolt. The girl's name, it seems, is Ray

Denison, and according to Gussie she does something which he describes as a single on the big time. What this degraded performance may be I have not the least notion. As a further recommendation he states that she lifted them out of their seats at Mosenstein's last week. Who she may be, and how or why, and who or what Mr Mosenstein may be, I cannot tell you.'

'By Jove,' I said, 'it's like a sort of thingummybob, isn't it? A sort of fate, what?'

'I fail to understand you.'

'Well, Aunt Julia, you know, don't you know? Heredity, and so forth. What's bred in the bone will come out in the wash, and all that kind of thing, you know.'

'Don't be absurd, Bertie.'

That was all very well, but it was a coincidence for all that. Nobody ever mentions it, and the family have been trying to forget it for twenty-five years, but it's a known fact that my Aunt Julia, Gussie's mother, was a vaudeville artist once, and a very good one, too, I'm told. She was playing in pantomime at Drury Lane when Uncle Cuthbert saw her first. It was before my time, of course, and long before I was old enough to take notice the family had made the best of it, and Aunt Agatha had pulled up her socks and put in a lot of educative work, and with a microscope you couldn't tell Aunt Julia from a genuine dyed-in-the-wool aristocrat. Women adapt themselves so quickly!

I have a pal who married Daisy Trimble of the Gaiety, and when I meet her now I feel like walking out of her presence backwards. But there the thing was, and you couldn't get away from it. Gussie had vaudeville blood in him, and it looked as if he were reverting to type, or whatever they call it.

'By Jove,' I said, for I am interested in this heredity stuff, 'perhaps the thing is going to be a regular family tradition, like you read about in books--a sort of Curse of the Mannering-Phippses, as it were. Perhaps each head of the family's going to marry into vaudeville for ever and ever. Unto the what-d'you-call-it generation, don't you know?'

'Please do not be quite idiotic, Bertie. There is one head of the family who is certainly not going to do it, and that is Gussie. And you are going to America to stop him.'

'Yes, but why me?'

'Why you? You are too vexing, Bertie. Have you no sort of feeling for the family? You are too lazy to try to be a credit to yourself, but at least you can exert yourself to prevent Gussie's disgracing us. You are going to America because you are Gussie's cousin, because you have always been his closest friend, because you are the only one of thefamily who has absolutely nothing to occupy his time except golf and

night clubs.'

'I play a lot of auction.'

'And as you say, idiotic gambling in low dens. If you require another reason, you are going because I ask you as a personal favour.'

What she meant was that, if I refused, she would exert the full bent of her natural genius to make life a Hades for me. She held me with her glittering eye. I have never met anyone who can give a better imitation of the Ancient Mariner.

'So you will start at once, won't you, Bertie?'

I didn't hesitate.

'Rather!' I said. 'Of course I will'

Jeeves came in with the tea.

'Jeeves,' I said, 'we start for America on Saturday.'

'Very good, sir,' he said; 'which suit will you wear?'

New York is a large city conveniently situated on the edge of America, so that you step off the liner right on to it without an effort. You can't lose your way. You go out of a barn and down some stairs, and there you are, right in among it. The only possible objection any reasonable chappie could find to the place is that they loose you into it from the boat at such an ungodly hour.

I left Jeeves to get my baggage safely past an aggregation of suspicious-minded pirates who were digging for buried treasures among my new shirts, and drove to Gussie's hotel, where I requested the squad of gentlemanly clerks behind the desk to produce him.

That's where I got my first shock. He wasn't there. I pleaded with them to think again, and they thought again, but it was no good. No Augustus Mannering-Phipps on the premises.

I admit I was hard hit. There I was alone in a strange city and no signs of Gussie. What was the next step? I am never one of the master minds in the early morning; the old bean doesn't somehow seem to get into its stride till pretty late in the p.m.s, and I couldn't think what to do. However, some instinct took me through a door at the back of the lobby, and I found myself in a large room with an enormous picture stretching across the whole of one wall, and under the picture a counter, and behind the counter divers chappies in white, serving drinks. They have barmen, don't you know, in New York, not barmaids. Rum idea!

I put myself unreservedly into the hands of one of the white chappies. He was a friendly soul, and I told him the whole state of affairs. I asked him what he thought would meet the case.

He said that in a situation of that sort he usually prescribed a 'lightning whizzer', an invention of his own. He said this was what rabbits trained on when they were matched against grizzly bears, and there was only one instance on record of the bear having lasted three rounds. So I tried a couple, and, by Jove! the man was perfectly right. As I drained the second a great load seemed to fall from my heart, and I went out in quite a braced way to have a look at the city.

I was surprised to find the streets quite full. People were bustling along as if it were some reasonable hour and not the grey dawn. In the tramcars they were absolutely standing on each other's necks. Going to business or something, I take it. Wonderful johnnies!

The odd part of it was that after the first shock of seeing all this frightful energy the thing didn't seem so strange. I've spoken to fellows since who have been to New York, and they tell me they found it just the same. Apparently there's something in the air, either the ozone or the phosphates or something, which makes you sit up and take notice. A kind of zip, as it were. A sort of bally freedom, if you know what I mean, that gets into your blood and bucks you up, and makes you feel that--

God's in His Heaven:
All's right with the world,

and you don't care if you've got odd socks on. I can't express it better than by saying that the thought uppermost in my mind, as I walked about the place they call Times Square, was that there were three thousand miles of deep water between me and my Aunt Agatha.

It's a funny thing about looking for things. If you hunt for a needle in a haystack you don't find it. If you don't give a darn whether you ever see the needle or not it runs into you the first time you lean against the stack. By the time I had strolled up and down once or twice, seeing the sights and letting the white chappie's corrective permeate my system, I was feeling that I wouldn't care if Gussie and I never met again, and I'm dashed if I didn't suddenly catch sight of the old lad, as large as life, just turning in at a doorway down the street.

I called after him, but he didn't hear me, so I legged it in pursuit and caught him going into an office on the first floor. The name on the door was Abe Riesbitter, Vaudeville Agent, and from the other side of the door came the sound of many voices.

He turned and stared at me.

'Bertie! What on earth are you doing? Where have you sprung from? When did you arrive?'

'Landed this morning. I went round to your hotel, but they said you weren't there. They had never heard of you.'

'I've changed my name. I call myself George Wilson.'

'Why on earth?'

'Well, you try calling yourself Augustus Mannering-Phipps over here, and see how it strikes you. You feel a perfect ass. I don't know what it is about America, but the broad fact is that it's not a place where you can call yourself Augustus Mannering-Phipps. And there's another reason. I'll tell you later. Bertie, I've fallen in love with the dearest girl in the world.'

The poor old nut looked at me in such a deuced cat-like way, standing with his mouth open, waiting to be congratulated, that I simply hadn't the heart to tell him that I knew all about that already, and had come over to the country for the express purpose of laying him a stymie.

So I congratulated him.

'Thanks awfully, old man,' he said. 'It's a bit premature, but I fancy it's going to be all right. Come along in here, and I'll tell you about it.'

'What do you want in this place? It looks a rummy spot.'

'Oh, that's part of the story. I'll tell you the whole thing.'

We opened the door marked 'Waiting Room'. I never saw such a crowded place in my life. The room was packed till the walls bulged.

Gussie explained.

'Pros,' he said, 'music-hall artistes, you know, waiting to see old Abe Riesbitter. This is September the first, vaudeville's opening day. The early fall,' said Gussie, who is a bit of a poet in his way, 'is vaudeville's springtime. All over the country, as August wanes, sparkling comediennes burst into bloom, the sap stirs in the veins of tramp cyclists, and last year's contortionists, waking from their summer sleep, tie themselves tentatively into knots. What I mean is, this is the beginning of the new season, and everybody's out hunting for bookings.'

'But what do you want here?'

'Oh, I've just got to see Abe about something. If you see a fat man with about fifty-seven chins come out of that door there grab him, for that'll be Abe. He's one of those fellows who advertise each step up they take in the world by growing another chin. I'm told that way back in the nineties he only had two. If you do grab Abe, remember that he knows me as George Wilson.'

'You said that you were going to explain that George Wilson business to me, Gussie, old man.'

'Well, it's this way--'

At this juncture dear old Gussie broke off short, rose from his seat, and sprang with indescribable vim at an extraordinarily stout chappie who had suddenly appeared. There was the deuce of a rush for him, but Gussie had got away to a good start, and the rest of the singers, dancers, jugglers, acrobats, and refined sketch teams seemed to recognize that he had won the trick, for they ebbed back into their places again, and Gussie and I went into the inner room.

Mr Riesbitter lit a cigar, and looked at us solemnly over his zareba of chins.

'Now, let me tell ya something,' he said to Gussie. 'You lizzun t' me.'

Gussie registered respectful attention. Mr Riesbitter mused for a moment and shelled the cuspidor with indirect fire over the edge of the desk.

'Lizzun t' me,' he said again. 'I seen you rehearse, as I promised Miss Denison I would. You ain't bad for an amateur. You gotta lot to learn, but it's in you. What it comes to is that I can fix you up in the four-a-day, if you'll take thirty-five per. I can't do better than that, and I wouldn't have done that if the little lady hadn't of kep' after me. Take it or leave it. What do you say?'

'I'll take it,' said Gussie, huskily. 'Thank you.'

In the passage outside, Gussie gurgled with joy and slapped me on the back. 'Bertie, old man, it's all right. I'm the happiest man in New York.'

'Now what?'

'Well, you see, as I was telling you when Abe came in, Ray's father used to be in the profession. He was before our time, but I remember hearing about him--Joe Danby. He used to be well known in London before he came over to America. Well, he's a fine old boy, but as obstinate as a mule, and he didn't like the idea of Ray marrying me because I wasn't in the profession. Wouldn't hear of it. Well, you remember at Oxford I could always sing a song pretty well; so Ray got hold of old Riesbitter and made him promise to come and hear me rehearse and get me bookings if he liked my work. She stands high with him. She coached me for weeks, the darling. And now, as you heard him say, he's booked me in the small time at thirty-five dollars a week.'

I steadied myself against the wall. The effects of the restoratives supplied by my pal at the hotel bar were beginning to work off, and I felt a little weak. Through a sort of mist I seemed to have a vision of Aunt Agatha hearing that the head of the Mannering-Phippses was about to appear on the vaudeville stage. Aunt Agatha's worship of the family name amounts to an obsession. The Mannering-Phippses were an old-established clan when William the Conqueror was a small boy going round with bare legs and a catapult. For centuries they have called kings by their first names and helped dukes with their weekly rent; and there's practically nothing a Mannering-Phipps can do that doesn't blot his escutcheon. So what Aunt Agatha would say-

-beyond saying that it was all my fault--when she learned the horrid news, it was beyond me to imagine.

'Come back to the hotel, Gussie,' I said. 'There's a sportsman there who mixes things he calls "lightning whizzers". Something tells me I need one now. And excuse me for one minute, Gussie. I want to send a cable.'

It was clear to me by now that Aunt Agatha had picked the wrong man for this job of disentangling Gussie from the clutches of the American vaudeville profession. What I needed was reinforcements. For a moment I thought of cabling Aunt Agatha to come over, but reason told me that this would be overdoing it. I wanted assistance, but not so badly as that. I hit what seemed to me the happy mean. I cabled to Gussie's mother and made it urgent.

'What were you cabling about?' asked Gussie, later.

'Oh just to say I had arrived safely, and all that sort of tosh,' I answered.

*　　*　　*　　*　　*

Gussie opened his vaudeville career on the following Monday at a rummy sort of place uptown where they had moving pictures some of the time and, in between, one or two vaudeville acts. It had taken a lot of careful handling to bring him up to scratch. He seemed to take my sympathy and assistance for granted, and I couldn't let him down. My only hope, which grew as I listened to him rehearsing, was that he would be such a frightful frost at his first appearance that he would never dare to perform again; and, as that would automatically squash the marriage, it seemed best to me to let the thing go on.

He wasn't taking any chances. On the Saturday and Sunday we practically lived in a beastly little music-room at the offices of the publishers whose songs he proposed to use. A little chappie with a hooked nose sucked a cigarette and played the piano all day. Nothing could tire that lad. He seemed to take a personal interest in the thing.

Gussie would cleat his throat and begin:

'There's a great big choo-choo waiting at the deepo.'

THE CHAPPIE (playing chords): 'Is that so? What's it waiting for?'

GUSSIE (rather rattled at the interruption): 'Waiting for me.'

THE CHAPPIE (surprised): For you?'
GUSSIE (sticking to it): 'Waiting for me-e-ee!'
THE CHAPPIE (sceptically): 'You don't say!'
GUSSIE: 'For I'm off to Tennessee.'
THE CHAPPIE (conceding a point): 'Now, I live at Yonkers.'

He did this all through the song. At first poor old Gussie asked him to stop, but the chappie said, No, it was always done. It helped to get pep into the thing. He appealed to me whether the thing didn't want a bit of pep, and I said it wanted all the pep it could get. And the chappie said to Gussie, 'There you are!' So Gussie had to stand it.

The other song that he intended to sing was one of those moon songs. He told me in a hushed voice that he was using it because it was one of the songs that the girl Ray sang when lifting them out of their seats at Mosenstein's and elsewhere. The fact seemed to give it sacred associations for him.

You will scarcely believe me, but the management expected Gussie to show up and start performing at one o'clock in the afternoon. I told him they couldn't be serious, as they must know that he would be rolling out for a bit of lunch at that hour, but Gussie said this was the usual thing in the four-a-day, and he didn't suppose he would ever get any lunch again until he landed on the big time. I was just condoling with him, when I found that he was taking it for granted that I should be there at one o'clock, too. My idea had been that I should look in at night, when--if he survived--he would be coming up for the fourth time; but I've never deserted a pal in distress, so I said good-bye to the little lunch I'd been planning at a rather decent tavern I'd discovered on Fifth Avenue, and trailed along. They were showing pictures when I reached my seat. It was one of those Western films, where the cowboy jumps on his horse and rides across country at a hundred and fifty miles an hour to escape the sheriff, not knowing, poor chump! that he might just as well stay where he is, the sheriff having a horse of his own which can do three hundred miles an hour without coughing. I was just going to close my eyes and try to forget till they put Gussie's name up when I discovered that I was sitting next to a deucedly pretty girl.

No, let me be honest. When I went in I had seen that there was a deucedly pretty girl sitting in that particular seat, so I had taken the next one. What happened now was that I began, as it were, to drink her in. I wished they would turn the lights up so that I could see her better. She was rather small, with great big eyes and a ripping smile.

It was a shame to let all that run to seed, so to speak, in semi-darkness.

Suddenly the lights did go up, and the orchestra began to play a tune which, though I haven't much of an ear for music, seemed somehow familiar. The next instant out pranced old Gussie from the wings in a purple frock-coat and a brown top-hat, grinned feebly at the audience, tripped over his feet blushed, and began to sing the Tennessee song.

It was rotten. The poor nut had got stage fright so badly that it practically eliminated his voice. He sounded like some far-off echo of the past 'yodelling' through a woollen blanket.

For the first time since I had heard that he was about to go into vaudeville I felt a faint hope creeping over me. I was sorry for the wretched chap, of course, but there was no denying that the thing had its bright side. No management on earth would go on paying thirty-five dollars a week for this sort of performance. This was going to be Gussie's first and only. He would have to leave the profession. The old boy would say, 'Unhand my daughter'. And, with decent luck, I saw myself leading Gussie on to the next England-bound liner and handing him over intact to Aunt Agatha.

He got through the song somehow and limped off amidst roars of silence from the audience. There was a brief respite, then out he came again.

He sang this time as if nobody loved him. As a song, it was not a very pathetic song, being all about coons spooning in June under the moon, and so and so forth, but Gussie handled it in such a sad, crushed way that there was genuine anguish in every line. By the time he reached the refrain I was nearly in tears. It seemed such a rotten sort of world with all that kind of thing going on in it.

He started the refrain, and then the most frightful thing happened. The girl next to me got up in her seat, chucked her head back, and began to sing too. I say 'too', but it wasn't really too, because her first note stopped Gussie dead, as if he had been pole-axed.

I never felt so bally conspicuous in my life. I huddled down in my seat and wished I could turn my collar up. Everybody seemed to be looking at me.

In the midst of my agony I caught sight of Gussie. A complete change had taken place in the old lad. He was looking most frightfully bucked.

I must say the girl was singing most awfully well, and it seemed to act on Gussie like a tonic. When she came to the end of the refrain, he took it up, and they sang it together, and the end of it was that he went off the popular hero. The audience yelled for more, and were only quieted when they turned down the lights and put on a film.

When I had recovered I tottered round to see Gussie. I found him sitting on a box behind the stage, looking like one who had seen visions.

'Isn't she a wonder, Bertie?' he said, devoutly. 'I hadn't a notion she was going to be there. She's playing at the Auditorium this week, and she can only just have had time to get back to her matinee. She risked being late, just to come and see me through. She's my good angel, Bertie. She saved me. If she hadn't helped me out I don't know what would have happened. I was so nervous I didn't know what I was doing. Now that I've got through the first show I shall be all right.'

I was glad I had sent that cable to his mother. I was going to need her. The thing had got beyond me.

*   *   *   *   *

During the next week I saw a lot of old Gussie, and was introduced to the girl. I also met her father, a formidable old boy with quick eyebrows and a sort of determined expression. On the following Wednesday Aunt Julia arrived. Mrs Mannering-Phipps, my aunt Julia, is, I think, the most dignified person I know. She lacks Aunt Agatha's punch, but in a quiet way she has always contrived to make me feel, from boyhood up, that I was a poor worm. Not that she harries me like Aunt Agatha. The difference between the two is that Aunt Agatha conveys the impression that she considers me personally responsible for all the sin and sorrow in the world, while

Aunt Julia's manner seems to suggest that I am more to be pitied than censured.

If it wasn't that the thing was a matter of historical fact, I should be inclined to believe that Aunt Julia had never been on the vaudeville stage. She is like a stage duchess.

She always seems to me to be in a perpetual state of being about to desire the butler to instruct the head footman to serve lunch in the blue-room overlooking the west terrace. She exudes dignity. Yet, twenty-five years ago, so I've been told by old boys who were lads about town in those days, she was knocking them cold at the Tivoli in a double act called 'Fun in a Tea-Shop', in which she wore tights and sang a song with a chorus that began, 'Rumpty-tiddley-umpty-ay'.

There are some things a chappie's mind absolutely refuses to picture, and Aunt Julia singing 'Rumpty-tiddley-umpty-ay' is one of them.

She got straight to the point within five minutes of our meeting.

'What is this about Gussie? Why did you cable for me, Bertie?'

'It's rather a long story,' I said, 'and complicated. If you don't mind, I'll let you have it in a series of motion pictures. Suppose we look in at the Auditorium for a few minutes.'

The girl, Ray, had been re-engaged for a second week at the Auditorium, owing to the big success of her first week. Her act consisted of three songs. She did herself well in the matter of costume and scenery. She had a ripping voice. She looked most awfully pretty; and altogether the act was, broadly speaking, a pippin.

Aunt Julia didn't speak till we were in our seats. Then she gave a sort of sigh.

'It's twenty-five years since I was in a music-hall!'

She didn't say any more, but sat there with her eyes glued on the stage.

After about half an hour the johnnies who work the card-index system at the side of the stage put up the name of Ray Denison, and there was a good deal of applause.

'Watch this act, Aunt Julia,' I said.

She didn't seem to hear me.

'Twenty-five years! What did you say, Bertie?'

'Watch this act and tell me what you think of it.'

'Who is it? Ray. Oh!'

'Exhibit A,' I said. 'The girl Gussie's engaged to.'

The girl did her act, and the house rose at her. They didn't want to let her go. She had to come back again and again. When she had finally disappeared I turned to Aunt Julia.

'Well?' I said.

'I like her work. She's an artist.'

'We will now, if you don't mind, step a goodish way uptown.'

And we took the subway to where Gussie, the human film, was earning his thirty-five per. As luck would have it, we hadn't been in the place ten minutes when out he came.

'Exhibit B,' I said. 'Gussie.'

I don't quite know what I had expected her to do, but I certainly didn't expect her to sit there without a word. She did not move a muscle, but just stared at Gussie as he drooled on about the moon. I was sorry for the woman, for it must have been a shock to her to see her only son in a mauve frockcoat and a brown top-hat, but I thought it best to let her get a strangle-hold on the intricacies of the situation as quickly as possible. If I had tried to explain the affair without the aid of illustrations I should have talked all day and left her muddled up as to who was going to marry whom, and why.

I was astonished at the improvement in dear old Gussie. He had got back his voice and was putting the stuff over well. It reminded me of the night at Oxford when, then but a lad of eighteen, he sang 'Let's All Go Down the Strand' after a bump supper, standing the while up to his knees in the college fountain. He was putting just the same zip into the thing now.

When he had gone off Aunt Julia sat perfectly still for a long time, and then she turned to me. Her eyes shone queerly.

'What does this mean, Bertie?'

She spoke quite quietly, but her voice shook a bit.

'Gussie went into the business,' I said, 'because the girl's father wouldn't let him marry her unless he did. If you feel up to it perhaps you wouldn't mind tottering round to One Hundred and Thirty-third Street and having a chat with him. He's an old boy with eyebrows, and he's Exhibit C on my list. When I've put you in touch with him I rather fancy my share of the business is concluded, and it's up to you.'

The Danbys lived in one of those big apartments uptown which look as if they cost the earth and really cost about half as much as a hall-room down in the forties. We were shown into the sitting-room, and presently old Danby came in.

'Good afternoon, Mr Danby,' I began.

I had got as far as that when there was a kind of gasping cry at my elbow.

'Joe!' cried Aunt Julia, and staggered against the sofa.

For a moment old Danby stared at her, and then his mouth fell open and his eyebrows shot up like rockets.

'Julie!'

And then they had got hold of each other's hands and were shaking them till I wondered their arms didn't come unscrewed.

I'm not equal to this sort of thing at such short notice. The change in Aunt Julia made me feel quite dizzy. She had shed her _grande-dame_ manner completely, and was blushing and smiling. I don't like to say such things of any aunt of mine, or I would go further and put it on record that she was giggling. And old Danby, who usually looked like a cross between a Roman emperor and Napoleon Bonaparte in a bad temper, was behaving like a small boy.

'Joe!'

'Julie!'

'Dear old Joe! Fancy meeting you again!'

'Wherever have you come from, Julie?'

Well, I didn't know what it was all about, but I felt a bit out of it. I butted in:

'Aunt Julia wants to have a talk with you, Mr Danby.'

'I knew you in a second, Joe!'

'It's twenty-five years since I saw you, kid, and you don't look a day older.'

'Oh, Joe! I'm an old woman!'

'What are you doing over here? I suppose'--old Danby's cheerfulness waned a trifle--'I suppose your husband is with you?'

'My husband died a long, long while ago, Joe.'

Old Danby shook his head.

'You never ought to have married out of the profession, Julie. I'm not saying a word against the late--I can't remember his name; never could--but you shouldn't have done it, an artist like you. Shall I ever forget the way you used to knock them with "Rumpty-tiddley-umpty-ay"?'

'Ah! how wonderful you were in that act, Joe.' Aunt Julia sighed. 'Do you remember the back-fall you used to do down the steps? I always have said that you did the best back-fall in the profession.'

'I couldn't do it now!'

'Do you remember how we put it across at the Canterbury, Joe? Think of it! The Canterbury's a moving-picture house now, and the old Mogul runs French revues.'

'I'm glad I'm not there to see them.'

'Joe, tell me, why did you leave England?'

'Well, I--I wanted a change. No I'll tell you the truth, kid. I wanted you, Julie. You went off and married that--whatever that stage-door johnny's name was--and it broke me all up.'

Aunt Julia was staring at him. She is what they call a well-preserved woman. It's easy to see that, twenty-five years ago, she must have been something quite extraordinary to look at. Even now she's almost beautiful. She has very large brown eyes, a mass of soft grey hair, and the complexion of a girl of seventeen.

'Joe, you aren't going to tell me you were fond of me yourself!'

'Of course I was fond of you. Why did I let you have all the fat in "Fun in a Tea-Shop"? Why did I hang about upstage while you sang "Rumpty-tiddley-umpty-ay"? Do you remember my giving you a bag of buns when we were on the road at Bristol?'

'Yes, but--'

'Do you remember my giving you the ham sandwiches at Portsmouth?'

'Joe!'

'Do you remember my giving you a seed-cake at Birmingham? What did you think all that meant, if not that I loved you? Why, I was working up by degrees to telling you straight out when you suddenly went off and married that cane-sucking dude. That's why I wouldn't let my daughter marry this young chap, Wilson, unless he went into the profession. She's an artist--'

'She certainly is, Joe.'

'You've seen her? Where?'

'At the Auditorium just now. But, Joe, you mustn't stand in the way of her marrying the man she's in love with. He's an artist, too.'

'In the small time.'

'You were in the small time once, Joe. You mustn't look down on him because he's a beginner. I know you feel that your daughter is marrying beneath her, but--'

'How on earth do you know anything about young Wilson?'

'He's my son.'

'Your son?'

'Yes, Joe. And I've just been watching him work. Oh, Joe, you can't think how proud I was of him! He's got it in him. It's fate. He's my son and he's in the profession! Joe, you don't know what I've been through for his sake. They made a lady of me. I never worked so hard in my life as I did to become a real lady. They kept telling me I had got to put it across, no matter what it cost, so that he wouldn't be ashamed of me. The study was something terrible. I had to watch myself every minute for years, and I never knew when I might fluff my lines or fall down on some bit of business. But I did it, because I didn't want him to be ashamed of me, though all the time I was just aching to be back where I belonged.'

Old Danby made a jump at her, and took her by the shoulders.

'Come back where you belong, Julie!' he cried. 'Your husband's dead, your son's a pro. Come back! It's twenty-five years ago, but I haven't changed. I want you still. I've always wanted you. You've got to come back, kid, where you belong.'

Aunt Julia gave a sort of gulp and looked at him.

'Joe!' she said in a kind of whisper.

'You're here, kid,' said Old Danby, huskily. 'You've come back.... Twenty-five years!... You've come back and you're going to stay!'

She pitched forward into his arms, and he caught her.

'Oh, Joe! Joe! Joe!' she said. 'Hold me. Don't let me go. Take care of me.'

And I edged for the door and slipped from the room. I felt weak. The old bean will stand a certain amount, but this was too much. I groped my way out into the street and wailed for a taxi.

Gussie called on me at the hotel that night. He curveted into the room as if he had bought it and the rest of the city.

'Bertie,' he said, 'I feel as if I were dreaming.'

'I wish I could feel like that, old top,' I said, and I took another glance at a cable that had arrived half an hour ago from Aunt Agatha. I had been looking at it at intervals ever since. 'Ray and I got back to her flat this evening. Who do you think was there? The mater! She was sitting hand in hand with old Danby.'

'Yes?'

'He was sitting hand in hand with her.'

'Really?'

'They are going to be married.'

'Exactly.'

'Ray and I are going to be married.'

'I suppose so.'

'Bertie, old man, I feel immense. I look round me, and everything seems to be absolutely corking. The change in the mater is marvellous. She is twenty-five years younger. She and old Danby are talking of reviving "Fun in a Tea-Shop", and going out on the road with it.'

I got up.

'Gussie, old top,' I said, 'leave me for a while. I would be alone. I think I've got brain fever or something.'

'Sorry, old man; perhaps New York doesn't agree with you. When do you expect to go back to England?'

I looked again at Aunt Agatha's cable.

'With luck,' I said, 'in about ten years.'

When he was gone I took up the cable and read it again.

'What is happening?' it read. 'Shall I come over?'

I sucked a pencil for a while, and then I wrote the reply.

It was not an easy cable to word, but I managed it.

'No,' I wrote, 'stay where you are. Profession overcrowded.'

■ THE END --

Made in the USA
Middletown, DE
10 September 2018